PRAISE

"Ava's story is witty and charming."
—Barbara Freethy #1 *NYT* bestselling author

Selected by USA Today as one of the Best Books of the
year alongside Nora Roberts' *Dark Witch* and
Julia Quinn's *Sum of all Kisses*.

"If you like Nora Roberts type books, this is a must-read."
—Readers' Favorite

Country Heaven
"If ever there was a contemporary romance that rated a 10
on a scale of 1 to 5 for me, this one is it!"
—The Romance Reviews

"*Country Heaven* made me laugh and cry...I could not
stop flipping the pages. I can't wait to read the next book
in this series." —Fresh Fiction

Country Heaven Cookbook
"Delicious, simple recipes... Comfort food, at its best."
—Fire Up The Oven Blog

The Bridge to a Better Life
Selected by *USA Today* as one of the Best Books of the
Summer.

"Miles offers a story of grief, healing and rediscovered love."
—*USA Today*

"I've read Susan Mallery and Debbie Macomber...but never have I been so moved by the books Ava Miles writes."
—Booktalk with Eileen Reviews

The Gate to Everything
"The constant love...bring a sensual, dynamic tension to
this appealing story." —Publisher's Weekly

MORE PRAISE FOR AVA

The Chocolate Garden
"On par with Nicholas Sparks' love stories."
—Jennifer's Corner Blog

"A must-read...a bit of fairy magic...a shelf full of happiness."
—Fab Fantasy Fiction

The Promise of Rainbows
"This is a story about grace, faith and the power of both..."
—The Book Nympho

French Roast
"Ms. Miles draws from her experience as an apprentice
chef...and it shows...I loved {the} authenticity of the food
references, and the recipes...looked divine." —BlogCritics

The Holiday Serenade
"This story is all romance, steam, and humor with a touch
of the holiday spirit..." —The Book Nympho

The Town Square
"Ms. Miles' words melted into each page until the world
receded around me..." —Tome Tender

The Park of Sunset Dreams
"Ava has done it again. I love the whole community of
Dare Valley..." —Travel Through The Pages Blog

The Calendar of New Beginnings
"A funny, inspirational friends to lovers story to pull on
your heartstrings." —Cullen House Reviews

The Fountain of Infinite Wishes
"A beautiful story... I love going back to Dare River."
—Goodreads Addict

The Grand Opening
"Ava Miles is fast becoming one of my favorite light contemporary romance writers." —Tome Tender

The Fountain

of

Infinite Wishes

THE DARE RIVER SERIES

AVA MILES

To Ian, Emma, and George, and Daria and Heath and
Sam and the rest of you precious ones:
I have so many wishes for you.
Thanks for bringing so many of mine into being.

And to my divine entourage,
who grants all my wishes from here to infinity.

Acknowledgements

My heartfelt thanks to the special people in my life who support my efforts:

Team Ava, who continues to expand and lives its highest version.

Eileen Rendahl and Gary Tabke who supplied all sorts of private investigation goodies.

T.F. For being a king among men.

CHAPTER 1

FINDING YOUR DADDY WAS A SCARY PROPOSITION. Especially when he'd abandoned you as a child. Shelby McGuiness was glad one of her sisters, Sadie, was joining her to kick off the search.

Hiring a private investigator was an equally scary proposition.

Shelby walked into the brass and glass lobby where Vander Montgomery's office was located in downtown Nashville. She'd purposely scheduled the meeting for Friday afternoon so she'd have the weekend to work through her emotions. Thank goodness for that—they weren't even in the P.I.'s office yet, and she'd had to forsake her morning cappuccino because her tummy was so upset.

Now that the family wedding season—three in three months—was behind them all, she and Sadie had decided it was time to move forward with their search. Their elder sister, Susannah, was well settled with her new husband, Jake; their brother, J.P., and his new wife, Tammy, already acted like they'd been married for years; and Tammy's sister, Amelia Ann, and her husband, Clayton, couldn't seem to get enough of each other. J.P. had given his blessing for the search, asking only to be informed of their progress, while Susannah had been dead set against it.

Their mama didn't know about their search for Daddy—something they'd all agreed was necessary, not that it washed away the guilt. J.P. was prepared to play peacemaker if everything went south. The McGuiness women could get riled up, especially when they didn't see eye to eye.

During their siblings' wedding preparations, Shelby had found herself wondering if their daddy would end up walking her down the aisle. Sadie had admitted she'd had the same thought. Of course, there was no telling if they'd even find Daddy. Shelby sure as shooting didn't know if he was sorry he'd abandoned them. But hope loomed large in her heart. What if they could form a real father/daughter relationship?

She and Sadie finally spotted each other in the crowd of worker bees meandering through the lobby. Her sister hurried over. She was a picture-perfect snapshot of summer in her white blouse and yellow skirt with navy wedges. Shelby had never been so happy to see anyone in her whole life. He sister must have felt the same way, because her hug was more like a clutch. Shelby clutched her right back.

"Are you ready for this?" Sadie asked in a rush.

"Yes," Shelby told her, releasing a long breath. "As we agreed, we can always decide Vander's not the right private investigator or pull the plug at any time."

Not that Shelby thought Vander could be the wrong choice. Her boss, Gail Hardcrew, had raved about the man after using him herself.

"I keep telling myself that," her sister said, locking arms with her. Together, they walked to the front desk and signed in with security. As if by silent agreement, they didn't loosen their clasp one bit until they reached the elevator.

While the car glided upward, Shelby said conversationally, "His office sure is located in a nice building." Southerners liked to be conversational when they were as nervous as a new soul approaching the gates of Hades.

"Yes, it's lovely," Sadie responded, following the cue. "Only a successful P.I. could afford rent in a place like this. I can't even imagine what he pays per month."

Working as Gail's accountant, Shelby had a pretty good idea what his rent went for. One of her boss' two restaurants was down the street. "It's pricy, that's for sure."

There were a few record companies located in this tony building as well, but that made sense to Shelby after reading some of Vander's endorsements. He ran background checks for country music stars. It was a sad fact that country singers had to delve into the backgrounds of those closest to them, but it was part of stardom. When J.P. had been in the business for a short time as a singer, his manager had handled such matters for him. And certainly mega-star Rye Crenshaw, J.P.'s best friend and Tammy's brother, did the same.

On the seventh floor, she let go of Sadie's arm as they exited the elevator and traversed the navy-carpeted hallway to the mahogany door bearing the brass nameplate of Montgomery Associates. The door clicked when Shelby opened it. The little touches of a high-class firm were everywhere, from the bold modern art on the walls to the plush furnishings Shelby knew cost an arm and a leg.

A woman stood from behind a sleek metal reception desk as they walked through the door. She was mid-thirties, blonde, and drop-dead gorgeous—the perfect counterpoint to the smoldering picture of Vander that Shelby had seen on his website. This was a pretty people's private investigation firm, Shelby decided. No wonder Gail had liked him. Her boss preferred her associates to be wicked smart *and* good-looking if at all possible, and she was bold enough to admit it out loud.

"You must be Shelby and Sadie McGuiness," the woman said with a genuine smile. "Welcome. Can I get you anything to drink?"

"Nothing for me," Shelby answered, wishing she could rub her jumping tummy without looking like a ninny.

"Water would be nice," Sadie said, and even to Shelby's ears, her sister's voice sounded raspy.

The receptionist disappeared and returned with her

water—in a Waterford crystal glass. Shelby had a hunch she could have asked for that cappuccino, and the woman would have reappeared just as quickly. "Please follow me."

They passed by three other offices. One woman was on the phone, her syrupy drawl audible, while the other two were hunched over their computers, picking at their keyboards like they were keying in numbers. Shelby knew that sound. It was the same one she made while doing Gail's accounting, different than the more fluid melody of composing emails.

Sadie reached for her hand, but Shelby gave her a look. Holding hands on the walk here was one thing, but they were both women in their twenties. Not little girls. They needed to stand tall as they did this.

Even if this monumental step made them both feel like scared girls all over again.

The woman opened the double mahogany door at the end of the hall and ushered them inside, discreetly closing the door behind her as she left. Vander looked up immediately and smiled at them.

Even though Shelby had seen his picture on the Internet, she wasn't prepared for the punch of attraction she felt. His eyes were as dark-lashed as they looked in his photo, and heavens if they weren't a brilliant aquamarine. His black hair seemed curlier somehow—almost as though he'd tamed it for the professional photo. But his suit was as crisply tailored as the one he'd been wearing in the shot and looked to be Italian, if she had to guess.

"Please come in, ladies," he told them, rising from his desk and coming around to greet them. The crisp way he shaped his consonants and vowels in that baritone voice of his pegged him as a Yankee. "I promise I don't bite."

Shelby wasn't too sure about that, but she held out her hand. Goodness, he was a tall man—she had to crane her neck to meet his steady gaze. "I'm Shelby McGuiness."

He shook her hand firmly, professionally, but she had to work hard to block the ping that fired up her arm from that brief contact. "Vander Montgomery. And that would make you Sadie." He immediately turned to her sister and shook Sadie's hand as perfunctorily as he'd shaken her own, giving Shelby time to pull herself together.

"Yes. That's me. It's good to meet you, Mr. Montgomery."

"Vander, please," he said, gesturing for them to take the two black leather chairs with decorative gold arms in front of his desk.

Shelby traced the leaf motif on the arm of the chair, taking in his office. He had expensive taste, but everything in the room was elegant. His desk was a sturdy Hepplewhite mahogany. A couple Montblanc pens in gold and red lay on his desk beside a day planner engraved in gold. A view of Nashville and the Cumberland River stretched out behind him. It all painted a picture that was as obvious as a tick on a hound dog. He was a powerful man who liked to make an impression, but who also felt comfortable working in a powerful setting.

As Vander resumed his seat behind the desk, Shelby's eyes lingered on the more inviting setup in the far corner of the room—a side table with gold-upholstered chairs. She wondered if he only met with clients there after they had officially hired him.

"You mentioned when we made this appointment that you're interested in locating your father," he said. "Tell me about him."

"His name is Preston McGuiness," Shelby said, clearing her throat when it seemed to fail her. "We don't know much about him. He left when we were children."

"How old were you both when that happened?" he asked, not bothering to offer his condolences, she noted.

"I was only two, and Sadie..." She gestured to her sister, wanting to include her in the conversation.

"I was a baby," her sister said, clutching her hands in her lap.

"And why are you interested in finding him now?" he asked. His posture was neither slouchy or ramrod, but he still exuded an intense interest she found compelling.

"We...ah...I..." Shelby was babbling and shut her mouth to compose herself.

"There's his medical history for one," Sadie blurted out with a huge gust of a breath. "You know, for family diseases and such."

He gave her a kind smile, and Shelby slowly blew her own breath out. Heaven help her, she hadn't expected to get this emotional.

"It's all right to be nervous," Vander said. "Looking for a father who left you over twenty years ago is a big deal."

Shelby nodded.

"The biggest!" Sadie blurted out. "Our other sister, Susannah, got married a few months back, which got us both to thinking. Our brother...you see...well, he escorted her down the aisle. She likely would have asked him to do it anyway—J.P.'s the best big brother there is—but she didn't have a choice."

Vander was still smiling, holding that steady gaze. "Congratulations. I hope your sister and her husband are very happy."

Her sister relaxed more in her chair. "They are. Thank you. And then there's...Shelby, you should tell him the rest."

That easy smile didn't alter as he turned it toward her.

"Well...we don't know why he left...or where he is." Shelby's heart was beating like one of those wind-up monkeys was pounding on it from the inside. "We don't even know if he's still alive."

"I see," Vander said, nodding. "Is your mother still alive?"

"Oh, yes!" Sadie said immediately. "Very much so. But she...doesn't like to talk about him."

He took their measure again. "You mentioned a brother and your sister, Susannah."

He earned at least ten points for remembering those facts after one casual mention. "Susannah doesn't approve of my wish," Shelby blurted out. "Our wish. Sorry, Sadie. She thinks it will open a can of worms and..." Gosh, it was awkward to tell someone their personal business like this. "She's afraid it will hurt Mama. I mean...we are too, but we want to know."

"J.P. is aware of our plans though," Sadie blurted out. "J.P.'s our big brother. He's given us his blessing, and that's... well, it means the world."

Vander smiled again at Sadie. "Thanks for clarifying that, Sadie. What do you think will happen when and if I find your father?"

"Ah—" Sadie exclaimed, looking at her for an answer.

"Is that question really necessary?" Shelby asked. "We're obviously here, and we want to hire you."

"I'm sorry if the questions seem personal," he said in that same even Yankee tone. "I know this must be hard for you. But in order for me to do my job to the highest standard, I need to know my clients' goals."

"It's simple," Shelby said with an edge in her voice. "We want to find our father. That's our goal."

Sadie looked over at her and shook her head as if to chide Shelby for being harsh. She couldn't help it. Questions like that might talk them right out of wanting to find Daddy. It was hard enough to dig into the past without considering the many ways in which it could go wrong.

"This is difficult for us," Sadie said, looking back at Vander. "I'm sorry Shelby was short with you."

"I can apologize for myself if it's needed," she said tersely, crossing her arms over her chest. She knew she was being difficult, but all of a sudden, she couldn't seem to help herself. Anger was pouring into her like water in a leaky boat—even though she knew it was misdirected.

"You don't need to apologize for anything," Vander said, rising and coming around his desk.

Shelby knew he meant it, and she released a pent-up breath. "I seem to be...emotional. I *am* sorry."

"Again, there's nothing to be sorry about," he said, sitting on the edge of his desk. "As I said before, kicking off a search like this is tough. It would be for anyone. I'm here to help you. We don't know each other yet, but if you agree to move forward with me, we will. I'll need to know everything you can remember about your father. Since you were so little when he left, most of what you know likely comes from other people. Am I correct?"

They both nodded.

"Most cases that involve an absence of this many years require a little more legwork. The databases I usually use to find someone only go back about twenty or twenty-five years—around when computers became mainstream. Your daddy disappeared on the cusp of that time if I've judged your ages right."

"You have," Sadie said. "I hadn't thought about the computer thing. Oh, goodness."

"It makes sense to me," Shelby said. "I didn't expect it to be easy. I've done my own Google searches and the like, and I'm pretty good at finding things out. I couldn't find anything."

"You seem incredibly smart...and brave," Vander said, gazing at her intently. "But I have access to information you wouldn't. We may get lucky with your father. We may input his name and last known address some twenty years back and get a hit."

"But you don't think it's likely?" Sadie asked, glancing Shelby's way, tension around her mouth.

"I have a gut feeling it might not be that easy," Vander said, resting his hand on his knee. "Otherwise, your mother wouldn't be so unwilling to discuss why he left or where he went."

"You think our mama might know all of that?" Sadie asked, blinking rapidly.

"Sometimes a parent keeps that kind of information a secret to protect her children."

That was impossible. "Our mama isn't secretive," Shelby told him, her mind spinning now. "She's a preacher."

His face didn't change, but Shelby thought his eyes

crinkled a fraction. "Was she a preacher when your father left?"

"No," Sadie said slowly, like she was thinking things over, "but both of them were good church-goin' people."

And yet, their daddy had up and left his wife and four children, Shelby could almost hear Vander thinking.

"What more can you tell me about your father and your family?" he asked.

Shelby let Sadie paint her version of the story, and while Vander kept his focus on her sister, she felt him glance her way every once in a while to take stock of her reaction.

"Is that how you remember things?" he asked her finally, shifting his large frame on the desk to give her his full attention.

"Sure...I mean...as you said, most of what we know is from J.P. and Susannah since we were so young." Truth be told, she and Sadie didn't really have their own memories of Daddy, and that bothered her more than she wanted to say.

"All right," Vander said. "I think I have a clear picture of things. Let me tell you what my services include. As I said, I'll use all the resources available to me to discover your father's whereabouts. Obviously, the greater the difficulty, the more resources I'll need to use, but I promise you, if you want me to, I will pursue every lead available. We won't know whether it will be easy or difficult to locate him until we start the search."

They both nodded. He pushed off the desk and walked around to sit in his office chair.

"Depending on how things go and what we find, we'll be in constant communication. If you need to reach me, I'm pretty much available day or night. Lucky for me, I don't need much sleep."

The thoughts that came into Shelby's head had nothing to do with Vander working a case to find their daddy. She imagined showing up at his front door in nothing but a trench coat. Goodness gracious, she really needed to stop watching murder mystery romances on TV. When she came back to the conversation, Vander was looking at her with that quiet intensity of his. Her mouth parted, and for a moment, she could have sworn he'd read her mind. Then he shifted his attention back to Sadie.

"And how much do you charge?" Sadie asked.

"Two hundred dollars an hour, plus expenses if there are any," he told them, handing them each a sheet of paper. "Here's my fee schedule so we're all on the same page."

His presentation was simple and flawless. Shelby felt Sadie waiting for her to make eye contact and knew her sister was worried about the money. Even though Sadie worked at a craft store and lived simply, she'd wanted to contribute to the cause. Shelby had agreed, but would be covering the lion's share.

"If you'd like to confer a moment," Vander said, standing again. "I can give you a few minutes."

Shelby suppressed her surprise. He obviously didn't have anything confidential in his office, or he'd never have offered to leave them alone here. Or maybe he had them pegged for trustworthy people. Most people assumed so, with their mama being a preacher and all. Then again, he might have a camera in his office. He was a P.I., after all. Gracious, she was overthinking things.

"Thank you for the offer to confer," Shelby said, knowing Sadie would do better if they chatted. "A moment would be *lovely.*"

He gave them that killer smile of his, as if he'd enjoyed every drop of sugar she'd poured into her Southern drawl. "Ladies, would you like anything else to drink?"

"No thank you, Vander," Sadie said, smiling at him as he turned and left them alone.

"I can handle his fees, Sadie," Shelby told her the moment the door closed.

"I didn't expect it to be so expensive," her sister said. "I guess I should have if Gail and all those politicians and celebrities use him. He's really nice, don't you think? I didn't expect that."

For some reason, Shelby hadn't either. She'd known he was handsome and successful, but Vander Montgomery also knew how to listen and manage client relationships better than many of the professionals she worked with. It only made him more attractive in her eyes.

"Do you think he can find Daddy?" Sadie asked.

Shelby took in the restrained power emanating from the room and nodded. "If anyone can, he can. But I think we're asking the wrong question. I rather hate admitting it, but Vander was right to press us about what we expect to find. Are we really prepared to learn things we're better off not knowing? I got mad at him, but really I...just got mad, is all. I feel like I'm poking a stick in my own hornet's nest, you know?"

"I know exactly what you mean," Sadie said softly. "I get angry, but it also makes me sad."

Suddenly Shelby wasn't sure what they should do. Vander had dredged up all the anger she'd shoved into a box a long time ago. Their daddy had abandoned their family. Their mama hadn't really ever explained it satisfactorily. Maybe she couldn't. But maybe Vander was right. Maybe Mama was being secretive to protect them.

"We were taught that pursuing the truth is always the best course of action." Sadie made a face. "Even though we weren't given that truth."

"Maybe Mama doesn't really know why Daddy left," Shelby said, as much to convince herself as her younger sister. "Maybe this would help her find closure too."

"She must suspect *something*," Sadie said, her voice raising. "A good man doesn't just up and leave his family without a word."

"No, you're right." That part of the puzzle had never made sense. If Mama had said he'd had a drinking problem or been in trouble with the law, Shelby might have understood. But no excuse had ever been given. He had been there one day, gone the next. That was all they knew.

"I sure wish Mama would answer our questions," Sadie said in exasperation. "It would save us a lot of money and heartache."

"But Mama hasn't said a word about him in all these years, even though she knows it's caused us heartache." Shelby felt her diaphragm tighten. "I don't see that changing."

"Neither do I," Sadie said. "And that scares me. Mama preaches about talking about things so they can heal, and all her silence has done is allow this hurt to fester and grow."

Truer words had never been spoken. Shelby didn't like to think about what it must cost their Mama not to live her values. Or why. In fact, it scared her spitless.

"What do we do if Susannah asks us about this again?" Sadie looked over her shoulder at the door to see if Vander had returned. "I'm terrible at hiding things."

"She's too happy with Jake to ask," Shelby said. "Besides, I think she's going to be an ostrich about this."

"But what if we find something?" Sadie asked, tears filling her eyes. "What if we find Daddy? Don't we have to tell her?"

Shelby's heartbeat ramped up, and she pressed her hand to her chest, taking deep breaths to quell its urgency.

"We'll tell J.P. first and see what he thinks is the best course of action," she said when she was able to speak. "Like we agreed."

"And Mama?" Sadie asked, wringing her hands now.

"If we all agree—and I mean even Susannah—we tell Mama we love her, but we needed answers."

Sadie got a little more teary-eyed at that. "I'm just going to pray God can soften this whole situation. We don't need any more hurt coming up from the past."

Yet, they both needed to find out the truth—or at least try to—in order to move forward with their lives. "So we hire Vander."

Her sister reached for her hand. "Yes. I still want to

contribute what I can."

"You really don't need to," Shelby said, patting her hand. "You know Gail pays me well."

"He's my daddy too," Sadie said with a stern nod. "I want to contribute *something.*"

Since Shelby knew better than to hurt anyone's pride—especially her sister's—she smiled. "I'll take them in baked goods and crafts."

"I can make you a quilt!" The corners of her sister's mouth tipped up.

"Sadie, you're always giving your quilts away. You should keep one for yourself." In fact, her sister usually thought of others before herself, just like Mama had taught them they should.

"I know you're right, but there's always someone who could use a quilt. Besides, the only reason I got good at them was because I made so many for the people at church. Now, I get to sell them at the craft shop. It's a blessing. Every quilt I make is stitched together with love."

Yes, every swatch her sister selected was done with intention. Her quilts were all the more special for it.

"I can make you peach jam too since we're just coming up on peach season," Sadie continued. J.P.'s wedding had been three weeks ago on the first Saturday of June, but because Tammy loved peaches so much, he'd found some early Eastern ones and asked Sadie to make a peach pie for the rehearsal dinner. It had been delicious.

Out of all of them, Sadie was the homiest. She'd even grown tomatoes for salsa last summer, and as if that hadn't been effort enough, she'd packaged jars for everyone in the family with hand-written labels and artful bows. She was a good sister to have around.

"Done," Shelby said, and they shook on it.

They hugged each other. The door opened, causing them to break apart.

Vander stuck his head inside. "Are you finished

conferring?"

"Yes," Sadie said brightly as he walked toward them.

He sat on the edge of his desk again and gave them that compelling smile. Her reaction to him was completely normal, she decided—the man was a chick magnet. His charm must come in handy with his job. People talked to nice, well-dressed handsome men—especially women.

"We'd like to hire you," Shelby said, giving him what she hoped was also a professional smile. "Thank you for letting us talk it through."

"This is a big decision. I want you to be one hundred percent sure you want to move forward."

"We do," Sadie said, nodding.

He gave them a measured look. "Let's go ahead and sign a service agreement so I can get started. You can tell me your father's last known address so I can include it at the bottom."

Sitting down at his desk, he typed for a minute, prompting Shelby when he needed the address, and then printed off the service agreement. He handed it to her when he was finished. Sure enough, their family's last address together loomed large at the bottom of the page.

They'd lived in that house for only a few more months after their daddy's abandonment, because Mama hadn't been able to afford the mortgage on her own. Shelby had been too young when they'd moved to miss the house on Meadow Grove Street, but she'd driven by it multiple times as an adult. It was something she'd never shared with her siblings, but every time she did it, she imagined what their life might have been if they'd remained whole. How she'd imagine Daddy pushing her on the tire swing. Or J.P. playing in a sandbox as a more carefree little boy.

Shelby wished she had more real memories of that simple white colonial house with the black front door and matching black shutters, but like everything else from that time in her life, she only knew it from pictures and her flights of imagination.

Sadie rummaged in her purse. "Do you need a photo of Daddy?" she asked, handing him the one of their family taken two months before he'd left.

Vander took the photo and studied it. "You have his likeness, Shelby." Then he locked gazes with her. "The eyebrow line is the same. And the mouth. Your bottom lip is... full...like his."

"Is it?" she asked, a little breathless. "I mean, do I...look like him?"

Sadie shot her a look, which she ignored. She needed to pull it together, but since no one ever talked about their daddy or so much as brought out a picture, she'd never been told she resembled him. J.P. resembled him more than the rest of them, not that the McGuiness siblings talked about it much. In fact, this photo was the only one they had of that time. Sadie had snuck it out of a photo album when she was a junior in high school and put it in her bedside stand. If Mama ever knew, she'd never said anything.

It rattled the heck out of Shelby to hear she looked like Daddy. Besides, Vander was staring at her with such intensity. Talking about her full bottom lip...

"You do. From this photo, Sadie takes more after your mother."

"Yes," her sister agreed, and Shelby wondered if she was longing to hear if any of her features resembled their daddy too. Those physical attributes were all they had of him—so far.

"The database I start with doesn't have any photos," Vander said. "I'll just plug in your father's name and last known address and see where things go from there. Sometimes I can use the local tax office to trace someone, but that's another step. If I end up needing to do some door-to-door visits at former residences, the photo might come in handy, although he's older now."

How many residences had their daddy had in the last twenty-plus years? There was so much they didn't know.

"This is a pretty precious photo, I imagine," Vander said.

"You two have a beautiful family. Would you like to keep it with you until I need it? Copies of photos aren't as effective in the field as originals. People tend to be more receptive and less suspicious if it's a real photo."

Sadie's lip trembled, and Shelby reached for her hand. She knew how important that photo was to her sister.

"You can keep it," Sadie said softly. "Maybe it will help inspire you…to see what he used to look like. Goodness, I… wonder if he even looks the same. It's been a long time, hasn't it?"

Vander nodded, and despite his polished façade, Shelby could feel the compassion in him. He might be a powerful man, but he had heart. Her interest in him was only building, and she wondered about him, personal things like where he'd gotten that accent, how he'd come to Nashville to be a P.I., and why in the world his parents had named him Vander.

"I promise I'll take good care of it, Sadie," he said, carefully laying the photo down on his desk. "Thank you for entrusting it to me."

Her sister gave him a teary smile, and Shelby knew they'd better hustle. Vander didn't need to see Sadie's waterworks during their first meeting.

"I'm happy to sign the agreement," Shelby said, taking out a pen from her purse.

When she looked up, Vander was handing Sadie a box of tissues.

"You go ahead and cry if you need to," he said quietly, still sitting on the edge of his desk. "Lots of people come into my office with difficult stories. You can't ruffle me, I promise."

The first tear slid down Sadie's face. Shelby had half a mind to shush her or stop her, but she knew better. When Sadie was like this, it was best if she let it out.

"You can leave us alone another spell if you'd like," she told Vander, taking her sister's hand and squeezing it.

He only spared her a quick glance. "No need. I told you. It

doesn't bother me."

And he seemed to mean it. Vander sat across from Sadie as she let loose a waterfall of tears, and Shelby busied herself with reading and signing the service agreement.

"Sadie," she said as she handed the signed agreement to Vander. "Let's let this poor man get on with his day and find you a cup of tea."

The look Vander shot her rooted her in her chair. His aquamarine eyes didn't look like calm waters now. There was heat—the kind that would scorch.

"Take all the time you need, Sadie," he said gently. *Don't listen to your sister*, Shelby all but heard him say, and if that didn't shame her...

"No, Shelby's right," her sister said, rising from her seat and handing him the box of tissues, which he set aside. "I'm sorry for that display."

"Pay it no mind," Vander said. "If you need to express your emotions at any time during this process, you just go right ahead. I have a broad shoulder. Sadie, I'd like you to sign our agreement too. Seems only right."

He shot Shelby a look that served as a silent message.

"But Shelby is...ah...paying for things," Sadie said.

"Payment is different," Vander said. "You're both my clients. He's your father too."

Sadie gave him a tremulous smile and signed it.

"When I have any news about your father," Vander said, setting the agreement aside, "I'll give you a call."

"I'll be your main point of contact," Shelby said, deciding it would be more efficient.

Sadie glanced her way, and there was hurt in her eyes.

Vander didn't respond immediately. "How about I text you both, and if you're able, we can set up a face-to-face? Once I confirm whether this is going to be easy or a little more challenging, we'll need to agree on next steps. I'll ask for your sign-off before I move ahead. Both of you."

He'd done it again. Impressed her with his ability to

manage his clients. Everything he did and said was carefully calibrated to ensure neither of them felt left out. Then she wondered if two people in the same family might develop different opinions during a process like this. That thought made her tummy burn. Surely she and Sadie would stay on the same page?

"That's fine," Shelby said, putting her arm around Sadie's shoulders to ensure he knew she cared about her sister.

"You've been wonderful, Vander," her sister said. "I'm... grateful."

"It's been a pleasure, Sadie," Vander said with that smile of his. "Shelby, it was good to meet you as well. I'll be in touch."

He gave her his total focus as he shook her hand, and she was firmer in her shake than she normally would have been. He didn't blink once, as if daring her to soften. She left his office quickly, determined not to quail.

Her sister hurried to keep up with her, and in the elevator, she didn't say a word. When they reached the parking lot, Sadie turned to her. "I know you're attracted to him."

Shelby didn't bother to deny it.

"I won't tell you what to do," her sister said, unlocking her older Honda. "I can't tell if he likes you or not. But he strikes me as a professional. I know you are too. Let's not make him... uncomfortable. We want him to find Daddy."

That hot anger rose up again, and Shelby took a moment before responding. Otherwise, she'd spew flames, and that wouldn't help anyone. "I won't make him uncomfortable. Besides, I got the distinct impression he didn't much like me."

It didn't matter, though.

She knew he wasn't the kind of man who would let anything affect his work.

CHAPTER 2

VANDER MONTGOMERY WALKED TO THE WINDOW AFTER closing the door behind his new clients. The view of the Cumberland River didn't calm him. Neither did the reminder that he'd earned this killer view of Nashville.

Every time a client hired him to find their father, he got all stirred up.

It didn't matter that he was thirty-five, and his father had been murdered twenty-five years ago this August. Part of what haunted him was that the crime remained unsolved after everything he'd done to find out who had murdered his father, Nashville detective Jed Montgomery. It didn't help that he was now the same age his father had been when he was murdered. He had no model for how a man was supposed to live past this age, and it bothered him. Acutely.

He shrugged out of his suit jacket, feeling constricted.

Vander had poured everything he had and was into finding his father's killer, until he'd been forced to face the conclusion there was nothing more he could do to find the man. After that, he'd poured himself into creating his detective agency and helping the people his father had served. That was something he'd succeeded at, *excelled* at. But it was no longer a challenge.

What was he supposed to pour himself into now?

Being a thirty-five-year-old successful bachelor in the South, he had plenty of people telling him it was time to find a good woman, settle down, and have a family. He'd never had much interest in that. After all, client after client had given him ample evidence that marriage and family didn't work out for everyone. It hadn't worked out for his parents either.

But work wasn't enough anymore. He knew how to deal with clients and handle their cases. Nothing felt like much of a challenge, except there was something about Shelby McGuiness...

As a P.I., Vander sized people up immediately—it was his gift and a key component of his success—but the man in him had sized her up as well when she'd sauntered into his office in her pale pink designer dress suit and sparkly chandelier earrings. She was as classic Southern as pecan pie, but with a modern edge. Her rose perfume dotted with a pinch of peony and musk suited her to a T, and her silky light-brown hair and whiskey-colored eyes had stirred something in him. Cream-colored Jimmy Choos with straps that wrapped up her calves like vines had showcased her knockout legs. He was a leg man, and he appreciated a woman who wore sexy heels. Sue him.

He'd even liked her strong and determined attitude until she'd turned it on her sister. Regardless of that fact, she'd fired something up inside him only his father's case and his business had fired up before.

He was going to need to keep a tight rein on himself while he worked on this case. It was counter to his personal code to show anything other than a professional interest in his clients. The curse word he uttered didn't ease his agitation.

A discreet knock sounded behind him, and Vander cursed again. He knew it was Charlie, coming to check on him. She was his number two, with the official title of vice president. He'd hired her for her sixth sense, but he hated it when she turned that uncanny perception of hers on him.

The door opened, but Vander didn't bother to turn

around. "I won't tell you to go back to work."

She snorted. "You know I'm too tenacious for that. Besides, I had those Southern belles pegged for a missing father the minute they walked into reception."

"It's a waste of company hours for you to monitor new client arrivals," he told her for the hundredth time.

"It's my way of testing my sixth sense," she answered like she always did. "Need to make sure it's one-hundred-percent accurate."

"It usually is," Vander said as she came up beside him, clad in simple black pants, low heels for running after people if needed, and a white button-down shirt.

All the detectives who worked for him were the best out there—he'd made sure of that. Gage Farris was an ex-cop who'd retired young, fed up with the bureaucracy and politics in Atlanta. Lawrence Patterson had run his own private detective outfit until he'd gotten tired of the paperwork and management and come to work for his biggest competitor— Vander. Then there was the support staff that Montgomery Associates used for the more routine work of background checks, something they had a slew of from their country singer celebrity and politician clients.

But Charlie was special. Somehow she'd become his best friend. It helped that they weren't remotely each other's type.

"Why don't you pass this case off to me?" Charlie asked him, putting her hands on her hips. "Give yourself a break for once. It's the twenty-fifth anniversary of your dad's death. I know it's on your mind more than usual."

It was. The thirtieth of August lived large in his mind. His nightmares had returned too. The ones where his mom told him his daddy had been hurt by a bad man and wouldn't be coming home ever again. Then there was the new dream that shook him to the core, where his dad's wounded corpse rose out of the morgue and asked him, *What are you going to do with the rest of your life, son?* before vanishing.

Vander tightened his muscles to fight off the shiver that

wanted to run through his body. He cleared his throat. "You know I can't do that, Charlie."

There was ultimately no choice for him. He'd returned to Nashville to go to Vanderbilt, where his parents had met and the place after which he'd been named, in the hopes of solving his father's murder one day. But while he'd failed himself, at least he could find other people's fathers—or mothers—or learn why they had been killed or had gone missing. It was the only redemption he'd found.

"You're a stubborn son of a bitch, Vander," Charlie said, frowning darkly.

"Don't I know it."

He had resigned himself to never knowing why his father had been left for dead in a downtown alley a stone's throw from one of Nashville's bottom-feeder music venues, the kind of place where washed out, hopeless musicians went to play and drink themselves to death, bemoaning their lost dreams.

The police report suggested his father had been undercover, looking into the selling of illegal substances onsite, and had been discovered somehow. No witnesses had ever surfaced. No prints were found on or around the body. And the murder weapon—a GLOCK 17—was never recovered.

"I was afraid you'd say that."

He was always reassuring her, but part of him liked that she cared enough to worry. Neither one of them had had much of that growing up.

"The girls were pretty," Charlie said in that practical way of hers.

"Were they?" he bluffed and immediately realized his mistake.

Before he could even register it, she was moving, and her hands were on his shoulders, turning him toward her. Her strength always surprised him since she was five foot nothing and weighed a mere one hundred and ten pounds, mostly muscle.

"Holy shit!" she said, staring into his eyes. "You're

attracted to one of them. You really need to give me the case now."

He frowned at her.

"The slightly older one, right? I'd peg them for Irish twins, but there's still an older/younger sister thing going on."

What the hell was he supposed to say? He'd felt that pull as soon as Shelby came striding through the door, trying to act like their appointment was just another business meeting.

"*Vander.*"

"Fine, she's hot," he said, brushing his shoulder. "But it's *not* a problem. Charlie, you know me. I wouldn't take the case otherwise. Shelby might be gorgeous, but I didn't like her much."

"Why not?" Charlie asked, studying him.

"Do you always have to ask so many questions?" he asked her in exasperation. "Forget I said that. Of course you do. It's your job." He'd best say it before she did.

"You're really riled up," she said, trying not to laugh. "What did this Shelby do to make you dislike her? Besides igniting some weird male attraction in you. Yuck. I think I need to wash my mouth out for saying that."

"Ditto for hearing it." But he decided to answer. "The younger sister, Sadie, has a soft heart, and I didn't like how Shelby treated her."

"Sadie cried, didn't she?"

"Yes, she did," he said, remembering how bravely the woman had tried to hide it in the beginning.

It pissed him off that Shelby had tried to stop her. The pain of losing a father was immeasurable, and his mother hadn't done him any favors by telling him to keep it locked up inside like his hurt heart was a bank vault. Her way of dealing with grief was to pretend none of it had happened. She'd moved them back to her rich family in Boston, who hadn't approved of her marrying a Nashville native, especially one who'd decided to go into law enforcement over the law.

His mother had soon fallen back into his grandparents'

mentality and had done everything in her power to beat the Southern out of him, even going as far as to make him take voice classes until all trace of his accent was eradicated.

For years, he'd fought the anger and the fathomless sorrow, but he'd erupted in high school, running wild, flirting with the law, all but daring his mother to throw him out like he felt she'd done emotionally.

It had taken his social studies teacher—also his lacrosse coach—pretty much busting his balls to get him back on track. Ruining his life wouldn't bring back his father, Mr. Hawkins had told him. Nor would it make his father happy if he was in heaven like people said. Why not position himself for a better life, so he could make his own choices once he turned eighteen? That advice had finally penetrated Vander's thick skull.

He'd stopped partying with the rough crowd, turned around his failing grades, and gotten into Vanderbilt University as a way to reconnect with his father and his roots. His mother and grandparents had been violently opposed to his return to Nashville, even more so the direction he'd taken with his studies, and it had been the last break in their already strained relationship.

Vander hadn't wanted to be a cop like his father, but he'd loved the idea of investigating things and uncovering secrets, so he'd majored in criminal justice. Becoming a private investigator had seemed the best course, and he'd pursued it wholeheartedly. He'd opened his own private investigation company in Nashville after securing his license, serving the same community his father had.

"Of the two sisters, *Shelby* looks more polished and tougher, although I bet they'd both still run in the opposite direction if I so much as said boo to them," Charlie said, leaving his side to open up the mini-fridge disguised as a cabinet.

She was tough, it was true, but something told him that Charlie might be wrong about the McGuiness sisters—or at least the older one.

"I'm not convinced Shelby would back down," Vander told her, following in her wake. "It took guts to come here. The mother doesn't know about their interest in finding their father, and their other sister is against it. The brother sounds like he's supportive."

"But he wasn't here today." Charlie handed him a bottle of Perrier—sue him, he liked the fizzy water—and grabbed a regular bottle of water for herself.

"No, he wasn't." And Vander wondered about that too.

"What's your gut tell you about this case?" Charlie asked.

"Home troubles, I'd bet," he told her, running through what little he knew of the case so far. "The mother is currently a preacher. Sounds like they all went to church together like a good Southern family before their father cut out on them."

"Going to church disguises a lot of deadbeats," Charlie said in that jaded tone of hers. "Foul play doesn't feel right to me."

"Me either," Vander said, and truth was, he could usually smell violence on a case before he had the facts to support it. "The reason isn't as important as the amount of time he's been gone. He went missing when Shelby was two, and from my guess of her age—"

"That was twenty-six years ago," Charlie told him with a smirk. "I looked up her driver's license."

"Of course you did, even though we're not supposed to use databases to look up our clients unless we suspect them of something," he said, rolling his eyes, doing the math. Shelby was seven years younger than him. Not that he had any business calculating things like that.

"Shelby Marie McGuiness also likes to speed," Charlie continued. "She got a ticket for doing eighty-eight on I-64 last month in a new white BMW convertible licensed to her and her alone."

The car suited her understated elegance. He ignored

Charlie's additional confirmation that Shelby wasn't married. Neither woman wore a wedding ring. Besides, any husband worth his chops would have been holding his wife's hand during an appointment as big as this one.

"I'm surprised she didn't talk her way out of it."

Charlie's smirk widened. "The officer was female."

"*Ah,*" was all he said.

"I'll run the father's name today," Vander said, taking a sip of his water. He hated to make clients wait on a case like this.

Charlie shook her head. "I already did."

"Dammit, Charlie! You didn't even have confirmation it was a lost father case."

"*Please.* You're insulting me. I always know. What was the use in waiting? It's a dead end, Vander. There are no records of any addresses or credit cards for Preston Matthias McGuiness after he left the Dare River area. He dropped off the face of the earth. He clearly didn't want to be found."

"You don't need to do my job for me, Charlie," Vander said, setting his water on the edge of his desk. "You have plenty of your own cases."

"Yes, but I knew those two were going to be trouble for you the minute they walked in," she told him, crossing her arms and staring at him with those determined hazel eyes of hers. "I'm going to help with this one, Vander, and you're not going to stop me. You need a friend right now more than ever with August 30th approaching, and since you're such a stubborn son of a bitch, I'm your best bet."

He cursed fluently, which only made her laugh.

"You can change your mind and give me the case," Charlie said, lifting her shoulder. "I promise to be gentle with the soft-hearted one."

This time he scoffed. "You couldn't be gentle with a koala bear. Dammit, you know I can't give up this case."

"I do," she told him, patting his shoulder before walking to the door. "Aren't you lucky I'm your best friend and don't listen to you when you're being a doofus?"

He didn't rise to the bait. "I'll let the McGuiness women know we want to take a look into his family and see whether they're up for it."

"I'll sit in on the next meeting with you," Charlie said, not posing it as a question.

The door closed behind her petite frame before he could respond—just like she'd intended. It looked like he was going to have a partner on this one. Of course, the sisters might decide not to move ahead after learning the official trail was a dead end. But something in Shelby's eyes told him she was ready to pursue the truth about her father as doggedly as he had tried to solve his own father's case. After meeting her and her sister, he had to admit he was pretty happy to have Charlie's support.

Not that he'd ever tell her that.

CHAPTER 3

SADIE WAS RIDICULOUSLY WORRIED SUSANNAH MIGHT SEE through her lame gift. She'd made extra peach jam to help pacify the guilt she felt every time she thought about hiring Vander without her eldest sister's blessing. Somehow telling J.P. she and Shelby had finally gone ahead and done it hadn't soothed her none.

Now she would have to join the rest of the family for their usual Sunday dinner and act like nothing was wrong. It was hard enough to lie at the best of times, which this wasn't. Vander had called them a couple of hours after Friday's meeting to say their daddy seemed to have disappeared without a trace. After the initial shock, Sadie and Shelby had confirmed with Vander that they wanted to dig deeper. J.P. had been supportive, thank God.

But the questions hadn't stopped racing through her head. How could anyone disappear like that? And why? Did it mean Daddy was dead?

Sadie headed into J.P.'s backyard, but while she'd gone around back in the hopes of getting a little more time to herself, Susannah stood there in the sun on the deck, her skin emitting a healthy glow. Heck, who could blame her—she and her husband, famous country-music star Jake Lassiter, were wrapped around each other. Susannah tugged away just enough to greet her, and Jake managed to kiss her cheek without letting go of his wife. She waved at the rest of the people lounging on the deck, and they returned the greeting before continuing their chatter, the melody of their voices blending together like the cicadas in the background.

"I brought y'all some jam," she said with a bright smile, thrusting the Mason jar out to Susannah.

The lime-green ribbon blew in the breeze. "Peach," Susannah said brightly. "Your favorite, honey."

"You're my favorite," Jake assured her before kissing her again.

It was something Sadie expected newlyweds should do, but it still embarrassed her a little. Kissing wasn't the only thing they were doing, of course, and it was weird to think of one of her siblings having sex. Of course, J.P. and his wife were too.

Sadie tried not to think about it. In fact, she tried not to think about sex, period. What was the point when you were a good girl and not supposed to have any before marriage? She'd blown that once, with a man she'd thought she would marry, but it hadn't worked out. No one had caught her eye since. She was still young, she told herself constantly—only twenty-seven—but the older women at church always reminded her that she wasn't getting any younger. It worried her some.

"What have you been up to, Sadie?" Susannah said, raising her face to the sun. "Could we have better weather?"

She latched onto the topic of weather like a child might embrace a teddy bear. "The weather is amazing! Hardly any humidity at all, and only eighty degrees. It's a blessing. How are your gardens coming along, Jake? Tammy told me they look real good."

Their sister-in-law was a marvel at creating gardens, which was how she'd connected with their brother, J.P. Of course, J.P. had hired his best friend's sister to design his gardens because he'd taken a shine to her. His strategy had worked because Tammy had felt the same way. Even better to Sadie's mind, Tammy's two children, Rory and Annabelle, adored him.

"The gardens look spectacular," Jake told her, grinning. "My favorite time of day is at dusk when your sister and I take a walk. I might have to ask Tammy to plant a chocolate garden for the little ones we're planning to have." The McGuiness siblings all shared a soft spot for chocolate, and Tammy had planted a garden full of chocolate-scented and colored plants for J.P. The two of them had created a magical story about fairies living in the garden to help Tammy's kids adjust after a traumatic experience.

Her sister's smile stretched wide across her face, and then she kissed her husband. Again. "I love it when you talk about kids."

Jake kissed her sweetly on the lips.

Sadie was over the moon that Jake's PTSD from his Army days was improved, but all the kissing was making her want to either roll her eyes or blush. She decided to make her excuses and head inside to help out with the last of the preparations for Sunday dinner.

"How are the newlyweds?" a familiar voice drawled from behind her. "We're gonna have three in the house today. I'm expecting a plague of bunnies or something."

Sadie didn't want to know what Rye meant by that, but she felt as jumpy as one of those bunnies, and she flinched a little when he snuck his hand around her waist and gave her a soft kiss on the top of her head.

"Hey, Sadie."

"Hello, Rye," Sadie said and hugged his wife, Tory, who was a few steps behind him. "You're looking more and more beautiful."

"I'm looking more and more *pregnant,*" Tory told her with a smile and pat to her enormous belly. "And I love it. This one," she said, nodding to her husband, "practically pounds his chest like a caveman whenever he talks about this kid. I've never seen anyone so primal."

Rye snorted while everyone else laughed. "It's why the women love me, honey. And why I look so good in tight jeans and nothing but a leather vest on stage."

Even though Rye was like a brother to her, Sadie had to agree with him. "No one stirs up a crowd of women quite like you do, Rye," she said. Turning to her brother-in-law, she added, "And Jake here makes us all cry buckets with his beautiful music." Of course, some of the songs Rye had written for his Yankee wife had made her tear up too. Come to think of it, there were plenty of things that made Sadie cry.

"I don't look good in tight jeans," Jake joked and extended his hand to his friend.

"Sure you do," Susannah said, resting her head against his shoulder. "You look handsome in everything."

"Love birds," Rye said to Sadie, sticking his thumb out and pointing it at the happy couple. "It's good to see it, isn't it? Speaking of love birds, who will bet me a hundred that my sister and *her* new husband are going to be a couple hours late to the party?"

Tory punched him in the gut, and Rye tried not to laugh as he pretended to double over.

"I think it's wonderful Amelia Ann and Clayton are acting like they just returned from their honeymoon," his wife told him.

"How can people keep acting like they're still on their honeymoon, Uncle Rye?" Rory asked, running off the deck and hugging his idol. "Are my mama and daddy acting like that too?"

Tory coughed and gave him a stern look. Sadie couldn't blame her. Rory might be wise beyond his years, but he was still a little boy.

Rye picked Rory up and tossed him into the air. "Remember how I'm always telling you about the idiosyncrasies of adults?"

Annabelle ran off the deck as well and hugged Jake's leg.

She'd taken him under her wing as soon as Susannah had started bringing him around to family events. Dressed in a pink dress with a blue ribbon running along the hem, she looked like a tiny version of her mama. "Are you talking about those idiot things adults do again, Uncle Rye?" she asked, clearly eavesdropping like she was wont to do.

Tory gave Rye a look. "Idiot, indeed. I know your uncle is hoping to expand your vocabulary because he thinks Southerners and idiosyncrasies go hand in hand, but it's still a pretty big word for kids your age."

Rory shook his head. "It sure is. I've been practicing and practicing it, but Annabelle's right. It's easier to remember idiot than idiosync—" His face scrunched up as he tried to pronounce it.

"And we can say that word," Annabelle told them with a conspiratorial smile. "Mama just won't let us say stupid. Because it's not nice. Right, Uncle Jake?"

He picked her up and kissed her on the cheek. "That's exactly right, sweet pea."

"Sweet pea," Annabelle all but purred. "I like that. We pick them right out of Mama's vegetable garden."

"Heavenly for sure," Sadie told her, tapping her on the nose and making her laugh. "I'm going inside to see if Tammy wants any last-minute help preparing dinner. Tory, you stay out here and sit a spell."

"Like that will work," Rye said, waggling his brows at his wife. "I keep telling her to sit down when she's cooking, but she won't listen, even though she's in her third trimester. I imagine she'll be cooking bread or something the day our baby makes its grand entrance."

"You met me when I was cooking in a diner, Rye Crenshaw, so you shouldn't act all surprised. Cooking relaxes me, and I need to keep myself occupied since you decided to push back your usual summer tour because you were afraid of traveling from city to city with me while I'm pregnant."

"I'm at a place in my career when I can hold off touring for a while," Rye said, cupping her cheek. "You and the baby are the most important things in my life."

Tory smiled and smoothed the hair from his forehead. "That's why I married you. But I'm still going inside with Sadie. I love being in the kitchen."

"I'll come along with you," Susannah offered.

"I'm staying with the men," Annabelle informed them all in a serious tone. "They need a woman's influence."

"Where in the world do you hear things like that, sugar?" Rye asked her, shaking his head.

"From you, Uncle Rye," Rory informed him. "It's in your latest song, 'Sons and Daughters.'"

"It sure is," Rye said, slapping his knee. "Y'all keep me on my toes. Come on, let's take a walk to your tree house before we're called in to eat."

The kids ran off, hooting and hollering like kids do, and Rye and Jake followed suit.

"They're going to make great fathers," Sadie said, turning toward her sister and Tory. "I'm so happy for y'all."

"Me too," Tory said, and Susannah simply gave her a stunning smile. "Anything interesting happen this week? I had a man at the grocery store try and touch my belly. What is it with people trying to touch pregnant women's bellies, anyway? I mean, would I go up to you and pat yours?"

"That sounds horrible," Sadie said, shivering at the thought of a stranger touching her so intimately. "Sometimes I have to wonder what people are thinking."

"I hope you gave him a what-for," Susannah said.

"I handled it," Tory said, "but since I'm trained as an anthropologist, I find it equally interesting *and* annoying. Okay, your turn."

Susannah got this moony look on her face that implied she was thinking of the kind of story that could not be shared, then blushed profusely and said, "I had a client ask for a wax figure of General Stonewall Jackson. The man's a Civil War buff and has more money than God. I told him I had no idea where I could commission a wax figure like that, but I'd look. Can you believe I actually found someone online?"

"That's crazy!" Tory exclaimed. "Beats my belly toucher hands down. Do you have any news, Sadie?"

Shelby and I hired a P.I. to find our daddy. She cleared her throat and looked away, trying to think of something else to say. Her mind seemed to be filled with sand. Oh, how she hated to lie, even by omission. "I...can't think of anything."

"Did you have any new quilt orders come in?" Susannah asked as they stepped back onto the deck to head inside through the back door.

Shelby waved at them from her seat on the patio furniture next to J.P., who also waved. Then their stepfather, Dale, and Rye's parents joined in. Suddenly it was a wave party.

"I'm making one for Shelby," she said absently, envisioning the purple and orange pattern she'd designed. It was the boldest one she'd ever created, but it suited Shelby to a T. Her middle sister had always been the most daring of the four of them, and their quest to find Daddy would require plenty of bravery from both of them.

"What are you making her one for?" Susannah asked. "Did she ask?"

She turned to look at her sister. Was that jealousy in her voice? Of course, the last time she'd made a quilt for Susannah had been for her birthday some four years ago. That year, she'd made all her siblings quilts. That was the year she'd finally decided her quilts were good enough to give as gifts.

"I..." Holy heck, she couldn't say it was her way of contributing to their Daddy Search Fund. "A pattern just came to me, and it's...perfect for Shelby."

Her sister's eyebrow rose. "Oh. I thought you were only making ones to sell now."

"I can make you one too if you'd like," she said immediately. "I thought you'd prefer the jam."

Susannah loved jam. Of course she'd made Shelby four jars of jam too, per their agreement. They hadn't heard from

Vander again since agreeing to meet with him on Monday to discuss their options for next steps, and while that made sense—it was the weekend, after all—Sadie had needed something to take her mind off the search. And the guilt. She'd given her mama jam too, professing it was a super late Mother's Day gift, choking on the words. She'd *lied*.

She was a horrible person.

"I'd like a quilt for our bed," Susannah said, her cheeks turning pink. "When you have the chance."

Sadie nodded over-enthusiastically. "Of course! Anything you want."

Her sister narrowed her eyes at her—she sensed something was off, all right—and Sadie turned to Tory to escape her regard. "I'm making one for the baby too, in case you were wondering."

Tory patted her arm. "I wasn't, but thank you. We'll cherish it, Sadie. I'm so happy you decided to sell your quilts through the craft shop. A talent like yours shouldn't be hidden away."

Her mama had always told her that too. She'd mentioned one of her projects—a cathedral window quilt she was making for a woman at church—to her boss, Debra Shumen, and the older woman had asked to see it. When Sadie had brought it in, Debra had exclaimed that her quilt making was more than a hobby. Sadie was a master at it. She'd asked her to bring some of her quilts to the store so they could showcase them by the register.

The four quilts had sold in two days.

Now, that hobby of hers was slowing turning into something more. People were buying her quilts at the store, and some were even commissioning custom-made designs. One woman had asked her to make a quilt from her deceased husband's old clothes, and Sadie had cried while making it. She didn't imagine she would ever make enough money to support herself through quilt making, but she had a nice nest egg starting.

Debra had even suggested Sadie start a quilting circle at the store, and darn it all if five women hadn't signed up immediately. And paid a class and materials fee too.

Mostly, Sadie loved giving people something from her heart, something that would touch their lives and have a place in their homes.

"Sadie!" Shelby called from the edge of the deck, a few yards off. "I need you!"

She smiled at Susannah and Tory. "I'll be right in."

As soon as she reached her sister, Shelby linked arms with her. "We're going to take a walk by the river before dinner," she called out to everyone as they took off across the backyard. "Be back in a jiffy."

Sadie had to hasten to keep up with her sister, who was moving like her tail was on fire.

"Are you *trying* to arouse Susannah and Mama's suspicions with all that peach jam you made them? Good heavens, Sadie! Mama said you were a jam-making fiend."

She had? "I'm sorry! I just had to keep myself occupied. I was going crazy. I also started your quilt."

"That's lovely, honey, but for heaven's sake! Keep it together, will you? I mean, we've barely started this process, and you're already buckling under the weight."

Sadie stopped on the path to the river and swatted at the gnats swirling around them. "It's a heavy weight, Shelby. Heck, Mama's sermon today about not telling the truth almost made me jump out of my seat. It's like she was reading our minds."

Her sister put her hands on her hips. "Preachers often speak about lying. It is the ninth commandment, after all. Mama doesn't suspect anything, but she *will* if you keep acting so guilty. Heck, you were wringing your hands the whole time you were talking to Tory and Susannah."

"I was?"

"You were. This is hard for me too. I pretty much cleaned my whole house yesterday, the closets too. Thank God Gail had a little party last night, or I would have gone plumb crazy."

"I can't stop thinking about it," Sadie said, looking down and seeing she was indeed wringing her hands. "Shelby, I keep imagining all sorts of things. Horrible things!"

"Me too," her sister admitted and hugged her.

"Y'all need another hug?" Sadie heard their brother say from behind them.

They jumped apart and stared at him, wide-eyed as two deer caught in the headlights of a big rig. He sauntered forward, his eyes narrowed.

"I was supposed to tell y'all to come in for dinner, but it looks like this is no casual walk by the river."

That was an understatement.

CHAPTER 4

IF SHELBY HADN'T BEEN WEARING HER FAVORITE GOLD sandals, she might have kicked at the rocks on the path to the river in pure frustration. Barely two days had passed since they'd met with Vander, and Sadie was already cracking up. J.P. clearly had enough intuition to notice, or he wouldn't be offering up hugs like he was the lead speaker at a hug-a-thon.

"I sure could use one, honey," Sadie said, all but flying into his arms. "We should have met with Vander on a Monday, J.P. This is pure torture, seeing everyone when we have news."

Here she goes, Shelby thought. "We don't have any more news, Sadie. Nothing we didn't already tell J.P. when we called him on Friday night."

"Tell her she's wrong, J.P.," Sadie said, giving their older brother an imploring look. "Learning there's no trace of Daddy *anywhere* after he left us is *huge* news if you ask me, and it's horrible. It has me imagining the worst."

"After we talked to Vander, you told me you were doing okay," Shelby said with a frown. "Why didn't you get all this emotion out with me before coming to family dinner?"

"It's not like I can turn it off," Sadie said. "I told you how I felt then, but I feel like a pressure cooker. All these feelings built up again."

"Sadie! You need to disguise what you're going through

better if we're going to keep this to just us three. Tell her, J.P."

Their brother gave a heartfelt sigh and wrapped an arm around Sadie's shoulders. "I'm not going to tell either of you how to act since I don't have a clue how to deal with this myself. I haven't slept much since you called me on Friday. I had to tell Tammy what was going on, and she's fretting too."

Well, wasn't that as terrific as key lime pie on a Wednesday? Shelby didn't begrudge J.P. for telling his wife, but this meant there was yet another person who had to hold it together at family occasions. It wasn't fair to Tammy somehow.

"I don't see how we're going to keep this a secret," Sadie said, her voice pitched a little higher than normal.

"Keep what secret?" a familiar voice asked, causing them all to spin around.

Susannah narrowed her eyes at them. "I knew something was going on. Peach jam out of the blue for me and Mama, and quilt making for Shelby. You'd better spill, Sadie."

Well, shoot. Susannah wasn't going to take this well, and then there was Mama to consider. "We're talking about doing something special for all the new brides—and that includes you," she said, hoping a fib would put a pin in it.

Sadie shot her a look, and she shot her one right back.

"I don't believe you," Susannah said in that definitive tone only big sisters could muster.

J.P. shook his head. "I don't think this is the way, Shelby."

Great. Their brother was going to be their moral compass again. Sometimes it was annoying.

Shelby faced her sister. "Fine! You want to know why we're flustered? We hired a P.I. to find Daddy. Since we know you are dead set against it, we didn't mention it. You need to decide if you want to be informed of the findings—like J.P. agreed to be."

Her elder sister flinched as if she'd been struck.

"I'm sorry, Susannah," Shelby said, already regretting her hasty words. There could have been a gentler way to share the news. Her fingers itched to hug her sister and soothe her. "We couldn't... We had to find out what happened to him."

"I'm really sorry, honey," Sadie said, walking over to their sister and putting a hand on her arm.

"You should be," Susannah told her, stepping back from her comfort. "What do you think this will do to Mama?"

Sadie hung her head.

J.P. strolled over to them, calm and steady as ever, and Shelby followed in his wake. Susannah had the right to get stirred up, but while Shelby didn't blame her for that, she wasn't sure where it would lead. Would she feel the need to spill the truth to Mama?

"I don't know how Mama will react if we end up telling her," J.P. said, as if reading her mind. "But it's not just Mama's first husband we're talking about. It's our daddy. I've struggled mightily with this, but Shelby and Sadie have a right to find him if they want to."

Susannah's eyes pretty much blazed fire. "I told y'all when it first came up that no good can come of it."

Shelby opened her mouth to respond, but J.P. put a soothing hand on her arm, stopping her. "No good has come from not knowing either. We're just more used to it, is all. There's already some news. Do you want to know what it is?"

Susannah put her hand to her forehead. "I just got married," she whispered. "I wanted to enjoy this bubble for a little while longer. I've been so happy."

"J.P. asked us to wait until after you were married," Shelby told her, swatting at the mosquitos biting her ankles. "We waited a spell. In fact, we waited until all of y'all got married."

"I appreciate that," J.P. said, "although y'all didn't have to wait for my wedding."

"You deserved it," Sadie said. "Please don't be mad, Susannah. I would hate that most of all."

"Well, I am," Susannah said, biting her lip. "And hurt too. This whole thing hurts me. Dredging up the past. Hearing you've gone along with them, J.P."

Their brother raised his brow. "They were brave to come

and talk to me about it. They could have done it behind my back after speaking with you, but they didn't. Their hearts are in the right place, Susannah. In the end, that's why I've given them my support." He paused for a long moment. "Our daddy might have up and left us," he finally continued, "but we stuck together and kept close. I'm not going to let this tear us apart. Are you?"

Tears popped into Shelby's eyes, and she noticed both of her sisters seemed choked up as well.

"You know I love y'all," Susannah said. "I just wish...y'all could have let this be. It's going to stir up so much hurt."

J.P. herded them all into a group hug. "All the more reason we face it head on so we can heal the rest of the way."

"I don't want to be wondering about Daddy on my wedding day," Sadie said.

"I'm sick of leaving a big blank whenever I have to fill out my father's medical history at the doctor's office," Shelby added.

"When Tammy and I have children of our own," J.P. said, squeezing them tight, "I don't want to get all upset whenever they ask where their original grandpa ran off to and why he's not around."

They all squeezed one another and pretty much sniffled, causing J.P. to pull out a few tissues from his pocket, the ones he kept for his women and the children.

"All right," Susannah finally said in a quiet voice as they eased back, their arms still wrapped around each other. "Tell me what you've learned."

As Shelby explained everything they'd talked about with Vander, both in the meeting and afterward, she could feel the muscles in her sister's back bunch up beneath her hand. Saying the words out loud somehow made it all worse, and Shelby felt like she was coming apart again. Where in the world could Daddy be? How could a person disappear without leaving a footprint in an age when everything was traceable by Social Security numbers or driver's licenses?

"So you're going to have this Vander keep looking?" Susannah asked after a spell.

"Yes," Sadie said. "I don't know what more he can find out, but there are other ways for him to search. He's going to meet with us again on Monday."

"What time?" Susannah asked.

"Why?" Shelby asked, shocked by the thought that her sister might join them.

"I want to pray, is all," Susannah said. "We're all going to need a lot of prayers to get through this."

"Amen," J.P. said.

The breeze blew through the trees, and Shelby shivered. Sometimes she felt something spiritual in these woods, and right now that sensation was stronger than ever.

"What do we tell Mama?" Susannah asked. "If I noticed something was up, so will she."

That was the God's honest truth. "I keep praying and asking if we're right to keep it from her, and I just don't know," Shelby said.

"What do you think, J.P.?" Susannah asked.

Their brother stayed silent for a long time, like he was prone to do when he was gathering his thoughts. "If she asks, we tell her. I have this feeling, though..."

"What?" Sadie asked anxiously.

He lifted his shoulder. "I don't think she's going to ask."

"That makes it easier, then," Shelby said. From a ways down the path, Rye shouted at them to come back to the house.

As they all looked in that direction, Sadie heaved out a sigh and said, "Does it? I'll still feel guilty as all get out."

"Me too," Susannah agreed.

"Let's see where things go," J.P. said. "We need to keep talking. If and when we learn anything more, we'll discuss it and come to a decision. Is that all right, Shelby? Sadie?"

Her younger sister nodded immediately, but Shelby took her time to think it through. When you gave your word to J.P., it was binding. What would happen if they didn't all agree about the best course to take with Mama? She suddenly had greater appreciation for why Vander had insisted that both she and Sadie sign his service agreement.

J.P. was looking at her with that patient gaze of his, and she finally nodded. "I promise."

"Let's head on back to the house to eat then," J.P. said. "The others will be wondering where we've gone off to."

When they returned for Sunday dinner, for which Amelia Ann and Clayton had finally shown up, they discovered J.P. was right.

Mama didn't ask them anything, but she watched them all night.

CHAPTER 5

WHENEVER GAIL HARDCREW INVITED HIM TO HER mammoth of a mansion in Nashville's tony Belle Meade neighborhood, Vander considered it a summons. He'd agreed to meet her, even though it was a Monday, a day he tried to stack with meetings that would start his week off right. With Gail, he never knew if a summons would cement or derail his week.

He'd done a lot of work for Gail over the years, everything from cleaning up her daddy's unfortunate death in the arms of his very young, gold-digging girlfriend to discovering the slutty blonde her recent ex-husband—that prissy asshole Calvin Henderson—was doing on the side. Beyond that, his firm conducted background checks and such for her business.

Vander liked having permanent clients, and Gail undoubtedly had connections, but he also simply enjoyed her company. She was like a one-person Southern theatre on crack.

The grounds of her ten-thousand-square-foot home were carefully manicured and tended like usual when he arrived, and the cherubs in the over-the-top Italian stone fountain in the center of her circular driveway looked like they were frolicking. Few people could display frolicking cherubs in their home without losing respect. Gail pulled it off with aplomb.

Gail's old-school English butler answered the door, and Vander gave him a nod of acknowledgement when he was allowed inside the mansion. Jeffries took his job seriously, to the tune of wearing old-school tails, and Vander did his best to indulge the older man.

"Ms. Hardcrew is in the informal parlor, Mr. Montgomery," Jeffries said in his lyrical English accent. "Please follow me."

Vander could find the informal parlor with a blindfold on—informal because it boasted a carved mahogany fireplace rather than a Carrera marble one like the formal parlor—and they both knew it. But that wasn't the point. Gail believed in maintaining appearances—until she had to fight dirty. He liked her best when she decided to go below the belt.

Not too many Southern women would stoop to the kind of measures Gail did, but that's what made her one of Nashville's leading female entrepreneurs. If Vander were back in Boston, he would have put it more bluntly: Gail didn't put up with anyone's shit.

"Vander, dahling," Gail said, rising in a low-cut pink dress that wouldn't have looked out of place on a contestant for the Miss Garden Rose beauty competition.

Her black curly hair bounced as she wrapped a white boa around her. She was dripping in jewels pretty much everywhere a woman could put them, and Vander had to bite his lip to hide his smile as he stepped forward to kiss the cheek she'd turned to the side so dramatically.

"Hello, Gail, it's good to see you," he said.

She swatted his chest and looked him straight in the eye, waggling her painted-in eyebrows. "But not good enough to take me up on my proposition."

She propositioned him every time they met. He told himself she was joking about them becoming lovers. Well, mostly. "Gail, you're one hell of a woman and gorgeous to boot, but alas, you're a client." This had been his script for years. Her scene was up next.

Her dramatic sigh made the white feathers on her boa

sway like a willow in a summer breeze. "Oh, Vander! You always disappoint me with that answer. I've been asking you since I got rid of that bastard ex-husband of mine. Need I remind you, I'm only ten years older than you. That's not much, is it, dahling?"

"Gail, you propositioned me after you divorced your first husband for stealing money from you for his horse gambling problem." Gail was nothing if not persistent.

She pushed at his chest flirtatiously. "Just imagine what might have happened if you'd taken me up on it! I might never have married Calvin, rot his soul."

Jeffries cleared his throat behind them, and Gail gave him the fish eye like she knew the butler was interrupting on purpose. Jeffries might be old-fashioned, but he was also protective—especially when it seemed like Gail was taking things too far.

"Well, fine, bring in the drinks, for heaven's sake, if you're going to interrupt us," Gail said to Jeffries, waving a hand in acceptance.

The silver tray the butler set down on the glass coffee table held a tumbler likely filled with Vander's current favorite bourbon, a green juice concoction he couldn't imagine Gail drinking, and some canapés.

"I can't drink this," Vander said. "It's not even noon."

She simply shrugged.

Without waiting to be asked, Vander sat down in the sofa chair with the pink, hibiscus-pattered cushions. He knew it was rude, but he couldn't lollygag with Gail for the rest of the day. There were cases for him to attend to, meetings to prepare for.

"What in the world are you drinking?" he asked Gail when she held her nose and sipped at her green drink.

"It's a kale and pineapple juice with a splash of lemon," she told him. "The doctors want me off alcohol for a spell, and I finally conceded. Every time I drink this concoction, it feels like the end of the world. You might as well engrave my tombstone now. Tell me, Vander, how am I supposed to enjoy life if I can't imbibe every now and again?"

Vander was hesitant to ask Gail why her doctors had her off the sauce, but since she was watching him so closely—almost daring him to give her permission to tell her sob story—he reached for his bourbon as a distraction. A few sips wouldn't hurt him.

Her face fell.

"All right," he said, giving in, "tell me why you're drinking that disgusting concoction."

Her smile was infectious as she launched into an emotional story about how the health of her heart was at risk due to a condition called hypertriglyceridemia. When she detoured into her family's medical history, waxing on about how blueblood Southerners never spoke about their health issues and how that tendency had almost killed her, he decided to take another sip of his bourbon. Gail was on a tear.

"And that's why I sent Shelby your way," she finished off, earning a sharp look. "She simply *has* to know about her daddy, Vander. Her very health could be at risk—and that of her siblings."

"Wait a minute," he said, setting his drink aside. "You sent Shelby to me? Shelby McGuiness? Related to Sadie McGuiness?"

"Good Lord, Vander!" Gail uttered. "How many Shelby McGuinesses do you think there are in Nashville, anyway? I mean, I know her mama named her after that Julia Roberts character in *Steel Magnolias*, but seriously. Of course I did!"

"This is unexpected. How do you know Shelby?" He didn't like being caught flat-footed—heck, he was the private investigator—but Gail was clearly loving this.

"She works for me, you fool!" she said, reaching for his bourbon. "I need a sip. To fortify me."

He rolled his eyes. "What does she do for you? I don't typically run a client's history unless it's related to the case."

He didn't need to know what she or Sadie did for a living to find their father. Then he remembered how Charlie had run both of the McGuiness women in their databases. Dammit, she must have discovered this. Why hadn't she told him? They were going to have a talk when he saw her.

"Oh, I love knowing something you don't," Gail said, pretty much finishing off his bourbon in two more healthy sips. "That must get your knickers in a wad. She's my personal accountant."

Shelby was an accountant? Somehow that intrigued him. She'd purposefully chosen an orderly profession, governed by legal structures like his was, even if hers was the IRS and his was the Tennessee Private Investigation and Polygraph Commission. But she also worked for Gail, the pinup girl for drama and chaos. What about Shelby had made her want to dance with both extremes on a daily basis?

"How did you two hook up?" he asked.

Gail picked up the silver bell she always carried around the mansion and rang it. "Jeffries! Excuse me a moment." When the man appeared, she gave him a radiant smile. "Another bourbon for Mr. Montgomery."

Vander shot her a look, which she pointedly ignored. "Thank you, Jeffries," he said. "I find myself thirsty."

When the butler was gone, she leaned forward, giving him a smile that could have made a Confederate general rethink his battle strategy, and whispered, "I only have a sip here and there. That won't kill me none."

His mouth twitched. "Nothing is going to put you in the grave unless you say so, Gail. That's one thing I know about you."

She slapped his knee. "That's why I love you so much. Vander, are you sure you don't want to knock boots with me?"

Vander shook his head. *"Gail."*

"I can't help it!" she said, fanning herself. "You're so handsome and compelling. I barely remember you're a Yankee when we chat."

He found himself chuckling, knowing she was mostly teasing. It didn't matter that he'd been born in Nashville and lived here his first ten years. He'd left—and then come back without a Southern accent. To some, that was heresy. "You were about to tell me how you happened to hire Shelby."

"Right! She applied for the advertisement pretty much right out of college, but she had grit—something I admire in people—and she was so earnest, what with her mama being a preacher and all. I just knew she'd never steal any money from me like my first husband did."

"How is it you haven't mentioned her to me before?" Vander asked.

"I don't have you investigate everyone who works for me, Vander," she said, "and since you refuse to come to my house parties, y'all have never crossed paths until now."

Gail's house parties pretty much terrified him, and Vander didn't scare easily. The engraved invitations were enough to make him queasy, partly because they reminded him of the kind of events his mother and grandparents used to hold in their Boston mansion. He'd never been allowed to attend any of the family parties because he was a reminder of his mother's greatest mistake. He'd been kept upstairs with his nanny, the orchestra music and laughter filtering in through the windows his only link to the events going on two stories below.

This past May, though, Gail had invited him to something his old-moneyed Boston family would never have imagined in a million years: a May Day celebration, the entertainment of which had included a painted yellow horse and dancing fairies. Of course, the fairies were actors from the local theatre scene, but still. There wasn't enough bourbon in all of Nashville to entice him to attend a party like that despite how unique the invitation had been.

"All right, I'm glad to know about the connection," Vander said. "It's interesting Shelby didn't tell me you referred her."

Gail gave Jeffries an innocent smile when he reappeared

with the bourbon. "Vander, your drink."

He took the drink and played along. "Thank you, Jeffries."

The man bowed and left, and Vander handed Gail the glass. After taking another healthy sip, she sighed and said, "Bourbon is so delicious, don't you think? Especially on a Monday morning."

"It's almost noon, Gail," Vander said to make her feel a little better.

"It is indeed," Gail replied, rearranging her boa. "I'm not surprised Shelby didn't mention that she works for me. The girl is special that way. She doesn't use her connection to me like she might. Because of that and all of the good she has done me over these years, I'd like to pay your fee. That's why I asked you to come in today, Vander."

He sat back in his chair. "You want to foot the bill? She must be special to you."

"She is," Gail said, patting her heart. "And pretty too."

While he agreed, he still rolled his eyes. "You're incorrigible."

"And you're getting too old to still be a bachelor around these parts," Gail said with a wink.

While he might be having a recurrent nightmare about his dad asking him what more he was going to do with his life, he wasn't prepared to give Gail any indication he was doing a personal inventory of it.

"I don't want to end up divorced and paying alimony to no-good exes like someone else I know," he said, both because it was partly true and because he could be balls-to-the-wall honest with Gail. "You're not my only client who's gotten screwed, blued, and tattooed by an ex."

"That's why I like you, Vander," she said, leaning forward and giving him an enchanting smile. "You tell it like it is. When you marry, and despite your cynicism, I expect you will—you're too handsome and kind-hearted to remain alone forever—you'll choose well. No mere girl would suit you. That's why I thought you might go for me. I'm a seasoned woman."

Hearing Gail refer to him as kind-hearted made him more than a little uncomfortable, so he tried to keep things light. He let a smile snake across his lips. "Seasoned, huh? Is that what they're calling it these days?"

She slapped him in the face with her white boa. "I'll ignore that unchivalrous remark. Now, tell me what you've found out about Shelby's daddy so far. I know y'all met on Friday. Plenty of time for you to run him."

"Gail," he said, leaning on the edge of his chair. "You might want to foot the bill for this case as a kindness to Shelby, but I can't share any information with you. It's unethical."

"Unethical," Gail harrumphed. "That's ridiculous! I'm only trying to be supportive."

Vander stood and buttoned his jacket, making a show of eyeing his watch. "I have another meeting. You can ask Shelby about the case, but not me. We need to get that straight right now. And no late-night calls or texts either."

Her mouth pursed, and she threw her white boa over her shoulder again. When a feather landed on her lips, making her cough to clear it, he couldn't help but chuckle.

"Fine!" She stood and fluffed her boa, sending more white feathers dancing into the air.

When she stuck out her hand, he shook it. "Deal."

Rather than release his hand, she pulled him closer. "It was good to see you, Vander."

He kissed her cheek. "You too, Gail. Behave for once."

"I'll go to my grave misbehaving," Gail said, picking up his bourbon and toasting him. "You know where I live if you change your mind."

She was as flirtatious as she was tenacious, but she'd never taken it any further, which is why he allowed it.

"Enjoy my bourbon," he said as he left the parlor.

"Oh, I plan to," she called out to him.

Jeffries appeared in the foyer as if by magic and opened the front door. Vander took note of the white BMW convertible cruising down the drive, but he didn't realize it was Shelby until he'd made it down the brick steps. She cut the engine and reached for her purse before swinging out of the car.

Vander tried not to notice the curves hugged by her sage green dress suit decorated with a simple strand of pearls. Her shoes and purse matched—a totally Southern thing that still mystified him after all these years—and were an off-white. That luscious brown hair of hers blew in the breeze, and his fingers twitched with the longing to touch it.

When she saw him, she immediately halted. "Oh!"

He fought a smile at her greeting. "Hello, Shelby. I was just calling on your boss."

She looked toward the house. "I didn't want to use her name. Gail has had too many people use her. It was enough that she recommended you."

Vander was seeing Shelby in a new light after his talk with Gail. There were layers there, and he suddenly wanted to discover them, everything from why she liked order to the kind of ethics that hadn't allowed her to use Gail's name. "On that, we agree. Some of the work I've done for Gail has been to protect her from just those kinds of people."

Her nod was perfunctory. "I'd imagine so. I'll...see you for our meeting later on."

He'd scheduled them for five-thirty since the rest of his day had already been booked. "I'm looking forward to it," she added, her voice a bit husky.

He wanted to linger, he realized, but that was exactly why he couldn't. After giving her a curt nod, he started off to his car.

"Would you like a penny?" she called out to him.

Turning, he watched as she opened her baby blue coin purse and extracted two coins. "What for?"

"The fountain," she said, holding the coin out. "So you can make a wish. You don't keep change in your pocket."

That was an interesting observation, and he found himself walking back toward her. "How did you know that?"

"Men jingle when they carry coins," she said matter-of-factly. "You don't."

Oh, the jokes he could make. "Indeed I don't."

Her cheeks pinkened prettily, and he realized she was blushing. He fought the urge to clear his throat. She extended the coin to him again, but he shook his head.

"I don't make wishes," he said flatly.

Her mouth parted in surprise. "Ever?"

"Ever."

She lowered her head and held the coin to her ample breasts for a moment, drawing his eyes somewhere they shouldn't go. Then she threw the coin in the fountain.

"I'm sorry you don't believe in making wishes," she said, studying him closely.

How was he supposed to explain himself to her without giving away too much? The day his mom had told him about his daddy, he'd gone to bed and made a wish that his father would rise from the dead like Jesus had.

Of course, his daddy hadn't risen, and Vander had wiped away tears at the graveside as the other officers lowered his daddy's coffin into the ground.

He'd wished a few times more. For his mommy to stop locking him out of her room and not coming out all day. For someone to find the man who had killed his father.

None of his wishes had been granted. And so he'd stopped believing.

"I make my own fate," he told Shelby, his voice a little harsher than usual.

"Wishes are like prayers," she said, fingering the coin still in her hand. "There's an infinite supply. You can never wish too much."

Anger rocked through him, and he ground his teeth to control it. "Wishing doesn't make anything happen. Shelby, I need to go now. I'm late for my next meeting. I'll see you and Sadie later."

He stalked past her to his black SUV and slammed the door once he was inside. She was watching him, a pretty picture in the sunlight. When she turned back toward the fountain with the frolicking cherubs and threw in the remaining coin, he made himself pull out of the driveway instead of gunning it down the lane as he was tempted to do.

CHAPTER 6

SHELBY WATCHED VANDER SPEED DOWN GAIL'S DRIVEWAY to the gates. Goodness, he'd gotten angry. What had made him so jaded? Shelby wasn't naïve enough to believe everyone prayed, but she had thought those who didn't at least wished for things.

Not Vander, apparently.

She headed to the front door, shaking off the image of Vander radiating intensity in the hot morning sun, looking both fierce and delicious in his Italian gray suit. Jeffries answered the door promptly, and they went through their usual comedic interaction.

"Hello, Jeffries," she said, giving him as regal a nod as she could muster. "Fine weather we're having." She used that line often because she'd heard it in British movies.

"Indeed it is, Ms. McGuiness," he answered, looking as if he might break his rule and smile for once.

Butlers from England apparently never smiled. They were like those guys with the tall black hats who guarded Buckingham Palace. Perhaps they endured the same no-smile training. Such a shame, if you asked her.

"Ms. Hardcrew is in the informal parlor."

Like normal, Shelby waited for him to show her the way. Just this once, she wished she could ask him if he'd ever thrown a coin into Gail's fountain. Vander's attitude about the whole thing had made her wonder how other people felt about wishing.

From the minute she'd thrown her first coin in Gail's Italian fountain all those years ago the day of her job interview, Jeffries had begrudgingly accepted her eccentricity. Apparently no one had thought to pollute Gail's precious Italian fountain with coins before, but people had begun to do so after seeing Shelby's coins at the bottom of the water. Jeffries pretended he didn't like it one bit, but Gail assured her it was all an act. Her boss, of course, found the tradition charming—so much so, she'd insisted that her butler leave the coins there. Over the last five years, the number of coins had multiplied until they took up more space at the bottom than the handmade blue Italian tiles.

Shelby liked to think of Gail's fountain as the fountain of infinite wishes. Her luck had changed for the better the moment she'd thrown that first coin into the water, wishing for a successful interview. Five years later, she had a fabulous salary that allowed her to afford the finer things in life, a convertible BMW named Pearl that she loved to hear purr on the road, and the best darn job an accountant could ever hope to find. With an incredible boss to boot.

When she stepped into the parlor, she couldn't help but smile at Gail. "Do you know how grateful I am to be working for you?" she said spontaneously.

Jeffries cleared his throat behind her, and she spared him a quick glance. Her wish had been granted. There was a slight uptick to his usually stern mouth. He was smiling!

"Shelby McGuiness, you're going to make me cry," Gail gushed, and Shelby turned to look at her boss, who wrapped her white boa around her.

"No need for that," she said, and then Shelby spotted the half-drunk bourbon on the table in front of her boss—a common occurrence despite Gail's protestation she wasn't drinking for health reasons. "I was just thinking about wishes and how important they are. If you don't wish for anything, you can never receive anything."

"Indeed, miss," she heard Jeffries mutter behind her before closing the door and leaving them alone.

Saints preserve her, but Jeffries seemed to believe in wishes too!

Only Vander didn't, and he was still successful, so there had to be some disconnect in her thinking. Well, he could continue to do things his way, wish-less, while she remained committed to hers.

"Shelby, I know why you didn't tell Vander you worked for me, but Lord Almighty, girl, you should have. He'll always do his best, but your connection to me gives him an added incentive."

"Is that why he was here?" Shelby asked, coming over and sitting down on the sofa next to her boss.

Gail gave her a decided wink. "Yes. Plus, I'll use any excuse to see that man. God knew what he was doing when he created that one."

Would *Amen* be an appropriate remark? Shelby bit her tongue.

"Oh!" Gail threw out her hand like she was prone to do when she got stirred up. "I almost forgot. I also told Vander I'm paying for his investigation into your daddy's whereabouts and the like."

"What?" Shelby said, blinking. "No, Gail. You don't need to do that. Really."

Gail grabbed her hand and squeezed it. "Shelby, you just said how grateful you are to have me in your life. This is my way of saying how grateful I am for all you do. Please don't fight me. You know you won't win."

Since Gail kept a pair of old Southern dueling pistols loaded in her office, Shelby knew she was serious. "It's hard for me to receive this."

"Land sakes, girl!" Gail exclaimed. "Think of it as a bonus. You were kind to me when I found out about this health condition. And you listened to me when I said how important it was for you to know your daddy's medical history. Plus, I know you throw coins into the fountain outside for me all the time. I'm doing this, Shelby McGuiness, so you'd just better accept it."

Shelby's mama had also raised her to be gracious, so she finally nodded. "Thank you, Gail. Truly."

"Good, then it's all settled." Gail traced the rim of the bourbon glass. "I might have one last sip. Now, since Vander won't tell me one eensy-weensy detail about your daddy's case, I'm supposed to ask you. Of course, you can keep it secret from me if you want."

Keep secrets from Gail? Shelby didn't think that was possible. "Why would I keep it from you? If you want to know something, just ask. All I can tell you right now is that the initial search on Vander's databases produced nothing. We're meeting later today to discuss our next steps." Which would mean more time and money. "Gail, are you sure I can't pay at least half of Vander's bill?"

Gail gave her the fish eye. "Give it up, girl. No way you're covering half when I offered to pay in full. You meet with Vander and tell him to use *all* his resources. Vander will find him or what happened to him, honey. He's tenacious, that one."

Under Vander's cool reserve, Shelby had felt a seething intensity. He'd been angry at the fountain today, not at her. She wondered again what had happened to him. To avoid thinking about him, she forced her mind toward practical matters. "Something's been bothering me a little."

"What is it?" her boss immediately asked, throwing off her boa and turning all business.

"Why haven't I seen any checks to Montgomery Associates on the books?" she asked.

Gail chuckled. "That's a good question, Shelby. When it came right down to it, I didn't want anyone to know I'd hired a private investigator to look into or clean up the...eccentricities in my marriages and families. I write Vander personal checks. None of the money comes through my business holdings. People might find out and not like it. Not that I did a check on you. You were as sweet as pie, so I knew I could trust you."

That made sense to Shelby, although she could have made some of it a tax deduction. "Okay, I just wanted to make sure I hadn't missed something or you hadn't—"

"Trusted you?" Gail asked, shaking her head. "Shelby McGuiness, there are few people I trust as much as you. I mean, I trust you enough to see me naked at the mortuary and dress me for my funeral. That's powerful trust for a vain Southern woman like me."

That image pretty much made Shelby's insides shrivel up, but since Gail was prone to dramatic metaphor, she managed a weak smile. "Thank you, Gail."

"All right," Gail said, ringing her silver bell for Jeffries. "Let's talk business over the lunch I had prepared, and you can walk me through the projections on the new restaurant. Then you can dash off to your meeting with Vander. Oh, how I wish I could be there. I never tire of looking at that man."

Shelby drew out her folders. Gail sure as shooting sounded like she had a thing for Vander. Good heavens, did he have a thing for her boss? Her stomach clenched, and she realized she didn't like the idea. Okay, that was wrong of her. There was nothing between her and Vander. He could like whomever he wanted. Plus, it was none of her business.

She opened the printouts of Gail's current budget projections as Jeffries brought in a silver tray with two spinach salads on Gail's gold-rimmed Bavarian china. They got down to business, and for the next few hours, Shelby forgot all about the search for her daddy and Vander Montgomery.

Of course, the minute she stepped outside into Nashville's humidity, her current worries were lying in wait for her. She drew out another coin from her purse—a quarter since it was a big wish—smiling a little at the thought of Jeffries' first smile earlier. She closed her eyes and pressed the coin to her heart. *Please, God. Let Vander find out what happened to our daddy. And please don't let his findings hurt anyone I love.*

She threw it in and started to walk away, but before she got more than a few steps she pulled out a simple penny and turned back to the fountain. This time, she threw the coin with all her might.

Please, God. Let Vander believe in wishes again.

Back in her car, Pearl, she cranked up an oldie but goodie by Madonna, singing "Like a Prayer" to distract herself all the way to Vander's office downtown.

When she arrived in the lobby, Sadie met her with an exuberant hug.

"I have news I think you'll like," Shelby told her sister. "Gail wants to pay Vander's fees. She wants us to find Daddy."

Tears filled Sadie's eyes. "That's the sweetest thing ever. I'll have to make her something to say thank you."

"Can you make a quilt with feathers?" Shelby asked with a smile. "Gail was wearing a white boa with her pink dress today. It was so her."

"I love that woman's fashion sense, but I'd be too scared to style myself that way. Imagine what some people would think. Especially at church."

Considering none of the McGuiness women wore white before Memorial Day, Shelby knew what her sister meant. "Let's head on up upstairs and see what these next steps are."

When they reached Vander's office, he greeted them with a smile. His bleak mood from this morning seemed to have drained out of him. A small but tough woman stood beside him as he greeted them.

"This is my colleague, Charlie Madison," Vander told them as the woman shook their hands. "She's going to help me with your case."

Charlie had a heck of a grip and pretty, intense eyes. Shelby wondered why in the world her people had given her such a masculine name. But perhaps they'd known she wasn't much on girl stuff when she was born. Her face was barely painted, and her clothes were downright simple. Not that she knew what female P.I.s typically wore.

"Nice to meet you both," the woman said, and while there was a touch of Southern in her voice, it wasn't pronounced. She also didn't say y'all.

Shelby smiled at her to be pleasant, wondering why Vander needed a helper.

"If you don't mind helping me bring in the drinks, Shelby, I'd appreciate it," Vander said, drawing her attention back to him.

"Of course," she said rising, wondering why he was making such a production of it. After all, his receptionist had already asked if they wanted something, and they'd both declined.

"Sadie, what would you like?" he asked.

"Tea," she responded, giving Shelby a shrug. "With lemon and honey if you have it."

His lips twitched, but he nodded. "I'll see what I can find."

In the kitchen, he made a couple of cups of coffee—likely for himself and Charlie since Shelby had told him she wanted tea as well—while she poured hot water into two tea cups.

"Did Gail mention she offered to foot the bill for my services?" he asked casually as she stirred in the honey he'd produced from one of the cabinets.

"Yes," she answered, taking her gaze off the cups and looking into his aquamarine eyes. "It was kind of her."

"It was, indeed," he said, dumping two sugar packets into the dark roast coffee. "I wanted to make sure she was transparent with you. The last thing I want is to be between Gail and a hard place."

"She also mentioned you wouldn't discuss the case with her. I appreciate your professionalism."

"I've known Gail a while now," he said, leaning back against the counter and sipping his coffee. "Despite her good intentions, she's the kind of woman who will run all over you if you don't establish a few boundaries."

"Gail is nothing but well intended," Shelby agreed. "Does

it make you uncomfortable? When she asked you about the case?"

"I can handle Gail," he told her. "I just wanted to make sure *you* were comfortable. This search is already difficult emotionally. You don't need to be concerned with anything else."

The regard he had for her feelings gave her a warm glow, but she told herself he was only being kind. "I'll be fine. I know how to handle Gail in my own way too."

His lips turned up at the corners. "I have to admit, I was surprised to hear that you work for her. I might have underestimated you some."

"*Indeed*," she said, her eyebrow rising as she studied him.

"You must be more adventurous than I realized, but you also long for order," he said, his aqua blue eyes intent. "I won't make the mistake of underestimating you again."

She felt like shifting on her feet. This man whom she'd known for only a few days had picked up on something few people ever perceived about her. She was drawn to the wild and eccentric in others—it energized her—but she also liked having a tidy, orderly space of her own to retreat to.

"You must enjoy Gail's company, or you wouldn't accept one of her outlandish summonses," Shelby said, lifting her mug of tea and taking a sip.

"She's greeted me wearing her Southern theatre costumes before," he said. "She might dance around the line of professionalism—that's why I like her—but she never crosses it. Or I wouldn't work for her."

Well, that answered Shelby's question, one she would never have asked either one of them. It took her a moment to recognize what she was feeling as relief. "You never date a client then?"

He set his mug aside and crossed his arms, looking at her intently. "No."

She felt oddly deflated somehow, even though she agreed it was the best course. It only made her think better of him to know he stuck to the rules of good business.

"Not that I'm not tempted like every other man," he added in a roughened voice that more than garnered her attention.

Her internal temperature heated like a tin pie plate left out in the sun at a church picnic. So he wasn't immune to her. Part of her wanted to throw her hands up and cheer like a ninny. "We should go back to your office."

"Yes, we should," Vander said, picking up the coffee mugs while she grabbed the tea for her and her sister. "I'm sorry I snapped at you earlier, by the way," he added. "About wishing at Gail's fountain. It wasn't about you."

They stopped at the kitchen door, or perhaps Shelby did. It took a lot for a strong man to apologize. She knew that from growing up with J.P. "I knew it was about something else."

He looked down, and there it was again, the flash of anger across his face. This time Shelby saw plenty of hurt there too.

"What happened to make you stop wishing?" she asked, unable to stop herself.

"I lost my family when I was a kid," Vander told her and then walked around her toward his office.

Shelby watched him walk down the hall, her throat thick with emotion from the no-nonsense way he'd said it.

That would make anyone stop wishing, she thought, including her.

CHAPTER 7

SHELBY SURE WAS TAKING HER SWEET TIME GETTING THEIR beverages with Vander. Sadie wondered if her sister had finally succumbed to flirting with the man. She saw how Shelby looked at him.

But when Vander walked back into the office and handed Charlie her coffee, it was obvious the last thing on his mind was flirting. Otherwise, he wouldn't be scowling like that. Shelby came through the door moments later, not meeting her eyes.

"Let's sit over at the table," Vander suggested. "That way, we can be more comfortable."

When Shelby sat beside her, Sadie noted her face was ghastly white. What in the world had those two said to each other? She drank her tea and reached for her sister, even though she knew Shelby thought it was unprofessional to hold hands in a meeting. But her sister took it like she needed a lifeline.

Sadie caught Charlie glancing at their clasped hands. That woman was as tough as rawhide if you asked her, with a name that suited her. Charlie didn't like women much, Sadie could tell, or at least not women like them. Sadie needed to quell the urge to make an ugly face.

"All right, let me walk you through what I think are the

best next steps," Vander said. "There are two paths we could take, so to speak. The formal route would take more time and resources. Charlie and I would check with some of our older police department contacts to see if they remember anyone matching your father's description. Maybe your mama or your father's family listed him as missing at some point."

"A missing person?" Sadie exclaimed. "I never thought of that."

"What's the other route?" Shelby asked, gripping her hand.

"We can run his family members in our databases and look up their social media accounts. You'd be amazed how much people put out there, and in some cases we've had more luck using Facebook and the like than our databases. Of course, you'd have to decide if it's worth reaching out to them directly to see what they know. Not everyone wants to go that route."

"Just because your mother doesn't know where your father is doesn't mean his family doesn't," Charlie told them, interjecting herself into the conversation for the first time.

Her words arrowed right into Sadie's heart. Would Daddy really have stayed in touch with the family he'd grown up with but not them, the family he'd made himself?

"So we might have to make contact with them," Shelby repeated in a soft tone.

"Goodness, that would be something, wouldn't it, Shelby?" Sadie said, wondering what his kin were like. Mama had always said they were mean, but maybe they'd changed. People did. Maybe they had another whole family waiting to embrace them.

"What do you know about your father's family?" Vander asked, studying them intently.

"His people are from Memphis," Shelby said, bouncing her knee, a clear sign she was anxious. "That's about all we were told. Mama never had any contact with them that we know of."

"They went to the wedding," Sadie offered. "I've seen the

photos."

Shelby nodded. "Right. I don't know why they never came around after that. I remember Mama saying his family was unkind to the core."

"Mean as rattlesnakes," Sadie interjected.

"Of course, we might not find anything," Charlie said, "but those are the best bets."

"You don't think he's dead, do you?" Sadie made herself say.

"We can't be one hundred percent sure," Vander said, "but there's no death certificate with his name on it in our databases. I wish I could offer you more assurances than that, Sadie, but right now I can't."

Sadie didn't like thinking her daddy might be dead—even if he had up and left them.

"We also can't be certain he's not incarcerated," Charlie added, and that statement was enough to elicit a gasp from both McGuiness sisters.

"Incarcerated?" Shelby croaked out.

"You mean prison?" Sadie asked, her heart contracting at the mere thought. "Good Lord above, I never even thought about that. Oh, Shelby, that would be the end of the world." Imagine that, their daddy behind bars for doing something illegal, wearing some horrible orange jumpsuit. She felt faint.

"But wouldn't the court know his real name?" Shelby asked in that logical way she had sometimes. "Wouldn't it be listed somewhere?"

"Yes, wouldn't it?" Sadie prodded.

"Not all the records go that far back," Charlie said. "He could have served his sentence and been released."

"But he still would have been on probation, right?" Sadie asked.

Shelby shot her a look.

"What?" she said. "I listen when Amelia Ann speaks about her work at the legal clinic."

Vander's eyes narrowed. "You know someone who works

at a legal clinic?"

"Yes," Shelby told him, reaching for her tea. "She's rather like our sister, I guess you could say. She's the sister of our sister-in-law. Amelia Ann's in law school at Vanderbilt and helps abused women."

Judging from the way Charlie's button nose rose in the air, she was surprised they knew a serious woman like that. "Amelia Ann almost got herself killed one time helping a client in East Nashville on a home visit," Sadie burst out. "It was scary."

Her sister cleared her throat, and Sadie knew it for the message it was. She shut up.

"We'd need to talk to our brother and other sister about contacting Daddy's family if you find anything," Shelby said, looking like she was barely breathing now. "But I say look there first. Sounds more efficient. Sadie, what do you think?"

Shelby would put it that way. "I agree." Plus, she wanted to know more about Daddy's family, even if it was only basic information. "You should know, we only agreed to tell them of developments. It'll be up to them whether or not they want to be a part of contacting a family member. Frankly, it's not going to stop me from doing it if I feel it's best."

"Or me," Shelby said, and they shared a look of solidarity.

"We'll start plugging right away," Vander said. "With Charlie helping, it's going to go a lot faster."

The woman rolled her eyes. "He's flattering me. But he's right. Vander has a lot on his plate, running the show here. I only do straight investigative work. I'll start tonight."

Sadie couldn't exactly imagine having lunch with Charlie, but the woman seemed more than competent—and dedicated. "Thank you, Charlie."

Vander stood. "I'll be in touch. I know the waiting is hard, but we'll keep pulling strings until there's nothing left to pull— if you want that."

"We appreciate it," Shelby said, standing as well and extending her hand to him.

He shook it, and Sadie stood and did the same despite how unnatural it felt. It got even weirder when Charlie shook both of their hands too. Business people mystified her. No one in the craft store or her quilting circle would have shaken her hand.

Shelby and Vander shared another look before they left his office, and Sadie had to bite her tongue until she and her sister were walking out of the building.

"Do you think he brought Charlie on to help because you two are attracted to each other?" Sadie asked her sister.

Shelby gave her a look and pushed the heavy glass door open. Sadie followed, gasping at the hot, damp air she encountered. Heavens, the weather was atrocious.

"I won't dignify that with a response," Shelby said, walking up the street to where she was parked. "Where are you?"

"I parked in the garage over there," Sadie said, pointing toward the area. "Shelby, do you think we should meet his kin if it comes down to it? If Mama had wanted them in our life, she would have made sure it happened. Part of me wants to meet them, and the other part is scared spitless. I'm a mess of contradictions."

Her sister put on her sunglasses, and Sadie rummaged for her own in her purse.

"Let's cross that bridge when we get there," Shelby said matter-of-factly.

Her sister was right. No use worrying over something that might not come to pass. "You and Vander took an awfully long time making tea and coffee," she pressed.

Her sister kissed her on the cheek. "I'm going to the gym. We can give J.P. and Susannah an update once we hear back from Vander and Charlie."

"Unless they ask us beforehand," Sadie said dryly. "If I were them, I wouldn't be able to wait past tonight."

"Well, you aren't them," her sister said, "which is why you're here with me. Thanks again, Sadie."

Her sister might be a little abrupt sometimes, but she had

a heart of gold. "You too. Have fun at the gym. I'm going to go home and design a quilt for Gail. Do you think Vander might like one too? Or is that silly?"

Shelby lowered her sunglasses to the edge of her nose. "Why ever would you want to make him a quilt?"

She shrugged. "Because it's how I say thank you."

"He's getting paid, Sadie," her sister told her. "It's not like he's doing this from the kindness of his heart."

"Goodness, you sound jaded when you speak like that," Sadie told her. "He's been kind to me, and I'd like to do something for him. Maybe some jam then. Men like food stuffs."

Her sister sighed. "He doesn't strike me as a quilt or jam kind of man, Sadie."

"What kind of man do you think he is then, Shelby?" she asked, hoping to get a little more out of her this time.

"Not the kind you'd know what to do with," she said, blowing her a kiss and taking off.

"What about you? Would you know what to do with him?"

Her sister ignored her, and she seemed to march rather than stroll off to Pearl, her convertible. Shelby was riled up by Vander, no doubt. She only sniped like that when she felt backed into a corner.

No good could come of it, if you asked her.

CHAPTER 8

"WHAT HAVE YOU FOUND OUT?" VANDER ASKED, pretty much stalking into Charlie's office.

She looked up from her computer and gave him the don't-rush-me look. "The McGuiness girls only left an hour ago—and from a meeting you could have easily had on the *phone*."

Her pointed remark about him making up a reason to see Shelby was best ignored. His motivations weren't completely pure, and he knew it. "I know how fast you are, Charlie." He sat on the edge of her desk, his favorite place when they were researching a case together. "Let me remind you that we don't call our clients *girls*."

She blew him a raspberry. "I'll add that to my list of Vander's Dos and Don'ts. So far, I've found a brother, Virgil, who died two years ago at age sixty in Tuscaloosa, Alabama. There's also the mother: seventy-eight-year-old Lenore McGuiness living outside Memphis. She has a handicap Tennessee license plate for a 1971 Ford LTD, and while she owns her own trailer, it looks like she's delinquent in paying her property tax."

"Good work." Memphis was only a three and a half hour drive. "What else?"

"The sister, Deedee, did some jail time for shoplifting. She lives out in Texas now, in Abilene. Tons of speeding tickets. She's the only one of the immediate family I've found on social media. Her Facebook page is a cautionary tale about bleached hair, the toll hard living takes on a woman, and drama of balancing multiple boyfriends and kids. The kids have Facebook pages, but all I've found are photos of their immediate family and various racist political opinions guaranteed to curl your toes."

"Wonderful," he said, shaking his head. As P.I.s, they were used to seeing the full swath of humanity from the seemingly well adjusted to the radical, militant elements. "They're probably not close then."

"Yeah," Charlie said, pushing back in her chair from her desk. "From my initial findings, Shelby and Sadie's mom did them a service by keeping their father's family away from them. Preston McGuiness' family is a peach. Of course, we don't know for certain if the family ever wanted to be connected in the first place."

Not everyone wanted to know their children or grandchildren, as Vander had discovered in his own version of the school of hard knocks after his mother had moved them in with his grandparents. "We know they didn't," Vander said, feeling it in his gut.

Charlie nodded. "Frankly, I think you visit the mother first and see what she knows. The sister looks volatile."

Neither one of them liked to start with volatile.

"I'll call our clients right now and see what they want to do." He found himself unduly excited by the prospect. "You go on home. Don't you have a kickboxing class tonight?"

She rose from her chair and put her hands on her petite hips. "I can be late if you want me to call them with you. Or are you looking for an excuse to hear Shelby's voice again today?"

Charlie busted his balls like none other. Shelby *did* have a lovely voice, smooth as spun sugar one moment and then firm as... Steel was the wrong term. Firm as something elegant... like marble. When he came back to the moment, Charlie was staring at him.

"You're worrying me," she said, her hazel eyes troubled. "First the in-person meeting today and now this. Please let me take over this case, Vander."

He just shrugged and said, "She's Gail Hardcrew's personal accountant."

Charlie sat back in her chair. *"Hmmm."*

He put his hand on his hips. "Don't *'hmmm'* me. Dammit, Charlie, why didn't you say anything? When Gail told me during our meeting, I was totally caught off guard."

She worried her lip. "I was hoping you wouldn't find out. I knew this would make you more curious about her. Heck, it made me more curious, and I'm not even into her."

Shit. "Gail had a reason for our meeting today. She thinks so much of Shelby she wants to pay my...our fee."

"Well, Ms. McGuiness becomes more interesting by the day," Charlie said, putting her finger to her lips. "I was hoping Gail's out-of-the-blue summons was about something else. A new lover to investigate, perhaps."

"I bet you did. That way you wouldn't get busted."

"You need to work on your glower, Vander. How was Gail dressed for your meeting today, by the way?"

He let her divert the conversation because he wasn't eager to discuss Charlie's instincts regarding his interest in Shelby. "She had on a low-cut pink number with a white feather boa, which got in her mouth a couple of times," he said, his lips twitching. "I really shouldn't talk about one of our clients this way."

"Please, it's Gail," Charlie said, rolling her eyes. "She loves the attention. But I suppose we should get back to Shelby. You're cogitating over what you might have missed the first time you met her, aren't you?"

He stared her down.

"Vander, you *really* need to give me this case. I know you. You can't stand learning someone has more layers than you originally suspected. It's your investigative nature. Add in your attraction to her, and you're toast."

He hoped he was stronger than that. He was a grown man, after all. "It's just a stupid infatuation. Embarrassing to admit really."

Charlie looked him up and down. "Are you sure?"

He stood. "I told you before. I don't even really like her."

Her eyes narrowed. "That was before you knew about Gail. Now, it makes more sense to you why Shelby was a little hard on her sister the other day. Gail is all drama, and Shelby must need to control her own emotions to work well with her. You know, like how you and I complement each other."

Shaking his head, he walked to the door. "I should never have had everyone take that stupid Myers-Briggs personality test. You love beating that drum when it's convenient to one of your arguments."

"And you run away because you have avoidance tendencies while I have confrontational ones," Charlie said, coming around her desk.

"Go kick something," he said, walking to the door. "And don't keep something as big as Shelby working for one of our clients from me ever again."

"I did it for your own good, you stubborn mule," he heard her mutter as he left her office.

When he reached his own desk, he fought his own urge to kick something himself. He wasn't prone to temper tantrums, but Charlie had a way of bringing them out in him. She pushed and pushed, holding up his faults in his face. Usually, it helped him break open a case or a personal limit. But seriously. So what if he sometimes avoided things? He'd learned avoidance in spades from his mother and her parents. Sometimes it was a good strategy.

Avoiding his growing attraction for Shelby McGuiness was the best thing for both of them.

He picked up the phone to call her.

CHAPTER 9

ALTHOUGH SHELBY HADN'T ADDED VANDER'S PHONE number to her contacts, she recognized the number. She was good with numbers, after all.

Her heart immediately started to race, so she took a deep breath before answering. "Hello."

"Shelby, it's Vander," he said, all business. "Charlie and I found your father's family, and I wanted to fill you in."

"Gracious, y'all do work fast," she said, her heart racing for a completely different reason now. "Okay, what did you find?"

"I'm headed out of the office right now," he said. "Can you and Sadie meet me somewhere for a drink, or do you want to wait until tomorrow?"

Did he really think they'd be capable of waiting that long? "We can meet you. Let me call Sadie. Wait! What's tonight?" She racked her brain for Sadie's schedule.

He chuckled, and the sound was as decadent and inviting as chocolate truffles dotted with fleur de sel. "Monday, remember?"

"Right." Goodness, she was frazzled. "She has her quilting circle."

"Her quilting circle, huh?" Vander said, and Shelby could hear the smile in his voice.

Hadn't she told Sadie that Vander wasn't a quilt kind of guy? "She's a master quilter if there is such a term. She teaches a group at the craft store on Mondays."

"Is that where she works?" Vander asked.

"Yes," she said, thinking about whether she should meet him alone. Her heart practically sang out the answer: *yes*. "Sadie's...on edge...like me, I guess, so she'll want to know what's going on as soon as possible. I'll meet you. Just tell me where."

Vander paused, then said, "It will just be me. Charlie did the searching, so I sent her off to her usual kickboxing class."

So it would be just the two of them? Good Lord, she needed to calm herself. "Fine. Where?"

"How about Oak Bar at the Hermitage?" he asked.

Shelby loved that classy cocktail bar in one of Nashville's most unique hotels. She should have guessed he'd suggest a spot like that. It had originally opened as a private gentleman's bar in 1910, and whenever Shelby went there, she could imagine it full of its original clientele—men in three-piece suits with gold timepieces smoking cigars and drinking bourbon. Vander was rather like the establishment himself, intriguing and compelling in an old-school way.

Checking the time, she calculated how far she was from the bar. "I can meet you there in half an hour. I'm finishing up some things for Gail."

"Are you sure? Gail's place is—"

"I have an offsite office and...sometimes work from home," she told him. Truthfully, she'd never get anything done working at Gail's house, and thankfully her boss agreed. She only went there for meetings.

"That works fine," he said. "I'll be at the bar. See you in few."

"Great," she answered as she hung up.

Was she really meeting Vander for a drink by herself? Heavens preserve her, she felt faint, like she'd drunk too much pink champagne and was walking along a cliff. In one word:

exciting. She texted Sadie to make herself feel better.

Vander called to say he has some news already. I'm meeting with him tonight even though I know you have your circle. I didn't think you'd want to wait. We're at Oak Bar if you get out early and want to join us. Call me when you're done.

Sadie's quilting circle ran from seven to nine thirty, and it was seven thirty now. They'd be long gone by then.

Wouldn't they?

She touched up her makeup like she would for any evening business meeting, telling herself she'd do the same no matter whom she was meeting. But she knew she was full of it.

"Oh, poo," she said in the mirror as she finished adding a nude pink lipstick to her lips. Heck, she'd even chosen a color with the word nude in it, she realized. The thought of seeing Vander nude made her cheeks hot...and did other things to her.

What in the world was she thinking?

She knew what she was thinking. She was about to have Vander all to herself for once, and part of her couldn't wait. There was trouble here. *Business*, she told herself again, *this is a business meeting.*

Still, Shelby made her hips sway a little extra as she walked into the cocktail bar perfectly on time. After all, she was a woman. Sure enough, he was already waiting for her, nursing a bourbon at the dark-wood paneled bar. A neat one, from the looks of it. His face was in profile, and she couldn't help but admire the hard line of his jaw. He was a handsome man, and he certainly filled out that suit he was wearing. The thought of him naked intruded again, and she imagined what those muscles must look like when he was shirtless.

Stick to business, she reminded herself as she approached him.

He must have sensed her presence because he suddenly turned when she was halfway to him. She stilled, unable to move. Then he smiled, and the way his mouth tilted up to the right was downright dangerous. Yeah, they were flirting with trouble, and they both knew it. She made herself continue forward with her head held high and her shoulders back like any Southern debutante fresh out of finishing school. "Hello, Vander," she said, sliding onto the vacant bar stool next to him.

"Shelby," he said, his aquamarine eyes taking her measure.

"I texted Sadie to let her know we're here in case her circle breaks up early," she found herself telling him.

His mouth crooked up. "Good thinking. What can I get you to drink?"

While she and her sisters normally drank white wine— something J.P. teased them about mercilessly—Oak Bar had one of the finest bourbon collections in Nashville. But did she really want to drink something that strong? No, she decided. Not for a meeting with Vander. "I'll have the Farmer's Daughter cocktail."

"I should have guessed," he said, signaling the bartender.

"Why?" she asked. "Because it's a girly drink?"

"You said it. Not me. Do you want a snack? I'm starved. I didn't have lunch."

She was hungry as well, but her stomach was too nervous for words. "Perhaps I'll order something after we've talked about the case."

He nodded. "Of course."

The bartender took her order, and Vander nursed his bourbon. When her drink arrived, she took a fortifying sip. "All right, I'm ready."

He turned to face her completely, and she did the same. Their knees brushed, sending a tingle shooting through her body.

"We found some of your kin, and the one we think we should interview first is your father's mother."

Her heart contracted as hurt welled up. "Oh," she managed to say. "She's still alive then?"

"Yes," he told her. "She's living in Memphis."

Her grandma was alive and living not three and a half hours away, and she'd never met her. "I just realized...I don't know her name."

His eyes turned somber. "It's Lenore, and she's seventy-eight years old."

She took a hasty drink of her cocktail. "And his other family?"

He told her about a deceased uncle, and her aunt living in Texas. It blew Shelby's mind to realize her grandmother had had her first child at sixteen. She'd been *married* at an age when Shelby's only thoughts had been about how to get random pimples under control or who might take her to prom.

"Hearing you have kin out there—even ones you've never heard of—does something powerful to you inside." In this case, it simply made her sad and even more curious. Vander had told her she looked more like her daddy. Did these other relatives look like her too?

"I imagine so," Vander said, fingering the edge of the napkin under his drink.

She paused, then said, "I mean, what could she tell us about our daddy? We don't know much about him beyond that he loved to sing. How did he grow up? Did he learn how to fish when he was a kid? Did he play sports? What *did* he like to do?" She realized Vander was watching her intently as her voice rose in volume. "I'm sorry. I'm babbling, aren't I?"

She took a breath as he laid a hand on her forearm. While it was a touch designed to comfort, they both started. He immediately removed it.

"Any time someone is abandoned, there are a lot of questions. It's natural, Shelby. What you and your sister have chosen to do isn't easy."

She remembered him saying he'd lost his family—she'd thought about it all evening—but it didn't seem like the right time to ask about it.

"It might not be easy, but it's necessary," she told him,

reaching for her drink and taking a sip. "Let me talk to Sadie. I think she'll want to meet our grandma too. I can't be sure about my brother and sister, but we'll ask them. Once we know, we'll figure out when we can get to Memphis to speak with her." Her mind was spinning at the mere thought.

His brow rose. "Ah...I wasn't thinking you'd meet her at first. I was planning on going."

Shelby sat back. "How could we *not* go? She's our grandmother."

He sighed. "Shelby, listen. You don't know how you might be received. So far the case has been all about gathering information, and as hard as that's been, meeting a member of your father's family in the flesh...it's a different ball of wax."

"But she's my daddy's mama," Shelby told him. "She birthed him, and that's a powerful bond. She'll know stories about him, even if she doesn't know where he is."

"I'm glad you realize she might not know your father's whereabouts, but meeting her might be tough. She might not welcome you with open arms."

But she might, and that was enough for her. She wasn't sure her other siblings would agree. "We won't know until we try. Whatever went down between my parents and Daddy's family is in the past. I'll tell her we McGuiness children want to start anew."

His jaw locked, and he turned away from her, facing the bar again. "Shelby, why don't we see how Lenore reacts to my questions about your father first? I don't want to put you and your sister in a hurtful situation unnecessarily."

This time she wanted to place her hand on his arm to assure him, but she knew better. The imprints of his fingers still felt burned into her arm. "We're tougher than you give us credit for."

He looked at her then, and his eyes were heated. "You work for Gail, which is evidence enough for me. I'm not so sure about Sadie, though. She has a soft heart, not that I'm saying you don't."

She took no offense. Sadie was a softer touch, and all the McGuinesses knew it. "Go on."

"Your grandmother..."

"What?" she asked when he trailed off.

"My gut tells me your grandmother isn't going to be an easy woman," he said, shaking his head. "It's just a feeling."

"My mama calls those feelings guidance," she said. How was she going to feel if her grandma was unpleasant? Surely it wouldn't be too awful. "All right, maybe you could come along with us."

He studied her as soft jazz played on the speakers, something she hadn't noticed until now. "*If* you're going to insist on going, I'm going to insist on coming. Shelby, that way I can step in and stop you from getting hurt any further, should things go with Lenore like I fear they will."

There was a warm feeling in her chest from his words. "I still don't see how can I be hurt by someone I don't know."

"We react all the time to people we don't know," he said, staring at her. "Sometimes we even find ourselves caring about them and their feelings without fully knowing why."

Oxygen backed up in her lungs as she realized he meant her. Or at least she thought he meant her. "*Oh.*"

He held her gaze a moment longer, and everything seemed to slow down. She was conscious of the buzz of other people's conversations in the background, a woman's sudden high-pitched laughter, and the smell of truffle parmesan fries wafting under her nose.

His aquamarine eyes had a gold ring around them, she realized, and sexy dark stubble lined his strong jaw. His gaze slid to her mouth, and she found herself unable to draw breath. Then, just like that, he was standing up and taking a money clip out of his pocket.

She fell back to earth.

"Talk to Sadie when she gets out of her quilting thing," he said, laying down a couple of twenties on the bar. "I imagine you'll speak with your brother and sister shortly as well. Once you know who's going, we can talk details and sync schedules."

His haste to leave was as unexpected as a summer tornado. "I thought you were hungry."

Those heated eyes of his met her own again, and she felt the punch all the way to her toes. "We both know that's not the best decision. Good night, Shelby."

She watched him walk out of the restaurant.

Shelby realized she was more unsettled by his abrupt exit than she was by the prospect of meeting her grandmother.

CHAPTER 10

SADIE HUGGED THE FIVE WOMEN IN HER QUILTING CIRCLE as they broke for the night. Each of them was at a different skill level, but they were all committed, which was all she asked. Teaching people how to quilt was as new to her as making quilts for people to buy.

She was experiencing some growing pains, like a girl who'd outgrown last year's Easter dress, but it felt good to share her talent. Especially after this afternoon's meeting.

When she checked her messages, her happiness popped like a birthday balloon. Vander had news *already?* Charlie had said she was getting started right away, but Sadie hadn't expected a same-day turnaround. Shelby had correctly assumed she wouldn't want to wait to hear the news, and goodness gracious, she was almost as curious about the meeting between her sister and Vander. Sparks flew between them in a professional setting, and Oak Bar was exactly the sort of sultry place suited to flirting.

She texted her sister to tell her she was finished with her circle, and Shelby immediately responded she was at home. Apparently, the meeting hadn't gone on for too long.

After locking up and getting in her car, she called her sister. "All right," she said with some urgency, "what did Vander say?"

"They found our grandmother in Memphis and think she's the best place to start," her sister said without beating around the bush. "I know we need to talk to the others first, but I told Vander that I want to go meet her. Do you?"

Sadie gripped the steering wheel, thinking hard about that. The softer tone of Shelby's voice indicated she was a little scared by the prospect too.

"I won't let you go alone," Sadie responded. "Besides, I have lots of questions myself."

"I wonder if J.P. will want to go," Shelby said.

Sadie found herself nodding even though her sister couldn't see her.

"What about Susannah?" she asked, her gut worrying over her eldest sister's reaction.

"We ask her," Shelby said, "but we can expect a lot of emotion all around. I'm afraid they might want to stop us, but I...I need to see this through. Even though I'm fixing to come undone about the prospect of seeing her. Sadie, I didn't even know her name. It's Lenore. That made me sad."

It brought tears to her eyes too. "I think we should all meet up tonight," Sadie said. "Neither of them go to bed early."

"They're newlyweds," Shelby reminded her, making her start to cough violently.

"Yuck. Did you have to go there? Darn it all, Shelby, I want to deal with this tonight. I won't be able to sleep a wink."

"All right, let's text them and see what they say." Shelby paused for a moment. "I should confess Vander isn't sold on the idea of us going. At all! He wanted to make the trip by himself, but I told him we have to go."

"But she's our grandmother!" Sadie exclaimed, deciding to pull into the parking lot of a Dairy Queen for some ice cream. She deserved a treat after all this stress. "Why wouldn't we go?"

"He doesn't want us to get hurt," Shelby told her, and that made Sadie's heart warm.

"Vander really is a good man," Sadie said, cutting the

engine. "How did your...ah...meeting go?"

Her sister sighed. "He pretty much bolted out of Oak Bar after sharing the news."

Wasn't that interesting? "Then he has ethics, which makes me like him even more. If you like him, you're going to have to be the one to make the move. I know I told you to be careful, but this changes my mind."

"Sadie McGuiness! Did you and your quilting circle up and smoke something tonight?"

"You know what I'm talking about." She grabbed her purse and headed inside. "I'm at the Dairy Queen. Why don't you call J.P. and Susannah? I'll see you in a few."

"You sure it's not too late?" her sister asked.

"No, there's a ton of people at Dairy Queen. They'll be awake." She took her place in line. "Do you want something?"

"I was too upset to eat earlier, but my stomach is growling at the thought of Dairy Queen," Shelby told her. "How about a burger and fries? A blizzard would melt."

"Done."

Pocketing her phone, Sadie waited until it was her turn to order. She decided to add in some chicken strips and more fries. Maybe J.P. and Susannah would like some if they were able to meet tonight. Who was she kidding? She was doing what every Southern woman did in a crisis. She was bringing food.

Her phone buzzed while she was paying. It was Shelby.

We're meeting at J.P.'s. Come immediately. They grumbled, but agree it's important.

When Sadie arrived at her brother's house, the porch light was on. As she made her way to the front door, Susannah pulled into the drive behind her and exited her vehicle.

She stopped and turned around. "Hey."

"Hey," her sister said, filling that one word with truculence.

"Did Shelby tell you the complete news?" she asked.

"Yes," Susannah replied. "I'm fixing to come undone."

Her hands were full with the food, but she leaned in and

pressed her cheek to her sister's. "Me too."

"Dairy Queen," her sister said, pointing to the bags. "That's a sure sign of stress."

"I already had a large Butterfinger Blizzard." In fact, she was fighting a downright unladylike belch. "We're scared too, Susannah."

"Let's go inside," her sister said, pressing a hand to her back and ushering her forward. They were on the porch when the headlights from another car illuminated them.

"Shelby's here," she said.

Sure enough, their other sister slammed her car door and rushed forward like there were hounds nipping at her heels.

"Are y'all going to come inside or dawdle out here all night?" J.P. asked from the doorway.

Goodness, J.P. was never grouchy. That didn't sit well with Sadie. No, not one bit.

"We were just coming in, honey," Susannah said, walking up the rest of the steps and wrapping her arms around him.

Sadie waited her turn, and when his strong hands drew her against his chest, she pretty much melted against him.

"All right, now," he said, patting her back. "It's going to be okay."

Stepping aside, he gave Shelby a hug too, and they went into the house together. Tammy was waiting to give them more hugs, and Sadie drew comfort from the flow of love.

"I'm going to let y'all talk by yourselves," she said, "but I'll be praying."

"We sure could use the prayers," Sadie said.

Her sisters nodded in agreement.

"Let's head into the kitchen," J.P. said as his wife left the room. "I see you brought Dairy Queen, Sadie."

After her blizzard, Sadie wasn't sure she could eat anything else. And Shelby might be hungry, but she looked a little green. Glasses of sweet tea garnished with fresh mint—likely from the garden—were already awaiting them on the kitchen table, probably Tammy's contribution to their siblings' meeting.

Sadie found a green serving plate in the cabinet and arranged the food on it while Shelby handed around napkins.

Once that was done, they all sat down and exchanged looks. The silence in the room was so intense Sadie could hear the moths hitting the screen door out back, seeking the light inside.

"All right," J.P. said. "We're all here now. Let's start from the beginning."

Sadie nodded to Shelby, and her sister laid out the current situation, including all the information Vander had given her about the kin he and Charlie had found. When she was finished, J.P. reached for his sweet tea and drained half the contents.

"It's a mighty big step," J.P. said, taking the mint off his glass and fiddling with it between his thumb and forefinger. "Seeing kin we've never met without knowing why we've never met them."

"What if Mama told them—our grandma and Daddy's siblings—that they couldn't see us?" Susannah asked. "Mama would have had her reasons. We should honor them."

"But this might be the only way we can find Daddy," Sadie said, reaching for a chicken finger.

"What if our grandma ends up contacting Mama after we visit her?" Susannah asked, her cheeks pink. "Worse, what if she wants to come around and visit us? What would Mama say?"

J.P. held up his hands and said, "I for one would be happy to have a grandma around if she wants a place in our lives. I say we all go meet her together and see what she knows."

Sadie shared a look with Shelby, and they smiled at each other. If J.P. was already on their side, they had a better chance of swaying their sister.

"You always believe in the best in people," Susannah said, elbows locked tight.

"You do too, darlin'," J.P. told her. "You're only scared like the rest of us are."

"I say we face this head on," Shelby said. "We go to Memphis together and tell her who we are and that we're looking for our daddy after all these years. I don't want to spend the rest of my life wondering. And I won't stop now out of fear."

"Life shouldn't be lived from a place of regret," J.P. said in that deep voice of his. "Susannah, you don't have to go. No one will think less of you."

Their sister leaned forward. "Like I could live with myself if all three of you went, and I stayed behind. I'm just worried this won't turn out well."

"But it might," Sadie said softly. "We won't know until we try."

"Then we go," Shelby said, reaching for her hand and J.P.'s. "We stick together like McGuinesses and get this done."

Susannah slowly joined their circle. "All right. The sooner the better. And I want Jake to come too, if that's okay with y'all."

They all nodded in agreement. It would help settle Susannah to have him there.

"We need to agree on a day to go," Shelby said.

"It's a three and a half hour drive," J.P. said. "We could do the whole trip in one day, or we could stay the night in Memphis to shake things off. I don't like bringing stuff like this home."

Sadie couldn't blame him. He was newly married, and there was Rory and Annabelle to consider. They were both sensitive to the moods of the adults in their lives.

"Might be good to have some time together...however this turns out," Shelby said. "We haven't done anything like that in a while."

It made Sadie a little sad to realize her sister was right. Now that Susannah and J.P. had families of their own, they didn't get to see them much except for Sunday dinner. "That's a good idea. I'll likely be...a mess, and I'd love to be with y'all."

"Me too," Shelby said, catching her eye. "Although I hate

to admit it."

"I'll bring plenty of tissues," J.P. said. "I expect meeting our grandma will be like pulling out a stinger. Any way we do it, it's gonna hurt."

"Let's agree on a few days," Shelby said. "Then I'll see what Vander's schedule looks like."

"Do you think he still needs to go with us?" J.P. asked, rubbing his jaw after some consideration.

"He feels pretty strongly about going," Sadie felt compelled to say. "Plus, he's more used to this kind of thing than we are. Vander has been good to us." His presence would make her feel better, she expected.

"He might also think of questions we either wouldn't or would be too...well, emotional to remember to ask." Shelby frowned after saying this, and Sadie knew she feared being a complete wreck.

"All right, we'll nail down a time that works for everyone," J.P. said, squeezing her hand before releasing it. "I'm glad you two reached out to us tonight."

"We promised we would," Shelby said.

"We don't break our promises," Sadie said.

But their daddy had. Was his mama any different?

CHAPTER 11

WHEN VANDER PULLED INTO THEIR GRANDMA'S trailer park, Shelby reached for Sadie's hand. She had never seen anything so run down or...frightening—well, except on television.

"Oh, my good Lord," Susannah said. "I know we used to live in a trailer park after Daddy left because Mama couldn't afford the house, but this is—"

"Squalor," Jake said, shaking his head. "I hate poverty like this. There's plenty of it in parts of Arkansas around where I grew up."

"But this is Memphis!" Sadie said, shrinking back from the window as three men with dirty wife beater shirts and neo-Nazi tattoos stepped out of a mobile home.

"Those men are armed," Vander told the group of them. "Aren't you glad you let me come along?"

Shelby nodded. Like he would have sat this one out. He'd been insistent from day one. He'd only expressed concern about Susannah's husband coming with them. Jake Lassiter was a celebrity, which meant he might get recognized. Susannah had been adamant, so Vander had said they would take every precaution.

He'd done some checking with local police on the trailer park where their grandma lived, and it had a dangerous reputation. To keep a low profile, he'd rented an old six-passenger Dodge in Memphis so they could all travel together. Vander was also armed, which Shelby had considered over-the-top until this very moment.

"I don't want y'all getting out of the car," Jake said. "You let J.P., Vander, and me handle this."

Shelby looked over her shoulder at him in the backseat with her sister. His tension was palpable, and his eyes were scanning the area like he was a soldier back in Iraq.

"I'm personally okay with that," Sadie said, her voice shaky. "I'm a little scared to get out of the SUV."

"I told y'all coming here wasn't a good idea," Susannah said, worry lacing her voice. "Jake, I don't like getting you upset."

Shelby heard what Susannah didn't say. She didn't want him to have another PTSD episode.

"I'll be all right, sugar," Jake said, but no one was convinced.

"Why don't you let me talk to your grandmother first?" Vander said from the driver's seat, looking at them in the rear view mirror. His eyes found Shelby's and pinned on them for an instant before he returned his gaze to the dirt road. "If I have a warm welcome, I'll usher you in. We just need to find her trailer."

There weren't any numbers on the mobile homes, and Shelby wondered if that was intentional. Vander continued to drive slowly as more men and women came out of their mobile homes to watch them.

"I don't expect they get a lot of visitors," Vander said, pulling to a stop. "Give me a minute to see what I can find out."

He put the car in park and hopped out before anyone could protest.

"I should go with him," Jake said, his fist resting on the seat.

"He'll be all right, Jake," J.P. said from his perch as copilot. "I have a feeling it'll only fire these folks up if more than one man gets out of our car. From the looks of it, there are a lot of scared people living in this park. I wonder how our grandma ended up here."

"Poverty, likely," Sadie said. "It breaks my heart to think of it."

Shelby was listening to their quiet conversation, but she only had eyes for Vander. He'd worn a wrinkled white T-shirt, a worn jean jacket to cover his gun, an even more worn pair of jeans, and scuffed-up work boots. He looked like the polar opposite of the elegant gentleman she'd believed him to be.

With his dark shades on, he seemed downright intimidating. Seeing these other facets of him made her wonder even more about him. Sure, it was all part of the P.I. cover he'd created, but it fit him like second skin. Who was Vander Montgomery anyway? She felt a growing compulsion to find out.

He'd told them upfront he was going in as Toby Parsons, Shelby's boyfriend. She'd almost choked on her own spit, hearing that, but she hadn't asked why he'd chosen her and not Sadie, and thankfully neither had anyone else.

The whole undercover thing was still a little scary. She didn't much like watching him talk to those men with the hateful tattoos on their arms, and she found herself offering up silent prayers for his safety.

When Vander came back to the car, he got in and tipped his hand at the men he'd talked to and started to drive.

"Your grandmother is home," Vander said, his voice crisp and all business. "Those men were helpful. I told them we were her kin from Nashville who hadn't seen her in ages. From the sound of it, she keeps to herself. She's just down the road here."

Vander stopped the car in front of a brown mobile home with torn window screens, a rusted-out septic tank in front, and a Confederate flag hanging from the front window. A car with rust stains to rival the septic tank sat in the dirt driveway.

"Do you think Grandma's a racist if she's flying that flag?" Sadie asked, cuddling closer to Shelby.

"In my experience, that's not true of everyone who has a Confederate flag," Jake said. "But many are. Vander, are you sure you don't want me to go in with you? I might not be armed, but the Army trained me well."

Vander turned in his seat and gave Jake a smile. "Thanks for having my back. I'd rather have someone with your training stay in the car with the women. No offense, ladies, but this is a rough neighborhood, and while my friends back there didn't express any hostility, who's to say that won't change? J.P., since you favor your father, I was hoping you might join me if I need some backup. That is, if she's not willing to talk to me about your father straight off."

J.P. nodded. "Happy to."

"I'll signal you in by waving," Vander said. "Casual. Like I'm one of you."

Suddenly this all felt too serious to Shelby. Someone could get seriously hurt, and that wasn't something she'd imagined when she'd suggested this trip.

"Maybe I was wrong to push this," she said. "Maybe we should just go and find another way."

"We're already here," J.P. said, meeting her eyes. "Let's see it through. We're in good hands."

Vander nodded and stepped out of the car. When he reached the front door, Shelby realized it was barely hanging on by the hinges. He rapped on the paint-faded brown wood and then stepped back when a dog started barking.

"Oh, my goodness," Sadie said, clutching her hand. "That dog sounds scary."

"It's a bulldog, from the sound of it," Jake told them, sitting on the edge of his seat.

Vander put a few yards between himself and the door and stood there. A full minute passed before the door opened. An older woman in a loose, baby blue polyester dress filled the doorway—one hand on a cane, the other wrapped around the collar of a black-and-white spotted bulldog.

Shelby wasn't the only one in the SUV who gasped.

"My God, she's morbidly obese," Sadie whispered, putting her free hand to her mouth. "She wasn't that way at Mama and Daddy's wedding!"

The woman at the door had to be over three hundred pounds, and her harshly dyed brown hair was gray at the temples and rolled up in curlers.

"Who the hell are you?" the woman shouted at Vander.

Shelby couldn't hear Vander's reply with the windows up and his back facing them, but her grandmother's response was all too audible.

"What do you mean you're a friend of my son's kin? Who? Virgil?"

Vander shook his head and said something. Once again, Shelby couldn't hear how he responded, but she saw the way it affected the woman. Her face crumpled and her hands balled into fists around their respective burdens.

"You mean that bitch Louisa's kids?" she asked, turning her gaze toward the car. "Are they in there?"

Vander nodded again, and since their grandma seemed to be paying attention to him, Shelby expected he was saying his piece.

"That good-for-nothing woman ruined my boy!" their grandma shouted. "I hope she rots in hell."

Sadie sucked in a breath, and Shelby felt her stomach quiver. She'd never heard anyone curse Mama.

"We should leave," Susannah said, her voice quavering. "She's a mean and hateful woman to be talking about Mama like that."

"I agree," J.P. said, "but we don't know the reasons for her venom or how she's come by it. Let's give Vander some more time."

They all fell silent.

Pretty soon, Vander was taking a few steps closer, and

their grandma wasn't shouting anymore. By the time he made it to her front door again, she was wiping tears from her eyes. Then Vander gave J.P. the signal, and Shelby tensed up.

"Be careful," Sadie said, reaching a hand out to clutch at his arm.

"I'll be fine," J.P. said, giving them a tight smile. "Be right back."

Their brother stepped out of the vehicle and walked to the door with his long-legged stride. The bulldog started barking again, but this time, their grandmother immediately shushed it. Then she awkwardly turned around and disappeared inside the trailer.

Vander and J.P. huddled together. After a few moments, they both turned and walked back to the SUV.

When they got back in the vehicle, J.P. looked at Vander, who nodded.

"She's invited us inside for sweet tea," J.P. said, turning in his seat to address them. "You don't have to come in if you don't want to. She doesn't know how many of us are here, so it won't offend her none."

Shelby gazed back at the house, her mind spinning horrifying images of what it might look like inside. Sadie clutched her hand so tight it hurt.

"I'm scared to go in there," her younger sister said in a soft voice. "That dog..."

"I told her it would make us feel more comfortable if she shut him in somewhere," Vander interjected, "and she agreed to put him in the back bedroom. Heck, it would even make me more comfortable. I thought it was going to take a bite out of me when she opened the door."

"I'll go," Shelby said, her heart pounding in her ears. "I've come this far, and I won't let fear stop me now." Besides, she knew Vander wouldn't let anything happen to her or any of them. His intensity was palpable.

J.P. gave her a hesitant smile. "All right."

"Every single one of us is scared to go in there," Sadie

said. "Maybe we'll feel better if we do it together."

"I can't promise you she won't say some pretty unpleasant things about your mother," Vander said. "She has a perspective on why your daddy left. It might not be true. Only your mother and father would know that. Either way, it won't be easy to hear what she has to say. She's...had a hard life. Not that I'm making excuses for her."

"That much is obvious," Susannah said. "Jake, what do you think?"

He let out a long sigh. "I think they're right, honey. You've come this far. I'll be with you every step of the way. That goes for the rest of y'all too."

That made tears pop into Shelby's eyes. "You're the best guy ever, Jake Lassiter. Right after our brother."

J.P. gave them an easier smile. "Let's head inside. Remember, we can leave whenever we want. I'll make sure of that."

"You leave that to me," Vander said. "I have a lot of experience in gracefully exiting uncomfortable interviews. If you all don't mind a word of advice..."

"Please," Shelby said, meeting his aquamarine eyes.

"Don't challenge what she says," he told them. "Let her say her piece. You aren't going to change her mind—and she isn't going to change yours."

"What he's saying is don't raise her hackles," J.P. said. "It's sound advice."

J.P. exited the vehicle and opened the passenger door. He helped Sadie out while Vander assisted Shelby, then Jake and Susannah followed.

"Stay beside me," Vander told Shelby, and she was more than happy to comply. "Sadie, stay close to your brother, and Jake—"

"I got my woman," he told Vander, giving him one of those alpha chin nods men gave each other.

"I also recommend you only use your first name, Jake," Vander said.

Another nod from him, and they walked forward en masse. Their grandma was at the front door waiting for them, but there wasn't a smile on her face.

When Vander's arm came around her, Shelby was beyond grateful to have his support, even if it was only as her pretend boyfriend.

CHAPTER 12

$\mathcal{V}$ANDER DIDN'T SEE ANY HARM IN LETTING LENORE McGuiness think he was attached to one of her granddaughters. In fact, it might keep her natural hostility in check. He'd suggested Shelby rather than Sadie since there was no denying that he and the middle McGuiness sister had chemistry. He'd find it easier to pull off his cover this way.

Plus, Shelby was shaking a bit anyway, and it had felt as natural as breathing to offer her some of his strength. This interview wasn't going to be easy for her. For any of them.

He made himself smile hesitantly at the older woman. It had shocked him to see how morbidly obese she was, and he could tell by the way she'd favored her right foot while holding the dog in check that it was painful to stand, even with a cane. He felt bad for her. Her feet were horribly bruised and swollen, which he suspected was why she didn't have on any shoes.

The dog was nowhere to be seen, and he breathed a sigh of relief. He'd dealt with enough protective dogs in his line of work to know that dog would kill for Lenore. She was enough of a handful without any backup.

"Are you really my Preston's girls?" she asked, shielding her eyes from the noonday sun. "I already told your brother— what was your name again, boy?"

"J.P., ma'am," he said, his arm around Sadie.

"Right," she said, her jowls like unbaked bread loaves tucked around her face. "You have his nose. What are your names?"

Sadie's eyes widened, and she pointed to herself. "Me?"

"Yes, you," Lenore said. "Spit it out, girl. I can't stand here all day."

"This is Sadie," J.P. said in a calm voice, "and that's Shelby. Susannah and her husband, Jake, are over there."

"Fine-looking man you have there," she told Susannah. "You too, Shelby. My, you resemble my Pres too."

The woman Vander had his arm around glanced up at him, and he could feel her muscles tighten even more. "She's a sweet one," he answered before she could. "Probably as sweet as your sweet tea. Can I help you pour, ma'am?"

Shelby turned to him with a puzzled look on her face, and he knew why. He was putting on a Southern accent as part of the act, something he'd decided to do after seeing the Confederate flags displayed all around the park. The people here had enough trust issues. They would rather spit on or shoot at a Yankee than shake hands with one.

He should have mentioned it, he supposed. He liked to think he would have talked this way naturally if he'd grown up in Nashville and never stepped foot in his grandparents' home.

"That would be nice," she said, turning and walking inside. "I'm feeling a little poorly today."

"I'm sorry to hear that, ma'am," Vander said, following her.

When he entered the front room, he had to lock down all his senses. The combined stench of body odor, cigarettes, and dog urine was overwhelming. The tan carpet was stained in spots, and the cream couch looked more dishwater-blonde than anything else. Half-eaten bags of potato chips and boxes of cookies lined the upholstery and the rickety liquor crate that served as a makeshift coffee table.

He heard Shelby clear her throat, and a few of the others

followed suit as they stepped inside. The dog was whining and barking on and off from the back room.

"Lenore," he said, "do you have somewhere we can all sit for a spell out back? It's mighty crowded in here."

Shelby glanced up at him again, and they shared a look. Yeah, she knew what he was doing. A few of the others looked like they were liable to gag if they stayed in here much longer.

"I have some old chairs out back," the older woman told him.

He gave Shelby one last squeeze before approaching Lenore. "If you show me where your keep your glasses, I can pour the tea for everyone. The others can go on outside."

"Those girls should be the ones to pour the tea," she told them with narrowed eyes. "I raised my girl to wait on the menfolk, not the other way around."

Vander made his mouth twitch. "I'm one of those modern kind of men. Hope that don't offend you none?"

She shook her head. "Modern, eh? You let him wait on you, girl?" Her question was directed at Shelby.

Shelby swallowed thickly and then shrugged. "There's no stopping him sometimes, but I like to help too. Why don't y'all go outside? Vander and I will bring out the drinks since he's a modern man and all."

Lenore snorted, but she led the way to the kitchen nonetheless, leaning heavily on her cane. Vander was impressed with the way Shelby had handled that. The part of her that loved order must be quailing from this miserable place, but there was also that other side of her, the one that enjoyed being around unusual folks like Gail. Lenore was certainly unusual, and Shelby had quickly stepped into the role-playing game with him. She was a good partner, and he liked knowing she could be counted on in tight spots. Not every woman could be, he'd discovered.

The grime on the kitchen countertops was as thick as dried tobacco juice, and there were roaches running across the floor. Vander saw Shelby shrink back when one scurried in front of her, but she managed not to outright squeal. Again, impressive.

"The glasses are in the cabinet to the left of the stove," Lenore called, opening the back door connected to the kitchen.

Vander fought a wince when the door gave an ear-piercing squeak.

"Don't go looking around my home while you're in there," Lenore said, shooting them a suspicious glance over her shoulder.

"We would never dishonor your hospitality," said J.P., who'd followed her. "What should we call you, ma'am?"

Lenore thought it over for a moment and then said, "I suppose Me-Mother since we're kin and all."

The rest of the group ambled out the door after her, Sadie giving them a nervous backward glance before stepping outside. The dog started another round of barking, and Vander struggled to tune it out.

He walked across the kitchen to the cabinet Lenore had indicated. The glasses he pulled out weren't much cleaner than the rest of her house, but there were no paper towels on the counter, so they'd just have to make do.

Shelby was pulling out tea from the ancient harvest gold refrigerator whose compressor was on its last legs from the sound of it. "I just can't..."

He crossed to her and took her shoulders in his hands. "I know it's a shock, but try and stay focused right now. You're doing great."

She bit her lip. "Okay."

Together, they poured the tea, and he listened to her take slow, even breaths to calm herself.

"We're not going to have enough for everyone. You'll have to pour water for the rest of us." He shuddered when rust-colored water emerged with a putrid smell when he turned the faucet on. Thankfully, the water ran purer after a spell, although a faint odor remained. "I think her septic tank needs to be flushed out."

Shelby gave another visible tremor and walked to the door. "Ah...Me-Mother? Do you have more ice tea fixings?"

There was a reply, and soon she was taking out the powdered tea from another cabinet. Her hands were shaking as she measured out the scoops, so Vander took over.

"Start handing out the glasses that are already full. I'll finish this."

She did as he'd asked, and he went through the motions of making the tea even though he knew it wouldn't do much to help the water. He hoped they wouldn't end up with some intestinal bug after this. With Shelby out of the kitchen, he scanned the area, looking for any family photos.

Lenore had been smart to warn them not to wander around in her home. If she hadn't...well, he would have gone on a little tour. He still planned to use the bathroom as a ruse to look around, especially if she chose not to be forthcoming.

He poured the rest of the tea and took the remaining glasses outside. Lenore was sitting on a rusted-out glider seat. J.P. had taken the patio chair next to her and was engaging her in small talk in that easygoing way of his. Vander liked him a lot already, and Jake Lassiter was the kind of guy he'd want for backup in an alley. Hopefully, Lenore wouldn't recognize him as a country music star. He couldn't be sure the woman wouldn't ask for money.

As he handed out glasses to those who needed them, he realized there weren't enough chairs. Jake was standing behind Susannah's chair, so Vander took a tip from him and stood in the same position behind Shelby. Sadie looked over at him, and he gave her an encouraging smile. The poor woman looked like she wasn't handling this well.

Lenore was watching everyone with keen, narrowed eyes while she chatted with J.P. about how long she'd been living in the trailer park. She continued to answer his questions for a while, sipping her tea, but when she wiggled on the glider to get more comfortable, Vander suspected she was ready to get down to business.

J.P. must have sensed it as well since he glanced at Vander with studied casualness.

He took the cue. "It won't surprise you none, Lenore, that your grandchildren have had questions about their daddy and his whereabouts for most of their lives. We were hoping you might shed some light. If it isn't too difficult for you, ma'am."

"Why not ask your mama?" she asked, bitterness lacing her tone. "That woman was a know-it-all long before she captured my boy's heart."

"As someone who lost a parent at a young age," Vander decided to share, "I can tell you that sometimes the parent who's left behind doesn't like to talk about the past."

He heard Shelby's sudden intake of breath, and without considering it, he reached down and squeezed her shoulder before returning his attention to Lenore.

"Your mama ran my boy off," she told the McGuinesses, scratching her sagging belly. "He never would tell me why. Only said he regretted having to leave."

It was only when Sadie reached for Shelby's hand that Vander realized he was still cupping his fake girlfriend's shoulder. He felt her trembling beneath his touch and couldn't bring himself to pull away. Comforting her was grounding him too. He was more anxious than usual for an interview like this.

"Preston's the youngest of my three, and he was a good boy. Sure, he raised some hell when he was young, but he was always kinder than his older brother. Virgil would kick a dog if he saw one in the street just for sport. And my girl... She shacks up with every Tom, Dick, and Harry who comes sniffing around. They take after the sorry man I ran off to marry at fifteen, who left me for a truck stop waitress outside Tulsa. He drove semis for a living until the drink done him in. May God rot his soul."

Susannah reached back to touch Jake's hand on her shoulder, and Sadie's bottom lip was quivering with emotion.

"Pres was the only one who wanted a better life," Lenore said. "That's why he packed up the guitar he'd bought in the dime store off Beale Street and used all his savings to go to Nashville."

J.P. gave her a smile. "I play the guitar, Me-Mother."

For the first time since they'd arrived, Lenore gave them a smile of her own, and it transformed her face. "I'll bet you play it good too. You remind me of Pres a good deal, boy. Your sister over there as well. It shakes me some."

Clearly it shook Shelby too, judging by the way her whole body trembled under his hand. He found himself rubbing her shoulder to calm her.

"I was too young to remember much when Daddy left," J.P. continued. "We've all lived with a lot of questions, so we're grateful for anything you can tell us. Do you know where he is?"

She sighed. "I haven't seen that boy since Virgil's funeral, and that's going on two years this September."

"So, he's alive then?" Sadie shot out, tears immediately filling her eyes.

"Well, of course he is, girl," Lenore said harshly, shaking her head. "Didn't I just say that?"

Vander watched the rest of the McGuiness children carefully. J.P. seemed to lower his head as if to say a prayer of thanks. Susannah gave an audible sniff while Shelby's frame started to shudder more violently. When she reached back and grabbed his hand, he clenched it hard. *You're okay,* he wanted to tell her, but stroked her back with his other hand instead. She leaned back into his touch, and he found his chest constricting in response.

"Land sakes," Lenore continued. "Pres is too sweet for the Good Lord to take him so early. Say whatever you want about how mean and ornery my boy Virgil was, but he was still my son. It's hard for a woman to lose her child."

"I'm sorry for your loss," J.P. was able to say after raising his head. He put a gentle hand on her arm. "Where was Daddy living when you saw him last?"

Lenore swatted a mosquito that landed on her face. "A small town outside Alamo. Not the one in Texas. But here in Tennessee. I can't recall the name. My boy has shied away from big cities after he lost all his dreams in Nashville. They never appreciated his talent out there."

"I wish I could have heard him sing," Shelby said, entering the conversation, which Vander thought was brave.

"He had a voice like a fallen angel," Lenore said a bit wistfully. "It wasn't right, him not getting his break."

"No, it wasn't," J.P. said. "Do you know if Daddy's still near Alamo?"

Vander had to give J.P. points for circling back to the questions they needed answered. It was exactly what he would have done.

"No," she said, scratching her belly again. "He doesn't like to stay in a place too long. I told him to send me a Christmas card at least. I'm his mama, after all. It's his Christian duty to be good to me."

Vander expected Lenore only used the Bible when it suited her needs. "Do you have his last Christmas card by chance? It would have the postal stamp on it."

"It's in my bedside drawer," Lenore said. "Didn't say much, but then again, my boy was always short on words. Except for his music. That's when he really spoke his mind."

Susannah looked over her shoulder at Jake. Vander hoped they would remain silent about him being a singer. Lenore might be softening, but they had a ways to go before he'd trust her with the full truth about anything.

"I don't want to rummage through your things, ma'am," Vander told her, taking a step forward. Shelby tightened her grip on him before letting go. He found himself oddly bereft. "But I'd be happy to bring the drawer out to you if that would help you some."

"So long as you can put the drawer back before you go," the woman said. "What's your mama doing now? How long did it take her to find another man to replace my boy?"

Vander stopped partway to the back door and turned around. He could sense the danger in the air. Hearing that Louisa McGuiness had divorced her husband on the grounds of desertion would only rile the older woman up.

"It took Mama a mighty long time, you'll be happy to hear," J.P. said quietly.

Lenore's penciled-in brows rose. "I'd be happier hearing she found no one. There was no man better than my boy, and she cut him down to size, or he'd have never have left y'all."

"Mama isn't—"

"What Sadie was starting to say, Me-Mother, is that Mama wasn't happy for a long spell after Daddy left us," J.P. said diplomatically. "It broke all our hearts."

"I'm sorry to hear that," Lenore said with a sigh, patting his hand. "It was terrible all around, for you children and my boy. I'm also sorry I never visited y'all. After my boy's wedding, there were words, but that's no excuse. It's...difficult for me to travel."

How long has she been morbidly obese? Vander wondered. Once again, he found himself feeling sorry for her.

"Are you going to get that drawer or do you intend to keep gawking, Toby?" Lenore finally spat at him.

He gave her a flirtatious wink since he suspected no one treated her with much charm these days. "I'm going, ma'am."

As he was opening the door, he heard Lenore say, "That man of yours could charm the pants off a snake, Shelby."

They shared a long look, and Vander felt acutely aware of the steady beating of his heart.

"And he probably has," Shelby answered easily, making Lenore laugh.

Her loud gusts of laughter followed Vander into the house, and he found himself smiling in spite of everything. The rest of the trailer wasn't much to write home about, and it was as filthy as the den and the kitchen. Her mattress sunk down in the middle, and the smell of urine hung in the air. The lamp on the nightstand had a dusty, stained shade, and he expected all of the furniture was from a thrift shop.

There was a faded photo on Lenore's dresser of her with three young children. While she looked completely different—large, sure, but in the way some people called curvaceous—she didn't look happy. Heck, no one in the picture looked happy. And the worthless man she'd married wasn't in the photo, he noted. He wondered when he'd abandoned the family. In so many of his cases, children made the exact same mistakes their parents had made before them. Seemed the McGuiness family was no different, but from what he had seen of the new generation, that pattern had been forever broken. None of these adults would abandon their families. It gave him hope.

He pulled out the drawer, noting it was stuffed with cream-filled cakes and rock candy. Lenore had already lost a few teeth, and it occurred to him that diabetes might have given her those bruises on her ankles. Well, it wasn't his concern. He was affected enough as it was. Taking the drawer, he headed back to join the others.

When he came through the door, Lenore was smiling as J.P. described his recent wedding and the two children he felt blessed to raise as his own.

"What about you, girl?" Lenore asked, turning to Susannah. "How long have y'all been married?"

Jake smiled. "Just a couple of months. Best months of my life."

"You're lucky," Lenore told Susannah. "And Shelby? When is that devil over there going to put a ring on your finger? Boy, don't just stand there with my treasures in your hand. Bring them over to me."

Shelby glanced at him as he made his way to Lenore. Clearly she didn't know how to answer, and who could blame her? He made himself smile at Shelby and punctuated it with a saucy wink.

"I'm still working on convincing her I'm good enough," he

told Lenore in his most honeyed Southern drawl.

He gave another wink, this time directed at Lenore. When he set the drawer on her lap, she slapped his hand. "You're a devil, through and through."

"You're going to have to work a lot harder to convince me to be with you forever, Toby," Shelby said in one of those sugary drawls she'd perfected, the kind that drove him wild. "I have pretty high standards."

Vander's brows rose, and he couldn't help but smile. "I'll keep that in mind, honey."

He knew they were flirting a little too easily, and from the intent way Sadie was watching them, it hadn't gone unnoticed. *This is just a job*, he reminded himself. But it was getting harder and harder to believe that.

Resuming his position behind Shelby's chair, he returned his attention to the group. J.P. was looking at him, and he had to wonder whether he'd noticed the same thing as Sadie. When Shelby didn't reach for one of the hands he put on her shoulder like she had before, he suspected her siblings had noticed. Even so, he kept his hands where they were.

"This is from Pres," Lenore said, pulling out an envelope wrinkled from many openings. "I always keep his cards together so I won't lose them. It's...my only connection to him. I don't have a phone, and I have a feeling Pres don't live in a place that has one either. He's been down on his luck most of his life. I wish....I could do more for him."

Vander watched tears fill Sadie's eyes. "We'll do what we can for him, Me-Mother," Sadie said. "If and when we find him."

"The postal stamp says Haines," Lenore said. "I wish my boy would come visit, but the bus doesn't get out this far. I have trouble driving, so it's near impossible for us to see each other."

Vander filed away those details. So Preston didn't have a car. Vander expected he was using a fake name now, but perhaps he also stuck to small towns because they were cheaper

and walkable. Sure, big cities had public transportation, but
they could be expensive. Plus, Lenore had said Preston didn't
like city life.

"I don't know that town offhand," J.P. said, "but we'll look
it up."

Lenore pressed the letter to her ample chest. "When you
find my boy, will you tell him I miss him? That we're due a
visit?"

"Of course, we will," J.P. said, folding his hand over hers.
"We'll also write you here and let you know what happens."

Vander knew he meant that and wondered if there would
be any more communication between this group after today.

"I'd like that," Lenore said. "Would you...tell me a little
more about yourselves? I feel so ashamed this is the first time
I've laid eyes on you. And...and I was so ugly to y'all earlier.
You were strangers, and there's still a lot of bad blood in me
from my time with your mama."

Vander was equally surprised and happy the woman
had softened. It would make this meeting so much easier for
everyone.

J.P. smiled at her and started to talk about himself, and
afterward, he turned to Shelby, who continued. Each of the
McGuinesses shared a little about their current profession
and a story or two about growing up together. All the while
Vander kept his hands on Shelby's shoulders, feeling so at
ease doing so, from time to time, he forgot they were there.

When Lenore included Vander and Jake in her questions,
both of them kept their answers as vague as possible.

Lenore spent the next hour sharing stories about
Preston as a boy. The McGuiness children lapped it up after
being denied details about their daddy for so long. Vander
remembered what Shelby had said at Oak Bar, how she didn't
even know if her daddy liked baseball or fishing, and he was
grateful her questions had finally been answered. Preston had
liked to play baseball, it turned out, but he'd hated fishing.

Seeing connections like this was what made Vander's

job worth it. Even if they didn't find Preston, at least these children had met their grandmother.

J.P. finally stood when Lenore started fanning herself. "We've stayed as long as we should. We don't want to tucker you out more. It was good to meet you, Me-Mother. I'm sorry it's taken this long."

She looked up and sniffed. "Me too, boy. You have a mighty fine family. Tell that wife of yours she's lucky to have a man like you."

"She already knows that," J.P. told her and helped her out of the glider while Sadie handed her the cane.

Vander took the dresser drawer, which Lenore had set on the ground, and held the door open for her. She ambled inside, and J.P. helped her get comfortable on her couch. Vander retraced his steps to her bedroom to replace the drawer. Before shutting it, he took a picture of the postal stamp on the envelope Preston had sent and then opened the card. It read:

Dear Mama,

Nothing much to say on this end. Working here and there and staying out of trouble. Wishing you a merry Christmas.

Your son,
Preston

Either Preston was a man of few words or he was sending the card out of a sense of obligation. Vander noted he didn't use a closing of love. Before he left the room, he took a picture of the photo of Lenore and her children.

When he returned, J.P. was smiling at Lenore as she handed him a photo. He caught a glimpse of it—and darn it all if it wasn't a more up-to-date photo of Preston. Vander wondered if it had been in the den since it was in a frame.

"This was taken at Virgil's funeral," Lenore told them, holding it out. "Deedee sent it to me. I wasn't as large then as

I am now, although some people around here might disagree. I've gotten so horribly fat. But when I lost my boy, I just..."

Tears ran down her face, and Shelby walked to the couch and knelt close to the woman. Vander felt his throat growing tight when Lenore reached for the hand her granddaughter had extended.

"I'm ashamed to have y'all see me like this," Lenore whispered. "I'm...I've grown into a monster."

"Oh, Me-Mother," Shelby said, capturing the woman's attention. "You have nothing to feel ashamed of. Certainly not with us."

Vander wanted to cross the room and kneel beside her in support. Just when he thought Shelby was the toughest of her sisters, she went and extended her compassion like this. Charlie had been right about one thing—this woman's layers intrigued him more than he would have liked.

"Thank you, child. Whatever I might think of your mama, she done raised y'all right." Lenore pointed to Preston in the photo. "He's always been skinny as a rail. Never ate much as a boy since we never had much. He takes after his daddy in that. That man was a skinny son of a bitch before he ran off. I take after my mama and her kin. They always were large, but I've gotten...out of hand. My health gets worse and worse...some days I don't want to get out of bed."

Shelby just kept holding her hand, and Vander was glad she didn't try comfort her with any meaningless platitudes. She was just giving her support, plain and simple. J.P. kept his hand on his grandmother's arm as she fought tears.

"Sure as shooting, y'all are good people," Lenore said, clearing her throat. "I'm happy to call you kin."

"Us too, Me-Mother," Sadie said, giving her a soft smile.

She returned her attention to the photo. "Pres is gray now, but he's got all his teeth—unlike me. He's still pretty handsome, if you ask me."

"Yes, he is," Susannah said, clutching her husband's hand.

Lenore glanced at J.P. "When I look at you, all I see is

Preston—not that you don't resemble him too, Shelby. There's just something about a father and son. It's...a good feeling. I want you to have this photo of him. So you know what he looks like currently. I hope it makes it easier for you to find him. He'd be lucky to know you."

"Thank you for giving this to us and for saying that," Shelby said.

"We can copy it and send it back to you, if you'd like," J.P. said. "We know this photo is precious to you."

"Thank you," she said as the dog started whining. "I'd like that."

Lenore looked over toward a closed door at the back of the trailer.

"I'd better take out No-no," she told them, making an awkward attempt to stand again, leaning hard on her cane. "He's been more than patient while we were visiting. I hope he didn't piss in the room, although it wouldn't be the first time. I sometimes can't let him out when I'm feeling poorly."

"I'd offer to get him," Vander said, "but I don't think your dog is used to strangers. How did you come to name him No-no?"

"Because when he was nothing but a whelp, all I did was say, 'no-no.' He got used to it being his name. Shoot, I've talked more today than I have in years. I should let y'all get back on the road."

"Would you mind if I gave you a hug, Me-Mother?" J.P. asked, helping her up.

Tears danced in her eyes. "I'd be mighty put out if you didn't."

He wrapped his arms around her as much as he could and kissed her cheek. Vander stepped forward to do the same because it felt right. He hoped the others in the group would gather their courage to follow suit.

He'd never hugged a woman as large as Lenore, and he felt that bone-deep compassion for her again. In his profession, he met plenty of people who'd given up after a lifetime of hard luck. Lenore might have been close to that before meeting her grandchildren. He wondered what she would do after they left. Sometimes all it took was a pivotal moment for someone to decide to turn their life around.

"You keep on keeping on, Lenore," he told her.

"You too, darlin'," she told him.

He let her go and nearly stepped on Shelby.

"It was real nice to finally meet you, Me-Mother," she said and leaned in to hug her gently.

Sadie gave her grandmother a sweet hug and actually wiped away her tears. Susannah was a little stiffer, but she pulled it off, and then Jake made Lenore laugh by whispering something in her ear as he embraced her.

"Boy, you might be as bad as Shelby's man over there," Lenore told the country singer.

J.P. started the procession out of the house. Lenore was dashing away her tears and waving goodbye when Vander looked back from the car. He waved at her too. She might have been mean when they'd arrived, but there was an unexpected kindness inside of her, like a bittersweet chocolate with a caramel filling. He was glad for the McGuiness family. The interview had gone a heck of a lot better than he'd hoped.

They had a real lead on Preston McGuiness.

CHAPTER 13

SHELBY WAS STRUNG OUT AFTER THEY LEFT ME-MOTHER, and she wasn't the only one. Hearing Daddy was alive had put a permanent lump in her throat. Sadie was weepy beside her, and Susannah couldn't stop shaking if the way her teeth were chattering was any indication. J.P. was silent, but she could see his chest rising and falling with deep breaths from her seat in the car. After all this time, after all her hopes, they finally had a lead on finding him.

She was a ball of emotion. Today had changed everything. They all knew it.

Vander found a roadside diner a few miles up the highway and suggested they stop and regroup. Maybe even eat something. While Shelby realized she should be hungry, she was too numb to have much of an appetite.

Vander took charge, finding them a table in the back of the rough wood building and then passing out menus taken from the metal holder in the center of the table. The lone waitress, who was working both the bar and the small eating area, ignored them. She looked fit to be tied. *Well, join the club*, Shelby thought.

She scanned the menu before settling on a hamburger and fries. In every crisis she'd ever experienced—and she'd had a few—she'd always been able to eat that classic. Maybe that's why some people called it the all-American meal. Good Lord, the thoughts she was entertaining after learning she might actually meet her daddy some day soon.

Vander took out a small notebook and jotted down everyone's orders. Shelby appreciated that he was taking care of them. Back at Me-Mother's, he'd more than taken care of her, comforting her with his strong presence behind her chair. She'd never forget that as long as she lived.

Her eyes followed Vander as he got up and approached the waitress. All he did was hand the dark-haired woman the list and say a few words to her, but her transformation was immediate. She was smiling by the time he walked back to their table.

Shelby had watched him pretty much transform their grandmother as well. Of course, J.P. had been wonderful with Me-Mother, but it was Vander's kindness that had caught her off-guard. That spark of empathy she'd seen in him the day he'd defended Sadie's right to take part in the investigation had burst into a full-blown fire today. That softer side of him was hard to resist.

She thought back to what Sadie had said about making the first move because she was a client, and it just might come to that after today. Gail's description of Vander came to mind: *men like that don't grow on trees, girl.*

Indeed, they didn't.

"Does everybody want to settle a bit or do you want to talk about what we discovered?" Vander asked. "I'm in no rush."

"Seems it might be prudent for us to stick with our plan and stay the night as opposed to rushing back," J.P. said. "I...I'm feeling a lot of extremes right now."

"Me too," Sadie said, letting out a thready breath while everyone nodded in agreement.

"I'm glad we made reservations downtown," Susannah said, gripping her husband's hand. Jake had suggested they stay at the Peabody since the hotel had protocols in place to give celebrities some privacy.

"How far is Haines from here?" Sadie asked.

"I already looked it up," Vander said, pulling out his phone. "It's a little over an hour away—not too far from Brownsville. The population is just shy of three hundred people."

"Me-Mother said Daddy liked to stay in small towns," Shelby said. "What do you think the next step is, Vander?"

"One thing about I noticed about the return address on that envelope is that he didn't use his name," he told her. "It spiked my curiosity. He might be using his real name, and he might not. People can avoid surfacing by using only cash, but since we haven't found any records of him for over twenty-five years, my guess is he has an alias."

It was weird to think of anyone having an alias, least of all her daddy.

"I agree," Jake said, and he and Vander shared a look.

"To answer your question, Shelby, I think I should go there undercover. Alone."

"But—"

"Shelby," Vander said, gazing her way, "I know you want to go. You might all want to go. But it might scare him off if a group our size comes into town looking for him."

"Couldn't you ask the local police for help?" Shelby asked.

"From my experience, some small-town local law enforcement officers aren't eager to help outsiders. Once I play my hand as a P.I., they could tell your dad. I don't want to take that chance. Undercover is better. Trust me."

"What are the chances he's still there?" J.P. asked, rocking back in his chair. "Christmas was months ago, and Me-Mother said he moves a lot. If he was in Alamo two years ago, and Haines now, he's moving at least once a year."

"I can visit Alamo if Haines is a dead end," Vander said. "But I'll start at his last known address."

"You really think Daddy would spook," Susannah said. "Even after all this time?"

The waitress interrupted them by bringing over their drinks, giving Vander an extra-helping of sunshine, which he returned.

After squeezing lemon into his tea and taking a sip, he said, "Like I told you, it's just a hunch. A man doesn't pull up roots this often for over three decades without a reason. It tells me he doesn't want to be found."

"Vander's spot on here," Jake said, tapping the table absently. "We learned some profiling in the Army. Your daddy has a pattern going, and I'd say he's running."

"Do you think that means he did something illegal?" Susannah asked, leaning closer to her husband.

"Charlie and I couldn't find any evidence he'd been convicted of a crime, but that's not to say nothing happened," Vander told them, making a point to look to the right and left of the table from his position in the middle of the group. "Honestly, I know it's hard not to want to think up different scenarios, but I've found it's a waste of energy. There are a hundred reasons why someone might move from one town to the next. I'd rather focus on pulling more threads to get the truth."

"Well put," J.P. said, patting Sadie on the arm since she looked like she was coming undone.

Shelby couldn't blame her. She just hoped her sister could keep it together until they got back to the hotel.

"I want to call Charlie and talk things through," Vander said. "I'm tempted to take a ride back to Lenore's by myself to get a photo with her. Something I could show your father if and when I find him. It might make him more amenable to listening to me. I think she'll be open to something like that after today. The timing and mood didn't feel right."

"I could go with you," J.P. said, and they shared a look. "She warmed up to me, and it might help if one of her kin joined you. Perhaps since I favor Daddy so, having a picture of me with y'all would help some."

"Good idea," Vander said. "You did a great job back there, especially asking for a recent photo of your father. Beat me to it. In fact, you all did an incredible job. From where I'm standing—or sitting—you're a pretty brave group."

"I didn't expect her to be so obese," Sadie whispered, speaking so softly Shelby had to strain to hear her. "It broke my heart."

"It broke all of us," J.P. said, heaving a sigh. "When I first entered her trailer, I...I wasn't sure I was going to measure up to the situation."

"We all felt that way, honey," Shelby said, reaching for his hand. "I've never seen anyone live like that. I...about came out of my skin."

"I thought about giving her all the cash I had in my wallet," Jake said, "but I didn't think it would be the right move."

"No," J.P. said, shaking his head. "She was ashamed enough as it was. But maybe when Vander and I go back, we can do something for her. Tell Me-Mother we took up an offering."

Everyone else was nodding in agreement, and Shelby's heart thumped double-time in her chest as she imagined Vander and J.P. going back to Me-Mother's and giving her some money. Would she even take it? Would it offend her? She didn't want anything to mar their meeting today, even though the thought of going back there scared the bejesus out of her.

She heard herself blurt out, "That's a great idea! I'd like to go along too." Besides, didn't she look like Daddy as well? Wouldn't he want to see his likeness in her if and when Vander showed him the photo? Shelby found she wanted that more than anything.

Before Vander could say a word, the waitress appeared with a tray of their food, and everyone waited to be served before turning their eyes toward Vander.

"Let me talk things through with Charlie," Vander said, not looking in Shelby's direction. "But I think it would be best if just the two of us go this time. It'll be a quick trip anyway."

It felt like a purposeful slight. Still, making an issue of it in front of everyone wasn't the way. She'd sound like a whiny baby if she asked why J.P. could go and not her.

But she certainly planned to ask him about it when they returned to the hotel.

There was no way she was staying behind.

CHAPTER 14

VANDER HAD A KNACK FOR KNOWING WHEN TROUBLE was brewing. He'd grown skilled at it after his father's murder, almost as if he could see inside his mother as the swirl of air started to whirl into a possible tornado.

He'd grown skilled at diffusing those dangerous storms, using everything from kindness to pacification to keep the peace.

Shelby's insides were swirling, and even though she'd gone off with the rest of her family after they'd all checked into their respective rooms at the hotel, he knew she wasn't finished with him. She hadn't liked it when he'd batted aside her request to accompany him to Lenore's, especially after he'd agreed to let J.P. go along.

They'd agreed to meet in Jake and Susannah's celebrity suite at eight a.m. for breakfast to discuss next steps, but Vander would be shocked if she waited that long. He'd given everyone his room number and cell phone so they could contact him if they needed anything—and so Shelby could tear into him in private.

What she didn't realize was that he was reluctant to bring one of the McGuiness women back to that trailer park. Those Neo-Nazis were up to something, and he'd bet the farm they were cooking up meth. Given what they were packing, he wasn't eager to put anyone in danger.

Least of all women.

Yes, he was being protective, but in this case, he also considered it smart. He respected a woman's ability to handle herself. Heck, Charlie was trained for it, but that was the operative word. *Trained.* None of the McGuiness women were.

He'd called Charlie from his hotel room, and she'd agreed with him—both about leaving Shelby behind and the next steps for their search. He had her checking for a Preston McGuiness online in both Alamo and Haines. They didn't expect to find anything, but sometimes they got surprised, which was why they pulled every thread.

When someone knocked on his door just shy of ten o'clock—it had to be her, and he felt a sense of anticipation despite himself—Vander rose from the desk in his room and walked over to it. He'd taken a shower, so his hair was slightly damp. He'd needed to rinse off the filth of the day, but he'd dressed in a clean pair of jeans and a black T-shirt Charlie had bought him as a white elephant gift for Christmas. He damn well knew how important it was to be fully dressed for this encounter, even if the logo across the front said in white block letters: *Private Eyes. They're Watching You.* Sue him, but he liked the Daryl Hall & John Oates classic.

He opened the door and leaned against the frame. "I can't believe you waited this long to chew me out, Shelby."

She'd changed into a fetching—way too fetching if he were being honest—pink dress made of cotton and silk that managed to look both sexy and comfortable. Had she chosen it to drive him wild or give this encounter a more professional veneer? He found he didn't care.

"We just broke up to go back to our rooms," she said, putting her hands on her waist.

"Of course," he said. He'd known they would need some time without him to process the day's events and talk about it as a family. That was why he'd left them alone when they'd finally arrived at the hotel.

"Can I come in?" she asked, looking down the hall floor. "I feel weird standing out here."

His brow rose. "Well, since you're a client, *I* would feel weird about you coming into my room. How about we go downstairs to the bar?"

Her whiskey-colored eyes seemed to shoot sparks as she pushed past him into his room. "I'm tired, and you're being ridiculous. What I have to say won't take long. Besides, you're flattering yourself."

Even though he knew he shouldn't poke at her, he said, "Am I?" Without moving away from the door he was holding open, he turned to face her.

"I don't jump into bed with every man I find attractive," she said, almost in a huff, a bright splash of color in the beige-heavy décor of the room. "Besides, I might find you attractive and sometimes even kind, but after the way you brushed aside my interest in going back to my grandma's house, I'm fixing to come undone."

He couldn't help it. His mouth twitched. "Fixing to come undone, huh? That is a problem."

"Vander, shut the damn door," she ordered, locking her arms at her waist.

He did her bidding after discarding the idea of propping it open with a chair so no one could assume they were up to no good. Who was he kidding? This woman threw his professionalism right out the window. She was cute when she got ticked off.

"Pink is your favorite color, right?" he asked her, strolling further into the room to the bar station. He was happy he'd opted for a suite at the Peabody. His bedroom was off the small parlor, out of reach. "And just so you know, I'm personally paying extra for the upgrade on my room. I'm always working, and I hate to do it in my bedroom."

"Thanks for clearing that up," she said, shaking her head like he'd thrown her off a little. "I can add honesty and fiscal responsibility to a list of your glowing traits."

"But you aren't here to talk about that, Shelby," he said, pulling two waters from the mini-bar. "Tell me what's on your mind."

"Why won't you let me go with you and J.P. tomorrow?" she asked, taking the bottle he handed her. "Is it because I froze up in the kitchen for a moment with the roaches? I *know* I didn't handle meeting Me-Mother as well as J.P. did, but I still...I still have compassion for her."

He sat in the armchair and gestured for her to take a seat on the couch to his right. Shelby wasn't just mad at him, he realized, she was feeling guilty about how she'd handled the meeting. "Are you beating yourself up? Anyone would have been poleaxed, seeing Lenore and the conditions she lives in. I was, and I've seen a lot more of this kind of thing than you have. That's not even taking into account how mean she acted at first. Give yourself a break."

"It's just J.P. is so much more easygoing and nicer than the rest of us," she said, setting her water on the coffee table. "I mean, Sadie and Susannah are nice too, but they're not easygoing."

"Shelby, you're nice too. Don't get down on yourself."

She looked at her lap. "I was afraid you..."

When she broke off, he leaned forward in his chair, sensing a real vulnerability in her. "You what?"

"I was afraid you didn't think I was as nice as J.P. or as... capable," she said, "and for some reason that really bothered me. Oh poo, I'm acting like such a baby. I should go."

She shot off the couch, and he got up just as quickly. Putting his hand to her arm was as much instinct as compassion, and she immediately stilled. When she looked up into his eyes, he felt his heart beat in deep, slow pounds. His fingers itched to trace the high cheekbones of her face, but he held back.

"Sit down, Shelby," he said, his voice octaves lower than usual.

"Why?" she asked in a soft tone, one that made the hairs

on the back of his neck stand on end.

They were moving into dangerous territory. He was tempted to answer her with a kiss.

"Because that's not why I don't want you to accompany J.P. and me. Will you listen to what I have to say?"

She heaved out a breath, nodding, and resumed her seat. He did the same.

"There's some bad shit going down in that trailer park," he told her, not wanting to delve any deeper into his suspicions. "I don't want to bring any of you women back there. I would have had reservations about Charlie going, even though she's trained to protect herself."

"That's sexist!" she cried out. "I can't believe Charlie lets you get away with that."

"Perhaps you're right," he said, drinking his water to cool his hot throat. "But we've both learned that sometimes equal opportunity doesn't get the job done. A redneck and a good ol' boy aren't likely to tell a woman jack shit. Excuse my French. And the reverse is true for me. Sometimes, we send her to get information from a man sitting at a bar because he wouldn't give me the time of day."

She unscrewed her water and drank a few sips, acting as though she was considering what he'd said. "Thank you for laying that out. I...hadn't thought of it that way."

He waggled his brows at her. "It's why you could talk your way out of a speeding ticket with most male officers, but you just got written up by a female one."

Her eyebrows shot to her hairline. "You looked *me* up?"

Admitting that probably hadn't been the best move, but for some reason, he wasn't bothered by it. "Charlie did. She likes to know what we're dealing with. Plus, it's public record. Nothing illegal. Some small-town newspapers even print information like that."

"*Hmmm...*" was all she said.

"Are you still mad at me?" he asked, aware that he was carrying some tightness in his diaphragm at the thought. It wasn't normal for him.

"I'm working on getting over it," she said, resting back against the sofa cushions. "It's been an emotional day. I'm... sorry if I overreacted."

He made himself stand. "No hard feelings. You should head on up. It's been a long day. Some rest will help."

That is, if anyone in her family managed to get some shut-eye. He knew how hard that could be in situations like this.

"I expect you're right," she said, pushing off the couch and setting her water back down on the table. "I'm so tangled up after learning Daddy is alive that I mostly wanted to go with you and J.P. to be in a picture with Me-Mother."

Oh shit.

"I wanted my daddy to see my resemblance to him—not just J.P.'s." She shook herself. "Don't mind me."

He was minding her way too much at this point, and delving into her daddy issues would open up an even greater connection between them. His control was slipping, he realized, because he wanted to reassure her. But she was a freaking client, and he'd made that rule for a reason.

They walked to the door together, but instead of putting her hand on the knob to open it, she turned around and leaned against the frame, studying him in the soft light. His balls seized up, more than aware of how alluring her pale skin was against the pink of her dress. He didn't think she'd done it to be alluring. She was just naturally that way. Still, her rose-and-musk perfume reached his nose, and he ground his teeth to keep from reaching for her.

"Shelby, you should go."

She looked down and fiddled with her manicure, suddenly shy. When she looked up, there was a rosy blush on her cheeks. It only made her more beautiful.

"I know," she whispered, "but I just can't get over one thing."

He wanted to know what it was.

He didn't want to know what it was.

Either way, whatever she said was going to change things. He was smart enough to realize that, so he asked, "What?" just as softly.

She laid a tentative hand on his chest, making everything inside him tighten up. "I was incredibly bothered you didn't think I was a nice person."

She wanted him to think she was *nice?* Well, he pretty much wanted to kiss her senseless against the door and hike her dress up so he could run his hands over her thighs.

"I think you're nice," Vander told her, immediately chastising himself for the idiotic response. He wanted to show her what else he thought of her, standing as she was with a gentle hand pressed to his chest, but he couldn't...

"I think you're nice too," she whispered.

And then she stepped forward until she was flush against his body, rose up on her tiptoes, and pressed her mouth to his. Her lips were a shock, not only because they were so soft, but also because they were so very warm. He closed his eyes, fighting for control, wanting to kiss her back but knowing he'd regret it if he did.

She put another hand to his chest, this one more certain, and he felt the electricity course down to his toes.

"Shelby," he said in a harsh voice against her mouth. "You're a client."

The siren in pink detoured to his jaw, running her fingers against the stubble there. "Technically, Gail is your client since she's the one footing the bill. Isn't that enough of a loophole for you?"

"No," he said, putting his hands on her waist and caressing her hips. "Shelby, I can't have sex with you. I have a code."

She snapped out of his arms in an instant. "Who was asking you to?" Her outrage was unmistakable.

"You were the one who kissed me," he pointed out.

She rolled her eyes dramatically. "Kissing isn't an invitation to sex."

His mouth dropped open before he could stop it. "Are you

kidding me?"

Her eyes narrowed. "I don't just jump into bed with anyone. You are so full of yourself!"

"Well, excuse me! You're the one who just kissed me in my hotel room after telling me how nice you think I am. I can't imagine why any man would get the wrong idea." Shit, had he just said that? She was clearly making him crazy. He never said things like that.

"Oh," she said, opening the door. "I can't believe I kissed you. You're impossible! You make me fit to be tied."

"Ditto," he told her, his lips finally twitching.

"Forget this ever happened," she said, turning with enough force to whip her hair around. "Good night!"

He watched her walk to the elevator and punch the up button. She ignored him while she waited, picking at her manicure. When the elevator arrived, she entered it like she had forgotten all about him—just like she'd said she would.

But he knew better.

Neither one of them was going to be able to forget what happened.

CHAPTER 15

SHELBY RETURNED TO NASHVILLE WITH A NEW HOPE IN her heart that they were one step closer to finding Daddy. He was alive, and that was something.

Vander was now in possession of photos of him and J.P. with Me-Mother. Even more wonderful, Me-Mother had accepted their small offering of support, and Shelby and her sisters and brother had all agreed to talk about what more they could do to help their grandmother move out of her squalid living conditions. It looked like they had a relationship with her now, and that was something to be grateful for—even if they didn't know how to broach the topic with Mama.

Even Susannah seemed to have come around after meeting Me-Mother. Her elder sister's compassion had overridden the fear and wariness in her heart. Of course, Shelby's heart had a dull ache from realizing their daddy had never reached out to them even though he'd been alive this whole time. She still wasn't sure how to process that.

When Vander called Shelby a couple of days later and asked if she could swing by his office, she'd been all a-flutter.

Just the way he'd said, "Hello, Shelby," had made warmth pool in her belly.

That night in his hotel room had played like a broken record in her mind. There was no way she was going to forget it, despite what she'd said. Heck, every time she thought about the feeling of his lips on hers, she shivered. And every time she thought about his presumption she had planned on sleeping with him, well, she got more than flustered. The nerve of that man, thinking she was some light skirt.

But it was also tempting to think of going that far with him.

Her one and only long-term boyfriend, Nick, whom she'd thought she would likely marry, had worn her down, saying how much he loved her and how he couldn't wait. She'd met him in college at a Bible mixer at their student Christian forum. It still ticked her off that she'd succumbed to him after five months, especially since the experience had been...disappointing. The flash and bang she'd seen in movies and read about in books had been more like a fizzled firework. The whole process had been awkward, and afterward, his attention had waned. So had hers.

He'd broken up with her a couple months later with the cliché excuse that they were going in different directions. She still hadn't completely forgiven herself for giving something so special to him.

Vander made her feel special. More so than she'd felt with Nick or any of the other guys she'd dated. From the depths of the emotions she experienced in his presence, everything from anger to passion to happiness, it was hard to deny that he would bring the flash and bang to bed. Her biggest problem was sex wasn't all that to her. She wanted to make love with someone she loved—someone who loved her back.

But she was going on twenty-eight, and her only experience had been akin to drinking the dreaded warm milk her mama used to insist upon before bedtime. Dammit, she wished she could just hop into bed with Vander and have a good time without analyzing it to death. But she couldn't. Sometimes, she hated being raised with the values her mama had always hammered home. As an adult, she could no longer blame it on her rearing.

"Do you want me to organize the rest of the clan?" Shelby finally asked Vander after what must have been a long pause. She needed to control her lustful thoughts.

"Not unless you want to," he said. "Charlie and I talked it through, and she agrees with my plan. When I go to Haines, I'm going to keep the cover I used with Lenore. I'm going in as your boyfriend."

Simply hearing him *talk* about being her boyfriend had her fanning herself. She pushed back from her desk and went to turn the air conditioner down. "You already mentioned that," she said, merely to push his buttons.

"I'm simply reminding," he answered back and cleared his throat.

"Okay," she said, not completely understanding. "Why are you and I meeting alone?"

He chuckled softly. "Since you asked me to forget about that kiss *and* you're a client, I won't give you the answer that comes to mind. I need you to swing by so we can take some photos of us together. People tend to be more sympathetic when they think a man is trying to find the father of the woman he loves."

That phrase—*the woman he loves*—made her take deep breaths, but she had to remind herself it was all an act. Vander didn't feel that way about her.

But he did feel something. So did she.

Damn him and his infernal code.

"I take it you've had some success with that sob story in the past?" she made herself say to fill the silence over the line.

"Yes," Vander said, a jaded edge in his voice. "People love helping others get their happy ending."

Of course, a man who didn't believe in wishes probably didn't believe in happy endings either.

"I also remember you mentioning you wanted your father to see the resemblance between the two of you, and I thought you might like...well, him to see a picture of you along with J.P.'s if and when I track him down."

Her heart pretty much stopped working. He'd *listened* to her. And he was actually doing something about it. She tried to think of a time anyone outside her family had ever been so sweet.

"I can stop by after work," she said, and she was probably going to kiss him on the cheek. How could she not help herself?

"How late do you work?" he asked. "I have this feeling you work as hard as I do."

"I like working."

"So do I."

Were they really shooting the breeze about their likes and dislikes? This ruse of a relationship felt more real than anything Shelby had experienced in months. No, years.

"I can meet you at your office at seven," she said, running through the final tasks she had on her daily to-do list.

"I know it's an odd request," he said, "but could you bring a couple changes of clothes? Nothing complicated. Oh, and a jacket too. So it shows we've been together for a while now. People internally catalogue time by the kind of clothing people wear."

"Should I bring a ball gown?" she asked, just to be contrary.

"No," he said, chuckling, "but I'd bet you look good in one. See you at seven, Cinderella."

"Vander," she said smiling at the unexpected endearment. "Thank you."

"For what?"

"You know what."

He was silent for a moment, and then said, "Shelby, I'm only doing my job."

But he wasn't, and they both knew it. When he hung up, she ended up closing up shop fifteen minutes early—after making a mistake that had required her to delete an entire row of expenses. Of course, he'd blown her concentration.

On top of that, he'd all but asked her for a fashion shoot with no warning. Did he know nothing about Southern women?

At seven o'clock, she wheeled her carry-on across his lobby. Her makeup bag was attached to the top, and her new cream and rhinestone Jimmy Choos clicked on the marble floor. The shoes were a perfect complement to the cream silk dress she'd cinched with a silver belt made of rhinestones. She'd fretted mightily over what to wear for the photos, wanting to show her daddy she was both beautiful and smart—somehow that mattered to her.

Vander's assistant wasn't present, so she headed down the hallway. As she passed the second doorway, someone called out her name. Poking her head in through the open door, she saw Charlie.

"Where in the world are you going?" the woman asked after closing her mouth. "Prom?"

Shelby narrowed her eyes. Of course a woman who only wore masculine-looking black pants and a white cotton shirt to work would say that about silk and rhinestones. "Vander wants to do some photos."

Charlie bit her lip, and Shelby could tell she was trying not to laugh. "Oh, brother. I wish I could stick around to watch. He's in his office."

Shelby took a step and then stopped. "I...want to thank you for everything you've been doing to find our daddy." She hadn't said it before, and her mama had raised them to thank the people who deserved it. With it only being the two of them, it felt like a good time.

"I like you better when you're snarky," Charlie said. "I need to keep remembering you work for Gail. You mustn't be a total goody two-shoes with her."

Considering Gail had bought a "genuine" Civil War cannon today from an antique dealer in Charleston and asked Shelby if she thought she could expense it under historical preservation, she couldn't deny she knew what Charlie was talking about. "She's zany sometimes, but she's also the smartest woman I've ever met."

Charlie made a gesture with her hands. "I'm not real good with the whole Southern beauty queen thing. Sorry about the prom comment. Those girls used to make fun of me in school."

"The girls in my school made fun of me for being a goody-goody and a preacher's kid. Everyone gets picked on for something."

"I suppose," Charlie said, sticking a pencil behind her ear. "I don't care now. I'm doing exactly what I want with my life, and a lot of them are probably unhappy. People who take out their frustrations on other people tend to be. I see that all the time in this job."

"I imagine so," Shelby said. "Well, I should get to Vander. I expect he likes things to be on time."

Charlie nodded, clearing her throat. "I have to do some undercover work myself tonight." She went over to a coat hanger dangling from cabinet and unzipped a garment bag hanging from it. "What do you think of my dress?"

All Shelby saw was a sea of blue sequins. She gaped at the woman. "You're wearing that?"

"Yeah," Charlie said with a feral smile. "The guy I'm pumping for information is a predictable pig. I even have matching shoes," Charlie added with a twinkle in her eye. "I'll be sure to let you see me as a Southern beauty queen before I leave. Vander likes to go all *King Lear* on me. He always says an over-feminine version of me makes him want to gouge his eyes out."

"That's terrible!"

"That's our relationship," she said with an easy smile, making Shelby wonder what it was like to be Vander's friend like that. Clearly, they had a rapport. One she didn't understand, perhaps, but she liked that they could work together and horse around like she would with Gail.

"Every time I dress this way—even if it's for work—I want to send it to my alumni network as an FU," Charlie continued, looking down in her lap. "Like I can be pretty too. And petty."

Shelby thought she was likely more hurt than petty. "You

should do it," she said, making the woman immediately raise her head and look at her. "They were wrong to make fun of you. I admire your toughness. Do you ever get worried about the men you have to face getting too fresh?"

"If they do, I knee them in the balls," she answered, cracking her knuckles. "But I don't put myself in that position. Vander runs a clean shop. We don't flirt with danger."

Shelby was happy to hear that. "Good luck."

"You too," Charlie said. "I can't wait to see the pictures of you and Vander." This time her smile was genuine.

When Shelby appeared in his doorway, he had his back to her, typing on his laptop.

"You're late," he said. "Did you plan it just to try and rile me up?"

She wheeled her luggage in and stopped by the set of chairs in front of his desk, wishing he would turn around. "No, I was talking with Charlie."

"Were you now?" He swiveled in his chair to face her. "Holy shit! You brought a suitcase?"

His response elicited her most flirtatious grin. "And makeup and hair accessory bags too."

Standing, he said, "I only need a few pictures, Shelby."

"And you need to understand, I don't let this—" she released the suitcase and made an up and down gesture, "—be captured on a mere whim. Besides, I am not going to let my daddy or anyone associated with him see me looking less than fabulous. It's the principle of the matter."

"Oh, for fu— sake, Shelby," Vander said, putting his hands on his hips.

"I also expect dinner since I look more beautiful when I'm not starving," she said, reaching into her purse and handing him the piece of paper she kept there. "This is a list of acceptable places."

His mouth dropped open before he snapped it shut. "You're kidding."

"No, honey," she drawled, wishing she could cross over to

him and kiss him right on his gaping mouth. "I'm not."

He scanned the list. "Jared's does take-out?" he asked.

She gave him a syrupy smile. "They do for me."

"Hmm. I'll bet." He stared at her, and his aquamarine eyes glinted with pure mischief. "Do they do take-out cocktails too?"

Her grin widened. "We call them sippy cups in my world."

"Of course you do," he said, and then his gaze shot to the door. "Dammit, Charlie! What did I tell you about prancing around like that in my presence? Do you want me to go blind?"

Shelby turned to see the P.I. biting her lip to contain her laughter. The woman before her was completely transformed. Her hair was twisted up in a side ponytail, her sequin dress displaying a hint of curve. The addition of lip gloss and mascara had done wonders to soften her face.

"Yes, Vander, I do. I live for the day you will have to rely on me to find your way. Have fun, you two."

"You look beautiful, Charlie," Shelby found herself saying.

The woman waved a hand out dismissively. "Nah, but I should be pretty enough for my mark."

"Check in with me later, beautiful," Vander drawled.

Charlie stuck her tongue out and left with an exaggerated swag of her hips, making Shelby laugh.

"That was nice of you," Vander said when they were alone.

"What?"

"She has...image issues. Not self-esteem exactly." He shook his head. "Never mind. I didn't say anything."

But he had, and his regard for his friend and colleague touched her deeply. "I didn't know if I liked her before," Shelby said, "but I do now."

He pressed his fingers to his forehead like she was giving him a headache. "I'm sure she'll be overjoyed to hear that. Let's re-focus."

Shelby walked to the phone sitting on the edge of his desk. "Shall we ring for dinner?"

"Let me get my silver bell," he quipped. "You really insist

on making a production of this?"

"I do," she said, picking up the phone.

He growled low in his throat. "Fine then. But *I* insist we head somewhere more comfortable."

"Where do you live?" she asked, giving him a dramatic look. "And does it have good lighting?"

His eyes narrowed immediately. "No."

"Oh, come on, Vander," she said, pouring charm into her voice. "We've already established I won't sleep with you, and you won't sleep with me because I'm your client. Don't you trust yourself?"

He stared at her. "Are you trying to piss me off?"

"Would little ol' me do something like that?" she asked, fighting a smile. Oh, how she loved teasing him.

"With interest," he growled, grabbing her bag. "All right. My house. Will you follow me, or do you plan on having me drive you back here once we're finished?"

"Whatever you prefer," she said, buffing her nails like she didn't care a whit. "But it seems like a waste of gas to take two cars if you ask me."

He muttered something under his breath, then, speaking louder, said, "Let's go, Shelby."

"I'd recommend we order from Jared's now so we won't have to wait too much longer," she said, tapping the phone's display. "I'm getting peckish."

"Peckish," he uttered, rolling the word around his tongue. "We wouldn't want that, would we? Do you have a menu? Or is this a magical line where I can ask for anything, and they'll deliver it?"

"You can bring up the menu online," she said. "I personally know it by heart. That is, except for the specials."

The look he gave her shot a bolt of fire through her. "Order me a steak, Shelby. Medium rare. Pick any sides you'd like to share. I'll close up the office while you're on the phone."

"Your address?" she asked.

He gave it to her with a wry twist to his gorgeous

mouth. She felt an all-body shiver as she watched him walk out. In some ways, she felt freer to flirt with him than she might have if they were dating. He couldn't push the envelope. Neither could she. It was almost the perfect arrangement.

By the time he returned, she'd called in their order. He grabbed his briefcase and rolled her carry-on out to the elevator.

"We're skirting the line here," he muttered.

"You worry too much," she said, even though she knew he was right.

Something about him made it impossible to follow the straight and narrow. Out of all her sisters, she'd always been the most daring.

Being with Vander was like playing in her own personal amusement park.

"Yet I seem to recall you saying we should forget about the kiss you gave me," he said as the doors closed to take them to the garage.

She casually leaned back against the wall and raised her brow. "We're eating and taking photos. Kissing is not on the menu."

While he didn't take his eyes off her face, they blazed with so much heat, she felt like he'd looked her up and down.

He didn't say anything as they walked to his car. She wasn't surprised to discover he drove a metallic gray Ferrari 360 with black leather seats.

"It suits you," she said when he opened her door.

"I like it," he said, waiting until she was settled to close it behind her.

They drove in silence, broken only by the sound of his rap playlist, which was playing at a soft volume. He stuck to the speed limit, which rather surprised her. She wondered whether he was doing that for her benefit.

Since he'd given her the address, she'd known they were heading to a swanky part of downtown. Vander pulled into the underground garage of a building of luxury loft apartments.

"I didn't see you as a house and picket fence kind of guy," she commented as he let her into his place.

The two-story loft had brick outer walls and tan interior ones. The staircase was a shiny chrome with black metal exposed steps. The open floor plan on the main level was composed of a large den with chocolate-colored leather furniture, a gourmet kitchen with a built-in eating space, a swanky dining room with a cast-iron chandelier, and what appeared to be an office judging from the desk and file cabinets facing the window that boasted a lovely view of a park.

Her gaze fastened onto a silver-framed photo sitting on the mantel above a hardwood fireplace. A man was throwing a young boy up in the air, and she wondered if it was Vander and his daddy. How would he react if she asked him? She bit her lip. It didn't seem like the right time.

"I detest yard work of any kind," he said, locking the door once they were inside. "Make yourself at home. What can I get you to drink?"

"I ordered us some cocktails," she told him, taking in the modern paintings hanging on the walls. He liked art. Somehow that surprised her. But he had good taste, something she already knew based on how he dressed and decorated his office.

"You weren't joking about that?" he asked her, setting his briefcase on the long white marble kitchen counter.

"I never joke about cocktails," she quipped.

He pulled out two sparkling waters from the Sub-Zero and poured them into water glasses. Then he pulled out his phone and crooked his finger at her.

"Let's take a picture of me in this suit before I change."

"Isn't that a little formal for Toby?" she asked.

"He has a professional job now that he's left the Army," he immediately responded. "Sales. Plus, you look like Imelda Marcos in that outfit."

She huffed a little, but made sure to get her fill of looking at him. He looked downright handsome in the gray Italian suit paired with a silk blue-gray tie and white shirt. From her perspective, he could keep it on for the rest of his life.

As she stepped close to him, he loosened his tie, brushing her arm and sending shivers down her body. Good heavens.

"Come here," he said, holding up the camera phone and sliding an arm around her.

Her unmentionables were going to start sweating if he kept putting his hands on her.

"Smile," he encouraged. "Smile like you mean it, Shelby."

All she wanted to do was stick her tongue out at him, but that would be both unladylike and childish.

He took a few pictures of them, and then she felt his fingers tickle her waist. She jolted, and he laughed.

"You're too stiff," he said. "We're supposed to be in love."

She turned her head and gave him her fish eye. "If you tickle me again, you'd better be prepared to meet your maker."

His lips twitched, but he didn't say anything. Only held the camera up and took some more pictures of them.

"I think we have enough in these outfits," she said.

He was smiling as he turned and laid his phone on the counter. Then he started taking off his tie. Followed by his jacket. When he started to open a few buttons of his white shirt, she gasped out, "What do you think you are doing?"

"Giving us another outfit to work with," he said, looking amused. "What did you think I was doing?"

Her dirty mind had thought he was getting undressed, and part of her had wanted to cheer things like *take it off; don't keep me waiting; strut it.*

"I couldn't rightly say," she said instead, walking over to her carry-on and pulling out one of the two light fall coats she'd brought.

"You brought all that?" he asked, peering into the suitcase. "Is that a white tank top? Oh, I'm liking this better and better."

She gently slapped him on the arm. "Don't look at my clothes yet! It's supposed to be a surprise." To show her daddy she was versatile, she'd brought several options, verging from formal outfits like the one she had on to simple looks like jeans and a tank top—something she'd wear at the lake.

"Holy shit! You brought a change of underwear too?" His mouth transformed into a crooked smile.

She snapped the top of her suitcase shut. "*Some* outfits require different underthings."

That infernal mouth of his twitched again. "I see."

"Do you have somewhere I can change?" she asked in as haughty of a voice as she could muster.

"I'm starting to see what you and Gail have in common," he said. "There are two bedrooms with bathrooms on the second level. Why don't you put on that pink jacket before you go up? I'd like to do one more photo like this."

Right. All casual-like after a day at the office. She liked seeing him like this. He looked just as powerful, but more approachable.

She shrugged on the jacket and leaned in next to him again. This time his hand slid a little lower around her waist, the contact accelerating her heart rate. Was he flirting? When she turned her head to look, he was already watching her. Heat and amusement danced in his aquamarine eyes. Oh, yeah, he was flirting. Well, so could she.

She settled herself even closer to him, realizing how well they fit together. Then she felt his muscles lock into place, and she knew he felt it too. His smile looked a little more forced on the screen this time, but he took a few more pictures before pulling away.

"All right, I'm going to change," he said, heading up the stairs with her bag. "Take as long as you need."

"I plan to do a hair and makeup change too," she said, following him.

"Whatever you need to do," he said, but she could tell he was humoring her.

The spare bedroom was painted a bright orange that contrasted perfectly with the fluffy white comforter on the bed, and there was a full-length antique gold mirror in the corner next to a rocking chair. Again, she liked the look.

He stood in the doorway as she opened the suitcase. "Are you planning on watching?" she asked.

He was chuckling as he shut the door, and she took a moment to hug herself in the center of the room. She didn't know what they were doing. All she knew was they were having fun.

A little fun never hurt anyone.

CHAPTER 16

VANDER WAS WONDERING WHAT IN THE HELL HE WAS doing as he shaved for the second time that day.

He told himself it was for the photos, but he was full of shit. He was couldn't stop thinking about kissing Shelby, but it was impossible while she was still a client. He needed to find her father stat. Maybe tomorrow he could cancel his meetings and head to Haines.

When a man put on aftershave for a woman, it forced him to face the truth. He liked Shelby McGuiness. He liked her a lot. Even the way she'd treated Charlie earlier in his office had done things to his heart.

He wanted to kiss Shelby McGuiness and not stop. He wanted to get naked with her. She might drive him a little batty, but it didn't infuriate him—far from it. It *amused* him when they pushed each other's buttons.

Yes, Shelby was one of a kind.

When he left his bedroom, the door to the spare bedroom was still closed. He shook his head and headed downstairs. There was no telling what she was doing in there. All he knew was she was going to emerge looking and smelling nice. He liked that a whole heck of a lot.

As he set the table for dinner to occupy his time, he considered lighting candles and then decided against it. That was way too date-like, so it would have to wait until they could date.

When the doorbell rang, he heard her call out from upstairs, "Would you get that, Vander? I'm still getting dressed. Tell Lamont hello."

He went to the door uncomfortably aroused by the thought of her in a state of undress.

A young man carrying not one but two bags of takeout grinned at him. "I've got your order, sir. Where's Shelby?" He looked over Vander's shoulder.

Vander wasn't the kind of man to besmirch a woman's reputation. "She said to say hello. She had to take a call. How much do I owe you?"

"Shelby has a running bill with us," Lamont told him brightly. "We just love her."

Apparently Gail wasn't her only fan, and he was starting to understand why. Shelby was kinder than he'd originally thought, and fun to boot. Vander handed the man a whopping tip, and he gawked.

"Thank you! Are you related to Gail by chance?"

"No, we're not related, but we're acquainted," Vander said.

"I knew it! Everyone Gail and Shelby know is cool. Well, I should run. Have a great dinner. Jared says hi too."

Vander nodded and shut the door. Shelby must have made an impression on the head chef as well. His mind brought up a scene of Shelby and Gail eating at the fancy restaurant. Gail would be wearing some outrageous outfit, and Shelby would saunter in, doing that thing with her hips that drove him wild. He started to take the food out of the bags and soon realized she'd ordered a feast. Including several desserts.

He heard someone clear their throat behind him, and he turned.

Shelby was in a pale yellow dress that hugged every curve and dipped between her beautiful breasts, her hand propped on the interior wall of his kitchen.

If they'd been on a date for real, he would have told her

she was beautiful and then kissed her senseless. If she'd been game, he'd have boosted her up onto the counter and taken her right there.

Instead he forced himself to say, "Did we need all these desserts?"

Her mouth turned pouty for a moment. "Sometimes Jared surprises me when he's of a mind. He's a dear man. What did he send over?"

She pushed away from the wall, and he caught a whiff of her perfume. The mixture of peonies, roses, and suede suited her, and he longed to bury his face in her neck. "See for yourself."

Her exclamations over a double-decker chocolate cake and profiteroles made him smile as he put their individual dinners on their plates. When she drew out four sippy cups, her smile was as happy as her dress.

"Two each," she said, uncapping the orange container. "I thought you might like their Southern Manhattan. It's like a normal one, but the bartender, Jeff, adds a kick with basil and hot pepper cherries."

He wasn't so sure about the wisdom of combining hot peppers and cherries, but he could pour himself a plain bourbon if he couldn't stomach it. "What did you order?"

"Their smoked ginger fizz," she all but purred.

Turning his back to her, he wondered how the hell he was supposed to get through the evening without shattering his own no-dating-clients policy. He took their plates over to the dining room table and turned on the chandelier.

"Oh, you set a fine table," she exclaimed. "Where are your glasses?"

"To the right of the Sub-Zero," he told her, watching as she poured their drinks carefully into the glasses as intently as a hot, albeit mad, scientist perfecting a concoction to save mankind.

When she was finished, they sat at the table, he at the head, and her to his right. She handed him his drink and touched his glass with her own.

"To finding my daddy," she said in a hushed voice.

He drank and watched her. The toast seemed to subdue her. Her see-sawing emotions captivated him somehow. She appeared so focused some moments. Then she got a little goofy. Now she clearly felt vulnerable.

"Let's eat," he suggested.

She didn't dive in with her earlier enthusiasm. He cut into his steak and all but groaned as he chewed. The meat was juicy and perfectly seasoned.

"Is the chicken not to your liking?" he asked, scooping up a few of the roasted potatoes with a fork.

"No, it's lovely," she said, pushing it around with her fork. "I just got to thinking about why we're really here. Vander," she said, nudging her asparagus into perfect rows, "what do you think the odds are of us finding Daddy? I mean, I deal in numbers, and right now, I simply don't have any sense of what we're facing."

When she looked down in her lap, he put his hand on her arm. "I don't know. Our chances are definitely better than before we met Lenore. Shelby, I'll do everything I can to find him. I promise you that."

She didn't shrug away from his touch, and he kept his hand there because she felt good. He also *needed* to touch her—even if this was the only way he could for now.

"I wanted to ask you something," she said, still not looking at him. "I got all flustered at the hotel the other night and plumb forgot. And then I saw the picture and I just—"

"What?" He set his own fork down, sensing a change in her.

"When we were vising Me-Mother, you told her you knew what it was like to lose a parent." Her head lifted, and her brown eyes were filled with so much warmth, his throat closed up. "I know a lot of what you do is acting, but this felt true… and I remember what you told me about losing your family. You said it was why you'd stopped believing in wishes."

A pocket of air lodged in his chest. He almost never told anyone about his family, but he was used to people shying away from the topic when he did, almost like it was too heavy or dark for them. But Shelby was asking for more details, and it completely disarmed him. "It was true."

Her hand moved to touch him in return. "How did it happen?"

While it was public information, Vander wanted Shelby to hear his story, the way he remembered it. "My dad was on the Nashville police force. He was murdered in the line of duty."

"Oh my goodness," she whispered, her eyes filling with tears. "How horrible for you and your family! How old were you?"

"I was ten," he said, trying to fight off the memories of that time. "They never found out why he was murdered." *I've never been able to find out.*

"Oh, Vander," she said, putting her hand to her mouth before lowering it to her heart. "I'm so sorry. There are no words for how sorry."

"It was a long time ago," he told her, unable to withstand the compassion in her eyes. A whole mess of emotion was rising in his chest, and he didn't want her to see him like this.

"I know a pat answer when I hear one," she said, her voice hoarse. "Daddy left me when I was two, and that was some twenty-six years ago. When people ask about my daddy, I tell them it's in the past. That I don't remember him. But it still hurts. I sometimes wonder how something that happened so long ago can still tie me up in knots until I'm fixing to come undone when I think about it."

Perhaps that's why he felt connected to Shelby. On some level, they understood each other.

"It's why you're so determined to help people," she said. "Now I understand. Your daddy would be so proud of the man you've become."

Shit, he actually felt tears burning behind his eyes. "My mother took me back to her parents' house in Boston after

Daddy was killed," he gushed out. "They'd met at Vanderbilt. Hence my name."

"I wondered," she said, comforting him with soothing circles of her fingers on his arm.

"I...ah...lost my Southern accent in Boston," he said. "Being there...wasn't a happy time. For any of us."

"Of course it wasn't," Shelby said. "How could it have been?"

Vander sometimes wondered how things might have been different if his mother had shared her grief with him and allowed him his. While he'd made peace with finding his own way in life—even though that had meant going against his mother and her family—there was still enough of that little boy who wished for a reconciliation. In that way, he was no different than Shelby.

"When I came of age," he continued, "I returned to Nashville, determined to find answers to my father's case."

"And did you?"

"I was left with more questions in the end," he said bitterly. "The case was more than cold. It was frostbitten. Every possible lead had dried up decades ago. I...all I wanted to know was why. Shit, that's not completely true. I wanted to find the son of a bitch who'd taken my dad from me and see him pay for it."

She pushed out of her chair and wrapped her arms around him. "For me, knowing why Daddy left us was as important as finding him," she whispered against his chest. "I'm sorry you don't have your answers. I can't imagine how hard that must be."

"Yes, you can," he said, pushing back and tracing her cheek. "You've lived your whole life knowing how hard that is."

A tear spilled down her cheek. "I'm sorry. I...seem to be more emotional than usual lately." She swiped at her tear.

He pulled her back against his chest. Holding her, comforting her, wasn't against his code.

"Is that picture over there of you and your daddy?" she asked softly.

He knew which one she meant. It was the only one he'd managed to keep out of his mother's grasp when she'd gone through their things and purged the past. "Yes."

"It looks like he loved you something fierce."

Hearing that squeezed his heart. "It was mutual."

She nodded against his chest, and they held each other in the silence for a long moment before she returned to her chair.

"Our dinner is cold," she said.

"I don't feel much like eating," he told her, eyeing his half-eaten steak.

"That's all the more reason to eat," she said, picking up her fork. "Gail says when you feel like life has kicked you in the gut, you feast like a queen. It was on the day she'd signed her divorce papers that she first asked Jared to surprise her with his favorite desserts. She told me to never let the past completely steal my joy in the present. I think she was on to something."

"I'll heat up the food," he said, taking their plates into the kitchen and popping them into the microwave.

"Vander," Shelby said, putting her arm on his shoulder and making him turn around. "Thank you for telling me about your daddy. I know it must have been hard for you."

"Seems we have more in common than we might have thought," he said, pushing one of her stray curls behind her ear. "Shelby, after I find your father, I'd like to go out with you for real."

Her mouth curved, and she rose on her tiptoes to kiss his cheek. "Great minds think alike."

"I'm leaving for Haines tomorrow," he told her, making the final decision. "How does your weekend look?"

"You think we're that close?" she asked him.

He prayed they were, because after tonight, he didn't think he could wait much longer to be with her.

CHAPTER 17

SADIE FELT LIKE SHE WAS IN THE CENTER OF A TILT-A-whirl. Meeting Me-Mother had been emotional enough. But then Shelby had told them that Vander was planning on going to Haines today to find their daddy...

She couldn't quilt fast enough. Purple and orange squares lay around her in what would look like a mess to other people, but she saw the pattern she'd designed for Shelby. She was pretty proud of it. The abacus pattern would make Shelby laugh, and given her love of numbers, it had seemed the perfect design.

Shelby was coming over for lunch, so she'd need to hide everything away soon. Sadie had invited all her siblings, but Susannah had promised to accompany Jake to some recording gig, and J.P. was meeting with a client about a new recording contract.

Right now, all she wanted to do was wrap her family up in the largest, most colorful quilt possible and hold them tight. Even though she wanted to find their daddy, with every step forward, she feared they would tear the stitches that had always held the fabric of their family together.

Her enchilada casserole was in the oven, the cream of chicken and mushroom soups bubbling with the enchilada sauce and cheddar cheese. Sadie wished she could have gone into the craft store this morning and stocked yarn or something—anything to keep busy—but she wasn't due there until one o'clock.

Her phone rang, and when she saw that it was her mama, she dropped it in her lap. It bounced off her knee and onto the floor. She wrung her hands, trying to decide if she should answer it. Her mama had left her a couple of voicemails, which Sadie had listened to and deleted promptly out of guilt. To appease her mama, she'd texted her, saying she was busy with the store and her quilting. She'd *lied*. Again. Surely she was going to hell in a hand basket.

But how in all that's sacred was she supposed to talk to Mama right now? She wasn't like Shelby—everyone in the family could see right through her.

The phone stopped ringing, and Sadie knew it was going to voicemail again. She picked up the phone and waited for a message to appear. When it did, she listened to it, her heart hammering in her chest.

Sadie, honey, I was hoping to catch you since it's your late day. I miss you. I was in between seeing people today and wanted to hear your voice. Give your mama a holler when you get the chance. Love you.

Guilt wrapped around her like tangled yarn. Oh, she was a horrible person.

Her doorbell rang, and she jumped. Her paranoid mind immediately jumped to the conclusion that it was Mama. Then she remembered Shelby was due to come over for lunch. She stuffed all her quilting materials back into her basket and hustled to the door.

When she opened it, her sister rushed inside and wrapped her up in a hug. "I'm coming apart."

Sadie squeezed her for all she was worth. "Me too!"

"How do people handle this?" Shelby asked, letting her go. "Wait! Is that enchilada casserole I smell?"

"I went all out!" Sadie said, ushering her inside. "I've done nothing but work on your quilt and cook since the crack of dawn. I'm not sleeping. I've never been on edge like this."

"I'm going out with Vander once we find Daddy," Shelby said in a rush, standing in the center of Sadie's small living room clutching her purse. "And that has me feeling crazy too. He asked me last night."

"Last night?" Sadie exclaimed. Even Susannah had noticed the attraction between Vander and Shelby. She'd asked Sadie about it when they'd gotten back from Memphis. "It makes sense now. You texting us last night that Vander was going today. I thought he'd only called you." "He kind of had," Shelby said. "Let me set my purse down, and I'll explain."

They sat on the couch, cuddled close. Her sister told her about the pictures and take-out and then pretty much blew her mind when she described Vander's tragic past with his own daddy.

"He was murdered?" she asked. "Good heavens! I feel for that man. I can't begin to imagine such a tragedy."

"I thought our daddy leaving us was awful, but can you imagine what it would have been liked if he'd been *murdered*?"

"That poor man. That makes me like him even more."

"I know!" Shelby said, patting her chest, a few breaths shy of a good panic attack if you asked Sadie. "I mean, I've been attracted to him since we first met, but I'm starting to really like him. Like big L like. He's a good man, and he isn't put off by me being sassy or over-the-top either. He gives as good as he gets. I can't wait until he kisses me for real."

"He kissed you?" Sadie squeaked.

"In his hotel room in Memphis," Shelby said. "Truth is, *I* kissed *him*. He's been very...honorable about everything. Talks about his code of conduct, not dating clients. But seriously, the way that man looks at me..."

"It's like you're the only birthday cake in a one hundred mile radius," Sadie said, fanning herself. "I've seen it. I'm glad he...you..."

"Oh, heavens, are you stuttering?" Shelby asked. "Of course, he thinks I'm planning on sleeping with him. I told him I'm not that kind of girl."

Sadie was sure her eyebrows shot straight up to her hairline. "How did he take that?"

"I think he laughed," Shelby said, falling back against the sofa. "I can't remember really. My head was buzzing after I told him not to flatter himself."

Sadie didn't know much about men—it was the part of her education she wished had been given more attention. But when your mama was a preacher and you went to a Christian school, no one really told you much of anything that was useful except to tell you what went where, that it was a sacred act, and you should never, ever do it outside of marriage.

Of course, she'd been in a three-year relationship in college she'd thought would lead to marriage. Randy, the boyfriend she'd met at a Christian social night, had been aptly named since all he'd done was talk about how randy he was for her. She'd finally told herself God would forgive her after getting randy herself. But then she'd caught Randy kissing the Vacation Bible School organizer their junior year and broken things off. Now she didn't date anyone at church.

Putting together hundreds of patches into a beautiful design for a quilt was easier than figuring out men. After Randy, Sadie wasn't sure she wanted to date a man who professed he was a good Christian man. Her daddy supposedly had been one too. They didn't seem to measure up. Better to go out with a man who didn't profess to have any such values. That way she couldn't be disappointed. Her only problem was looking for men like that. She didn't know exactly where to find them. Tattoo parlors? Dive bars? She was scared of those places. Sure as shooting, it wasn't easy to find men in the circles she normally hung out in—quilting, crafting, and the like.

"At least Vander is honest," Sadie said. "All men want sex. I'd be suspicious of a man who says he doesn't want sex in the beginning. That's what Randy said to me, and I fell for it. I bet he was getting it from someone else at church."

"Randy the Dandy," Shelby said, using their nickname for him. "Beats Nick the Prick."

All the pent-up emotion was making her kooky, and she started laughing. "We're a pair, talking about the sorry excuses for men we've had. We're so college cliché, giving it up as soon as we left home. What were we thinking?"

"We were curious, in love, and thinking we wanted sex," her sister replied.

They continued to laugh hysterically, but soon they wound down.

"Now, I understand why Vander left for Haines today," Sadie said. "He was eager to get started with you. I think that's lovely."

"Me too, actually," Shelby said. "I get all girly whenever I think about it, but then I remember he's going there to find Daddy."

"At least you have that half a minute of joy," Sadie said, the bubble from their laughter bursting. "I'm having trouble finding anything to be grateful about. I ducked another call from Mama."

"Me too," Shelby admitted. "It's like we're so close to knowing...the full truth...meeting Daddy. I'm...holding out until I have all the facts, I guess."

"Once we have all the facts, what are we going to tell her?" Sadie still didn't know.

"I know we agreed to talk about what more we might do for Me-Mother," Shelby said, "but it will get mighty complicated with Mama if we keep seeing her."

Sadie thought about it a moment. "It will, but she surprised me so much in that one meeting. I'd like to get to know her more."

Shelby nodded. "I want to find her another place to live, no matter how much trouble it causes us with Mama."

"That's a possibility to discuss another time," Sadie said, worrying about how she might contribute financially. "I still wonder what happened between her and Mama. When I think about her vehemence, it's like I'm looking at circles instead of squares for a quilt."

"I'm confused too," Shelby said, pulling a pillow against her chest. "I keep wondering if Mama could have done something. I mean, she was basically our age when this happened. Look at me. I make mistakes all the time."

"Me too! Like ducking Mama." Sadie hung her head.

"This will be over soon," Shelby told her sister. "Vander will find Daddy. I just know it!"

Sadie's insides lurched. "I know he will. It's just...I don't know what we're supposed to do *after* Vander finds him, now that we know he's alive. I hated not knowing that."

"I suppose all we can do is take it one day at a time," Shelby said.

"Serenity now," Sadie breathed out.

"Amen, sister," Shelby said, taking her hand. "We'll know soon enough."

Yes, if there was one thing Sadie knew about Vander... He was not a man to waste time.

Her sister was one lucky woman.

Sadie hated that she felt a little left behind in the love department herself.

CHAPTER 18

HAINES, TENNESSEE WASN'T THE KIND OF CHARMING small town that made city folk reconsider their lifestyle. The sidewalks had been cracked by too many weary footsteps along the dusty Main Street. A hodgepodge of water-starved weeds wound out of those puzzle-like pieces of concrete.

Vander had seen towns like this before. The people were hurting for work, struggling through each day. As he parked the pickup truck he'd rented in front of the small whitewashed building this town called a police department, he was conscious of the eyes on him. It was a hot and muggy day, and people were hustling into the few businesses still clinging to life, mostly the bank and the diner and the beauty parlor, it seemed. Maybe they were just seeking air conditioning.

A stranger was in town, and the whole town was likely already abuzz with speculation about who had come calling. He fitted his cowboy hat on his head a little better as he walked into the police station, completely in his cover, only this time he was going to say he was Shelby's fiancé. Charlie had thought folks would respond better if it looked like he was joining the family.

"Can I help you?" a fire-haired woman asked when he crossed the worn threshold.

"Yes, ma'am," he said, coming over and taking his hat

off, worrying the rim to appear nervous. "I'm looking for my fiancée's daddy, and his mama mentioned he'd sent her a card from this town. I'm... My girl, Shelby, she's never met her daddy, and I was kind of hoping I could bring her to him as a wedding gift. Do you think...do you think you could help me? I didn't know where else to start, being a stranger in these parts."

His accent was one of the many he'd honed for work in rural areas, and judging by the way she'd tilted her head to the right, the fire-haired woman was already eating out of his hand. "Oh, that poor thing," she said.

"I'm Toby, by the way," he said, thrusting out his hand. He never gave a last name unless pressed for it. If she were to look up his name, which she had the resources to do, she would discover he'd lied. Not helpful. The truck was from Enterprise, so he couldn't be traced easily. Vander could always say his car was in the shop if someone pressed him about why he was riding around in a rental. "And my girl is named Shelby, Shelby McGuiness. Her daddy is named Preston McGuiness."

One of the deputies moseyed out—moseyed because he sauntered with his hands on his police belt like he was the shit around here. "What's going on out here, May?"

"This man is trying to find his fiancée's daddy as a wedding gift," May explained. "It's the sweetest thing I've ever heard."

Vander made himself duck his head and kick at the ground. "I'd do anything to make my Shelby happy. Here, let me show you a picture of her."

Pulling a worn photo from his pocket, he handed it to May. After making a copy of one of the photos he'd taken the other day, he'd worried it with his fingers most of the way here to give it the appearance of age and care.

"She and I have good jobs in the city, but we're both small-town people at heart. I miss being out in the country. Isn't my Shelby beautiful?"

"She's lovely," May said, handing it to the deputy. "What's her daddy's name again?"

"Preston," Vander said. "Preston McGuiness."

The deputy handed the photo back to him. "Don't know of anyone by that name in this here parts."

"His mama was afraid of that. That's why she done gave me this here photo of him," Vander said, patting his other jean pocket as if looking for the photo. After a moment of "searching," he took it out. "It was taken two years ago."

He made sure to hand it to May since she was so eager to help him. When she looked at it, her eyes widened to the size of coins. "Why, that's Wallie Blevins! Isn't it, Greg?"

The man peered at it closely. "That's Wallie, all right. What did you say—"

"Lenore thought he might be using a different name," he said, heading off the deputy. "Can't say why. And honestly, I can't say I care. All I want is to reconnect my Shelby with her daddy. If the reconciliation goes like she hopes, she wants him to walk her down the aisle at our wedding."

Vander experienced an odd shiver at the thought. It wasn't...unappealing. He forced himself back to the task at hand. Falling into character was a little too easy, and he needed to keep his wits about him. Greg still had questions about his veracity.

"Wallie keeps to himself mostly," Greg said, running his hand across his mouth like he was ruminating. "I wonder why he's using a different name."

"Maybe he's running from something," May said, taking the pencil from behind her ear and doodling absently on the steno notepad on her desk.

"His mama doesn't think it's anything like that," Vander rushed to say in his fake accent. "Like I said, I don't care about his past none, anyway. I just want to talk to him and see if he'll meet my Shelby. She's got a big heart."

He thought back to last night, how he'd opened up about his father's murder. She *did* have a big heart, and he was starting to like it as much as he did her playfulness and her beauty. All together, it was a killer combination, and one he was falling for pretty fast.

"Wallie takes his lunch in the diner most days," May said, pointing to the faded red sign across the street. "He and Pauline Talbot have been seeing each other for a while now. She's been a waitress there for some thirty years, and all her kids have left the nest. I'll take you over there. Greg, can you mind the phones while I step out?"

The man nodded, and Vander extended his hand. "Thank you for your help."

Vander opened the door for May, and they walked outside together. He put on his cowboy hat even though they were crossing a short distance because he was still in character, and it was what men who wore them did. May made small talk, asking where he was from originally, where he lived now, and what he did for a living. He did his best to keep his responses brief, turning the topic to her whenever possible.

When they entered the diner, May called out, "Pauline, come on over here. I want you to meet someone."

There were eight people seated in the small diner, and all of them turned to look at the new arrivals. Vander made himself doff his cowboy hat and nod in their direction.

A blonde-haired woman thin as a rail, likely from being the only waitress in this washed-out joint, rushed forward. "Hello, May. And who's this here handsome man with you?"

She said it in a way that was complimentary and not flirtatious, something a long-time waitress might do to garner tips and keep the patrons coming back.

"This here is Toby, and he's looking for his fiancée's daddy as a wedding present."

Pauline gave a heartfelt smile. "Well, if that isn't the most romantic thing I've ever heard. What about you, Amos? Ever hear anything more romantic?"

"Can't say I have," the older man sitting at the counter said, paused over his French dip, not bothering to pretend he wasn't listening.

"Turns out, his fiancée's daddy is your Wallie," May said

brightly. "Isn't that the most incredible coincidence?"

The woman's smile faltered. "I...of course it is."

Vander watched as she swallowed thickly. He suspected she didn't know Wallie had children. She likely didn't know he was living under a false name.

"Of course, Toby here said Wallie's real name is... What was it, honey?"

He made himself smile, seeing the woman's shoulders tense up. "Preston McGuiness, ma'am. His mama told Shelby—that's my girl—that he sent her a letter from here in town last Christmas. As I told May, I don't care about why he's calling himself Wallie. All I want to do is talk to him for my Shelby. She's wanted to find her daddy her whole life. May said he sometimes stops in here for lunch. Is he coming today? Because I would be happy to wait for him."

The woman's eyes were darting around now, like a rabbit ready to run. Was it because she'd just learned her boyfriend had lied to her from the start? Vander couldn't blame her there. Trust between two people was hard enough. Add in the tough life Pauline looked to have led, and trust was likely as difficult for her as climbing Kilimanjaro.

"Wallie's...ah..." She fidgeted with the collar of her waitress outfit, stained yellow from overuse and numerous washings. "He's been helping Old Red Waback on his farm. I...he's not coming into town today."

"Oh, shoot," Vander made himself say as he slapped his hat against his legs. "Could you give me his address then? I could leave him a message or something. I'll do whatever it takes to make my Shelby happy."

May put her arm around Pauline. "Why don't you call Wallie and tell him to come on in here for lunch? We both know Old Red would love a romantic story like this and wouldn't mind him leaving the farm for a chat. Heck, this is the best thing that's happened in town since Mayor Harris proposed to Widow Keller in front of the library by reading that Shakespeare sonnet she loves so much."

Vander gave May a winning smile, but poor Pauline looked green now. "I'll—"

"Pauline! Where in tarnation are you, girl? I've got orders up, and they're growing cold." A burly bearded man in a black apron stood in the doorway to the kitchen. "Stop yapping yer gums and get back to work."

"Oh, shut your trap, Cletis," May shot back. "Pauline's helping this nice man here. I'll get your orders up if you tell me who has what. Land sakes, you grow more ornery every year."

May paddled over to the kitchen, and soon she was laying four plates of food in front of gawking patrons.

Vander leaned in to Pauline and lowered his voice, saying, "I don't want you to get yelled at any more, ma'am. If you'd like, I can call Wallie and explain about my Shelby. Might be better coming from me. Whatever you think is best. I don't want to impose."

She dug out her phone and brought up her call list. "Here's his number."

Vander memorized the number and dug out his phone, an older model he used on assignments in poorer areas. It wasn't a wise move to flash the latest technology. Folks got suspicious.

"Thank you, ma'am," he said, digging out a photo of him and Shelby and handing it out to her. "That's my girl."

He ignored her gasp, sensing Pauline had noticed how much Shelby favored her father.

"Isn't she beautiful? I'm the luckiest man in the world. Never imagined she'd marry me, but I plan on making her the happiest woman out there. Not like my mama. She had a tough life. Worked three jobs to put food on the table after my dad left, but she never complained." He was laying it on a little thick, but he sensed it would strengthen his connection with Pauline.

The woman finally took the picture of him and Shelby. "You look good together."

Keeping faithful to his cover was critical to getting hard-to-come-by information. He wouldn't have dared to show anyone one of the digital photos they'd taken yesterday on his phone because someone might have noticed how new they were. Vander liked to cover all his bases.

"Yeah, we do," he said, studying the picture of them. Of all of the ones he'd taken, this was his favorite. They were in his kitchen, and she'd turned her face to say something to him. If he hadn't seen her interest in him before, there would have been no mistaking it in this photo. He'd blurred out the rest of the surroundings so anyone looking at the photo wouldn't focus on his apartment or even the clothes they were wearing. He'd worked on the photos after he'd driven Shelby back to her car and then printed them out on his special printer.

"Do you..." Pauline fiddled with her collar again. "Do you really not know why Wallie is using a different name?"

Vander shook his head. "No, ma'am, and neither did his mama. She said he's always been a good man. Just made a mistake with his family when he was mostly a kid himself. You know."

Pauline lowered her head. "My husband ran off on me and my two girls. It was...hard. Thank God, Cletis gave me this job. I've been working here ever since."

He'd had a hunch that her story would go something like that. Again, it was one of those instincts he had about people—part of what made him a great detective. "Did he ever come back?"

"No," she said, looking out the front windows of the diner. "My baby girls cried when they had to ask their uncle to walk them down the aisle even though their daddy didn't deserve to share their joy after what he'd done."

He put his hand on her shoulder. "That's why I'm hoping my Shelby and her daddy can reconcile. Life is too short."

"Preacher says that every week," Pauline said, sniffing. "I'm sorry. All of this...it's a shock."

"Of course it is, and I'm sorry for it." He was, but it

wouldn't sway him from his goal of finding Preston. Even so, he was aware he'd changed Preston's relationship with this woman and the whole town. In his business, he couldn't always keep those kinds of consequences from occurring, especially if people didn't give him any other choice. Besides, the lies Preston had told would be his undoing.

Vander gave May a smile as she rejoined them. "I should give ah...Wallie a call. Ask him to meet me here for lunch. How late are y'all open?"

"We usually close at two," Pauline said, "but I can ask Cletis to keep the diner open longer if you'd like. Wallie's place...he's renting a small room above Myrtle Glories' garage. It's...not for entertaining."

Vander nodded. Now he knew where the man lived. If this phone call went south, he could swing by Wallie's place, maybe give Myrtle his speech if need be.

"Go ahead and give Wallie or whatever his name is a call, Toby," May said, nodding briskly. "I love it when miracles happen, and reuniting your Shelby with her daddy is certainly up that alley if I ever heard one. Even though it brings to mind all sorts of questions. Goodness, Pauline, you never seem to settle on a man without some troubled past."

The woman hung her head, and May put an arm around her.

Thinking through the best approach, Vander pulled out his phone and dialed the number Pauline had given him. "I'll just step out for a moment. Don't want to disturb everyone eating."

No one was eating anymore, but that didn't matter. The chime on the door rang as he let himself out onto the sidewalk.

"Hello," a rough voice answered after a few rings.

"Hello," Vander said, pouring more Southern charm into his voice. "My name is Toby, and Pauline gave me your number. She said you weren't coming into the diner for lunch today, but I was hoping I might meet you, sir."

"What about?" the man asked hesitantly. "You need

someone to work for you?"

Ah...Vander had wondered if the man would answer an unknown number—the phone was calibrated so all the calls it made would show up as Anonymous. If he hadn't picked up, Vander would have talked Pauline into using hers.

Now for the tricky part. "No, sir, I'm not. I...well...there's no easy way to say this, but my girl—heck, the woman who agreed to marry me—wants to see you. I was hoping to... arrange that." He made sure not to use Shelby's name yet, wanting to weave more of a story.

"Your girl? I don't recall knowing you or your girl. Are you a friend of Pauline's?"

"No sir, but I'm a friend of your mama. Lenore. She said to give you her best. She told me you were living in Haines based on the Christmas card you sent her this year."

"You know my mama?" the man asked, his voice ripe with suspicion. "Is anything the matter?"

Other than Lenore living in abject poverty and ill health? "She was feeling a little poorly when we visited, but there was nothing gravely wrong."

"I'm sorry, but who are you again?"

"I'm Shelby's fiancé," he said in as even a tone as he could muster.

"Shelby!" The man sounded like he'd run into a wall while walking.

"Yes, your Shelby," Vander continued. "We're getting married, you see, and she...ah heck, sir...she's wanted to meet you all her life, and with the wedding coming up, that feeling's only gotten stronger. You know, walking down the aisle stuff. I was hoping to reunite the two of you. I don't know your reasons for leaving, sir, but your daughter wants to meet you. She has the biggest heart. So do the rest of her siblings."

The silence on the line went on for so long Vander had to strain to hear the man's breathing over the air conditioner humming in the diner's window. "You still there, sir?"

"Yes," he said roughly. "Does Louisa know about this,

boy?"

Vander could hear the man's voice quaver when he said his ex-wife's name. "No, sir, and the kids aren't planning on saying nothing." He wasn't sure if that was true, but for the moment, he was going to say whatever it took to get this man to meet with him.

"You tell my girl I'm sorry, but I can't meet with her. Or any of them. Don't contact me again."

The line went dead.

Vander fought a curse. That man was going to run. He knew it to the core. He had to find out where Myrtle lived stat.

He went inside to say goodbye to Pauline and May and report that Wallie hadn't been very encouraging on the phone. Sure as shooting, May gave him Myrtle's address, which was only three blocks from the diner.

"I'll stop back in on my way out of town, Pauline," he told her, knowing she was the strongest link to Preston. She was shaking when he put his hand on her shoulder. "Thank you for your help."

"If it's after two, I'll be at the beauty parlor," she told him.

He kissed May on the cheek for good measure. "You've been a peach. Would you mind calling Myrtle and telling her I'll be dropping by her garage? I'd hate to scare her or get shot at if she's opposed to trespassers."

She laughed. "Myrtle couldn't hit the side of a barn. Don't worry. Happy to call her, Toby. You pop on by the station before you leave to give me a proper goodbye."

"You bet, ma'am," he said, fighting his impatience to jog to Myrtle's.

He decided not to drive there. He didn't want Preston to see an unfamiliar truck and run off. The gravel road to the woman's house was hot and dusty, and Vander wished he had a bottle of water with him to swallow the grime coating his throat. When he arrived, he surveyed the woman's home. The white paint was peeling, and the roof line was sagging although she had pretty rose bushes in her front lawn.

When he opened her rickety gate, an older woman appeared on the porch in a purple muumuu with flowers on it. "You that boy May said would be coming by to see Wallie?"

"Yes, ma'am," he said, tipping his finger to his hat as a greeting. "Had May call so as to not alarm you."

"That was a good idea, boy," she said with narrowed eyes. "I still have my husband's Colt, God rest his soul."

Given the old woman's frail body, a weapon like that would knock her flat on her back. "I'll just be waiting in his room then. Out of this infernal heat. If that's all right with you, ma'am."

She nodded. "You'll need the key. Come on up here, boy. I'll get it for you."

He waited a few steps off the porch and smiled when she returned. "Thank you, ma'am."

"Wallie doesn't have a pot to piss in, but I'm still telling you not to steal nothing—even if May thinks you're an angel of a man sent from on high. That woman is a moron about men, if you ask me."

"I appreciate May's confidence in my character. You have nothing to worry about, ma'am."

She huffed. "Seems I might if Wallie isn't using his real name. I plan to have words with him after you leave. And bring my key back, mind you. Best get back inside. It's hot as Hades out here."

He tipped his hat again as she opened the front door. Once she had disappeared inside, he headed around to the garage and unlocked the side entrance. He climbed the uncarpeted wood stairs. The apartment was a clean and bare bones studio.

The rafters were painted white like the four walls. There was a hot plate on the counter by the kitchen sink. A pullout couch served as the bed. There wasn't much of anything in the room save worn furniture. There wasn't even a TV. Vander spotted a black suitcase in the corner by the couch and carefully lifted the lid. Clothes were stacked inside all orderly like: jeans, work shirts, underwear, socks. Nothing fancy, not even a Sunday suit. He didn't see any other shoes, so he had to wonder if the man only owned one pair.

He stood by the window discreetly, watching the front. He supposed Preston could come around the back. If he'd had backup, he would have sent Charlie out to Old Red's place. Fifteen minutes passed. Then thirty. Vander's gut started to burn.

When Pauline opened up Myrtle's white gate an hour after he'd arrived and walked toward the garage, Vander decided to go down and meet her. People didn't trust skulking characters, and his cover had gotten him plenty of useful information so far.

He opened the door to the apartment before she could knock. "Hello, Pauline. Myrtle let me wait inside since it's so hot out. I was waiting for Preston—or Wallie—to come back."

Tears popped into Pauline's eyes, and she dug into her tan purse for a tissue. "I thought I'd come by and tell you in person since I knew you were here."

He already knew what she was going to say.

"Wallie called and told me y'all had spoken. He said he was leaving town and never coming back. Said he was sorry, but the past can't be undone. He's been running from it all his life."

Vander leaned against the doorway, fighting the urge to curse. If Preston wanted to run, wouldn't he have at least come back for his suitcase?

"That's terrible," he said, tugging on his hat. "I don't understand."

"Neither do I."

He could tell she meant it. "I just don't know what I'll tell Shelby. I...did he say where he was going, ma'am? I keep thinking if I can talk to him, show him his daughter's picture, he'd come around, you know?"

"I know," she said, mascara streaking her tissue. "I'm disappointed too. We'd been seeing each other since last October when he came to town. I thought we might..."

She didn't have to say what she'd thought. "I'm sorry for you too, ma'am. More than I can say. I'm sorry I might have caused this."

"Don't blame yourself none." She inhaled jaggedly. "Guess it's best for this to happen now, before I could get in any deeper with him. He said he loved me, that he hadn't loved anyone for so long. I...believed him."

Vander wondered if Preston was the kind of man to say that easily. Some men did. Anger took hold of him. He'd lost the last of his objectivity, it seemed. He often fought with his own judgments on cases like these—the ones that hit so close to home—but the kind of rage he was experiencing made him want to punch the man. Preston McGuiness didn't deserve Shelby or the rest of her siblings, but that wasn't his call.

"Do you know how he was planning to leave town?" Vander asked. "His mama said he didn't have a car."

"He didn't say," she said, wiping away more tears. "At first I thought he might have had too many DUIs, but...he just couldn't afford one."

Was the man planning to head out of town on foot? If so, Vander needed to search the area.

"He hitchhiked a lot," Pauline said, pressing her tissue to her chest. "I just can't believe this. I thought I knew him."

Vander patted her back, fighting the urge to run to his car and get going.

Then he realized the full extent of his problem.

Preston didn't want to be found, and when someone who'd been hiding for years set their mind to staying hidden, it was near impossible to chase them out.

CHAPTER 19

SHELBY DIDN'T TAKE IT AS A GOOD SIGN WHEN CHARLIE texted her and Sadie asking if the entire McGuiness clan could meet with her and Vander at five o'clock that day at one of their houses.

It had been two days since Vander had left for Haines. On day two after no word, she'd broken down and texted him. His response: *I'm on it.*

She'd stewed and told everyone there was no word. That had apparently changed. Shelby volunteered Susannah and Jake's house after conferring with everyone.

Somehow it made her worry that Vander hadn't called her personally. Was the news so bad he didn't want to share it alone with her on the phone? Had he changed his mind about them?

When she arrived ten minutes before five o'clock, cars lined the driveway. Everyone was eager to hear the news. Susannah answered the door and hugged her.

"I'm so nervous, I can barely sit down," she said.

"I feel the exact same way," Shelby replied, giving Sadie a smile when her younger sister barged into the entryway.

"I feel like I'm poised to leap off a cliff," Sadie said, squeezing both of them tight.

"Best put on a helmet so you won't get hurt," J.P. said in

that matter-of-fact way of his, but Shelby couldn't help but notice that his mouth was tight around the edges.

She hugged her brother and then Jake. A car door slammed outside.

"They're here!" Sadie said, throwing the door open dramatically.

The whole lot of them clustered around her to watch. Vander and Charlie walked forward, looking like characters from *Men in Black*. Both had on dark suits with white shirts, although Vander was sporting a red tie. Neither was smiling beneath their reflective shades.

They had bad news. Shelby knew it. Her stomach gripped, and Sadie squeezed her hand like it was a stress ball.

"You didn't find him," her younger sister said to Vander when he arrived on the threshold.

He took his sunglasses off and tucked them into his pocket. Charlie did the same.

"Let me tell you everything from start to finish," Vander said simply. "It will be easier that way."

The McGuinesses comforted one another with looks, arm pats, and squeezes as they made their way into the house. Once they were all settled in the den, Charlie stood off to the side as Vander took the center of the room.

"I'll tell you the news you all want to know first," Vander said, unbuttoning his jacket and shoving his hand in his pocket. "Your father was in Haines when I arrived. When I spoke to him, he said he couldn't meet with any of you. He asked that you not try to contact him again, and then disappeared from town shortly thereafter, leaving everything behind."

Shelby felt like a car had crashed into her middle. Distantly, she heard Sadie make a whimpering sound, and noticed Susannah turning to Jake, and J.P. pinching the bridge of his nose.

"I arrived in town under cover as Shelby's fiancé. Charlie thought that storyline would be more effective than if I went in as a mere boyfriend."

He said that word while looking into Shelby's eyes, and a ripple of heat shot through her. She found herself on the edge of her seat waiting for him to continue.

"The administrative assistant to the local police department was moved by the story about wanting to reconnect Shelby with her daddy as a wedding present. She and the deputy recognized your father immediately from Lenore's picture. He was going by the name of Wallie Blevins. May, the assistant, proceeded to take me over to the town diner to meet the waitress Wallie was seeing. Her name was Pauline. She was the one who gave me your daddy's phone number."

Shelby's chest grew tight as he described waiting at Daddy's apartment, only to learn from Pauline that he'd left town. Sadie leaned her head against her shoulder, and she put her arm around her sister. J.P. grabbed her hand as she was sitting in between them.

Vander described his actions after he'd learned the news. He'd worked with the Haines police to speak with other law enforcement in nearby towns, asking them to be on the lookout for Preston, explaining that the man's family simply wanted to be in touch with him. They'd agreed to help, something small town police forces were more liable to do, Vander said. They'd canvassed a few local truck stops and rest stops, but there'd been no hits. On the third day, Vander and Charlie had conferred and decided to call off the search.

"One of the hardest things about my profession is tracking down someone who doesn't want to be found," Vander said, gazing thoughtfully at all of them. "There isn't a warrant out for him. Local law enforcement doesn't have the interest or the manpower to find someone who simply takes off."

No, why would they? Shelby thought, the shock of everything making her head spin. There were enough people who were truly missing and in need of help.

"I don't know why your father leads this kind of life or why he's unwilling to speak with you," Vander said, shaking his head.

Shelby couldn't fathom any of it. It was like their daddy had slammed the door in their faces. But *why*?

"Since Preston likely hitchhiked out of town, there isn't much more we can do. I could have Charlie stake out where he was living or follow Pauline around in the hopes he returns, but it's highly unlikely he'll return now that everyone in town knows he's not who he claimed to be. Besides, everyone in Haines knows we're looking for him. If he does return, I expect May will call me."

"But he was seeing that woman," Sadie said, tears running down her face. "How could he simply leave without another word to her?"

Shelby bitterly thought it was no different than what their daddy had done to their mama.

"Seems he hasn't changed after all these years," J.P. said, sighing heavily. "I suppose it's best we know his nature so we don't cling to any false hope."

"I never had false hope," Susannah said, sitting up straighter next to Jake. "We already knew his true colors when he left us. I say we put this behind us and never tell Mama."

A hot rush of anger rose up inside Shelby, and she had to bite her tongue to hold back a harsh comeback. She wasn't mad at Susannah. She was mad at Daddy.

"Vander and Charlie don't need to hear us discuss what we want to do about Mama," J.P. said, sounding ever like their older brother. "I agree there is nothing more we can do here. We did our part to try and find him."

"And he ran away from us again," Sadie said, crying softly. "How could he be so cruel?"

Shelby didn't think it was just cruel. It was downright cowardly.

"A kind man doesn't leave his family in the first place," Susannah said in a hard tone. "I don't care what Me-Mother said. She doesn't see the real him."

"All right now," Jake said, bringing her back against his

chest and rocking her.

"We never should have looked for him in the first place," Susannah said, grabbing a handful of his shirt.

"That's water under the bridge, Susannah," J.P. said. "We're all hurting here. No need to make it worse by throwing around blame. Vander, I want to thank you and Charlie for everything you did."

"Yes," Sadie said, rising from the couch and crossing to hug Vander. "Thank you."

"I wish I had better news," Vander said, awkwardly patting her on the back. "I'm sorry."

Again, he looked in Shelby's direction. She could feel his regret. It surprised her that in her own distress she wanted to comfort him and tell him he'd gone above and beyond.

Her sister sniffled. "It's not your fault. You found him. I'm...going to head home. I want to lie down."

Shelby understood the feeling. A part of her wanted to shut herself in her bedroom, close the drapes, and become a recluse. She couldn't stop thinking about what her daddy had said to Vander, the phrase he'd memorized to share with them.

You tell my girl I'm sorry, but I can't meet with her. With any of them.

How could he run off like that, knowing how desperate she was to find him?

"I'm going to leave too," Shelby choked out. "J.P., you should get back to your family."

He chucked her under the chin and smiled. "Tammy's with the kids. I can stay if y'all want to hang around."

"Well, I'm going upstairs," Susannah told them, hands fisted by her side. "The faster we put this behind us the better. This family has a lot to be grateful for, and I, for one, want to focus on our blessings. We can discuss what to do with Mama later."

"It's pretty simple if you ask me," Shelby said. "We don't say anything to Mama since there's nothing to say." The faster they closed this unfortunate chapter, the better.

"Good, I'm glad we're on the same page," Susannah said.

"What about Me-Mother?" Sadie asked. "Shouldn't we tell Mama we met her? We still haven't talked about doing anything more for her."

"I can't think about that right now," Susannah said, putting a hand over her temple like she had a headache coming on.

"I say we take a couple of days to let this all settle," J.P. said, rising from the couch. "We can circle back when everyone isn't so raw."

"Fine," Susannah said with a terse nod. "Vander. Charlie. Thank you for your help."

Jake stood. "Let me walk y'all out."

"I'll do it," Shelby said.

Vander looked over at her. Their eyes held contact for a long moment.

J.P. shook their hands and then went over to Sadie and wrapped his arm around her. She immediately started to cry. The pressure in Shelby's chest was building with each second. She knew she was going to have a long cry herself, berating worthless daddys and wishes gone unanswered.

Vander was a few steps behind Shelby and Charlie as they walked to the door. "I'm sorry, Shelby," Charlie said. "People suck sometimes."

If she hadn't been close to tears, she might have laughed. "Thanks for your help."

"I didn't do much. Vander was out there acting like Boy Wonder," Charlie said. "I'm sure I'll be seeing you, Shelby. Vander, I'll be in the car. Take your time."

With that, she strode off, and Shelby turned to see Vander closing the front door behind him. She was acutely aware they were alone together for the first time since she'd left his apartment the other night.

"I'm sorry I wasn't in touch while I was gone," Vander said. "I didn't want to tell you anything over the phone, not until I was sure there was nothing more I could do."

"You did everything you could." She swallowed thickly. "Did he even sound sorry? I know he said he was, but you can usually hear it in a person's voice…" She broke off, unable to continue, and hung her head. How could a daughter live with the knowledge her daddy disliked his children so much, he'd run away from them twice?

"He was sorry, Shelby," Vander said, cupping her upper arm. "I don't know what set him running, but intuition tells me he's trying to escape himself. It doesn't have anything to do with you."

She pressed her lips together to keep from crying. "It sure doesn't feel that way right now."

"I know it doesn't. I wish I could tell you it gets easier, but I can't."

No, he was still hurting inside over his daddy's murder. "Time doesn't heal all things, does it?"

Vander shrugged. "Maybe not. I should let you get back inside to your family. I don't expect you'll want to go out this weekend, but you know where I am when you feel up to it. I'd still like to."

She appreciated his consideration. "Thank you. I'd…like to go out this weekend. There's nothing I can do to change any of this, and I always feel better when I focus on the good things in life."

He gave a soft smile. "I like knowing you consider me one of them." Leaning down, he kissed her cheek. "I'll call you, and we can set something up."

She put her hand on his arm. "Just so you know going forward, I don't take kindly to not having my texts or phone calls returned properly."

His lips twitched. "I'll keep that in mind. Bye, Shelby."

"Bye, Vander." With one last thoughtful look at her, he slid his sunglasses back into place and strode toward his car.

When she went inside, J.P. was still soothing Sadie, who had thrown a whole wad of tissues on the floor. When Sadie saw Shelby, she pulled away from J.P. and ran to her.

"Oh, it's so awful," Sadie said, wrapping her arms around her. "I wish we'd never looked for him."

Shelby put her chin on her sister's shoulder, tears starting to burn down her face. "Me either."

They held each other as they cried out all the hurt.

CHAPTER 20

VANDER TOOK EXTRA CARE TO PLAN SOMETHING enjoyable for his date with Shelby, wanting to cheer her up. Even though he knew her address from her file, he texted her for it. When he showed up in front of her quaint townhouse, he couldn't help but smile. The door was buttressed by bright containers filled with Gerbera daisies and trumpet-shaped flowers ready to be a hummingbird's happy hour. It suited her perfectly.

Tucking the sunflowers he'd bought her under his arm, he walked to her door and knocked. And waited and waited while the sun beat down on his neck.

When she finally opened it, she pretty much took his breath away in her red halter cotton dress that flirted with her knees.

"Did you wait so long to open the door on purpose?" he asked, deciding to kick off their banter right away.

"I did," she said. "I hope you don't mind."

"And if I said I do?" he asked, handing her the sunflowers.

She gave him a playful wink and shrugged. "Thank you for the flowers. I have to admit to being a little surprised. I didn't think you'd bring me flowers on our first date."

So she was already thinking they'd have more than one. Good, he did too. "I thought they might lift your spirits. How have you been holding up?"

From the way her shoulders slumped, he had his answer. "We're not going to talk about that tonight. We're going to go out for a delicious dinner and have some fun."

He gave her a look. "Shelby, I don't want you to pretend nothing happened. How are we supposed to get to know each other if we're not honest right off?"

She worried her bubble-gum-pink lips. "I don't want to be a downer. Besides, I thought we weren't acting like I've been your client."

"I don't see any reason to ignore the elephant in the room," he said, reaching out a hand to touch her bare arm.

"And I don't see any reason to put a magnifying glass in front of it," she said, playing with the sunflowers' petals.

"Are you going to argue with me all night?" he asked.

"I don't want to." She put her hand on his chest. "But talking about this week will make me get all emotional. You don't want that."

"That's where you're wrong," he said, cupping her shoulders in his hands. "I don't want you to hide how you feel from me. Especially since I have my own feelings about how things went down with your father."

She pressed the flowers to her chest, crinkling the plastic wrapping. "I hadn't thought about that."

"I was pretty upset too," he admitted. "I...Shelby, I wanted to find him for you. For all of you. I haven't been this upset about failing to meet a client's request in some time."

Rising on her tiptoes, she kissed his cheek. The flowers were getting squished between them, but he didn't care. He slid his hand around her waist.

"This isn't going to be a normal first date, is it?" she asked, her perfume intoxicating him.

"No," he said, nudging her back a few steps until they were inside her townhouse. "Especially since I already want to kiss you senseless."

He closed the door, set the flowers on the entry table, and

brought her back against his body. Cradling her face in his hands, he stared into her brown eyes.

"I'm a little scared," she whispered. "Even though I'm happy we don't have to wait anymore."

His heart was beating hard in his chest. He couldn't remember reacting this way with anyone. Particularly this soon. "I'm a little scared too," he said, right before he kissed her.

Those luscious pink lips stole all his senses. Her hands came up around him, and she settled closer to his body, her body fitting perfectly against his. Changing the angle of their kiss, he kept it light until she moved forward and demanded more. He should have known. She'd been the one to make the first move, after all.

Her tongue teased him and then proceeded to invite him to dance. Suddenly he had to caress her curves, which had driven him wild since she'd first entered his office. He ran his hand down her waist and cupped her bottom. She started against him and then let out an earthy moan.

She edged back, her breath warm on his lips. "I'm still not sleeping with you tonight."

He chuckled. "Who asked you?" he said, using the response she'd given him back in the hotel.

Their mouths found each other again, and she seemed to grow lusher, hotter with every kiss, every caress. He needed to touch more skin, so he trailed kisses down her neck and across her bare shoulders. His fingers itched to untie her halter, but he expected she'd slap him for it just because she could.

"Have I told you how beautiful you are?" he asked as he gave particular attention to the place where her shoulder met her arm.

"I can't...remember," she answered breathlessly, fitting her hand inside his suit jacket and caressing his chest through his white shirt. "We should probably stop this."

"Probably," he said, with no intention of doing so. "I've been thinking about this."

"Me too," she confessed. "Even when I was upset about family stuff. The thought of being with you tonight helped me get through my day."

"I'm glad," he said, taking her mouth again.

This time the kiss swelled between them, going from hot to scorching. He cupped her hips in his hands and brought her closer to his erection. She put her hands on his shoulders.

"Okay, now we really need to slow down," she said, edging back. "I was serious about what I said, Vander. I...I might not have waited for marriage, but the next time I make love with someone I want to be in love with him—and him with me. That's...not easy to say to you right now."

He stroked her cheek to ease her obvious embarrassment. Sure, he wished she was a little more open about having sex with him, but he rather liked that she wouldn't do it with just anyone. He'd gone out with plenty of women in Nashville, and many of them had proved all too eager to hop from his bed to someone else's. He wasn't a prude. Never had been. But as he'd grown older, he'd gotten more discriminating.

"I'm glad you're being honest with me," he said softly. "I told you I want that. More than anything."

She took a deep breath and smoothed her dress. Not that he'd gotten much of anything out of place. But she was flushed and looked well-kissed. He liked that.

"Is honesty all the more important to you because of your profession?" she asked.

He nodded, happy she'd intuited that. Some of the women he'd dated had wrongly thought he liked subterfuge and mystery in his personal life. He'd had a belly full of that with his father's murder, notwithstanding his line of work.

"I don't ask for much. But honesty and mutual respect is important to me."

"Me too," she said, standing a few feet from him with her hands at her sides. "I suppose we should go."

"I suppose so," he said, reaching out to push her silken brown hair behind her ear. "Although I don't want to. I could stay here and kiss you all night."

Her brow arched. "As tempting as that is, let's go to dinner. I find myself hungry."

"Not much of an appetite this week, huh?" he asked.

She shook her head. "Where are you taking me? You didn't say."

"It's a surprise. Grab your purse."

"Let me put the flowers in some water first," she said, giving him the opportunity to study the sliver of her place he could see from his position in the entryway. A cherry-wood staircase led upstairs. The walls were decorated with either landscape or floral designs in bold metallic frames. There was a horse sculpture on the entry table and an Art Deco mirror above it.

"You can look around," she called out. "I know your curiosity must be killing you."

He laughed and headed in the direction of her voice. Her living room furniture was cream-colored leather piled with bright purple pillows crisscrossed with orange stripes. The den had a fireplace, and the mantel was lined with family photos. He picked up one of Shelby with an older woman she favored in looks and knew this had to be the infamous Louisa.

"That's Mama," she said quietly in the doorway.

"I figured," he said, placing the photograph back. "Sadie and Susannah resemble her more."

She rubbed the back of her neck. "I wonder what Mama thinks sometimes, seeing me and J.P., but him especially. Does she see the man who abandoned her? Don't mind me. I'm..."

"It's okay, Shelby," he said, turning to face her. "Perfectly normal questions."

"You've had them?" she asked.

He met her gaze. "Of course. It's only human to have questions. Especially when there aren't any obvious answers. I've wondered the same about my mother. I resemble my dad too."

"Have you...well, ever looked in the mirror and wondered how much the likeness you share carries past looks?"

For a moment, he looked away, not sure of how much to share. She was vulnerable, and he didn't want to heap more weight on her shoulders. "Yes, but I'm the same age as he was when he died. After this...I'll be aging in a way he never had the chance to. It's bothered me more than I like to admit."

She wrung her hands—something Sadie usually did—like she was flailing to find an appropriate response. "I wish I could say something to make you feel better."

He shrugged, as much to shrug off the downturn in the conversation for her as for himself. "It's just the mind wanting to fill in the blanks."

"It does, more's the pity," she said, crossing to him. "That doesn't mean it hurts any less. We can go."

He pulled her to his chest. "In a minute."

She put her arms around him. "I'm fine."

"You don't have to be anything but what you are right now," he said, running his hands up and down her back. "In fact, we don't have to go anywhere. I'd be perfectly happy ordering takeout again and watching a movie." He was feeling a little raw himself after those admissions.

"Don't you have reservations?" she asked.

He thought about lying. For a second. "They can be canceled."

"No, we should go," she said, linking their arms and leading him to the door.

She picked up her purse and studied him. "I...didn't expect it to be like this. With you. I mean I don't really know you, but I feel..."

He looked deep into her eyes. "How do you feel?"

Her chest rose as she sucked in a deep breath. "I feel really good around you."

Unable to help himself, he kissed her lightly on the lips. "I didn't expect this either." In fact, he'd shared more with her than he had with any woman. It was more than a little surprising how easy it had been to open up.

"How do you feel?" she asked softly. "If you don't mind me asking."

She worried her lip then, and he dug deep for the truth.

"I feel...calm in one moment. Happy when you smile at me. Intrigued when you play your Southern belle act. Hot when you kiss me."

Her sudden blush delighted him.

"How's that for honesty?" he asked.

She gave him a long look before drawling, "Not bad, honey," and headed out the front door.

CHAPTER 21

WHEN VANDER PULLED TO A STOP IN FRONT OF A racetrack, Shelby turned in her seat and raised an eyebrow. They weren't having dinner quite yet, it seemed. "What *are* you thinking?"

"I know you're a woman who likes speed, so I thought this might get your mind off things," he said, tracing her cheekbone. "This company specializes in providing a racing experience for novices with hot, dreamy cars. As far as I'm concerned, this is better than a regular Friday night date. Have you ever ridden in a Lamborghini Gallardo LP550?"

Her mouth went dry, and she shook her head. "No."

"You sound breathless," he said, looking very pleased with himself. "I take it you're up for some fun."

She let her imagination fly as she looked out the window at the circular track. Was she really going to do this? Heck yeah, she was. "Where do we start? Wait, I'm not exactly dressed for it." She swatted him. "Why didn't you *say* something?"

"So you could pack another suitcase or insist on shopping for race-appropriate clothing?" he asked. "Thanks, but I've experienced that routine already. Besides, they give you an outfit to wear. Trust me, you'll look cute in it."

He wisely got out of the car after delivering that comment. "Cute?" she muttered to herself. She'd show him cute.

He opened her door and lounged against the frame. "Afraid to get a little dirty?" he taunted.

She swung her legs out of the bucket seat but stayed where she was, running her hand up her legs as if adjusting her skirt, which had ridden up. She tugged on the material slowly, staring him down. Her internal temperature was rising to meet the hot, muggy air as his eyes made a leisurely sweep of her body.

She liked that he challenged her. No man had ever done that before. All her previous dates had consisted of meetings in coffee shops and restaurants, punctuated with conversation and food. In fact, she'd felt obligated to conduct that same worn-out dance with Vander, but he clearly didn't want that. And this...

"Not if you're not," she said, taking the hand he'd extended to assist her out of the car.

Of course, he pulled her against his tall, hard body and ran a hand down her hip. "We can always shower later."

She pursed her lip. "We can stop at a toy store and find you a rubber ducky because that's the only company you're getting in the shower later."

He laughed. "I already have a rubber ducky, thank you."

"Lucky duck." Oh, the sparring. She was starting to crave their rapport like she did chocolate. Patting him on the shoulder, she stepped away and started walking toward the front door of the building. "Coming?" she called over her shoulder.

She knew he was right behind her. Heavens, her palms were damp. How in the world was she supposed to resist this man? She'd never desired anyone this much. This was the kind of man her Bible school teachers had warned her about. Except that wasn't completely true. He was a good man, straight down the line, and that only made him more tempting.

They were met inside by a man named Luke, the driver who would be bringing her on a ride-along in the car of her choice. His official title was a professional drifter, which Shelby thought was a bit odd since it made him sound like a hobo.

She chose a lime green Gallardo and signed a whole stack of forms saying she wouldn't sue them if the car turned into a fireball and she died. Wonderful thoughts. She said a prayer that everything would work out because she didn't let fear rule her life. When Vander chose an orange McLaren 570S, she shot him a glance.

"You're going for a ride too?" she drawled.

He rolled his eyes and scratched his signature at the bottom of his forms. "I believe in mutual fun on a date. Although I do like to watch."

Her mouth dropped open, and she socked him again. "Are you crazy? Luke is..."

"Not listening," Vander said with a grin. "Are you, Luke?"

The man shook his head, but she didn't miss his restrained smile. "I'll show you where you can change, Shelby. We have a few suits that will fit you, I think."

She wanted to cringe, thinking about wearing a suit someone else had worn, least of all sweated in. Yuck. But she wasn't going to balk. This was going to be so fun. Hadn't she bought Pearl with her bonus because she'd always wanted a sleek, fast car? Growing up, she'd always played it safe. They all had. While they hadn't had a daddy, their upbringing had been pretty conventional. One of the reasons she'd first wanted to work for Gail was because the woman lived large. But while she did things her own way always, she was still a successful, respected businesswoman.

Shelby secretly wanted to be like Gail. Minus all the ex-husbands, some of her boss' more outlandish outfits—like the real snakeskin bikini, and unconventional ideas—like the recent cannon she'd bought to fire off at noon every day, her Civil War version of a church bell.

After donning the hideous yellow and white suit, Shelby emerged to see Vander already dressed in a red and black one.

"Didn't I say you'd look cute?" Vander gestured to her and asked Luke, "Cute as a button, right?"

"More like a cat on a hot tin roof liable to dig her claws into you if you keep calling her that," the older man said, handing Vander a helmet, which he tucked under his arm. Turning to Shelby, Luke quipped, "Here's yours. Cutie."

She shot them both the fish eye and took the black helmet he offered her. Again, she shut down all thoughts about someone else's hair being inside the helmet. *Eww.*

"Your man bought you extra drifting laps," Luke told her, gesturing to the back door that led to a garage so palatial it felt more like a warehouse.

"You were that sure I was going to enjoy myself?" she asked Vander as they walked to the line of cars waiting for them.

It was like a scene in *Fast and Furious*. Heavens, she loved those movies.

"I had a hunch," he said, "and I'm usually right about them. Part of the deal is a personal video of the experience. I can't wait to watch yours afterward."

Great. She was going to be screaming like a girl from the speed. "So you get to watch, after all," she boldly said, falling into the fun of the moment.

"I like it when you talk back to me," he said, his aquamarine eyes darkening. "I'm used to women fawning all over me."

She could imagine that. "They probably fall into bed with you easily too."

"I've grown more discerning." He stopped her with a hand and zipped her suit up the rest of the way. "Have fun, Shelby."

"I plan to," she replied and rose on her tiptoes to kiss his cheek.

Luke walked her through the details of the car she'd chosen, everything from how it could go from zero to sixty in three point nine seconds to the fact that the V-10 engine was five hundred and fifty horsepower. He helped buckle her in and put on her helmet, saying they could communicate using the built-in communication system.

She took note of the video camera on the dashboard and crossed her hands to compose herself, doing her best to smile as Luke started the engine and drove them onto the track. Then Luke punched the gas. The tires screamed, and she slammed back against her seat. Everything flew by in a blur as she clutched the handle bars in front of her, her fingers gripping with all their might. He punched it again around the first turn, and she screamed. She couldn't help it. It had felt like she was about to fall sideways out of the car.

"You ready to go full out, Shelby?" Luke asked, skillfully maneuvering the car as it thundered down the track.

"Okay," she said, tightening her grip on the handle bars.

The engine roared as they shot forward. Her eyes frantically shot to the odometer, and she noted they were approaching two hundred miles per hour. Holy Moses! She screamed again as he took another curve, and that was pretty much how the rest of the drive went. Except she wasn't really screaming from fear, it was exhilaration. Freedom. Luke let them drift a little once he let the speed drop some, and she could feel the pull of the car.

"I love this!" she shouted as he cruised around another curve.

She had lost count of the number of laps they'd made. Her face felt tight from screaming and smiling and shouting, and her body... It didn't know which way was up anymore.

"Last lap, Shelby," Luke said. "Shall we give it all it's got?"

He'd been holding back? "Go for it!"

As the car shot forward, everything around her started vibrating. He whipped around the curves, making her squeal and laugh all over again. When he finally pulled to a halt in front of the warehouse, she sagged back in the seat. She had to make her fingers unlock from the bars she'd been holding.

Luke turned to her. "How do you feel?"

"Terrific!" she said, giving him a thumbs up. "Thank you!"

He exited the vehicle, and she took one last look at the

interior of the Lamborghini. Goodness, she'd thought Pearl was fast.

Vander sauntered forward as she got out and took her helmet off. "How was it?"

"Incredible!" She ran forward on unsteady legs and threw her arms around him. "Thank you so much for this!"

He wrapped his arms around her. "You're welcome. Glad you had fun."

"There's only one problem," she said, edging back.

His brow furrowed. "What? You're okay, aren't you? You didn't get sick?"

"Sick? Of course not. Who do you think I am?" She swept her hand toward the car. "How am I supposed to drive my BMW after I've driven in this?"

He chucked her under her chin. "When you get all nostalgic, remember how many speeding tickets you're avoiding."

"Haha," she said. "You have fun yourself."

"I intend to," Vander said.

Pretty soon she was watching the orange McLaren race around the course. She cheered as they whizzed by even though she knew Vander couldn't hear her. But it gave her a funny feeling, realizing how much she wanted to support him—even though he wouldn't know it.

She was falling for him. Hard.

Is this the man God designed for me? That thought seemed to come out of nowhere, and it made her legs even more unsteady than going two hundred miles an hour in that Lamborghini. Holy heavens! What in the world was she thinking? This was only their first official date. Then the orange car pulled to a stop in front of her, and she watched as Vander emerged. The grin he had on his face seemed to light every cell in her body, almost like he'd become the nucleus of her being.

Yes, it was early, much too early to know if he was the one, and yet she'd never felt this way before, and she couldn't imagine feeling this way about someone else.

When he reached her, he pulled her to him and kissed her without compunction, making her knees turn to jello. She fell against him, and his strong arms held her in place as his mouth ate at her lips with hunger. Somehow she managed to raise her tingling arms and wrap them around his neck.

He groaned in his throat and pulled her even closer. Their suits scratched against each other, and part of her wanted to rip it off so she could feel the angles of his body better. But he continued to kiss her, and she continued to kiss him.

"Y'all need to get a room," she heard Luke say wryly with a chuckle.

Vander must have heard him because he edged back, keeping his arms around her. That was a good thing since she wasn't feeling very steady on her feet.

"Shelby," he said softly, looking straight into her eyes.

"Vander," she whispered back, seeing his hunger for her, but also a simple sense of joy—a joy she realized was simply because of her.

"I'm…" He cut off whatever he'd intended to say, and she knew it.

"What?" she asked, tracing his dark eyebrows.

"I'm in deep waters here, Shelby," he said, his voice grave.

"Me too." Then she smiled. "But I'm not scared."

CHAPTER 22

WHEN SHELBY STEPPED ONTO THE BACK PORCH AT Rye's house for Sunday family dinner, her easy smile and radiant skin told Sadie the whole story. Her sister was completely infatuated with Vander. Of course, Shelby had called her to tell her about the dates they'd been on—they'd gone to the racetrack on Friday, then an art show the next night. It seemed like Vander was going out of his way to woo her by indulging in their common interests.

"You look so happy!" Sadie declared, hugging her sister. "I wish I felt like that. My stomach has been upset all day, what with seeing Mama." Of course, she'd done her best to chat with other people at church after services. She was still avoiding Mama, and she hated that.

"I know what you mean," Shelby said, glancing at the rest of their clan tucked away on the deck. "But it's over now, and we need to do our best to not dwell on it."

"I don't have the same handsome distraction as you do," Sadie said, earning a playful jab from her sister.

"I know." Shelby got a far-off look in her eyes. "He's amazing. I've never met anyone like him. He makes me feel... so alive. Oh, Sadie, I can't wait until you meet your special someone."

Sadie couldn't either, but she was determined to have her

eyes wide open the next time she got involved with a man. In truth, she'd rather be alone than with someone who didn't make her shine the way her sister was doing right now.

"You're looking pretty happy, Shelby," Amelia Ann said, joining their group. "Are you seeing someone? Because I know that look. I see it every day in the mirror. I don't care if that sounds smug. Hah."

"There is someone," Shelby said cagily, "but it's early yet."

"Sometimes all it takes is one look at a man for you to know he's the one," Amelia Ann said, fanning her neck with her hair in response to the heat. "That's how I felt with Clayton."

Shelby nodded. "Fine, I do feel like he's different. I'm trying to not to get ahead of myself. He says this is unusual for him too, but... I'm trying to stay in the moment."

Sadie knew better. Her sister had never spoken about another man this way, and since Sadie already thought Vander was wonderful, she hoped it worked out between them.

"What's his name and what does he do?" Amelia Ann asked.

"I'm missing out on something, aren't I?" Tammy said, walking out the back door and coming over to join them. "Shelby, you look amazingly great."

Sadie heard what she wasn't saying: *For the kind of week you had.*

"There's a man," Amelia Ann confessed with a grin.

"Really?" Tammy drawled. "Who?"

"We were just getting to that," Amelia Ann told her sister.

Shelby gave Sadie a look and then fiddled with her manicure. "Maybe it's too early to talk details."

Rye bounced over and wrapped his arms around his sisters. "What are y'all talking about?"

"Shelby's new beau," Amelia Ann told him. "Come on, girl. We're family. You can tell us his name and profession at least."

"Good idea," Rye said. "Then I can have my security manager run a check on him to make sure he's good enough for you."

Shelby's natural glow was fading fast, and Sadie linked arms to support her. "Doesn't Tory need help in the kitchen?"

Rye shook his head. "No, I finally talked her into lying down a bit before dinner. Why that woman insists on cooking and hosting family dinner when she's so close to popping, I'll never know. But you're evading. Shelby, honey, who are you seeing? Don't make me call J.P. over here. He'll want to do his big brother act, although mine is much more effective. I have a shotgun."

Sadie felt Shelby tense up beside her.

"All right," her sister finally said, making an attempt to smile. "His name is Vander Montgomery, and he's a private investigator."

"Vander Montgomery?" Rye asked, shaking his head. "He and his firm did some work for me early on before I needed a full-time security team. He's a good guy, but how in the world did you meet him? He runs in pretty different circles."

Sadie all but heard her sister gulp. "Ah...Gail."

Rye nodded. "Of course. How is that loony ol' girl? Now, there's a woman who knows how to mix it up."

"She's fine," Shelby said, and Sadie could feel them all walking on shallow ice.

Tammy was looking at everyone with concern, and Sadie knew why. It hurt to keep such a whopping secret from their loved ones, but they could hardly justify concealing the truth from Mama if they told the rest of their extended family.

"I'm feeling all this heat suddenly," Shelby said, fanning herself. "Sadie, why don't you come inside and help me pour out some sweet tea?"

"Good idea," Rye said, "I've got a powerful thirst. Shelby, you tell Vander I said hey when you see him next. I'll hold back the gun threats until Vander does something naughty." Then he gave a knowing wink.

She gave him the fish eye. "I'll pass along your regards, you silly man."

Sadie drew her sister to the back door as Rory and Annabelle raced out, almost bowling them over.

"Excuse us!" Annabelle called, waving a sparkly yellow fairy wand. "Rory and I have flowers to pick before dinner. Aunt Tory told us we could choose anything we wanted."

"Mind the thorns on the roses, Annabelle," Tammy hollered as her children raced off. "That girl. I tell you. She'll walk right into brambles if there's a pretty flower. I've even gotten her child gardening gloves, but she doesn't wear them."

"Too busy running so fast," Rye said, smiling at his niece and nephew. "They're a pair. I can't wait for them to play with our baby. It's going to be great for him or her to have cousins around."

Tammy put her arm around her brother. "Indeed it is."

Shelby tugged on Sadie's arm to draw her inside. When she closed the door behind them, she all but slumped against it. "I shouldn't have glowed."

"Oh, good heavens," Sadie told her as they wandered through Rye's house to the kitchen. "You can't keep yourself from glowing. Nor should you."

"I hate this!" Shelby said, reaching for the plastic cups on the counter. "I don't like holding back from everyone."

"What are you holding back?" Amelia Ann asked from the doorway, still yards away but closing on them fast. "If you think I can't smell when something is up, you're crazy."

Shelby sighed and looked over at Sadie. "I don't know what to do," she said.

"Well, I do," Amelia Ann informed them. "You'll tell me because Tammy already knows about whatever's going on with your beau. I could see it on her face. She's my sister, after all."

"*Amelia Ann...*"

"You're going to hurt my feelings, Shelby," she said. "I thought we were friends if not sisters."

Her expression was so crestfallen Sadie crossed the room to her and rubbed her arms. "Of course you are. It's just...we haven't even told Mama. It's...delicate."

Amelia Ann's eyes grew wide. "You know you can trust me. I'd like to tell Clayton since I don't like secrets between married folk, but if you don't rather I didn't, I won't."

Shelby glanced around the kitchen, then walked to all the doorways to make sure no one was hovering. "All right, we'll tell you."

And so she did, dredging up all the heartbreak and guilt Sadie suspected would never leave her. Even after hearing her sister recount their search for their daddy, Sadie couldn't help but wonder for the thousandth time why the man who'd sired them had run from everything he knew at the prospect of seeing them. It was the worst hurt she'd ever felt.

"Oh, honey," Amelia Ann said, wrapping her arms around Shelby when she finished the tale. "And Sadie. Come here, girl."

They shared a long hug, and Sadie felt tears start to drip down her cheeks again. They'd hardly stopped these last few days.

"I wish there was something I could say to help," Amelia Ann said, patting them both on the backs, "but if there's one thing I've learned from working at the law clinic, it's that there are no words to soothe the pain of abandonment. You were brave to look for him after all this time. More open-hearted than I could be. At least you'll never regret it."

"That's the only blessing in all this," Sadie found herself saying.

"And Vander," Amelia Ann said, releasing her hold on them. "Meeting him sounds like a blessing."

Shelby nodded. "Yes, you're right."

"God does work in mysterious ways," Sadie found herself saying. "Maybe that's what we need to focus on."

"Maybe so," Shelby agreed. "We aren't going to tell Mama, which is why we haven't told anyone outside of our siblings—and Tammy and Jake."

"Of course," Amelia Ann said. "I understand. That's likely

best."

"Do you think so?" Sadie asked. "We never settled things completely. I know Susannah would like to forget about the whole thing."

Their eldest sister hadn't even risen from her deck chair to come over and talk with them, sticking close to her new husband. Susannah was keeping to herself after everything, and Sadie was trying to respect that.

"What are y'all doing?" Rye asked, coming in from the mud room. "I know trouble when I see it."

Amelia Ann put her hands on her hips. "Women stuff."

"*Oh,*" Rye said. "Well, excuse me. I was coming in for that sweet tea y'all promised me."

"You're excused," Amelia Ann said, walking over to the kitchen counter and pouring her brother a glass from the pitcher. "Now, off with you."

"You sure have gotten bossy," Rye told her with a wink. "Keep it up. It sure beats the shy wallflower you used to be. I'll leave you to your women stuff. I'm going to check on my beautiful wife and baby."

He left the room, and Sadie took a breath. "That was close. We need to be wiser about where we speak about this."

Shelby nodded. "Hopefully this is the last of the discussion."

"You can talk to me anytime, y'all," Amelia Ann said, pouring everyone sweet tea. "I hope you know that."

"You can talk to me too," said a familiar voice from behind them.

Sadie turned, her belly looping into sail knots. "Mama."

"Yes, *Mama,*" she said with narrowed eyes. "Y'all have been ducking me, and I can't see as I understand why."

Amelia Ann cleared her throat. "I'll just go deliver this sweet tea."

Frankly, Shelby couldn't blame her. In the face of Mama's glower, she was speechless.

"Shelby is dating someone new," Sadie blurted out, "and

we didn't want to raise everyone's hopes she's finally getting hitched." Had that really popped out of her mouth?

Her sister glared at her.

"Is that all?" Mama asked, shaking her head. "Shelby, is this man anything to be ashamed of?"

Her sister shook her head fiercely. "No, Mama."

"Then why in the world would you think I wouldn't be happy for you?" Mama said, walking over to her sister and putting her hands on her shoulders. "Are you feeling a mite tempted by him?"

Oh, Good Lord, Mama was going *there*.

"Mama!" Shelby gasped, blushing to her roots.

"Honey," Mama said, "when a new man comes into your life, especially one you care about a lot, there's always temptation. You know how I feel about things, but you're a grown woman. It's up to you to decide what's best for you. I hope you know I would never judge you for your choice. I'm always here to listen or share my insights with you."

Sadie was sure her eyes were as wide as quarters. This was the kind of embarrassing chat that made her cringe from the thought of finding someone special. And it kind of ticked her off some too. Would Mama have said the same thing to J.P.?

"Thank you, Mama," Shelby said, clearing her throat.

"So, when are we going to meet this man?" Mama asked. "If you set so much store by him, I surely will too."

"Ah... As I was telling Amelia Ann, it's early yet. We haven't...talked about meeting each other's families."

Mama patted her on the back. "Well, yours is important to you. I hope your man knows that."

Oh, he knew. Mama had no idea how much.

"What is his name, Shelby?"

"Vander, Mama," she said, clearing her throat again.

"Vander, huh." She shook her head. "An interesting name."

"He's named after the school," Shelby shot out. "It's a family thing."

"Are his people here?" Mama asked.

"They used to be," Shelby said. "His daddy died when he was a boy, and then his mama moved them back East. We haven't much talked beyond that."

"Well, you can tell a lot about a man from the way he treats his family," Mama said. "Too bad about his daddy. You have him come to Sunday dinner next week so we can all meet him."

"I don't know, Mama," Shelby said, her shoulders slumping.

"I won't take no for an answer," Mama said. "You bring him by and let us get a good look at him. I don't want either of you girls to get taken advantage of."

Sadie was sure her mouth opened a touch. She remembered Mama saying things like that when they were growing up. The full reason hadn't hit her until now. Mama didn't want them to make the same mistakes she had. This was her way of talking around it like she always did.

"You mean like you did with Daddy?" Sadie asked softly.

Her mama turned her full attention toward her. "Yes, and that's all we'll speak about it. You just need to trust me on this, girls."

Sadie felt herself wither like a flower in the first frost. Her eyes tracked to Shelby. There was a stricken look on her sister's face, and she had her hand on her heart.

Mama patted Shelby on the back. "I look forward to meeting your man, honey."

Then she walked out of the kitchen.

Sadie could feel tears well up in her eyes, and Shelby wrapped her up in a hug.

"I'm sorry," Sadie whispered. "That just popped out of my mouth."

"No, I'm glad," Shelby said, holding her tight. "I was paralyzed."

"We can never tell her what we did," Sadie said, fighting the powerful urge to let those tears loose.

"I know," her sister said. "There's no question now."

CHAPTER 23

"YOU'VE GOT A SPRING IN YOUR STEP THESE DAYS," Charlie said to Vander as he stopped by her office to say goodnight for the evening.

Like usual, his best friend and top detective was eating at her desk with her shoes off. "Do you ever go home?"

"You're one to talk," Charlie said, kicking her bare feet up on her desk. "Until recently, you were all work, work, work. Now you're running off at... What time is it? Just before seven o'clock. Wait. I think hell might have frozen over. I take it things are going great with Shelby."

Things were going more than great. He was a little freaked out by how much he thought of her when they weren't together, by how much he enjoyed being with her, and yes, by how early he'd been leaving the office to see more of her. "Yes. I need to run."

"That's *all* you're going to say?" Charlie asked, swinging her legs to the floor and standing. "Dammit, Vander! We've known each other for a long time now. You've *never* acted this way over a woman."

She wasn't wrong. "I don't want to discuss this, Charlie. Shelby and I are seeing each other and having a good time. I'm trying not to think about anything else."

"Oh, come on, Vander," Charlie said. "Who are you

kidding? Shelby's mom is a preacher, and her siblings are some of the nicest, most down-to-earth people we've come across. This isn't your run-of-the-mill girl to have fun with."

It was like Charlie was reading his mind. He'd seen Shelby every day since their first racetrack date, and they still hadn't slept together. "I know. Shelby's..." He broke off, not sure what the hell to say. Special? "I don't like it when you talk like a girl. It freaks me out."

"I don't *like* talking like a girl with you either," Charlie said. "I'm really talking as your friend. You're being abnormally close-mouthed about this situation, Vander, and it's not like you."

"What do you want me to say?" he asked. "Do I know Shelby is the settle-down type? Yes! Do I get a little queasy thinking about that? Yes."

Charlie sat on the edge of her desk. "I know we both had shit happen to us when we were growing up that makes us run like rabbits at the thought of marriage."

"Who's talking about marriage? Jesus, Charlie, we've only been going out for less than a week." Of course, they'd been spending practically every free moment together.

She rolled her eyes. "Vander, you're a man who knows what he wants. I've never known time to be a factor in your decision making."

Shit. She knew him too well.

"You need some help," Charlie went on. "Maybe if I find someone I want to leave work for early, you'll be the one to help talk it out. I... Vander, do you ever think about growing old?"

He started at that. "Not really." But that wasn't entirely true. He'd thought about it a little this year, thanks in no small part to that damn nightmare about his dad. *What are you going to do with the rest of your life, son?* Thank God, he hadn't had it in weeks. Shelby was filling his dreamtime now.

"Well, I do," Charlie said. "I suppose it's because of what happened to me. I...when I was a kid, there were days when

I wanted to die. I...shit...this is heavy. I wasn't sure if I even wanted to grow old, you know, like gray-haired-old-lady old. The more years I rack up, the more I wonder if I'll get there. But if I do, I'd rather not do it alone. Don't get me wrong—I like being on my own. I'm just not sure I'd like being alone *and* old. Do you understand what I'm saying?"

He walked forward and put his hands on her shoulders. "I promise you can sit in a rocking chair beside me on a front porch when we're old and gray. We'll read the newspaper and listen to the police scanner and look for clues. Maybe we can change the company name to the Geriatric Crime Busters."

She smiled at him, a soft one for her. Though he rarely saw her like this, his tough, no-nonsense friend was like everyone else beneath it all. Human.

"I'd like that," Charlie said. "Thanks for not laughing at me."

He rubbed her shoulder. "I'd never laugh at you."

"I know that, and I'm also trusting you not to get pissed at what I'm about to say." She took a deep breath. "Usually as we get closer to August 30th, I have to start walking on egg shells around you...and worrying about you working too late, eating enough, and sleeping more than a few hours a night. I don't feel that way this year. You're...lighter somehow."

It was her way of crediting Shelby for the change, and he couldn't disagree. "I've noticed it too. Do you really worry about me eating and sleeping? Charlie, that's pretty fucking weird."

"I know it is," she said with a smile, giving him a hard shove toward the door. "Girl talk is over."

"Thank God," he said, resting his hand on the doorframe. "Don't work too late, Charlie. Sometimes I worry about you too."

"Yeah, yeah, yeah," she said and turned back to her computer, ignoring him.

As he drove to Shelby's house, he couldn't help but think about what Charlie had said. Did he need to think more about the future? Is that why his dad kept rising up in his subconscious mind?

He was content on his own—like Charlie had said. He'd created a successful business, made a name for himself. He was well respected and knew interesting people. Like Gail. That thought made him smile. He wondered if Shelby had mentioned they were dating yet. What would Gail think of that after chasing him all these years? Surely she wouldn't be jealous? She wouldn't go off the deep end about it and hurt Shelby, would she?

Shit. He was in crazy deep if he was worrying about that.

Somehow he didn't mind at all.

When he finally knocked on her door, and she answered, the light from the fading sun seemed to cast her in a magical glow. His throat got thick as she smiled and rose on her tiptoes to kiss him sweetly on the lips. She smelled delicious, and her curvy body was so soft against him. His heart started thudding in his chest.

"Hi," she said, her lips an inch from his mouth.

"Hi," he said in a hoarse voice.

"You all right?" she asked, putting a hand to his forehead. "Tough day?"

It hadn't been. He'd closed a few cases. Made some clients happy. Work wasn't making his stomach do flip-flops. That was all Shelby and the epic effect she was having on his life. "I'm fine. Happy to see you."

"I'm happy to see you too," she all but purred, making him rock hard in an instant. "Do you want to come inside for a bit? Our reservation isn't until eight, right?"

"Right," he said, considering the wisdom of being alone with her right now. This was the first time he'd ever dated a woman who wouldn't put out. He wasn't a dog, but most of the women he'd dated didn't have the kind of internal struggle Shelby seemed to have with him. She wanted him and was honest about that. But when it came to sex, she wanted to be in a committed, loving relationship. He couldn't fault her that.

In fact, he respected her decision.

Didn't make him less horny, though. It also didn't make him less eager to be with her, even if he was aching by the end of each evening.

"Well, come on in," she said, grabbing his hand. "I'll pour you some of my sweet tea."

"Shelby, I hate sweet tea."

She turned around as he was closing the front door. "But that's sacrilege!"

He laughed. "Sacrilege? You forget. I wasn't primarily raised here."

In fact, he hadn't had run across sweet tea for eight years while in Boston. After moving back to Nashville, he'd ordered some iced tea at a pizza hangout, and the taste had given him a horrible coughing fit. It had brought back a memory he'd somehow lost along the way. Vander's mother had forbidden him to drink sweet tea when he was a kid, claiming it had too much sugar, but his daddy used to sneak him sips from his glass at suppertime. He couldn't drink it to this day without feeling angry at his mother, so he avoided it.

"But you've lived here long enough," she said, cocking her brow. "Vander, I'm not so sure about you now."

"That's all right," he said, taking off his suit jacket due to the sudden heat raining through his body from the memories. "There are things I like I'm sure you don't."

"Like what?" she asked, wandering into the kitchen, her curvy body distracting him from his dark thoughts. He let himself look his fill.

"I guess we'll find out in time." He followed her and put his arms around her from behind. "You always smell so good. You feel even better."

She sighed and let herself soften against him. "I feel the same way about you." Her phone rang. "Let me make sure that isn't Gail. She actually bought antique cannonballs from some moron of an antique dealer. She's been looking for gunpowder. I told her she can't fire actual cannonballs from her cannon.

Of course, she wants me to look into whether there's a permit or something we can apply for. My duties often extend beyond straight accounting with her."

"That sounds like Gail," he said, laughing, happy she could affect him so.

When Shelby checked her phone, her happiness seemed to fade. She turned her ringer off and flipped her phone facedown onto the counter.

"Who are you evading?" he asked, going over to rub her shoulders.

She tilted her head to the side to give him better access. "Mama."

Shelby had told him about her and Sadie's interaction with Mama at Rye's house. It roused the suspicion Vander had held since he first took their case—Louisa was hiding something.

"What does she want?"

She moved out of his arms and opened the refrigerator, grabbing a pitcher of sweet tea. "Nothing."

Shelby was one of the most outspoken women he'd met, one of the many things he enjoyed about her. "It's not like you to hold back from me."

Pouring the tea into not one but two glasses she'd selected from the cabinet, she made a face. "Trust me. This is one thing you'll be happy I don't share."

He didn't like the sound of that. "We agreed to be honest with each other. I don't want that to change. Why don't you let me be the judge of what I want to hear?"

She slid an infernal glass of sweet tea his way, and he took it because she was clearly on autopilot. "My mama is insisting you come to Sunday family dinner this weekend to meet everyone. She's called me every day about it. I mean, she basically strong-armed Jake into coming even before he started dating Susannah, but this is ridiculous."

Family dinner? Already? "Doesn't she think it's a little early for that?"

Shelby ran her finger around the rim of her glass. "Apparently not. I've..."

"You," he encouraged, taking her hand and searching her brown eyes.

"I've apparently never looked like I do right now," she said, releasing a huge breath. "I wish everyone would leave me alone."

"How do you look?" he asked, although he knew. He'd seen her when she was all business at Gail's, and on the other end of the spectrum, he'd watched her come undone over her father. Lately, all he'd seen was a happy, sexy, beautiful woman. Seeing her like that made him feel like he'd taken his own happy pill.

"Like I have someone special," she drawled. "Are you having fun teasing me?"

"Shelby, I'm not teasing you," he said. "If it makes you feel any better, Charlie told me I was acting differently too."

"She did?" Her question was flush with hope.

"Yes," he said. "I was embarrassed."

"I understand that," she said. "I know we've just started dating—"

"But we both have said this is different for us," he finished for her. "You know I'll come on Sunday. My only concern is how we're going to handle me already knowing your sisters and brother."

"It's an uncomfortable situation all around, isn't it? That's why I was trying to think of some way out of it."

But if they kept seeing each other—and he had no reason to believe they wouldn't—it was inevitable he'd meet her family. It was what people who cared about each other did, especially when someone's family was as important to them as Shelby's was to her.

"Maybe we face it straight away. Then it will lose its bite."

"It's as bad as a bite from a rabid pit bull, if you ask me," Shelby said, making him laugh.

"You do have a colorful way of saying things," he said,

bringing her close to him and running his hands up and down her arms. "Why don't you talk to J.P., Susannah, and Sadie about it? I think the cover Sadie gave Rye works just fine. Gail did refer you to me, after all. There's no lie in that."

"But it's not the full truth, either," she said, resting her head against his chest. "I don't want to lie about how we met, Vander. It's not a good way to start things off."

"Do you see a way around it? Why don't you ask J.P? He has a good head on his shoulders. We can talk to him together if you'd like. He's a great guy." Someone he could imagine calling a friend.

"Yes, he is," she agreed. "I'll talk to him. Dagnabit, I wish Mama felt differently about all this. Sometimes I want to yell at her."

She was heating up in his arms. "Maybe yelling would do you good. You seem to have a lot of anger. How about you yell at me? Tell me what you'd tell your mother if you could say anything to her."

There were tears in her eyes when she pushed away. He wanted to take back his words, but it was too late. "Never mind that," he said instead. "How about I just hold you a bit? Then we can go to dinner and order a whole bunch of desserts?"

"I really must be worrying you," she said, wiping at a tear.

She was, but only because he cared about her. "How about I find a way to make you feel better?"

He lowered his mouth to hers and made her sigh.

They were late for their reservation, but they made up for it by feasting on every chocolate dessert the restaurant had to offer.

CHAPTER 24

THE PROSPECT OF MEETING SHELBY'S FAMILY MADE Vander's belly quiver as he drove to her house. Normally, the only thing that made that happen was when someone pulled a gun or a knife on him when he was working, which was thankfully a rarity.

Was he really doing this? It seemed too soon if he took a step back and looked at things logically. Somewhere inside him, though, there was a deep certainty he was right where he was supposed to be.

Funny, that's how he'd felt after retuning to Nashville against his mother's wishes. He'd seen the Cumberland River and known deep down in his bones he'd been right to listen to his gut and return to the place of his birth, the place of his father's murder.

He'd never regretted the breach his decision had caused with his mother and her family. They rarely spoke. She'd tried to forget everything that had happened in Nashville—like she'd tried to make him do—and stunted herself into a shallow, bitter woman. It hurt that she'd chosen to live that way, but he couldn't do the same.

When Vander arrived at Shelby's place, he was filled with a crazy sense of elation at the thought of seeing her, holding her, kissing her. He felt like hundreds of fireworks had exploded inside him when she opened the door after his first knock. There was a sassy grin on her face, and she was wearing a yellow cotton dress.

"Hi there," she said in her most syrupy drawl, grabbing his tie and pulling his mouth to hers.

He groaned as her lips fitted against his and her perfume wafted over him. This whole week they'd taken a liberal interpretation of the goodnight kiss, devoting an hour to it each night, and while he was aching with desire for her, he wouldn't have it any other way. But Christ, he had never wanted a woman this much. He wasn't sure how much more he could take.

Since he didn't want to start their outing with a hard-on, he pulled back. Her mouth followed, and he found himself kissing her again, that lush, sweet mouth that held nothing back.

"All right," he said, finally putting his hands on her shoulders and creating space between them. "That's enough."

She gave a pout. "Oh, poo. You're such a spoilsport sometimes."

His brow rose. "Oh, poo?" he asked. "Tell me you just didn't say that."

"I don't need you making fun of my colloquialisms." Crossing to the entryway table, she checked her makeup and picked up her purse. "Are you as nervous as I am? I wish Mama hadn't pushed this. She even asked me where you were this morning when I went to church. I told her I didn't know if you were a church-going man. You aren't, are you?"

He took a moment to answer, knowing this was the kind of question that could change things between them. But he had to be truthful. "No, I'm not. We went when I was a kid, but after my father's murder, my mother stopped attending. I respect other people's beliefs, but the whole God thing isn't for me. I still can't reconcile how a God who is supposed to be loving and kind would allow a man like my father to be murdered. Or millions of other people to suffer like they do."

She nodded, and he could feel her mood shift as surely as the wind. "I don't understand that either, honestly. I try and focus on the good things in life and ask God for help when times are tough. I find comfort in that, knowing there's divine support."

He needed to touch her, to assure them both that their different viewpoints weren't an obstacle. His finger caressed her cheek. "Does it change how you feel about me?"

When she put her hand on his chest and looked into his eyes, he released the breath he'd been holding. She hadn't said the words, but he knew she was falling in love with him—just as he was falling for her.

"My daddy was a church-going man. Look how that turned out. So was my only long-term boyfriend in college, and he showed his true colors too. I'd...rather be with a good, honest man. That's what you are."

Relief washed over him as he kissed her softly, slowly on the lips. "I'm glad."

"I'll warn you, though, Mama will work on you about the church thing," she told him with a frown. "She did it with Jake, but then again, Jake was hurting pretty bad from PTSD. His best friend was killed in Iraq, and he survived. It's haunted him, but Mama helped him find his way."

"Violence and death leave deep scars," he said, feeling the pain in his own heart. "It's the twenty-fifth anniversary of my father's death this year, and I'm...always thinking about it, especially this time of year." Except he wasn't as much. Suddenly he felt guilty for that.

She caressed his face. "How could you not think about it? He was taken from you in the worst way possible when you were just a boy."

His chest was growing tight. The hurt he hadn't been thinking much about since Shelby had come into his life loomed large in his mind, as if waiting for him to give it attention.

"Charlie thinks I need to let him go, but I can't." He looked into Shelby's eyes and found himself wanting to share the memories he did have, the only ones he had left. "I remember how he'd come home in his uniform and read me a book before bed. He'd do all the voices. He was great at that." And then he would call Vander his little bear and wish him happy dreams before kissing him goodnight.

Vander hadn't had happy dreams since his daddy's murder.

"He was a great dad. I wish I'd told him that more."

Shelby wrapped her arms around him, and he felt comforted by the hands soothing the tight muscles of his back. "I'm not a good person to talk about letting go," she told him. "J.P. said he's mostly made his peace with Daddy leaving, but this search dredged things up. Mostly, I can't seem to stop asking questions that start with why. Mama says they're the worst kind you can ask. They kill your joy."

Her mother wasn't wrong, but it was human nature to ask them. "Maybe we can help each other let go. I haven't thought about his anniversary as much because of you."

She leaned back and gazed at him. "I'm glad."

"I...don't go to his gravesite to remember him," Vander confessed. "Only Charlie knows where I go."

Her hand came to rest on his cheek, and he found the courage to keep going. "I have a drink of his favorite bourbon—Bulleit—from his flask in the alley where he was murdered."

"Oh, honey," Shelby said, fitting him to her again.

"I remember teasing him about drinking something named after the bullets he put in his gun," he continued, feeling raw to the core. "Dad used to say drinking bullets in liquid form made him invincible to the real ones. It was his way of assuring me he'd be safe on the streets when I'd cling to him before he left for work. Of course, it didn't make him invincible at all."

"What about your mama?" she asked.

"She wasn't invincible either," he said sadly and proceeded to tell her the rest, everything from their move to Boston and her and her family's indifference about the past to their ultimate rift when he'd decided to go back to Nashville for college.

"Come with me," Shelby said when he was finished, taking his hand and leading him into the family room. She laid on the couch and stretched out her arms. "You need some holding."

His chest was growing tighter by the moment, and he needed to regain control of himself, especially before they left to meet her family. "I'm fine."

The look she gave him could have scorched the sidewalk and left a mark. "Come here, Vander."

He put his hands on his hips. "Shelby, I'm fine."

"I said, 'Come here.' You don't want to mess with me just now."

There was no mistaking her will. He'd seen her assert it before, but never quite like this. He decided not to fight her and let himself settle against her on the couch.

"Put your head on my chest," she said, guiding him.

"My favorite place," he joked.

He couldn't help but grin when she swatted him. "Be quiet and let me... Oh, you're such a man."

"Thank you," he said, his head resting on the best pillows in all of Tennessee if not all of the United States of America. "I seem to remember you trying to talk Sadie out of crying."

"That was because it was in front of you," she told him, massaging his temples softly. "You were a stranger then, and it wasn't professional."

Being professional was so important to her. She prided herself on it, and why shouldn't she? She'd worked hard for all she had.

"Shelby—"

"Oh, be quiet, you infernal man," she ground out. "I'm trying to comfort you."

The funny thing was, he actually did feel better. His chest wasn't as tight, and his throat had eased up some. Since she was getting all riled up, he decided to shut up and enjoy the feel of her hands soothing his temples. Her heart beat strong and sure under him, and he finally sighed.

"There," she said, twining her arms around him. "That's better."

They stayed that way for a long while, and when he glanced at the clock, he rose onto an elbow over her. Her long brown hair was flowing over her shoulders, and her eyes were wet at the creases.

"Were you crying for me?" he asked, astounded.

"I was crying for you and me and all of us," she said. "We deserved to have our daddys. I don't know why we didn't, and we sure as heck can't change the past, but it's still sucky, if you ask me."

He loved how she used the word sucky instead of shitty and a whole host of other phrases. "I'm falling completely under your spell," he said in a deep voice. "I think I'm in love with you."

"Oh, me too," she said, caressing his jaw. "Vander, I...I want to be with you. I've...decided."

He felt the punch of her statement all the way to his toes. He knew what that meant.

"Are you going to say the words?" he asked, aware of how she lowered her eyes to break their gaze.

"I thought it might be too soon. Oh, good heavens, I need to sit up. I can't breathe."

He rearranged them on the couch and watched as she sucked in air, her hand pressed to her brow.

"You don't have to make love with me, Shelby," he said. "I'm not pressuring you."

Her eyes shot to his. "I said I wanted to, didn't I? And I know you're not pressuring me. Thank you for that. Maybe I want to. All right?"

When she started to feel like she was coming undone, as she liked to say, she always stoked up her internal fire. He'd paid attention. "I'm glad you want to. I want to too. So, let me understand. You aren't going to say the words just yet?" He could feel a slow smile cross his face.

The look she gave him was coupled with a head shake that would have put the fear of God in some. Not him.

"Oh, you're an odious man," she said, shoving him away from her on the couch.

He clasped her to him. "I told you I'm falling in love with you too."

She stilled in his arms. Her gaze latched on to his. "Well, I'm not falling. I *am* in love with you."

"Leave it to you to quibble over the right way to say it." He bit his lip to keep from smiling.

She glared at him. "*Why* I love you, I couldn't tell you. Part of me wants to talk myself out of it. Say it's too soon. Say I'm just making excuses to get naked with you."

He didn't dare laugh. "But it's not that simple, is it?"

"We should go," she said, trying to pull away.

He brought her to his chest. "I thought it was too soon too, but I promised myself I wouldn't be blind to how I feel. Shelby, I love you. I love pretty much everything about you, from the way you say 'oh poo' to how brave you are. But mostly, I love how big your heart is and how you keep throwing coins into Gail's fountain and wishing for things." He still didn't believe in wishes, but he liked that she did.

She reared back, her eyes wide and sparkly. "You really mean it? You're not still in the falling-for stage?"

"Would I say something like all that without meaning it?" he asked.

She studied his face before shaking her head. "No, you wouldn't. You always tell the truth. I love you too."

"I know," he said, cupping her cheek. "You wouldn't have decided to make love with me if you'd felt otherwise."

Her chest rose with a huge breath again. "I'm a little nervous about it all. I...don't have much experience. I *want* to please you."

He kissed her gently on the lips. "You don't need to worry about that. We're going to be incredible together. Can't you feel it?"

That made her smile. "Wait a minute. You said you *pretty much* love everything about me. What don't you love?"

"Are you kidding me?" he asked, laughing. "It's a turn of phrase, Shelby." But he knew she liked to turn phrases until they couldn't turn anymore. She was Southern like that.

"Are you sure about that?" she asked, poking him in the ribs.

"I'm sure," he said, tugging her off the couch. "Of course you would tell me you love me and want to make love with me right before we leave to meet your family."

Her grin was pure mischief. "Gives you some incentive to get through this evening, doesn't it?"

"You had a strategy?" He shook his head. "How could I not love you when you think like that?"

"Stick with me, honey," she said, smoothing her dress down her body like it was a meditation. "You're going to learn even more ways you love me."

He gulped. "For a woman without a lot of experience, you sure as hell know how to bring me to my knees."

She waggled her brows. "There's a lot of ways to learn things. There's book learning, and then there's actual experience. I might be a little heavy on the former, but I plan to change all that. Can you take off work tomorrow?"

He thought through his schedule. His calendar pretty much boasted back-to-back meetings with clients. Would it be irresponsible to cancel everything? He could call in sick. Hah. No one would believe that, least of all Charlie. "Sure. Why not?"

"Really?" Her grin sailed across her face. "Great, I'll call Gail and tell her I'm taking the day off too."

"Have you told Gail about us yet?" he asked.

She shook her head. "No. I wanted to..."

"Give it a little more time," he finished for her. "You might want to tell her this week. There's something I need to share too. Gail has been jokingly coming on to me for years. I've never thought she was serious, or I wouldn't have continued a professional relationship with her."

"Coming on to you, huh?" Shelby said, sauntering over to him. "Well, she certainly talks about what a man you are. I'm glad you said something." She ran her hands up his chest and twined her arms around his neck.

"We really need to go, Shelby," he uttered in a deep voice, visions of them tangled up in the sheets later tonight playing in Technicolor in his head.

"I know," she said. "I'm prepared, by the way."

"What does that mean?" he asked.

She flushed. "I bought a selection of condoms."

He bit his lip to keep from laughing. "A selection, huh?"

Her fist punched him in the gut. "Do you have any idea how many choices there are? I had no idea what you liked. I mean, seriously! There are as many choices of condoms as there are types of yogurt. I had no idea!"

"Yogurt," he managed, but he couldn't keep a straight face. "Oh, Shelby, you're so funny sometimes."

"Don't you dare make fun of me," she said, giving him another playful swat. "I thought everyone in the drugstore was looking at me, judging me. Vander, I've made an appointment with my doctor, but it takes—"

"Time," he answered, holding her in place when she tried to push away from him. "I'm clean, by the way."

"I thought you would be," she said, "but thanks for telling me before I asked. I haven't been with anyone since college. I suppose you should know there was only one guy, and his attention waned pretty soon after we'd... With him, I never felt like I was...oh, heavens, this is embarrassing...eager to do it every time. I'm rather hoping I feel that way with you."

Since she was beet red to the roots of her hair, he took his time kissing her softly until she relaxed against him. "I don't think we're going to have any trouble in that department. Shelby, you can trust me to make it hot for you."

She shivered all over. "Oh, I like hearing you promise that. Now, we'd really better go. I'd call and say we got caught up, but Mama will be on me like a swarm of angry bees. She's determined to meet you and make sure you're not a wolf in sheep's clothing."

"The sooner we get there, the sooner we can come back here," he told her.

"Just promise..." she said, taking his hand.

"What?"

"That you won't change your mind about wanting to be with me after meeting Mama. I'm afraid she's going to put you through the wringer. You just...stand your ground and tell her the truth. Mama believes in church-going and community, but I think she'll respect your beliefs. She's generally open-minded."

Except where it concerned her children. He'd seen it a thousand times with clients. They treated the rest of the world differently than they treated their families. He had a feeling Louisa was going to be the same.

"I won't change my mind about you, Shelby," he said. "I can't imagine not wanting to be with you. That's how I knew I loved you. I've never...longed for anyone's company like I do for yours." And no one else had ever lessened his grief about his father. Not even Charlie.

"I long for you too," she said in a hushed voice, her brown eyes shining. "I'm glad we found each other, Vander."

"Me too."

CHAPTER 25

SHELBY FELT LIKE SHE WAS COMING OUT OF HER SKIN IN the best way ever as Vander drove them out to Jake and Susannah's house. He loved her. He really did! And he'd opened up even more about his daddy. Her heart felt like a wine skin ready to burst.

Oh, she couldn't wait to be with him tonight. It was going to be delicious.

They just needed to get through the next couple of hours.

When they arrived, Rory and Annabelle were waiting for them in the driveway. Annabelle looked pretty as a peach in a purple dress decorated with ice cream cones. Rory was riding a bright blue bike.

"Hi!" Annabelle said, running over. Shelby realized there was a butterfly catcher clutched in her small hand. "Are you Shelby's boyfriend? Folks have been talking about you. I'm Annabelle. I'm six. I'm going to be in first grade when we go back to school."

"Good to meet you, Annabelle. I'm Vander." He crouched down and smiled. "Catch any butterflies yet?"

She held out the catcher. "I think it's broken. Every time I get one inside, it manages to sneak back out. Uncle Rye said he'll help me later, but he's keeping an eye on Aunt Tory. She's working too hard even though she doesn't live here. Uncle Rye says no woman about ready to have a baby should cook. What do you think?"

Vander's lips twitched. "I think your Uncle Rye is a smart man," he said.

"He's the smartest," Rory said, jumping off his bike and propping it up with the kickstand. "Except for our daddy. He's pretty smart too. Uncle Rye said you must be pretty smart yourself to get Aunt Shelby to give you the time of day."

Vander grabbed Shelby's hand as he stood, and both of them burst out laughing. "Yes, she is pretty particular about who she spends her time with," he finally said.

"Women are supposed to be particular," Annabelle informed him, shaking her catcher dangerously in his direction. "That's what makes us special. Aunt Amelia says that all the time."

"I can't wait to meet your Aunt Amelia," Vander said. "Sounds like she and your Aunt Shelby are two peas in a pod."

"There are more than two peas in a pod," Annabelle told Vander seriously. "Mama is growing some in our garden out back. There's like a whole bunch of peas in one pod."

His lips twitched. "You're absolutely right."

She tilted her head to the side. "Are you humoring me because you're Aunt Shelby's boyfriend?"

"Annabelle!" Shelby said, giving her a look. "Of course he isn't."

"I tend to call a spade a spade," Vander answered. "Seems you do the same."

"I do," she told him seriously. "Uncle Rye says it stops trouble from breaking out."

Vander cleared his throat, and Shelby had to bite the inside of her mouth to keep from laughing out loud.

"Uncle Rye said you did some work for him and that he likes you," Rory said. "That means you're okay by me."

"Me too!" the little girl agreed.

"Come on, Annabelle," Rory said. "Best let them head on inside."

"We'll see you later," the little girl said, running off with her catcher, slashing it through the air.

"Those butterflies had better watch out," Vander said under his breath.

"Indeed," Shelby said as they went inside. "She's a handful. Tammy was in an abusive relationship before coming to Dare River with Rye. The kids act older than their age."

"I saw a newspaper article about the concert Rye threw to raise money for domestic violence," Vander said as they walked toward the kitchen, where Shelby knew they'd find some people. "I recall mention of his sister."

"Yes," she said, reaching for his hand when they were a foot outside the kitchen. "I'm so glad she and J.P. found each other. Now, are you ready?"

"You don't need to worry about me," Vander assured her. "I'm good with people, and I can handle myself."

"You haven't met Mama," she said, pasting a smile on her face and kissing her finger and tapping it to his lips. "For luck."

"I'll hold out for a better kiss later," he said as they entered the hustle and bustle.

Rye was hovering over Tory at the kitchen island as she loaded up vegetables on top of what looked like pulled-pork nachos. "I don't understand why you won't let me or someone else assemble the nachos. It's not like they're difficult to make."

She wiggled around him, her pregnant belly looking like a prize watermelon. "I've seen the way you dump fixings. You have no sense of presentation—despite how much you love food."

"I love to eat," he said, his mouth tight with worry. "I've never said I love to present. It all ends up in the same place anyway. Tory, honey, won't you please sit down and let someone help you? You'll only be tired later."

"I'm tired at night because I'm carrying an extra fifteen pounds and your baby, Rye Crenshaw." She stopped and put her hands out. "Will you please stop fussing over me? You're driving me crazy!"

"I love you!" he said, taking her shoulders in his hands. Then he looked over his shoulder and spotted them. "Oh, hi. Sorry you had to hear our little tiff. My wife here is being stubborn. Like usual. Vander, it's good to see you again, man."

While the men shook hands, Shelby hustled over to hug Tory.

"He makes me want to smack him sometimes," Tory whispered in her ear. "I'm pregnant, not dying. I swear."

"He means well," Shelby said, to which Tory gave an emphatic, "*Humph.* But I like the look of your man just fine."

"Me too," she whispered back before releasing her.

"It's good to see you too, Rye," Vander said. "Congratulations on the baby."

"Thank you," Rye said. "I'd like you to meet my wife. Tory, this is Vander Montgomery, one of the best private investigators in the South. Before I needed full-time support, he used to do some great work for me. Runs a top-notch firm here in Nashville."

Shelby expected Rye had already told Tory that and a heck of a lot more, but he was just observing the pleasantries.

"It's a pleasure to meet you, Vander," Tory said, shaking his hand. "We're glad you could join us today."

"Yes, we are," Rye said, stroking his jaw. "I wish I'd known y'all were seeing each other earlier—not that anyone tells me anything around here."

"I didn't know either," Tory said, handing him a chip. "Eat that. It might improve your disposition."

Rye crunched happily on the chip. "Come with me, Vander. I'll introduce you around. Shelby, maybe you can talk Tory into letting you help her?"

"I'd...rather go with Vander, Rye," Shelby said. "If you don't mind."

"Oh, of course," Rye answered with a knowing wink. "Your mama has been hot to meet him. I've never seen her fret about much of anything. Guess it's different when it's your own child. My kid's not even born yet, and when I think about the baby being a girl and dating anyone, I want to puke my guts out—or take out my shotgun."

Shelby swallowed thickly. "Aren't you just making us both feel better, Rye? Come on, Vander."

"Everyone is out back," Tory said. "The weather isn't too oppressive for once."

Shelby nodded and led Vander through the massive house to the French doors that led to the deck. Sadie was the first to see them and jumped out of her chair to rush over.

"Hello, there," she said, her smile as bright as her lime green dress. "Welcome, Vander."

Shelby leaned in and hissed, "You're supposed to pretend you don't know him." Apparently, Sadie had forgotten the chat she'd had with J.P. and the rest of them about their "cover." Heavens, she hated the thought of it.

Sadie gave a pout. "I'm only being friendly." She stuck out her hand. "Hello. I'm Sadie."

Vander was fighting a smile. "Hello, Sadie."

Amelia Ann bounded over with Clayton in tow.

"Good to see you again, Vander," Clayton said before Shelby could make the introductions. "Been a while."

"You two know each other?" Sadie asked. "Right, if you worked for Rye..."

"Goodness, the way people are connected sometimes," Sadie said.

"We're happy to have you join us," Amelia Ann said. "You have friends here. I for one am pleased to make your acquaintance. Clayton sings your praises, and he's a tough customer."

"Shelby told me about your work at the legal clinic," Vander said. "I'm always happy to meet someone committed to justice. Clayton is a lucky man from where I'm sitting."

She linked her arm through his. "Oh, I like you already. Come, let me introduce you to my parents. Shelby, the rest of your clan is out in the gardens looking at how Tammy has transformed this place. The roses are pretty stunning."

After meeting Hampton and Margaret Hollins, who only seemed to get happier with each other as each month of their reconciliation passed, Shelby took a deep breath and walked with Vander to the rose garden.

Sure enough, the rest of her family was there, exclaiming over the various colors and scents of roses. J.P. caught sight of them first and strode over.

"Welcome, Vander," he said, shaking his hand. "It's good to have you here."

Vander put his hand to the center of Shelby's back and rubbed the tension there, and she realized he was trying to comfort *her*. Oh, she was going to kiss that man senseless when they got home.

Everyone else wandered forward, and Shelby made the introductions, saving her mama, who was watching everyone like a hawk, for last.

"And this is my mama, Reverend Louisa," Shelby said, giving her mama what she hoped was an easy smile despite the fact that her insides felt like sour cream.

"It's a pleasure to meet you," Vander said, shaking her hand when she held it out. "What would you prefer I call you? Reverend? Louisa?"

"Louisa is fine," she told him. "Rye speaks highly of you. So does Clayton."

"It's been fun to watch his career explode," Vander said. "He was just getting hot when he and Clayton contracted my firm."

"You own your own business, I hear," Mama said, fingering a few white rose petals she was holding in her hand. "And Gail uses you still, I understand."

"I don't advertise my client list," Vander said, "but I don't think Gail would mind me saying I've done work for her. She's a heck of a businesswoman."

"Indeed," Mama said, nodding. "She hired my daughter."

"Gail might be a little eccentric," Shelby's stepfather,

Dale, added, smiling at her, "but you can't pull the wool over her head."

Shelby refrained from mentioning her boss' two ex-husbands. "Gail has taught me so much." Oh, how much small talk were they going to suffer through before Mama relaxed her eager-beaver interest?

"Gail's been good to you," Mama said, nodding. "Are your people from here, Vander? Shelby didn't say."

That wasn't entirely true. Mama wanted to see how Vander answered. "My mother moved out here from back east to go to Vanderbilt. It's where she and my father met. He was from Nashville."

"Was?" her mama asked. Susannah shot Shelby a compassionate glance. Yeah, she'd been through this too.

"Mama, I mentioned Vander had lost his daddy as a boy," she said, reaching for his hand, peeved beyond belief.

"It's okay, Shelby," Vander said. "He was a local police detective, Louisa."

"I see," Mama said, gazing at him in that unflinching way she had. Growing up, they used to call it her way of playing chicken with folks. "I'm sorry for your loss."

Well, at least she'd said something nice. For a moment there, Shelby had worried Mama was growing horns.

"Dinner should be ready soon," Susannah said, reaching for Jake's hand. "We should head back to the house and finish up."

Vander held her mama's stare as the others started walking back to the house.

"Come on, Louisa," Dale said, clearing his throat to get her attention. "Vander and Shelby don't have a drink yet, and it's hot out here."

Shelby wished she could give Dale a kiss. Mama had met Dale Adams when he'd joined her church after moving to town. He'd just gotten divorced and had no children. A few years later, not long after Shelby turned twelve, he and Mama had gotten hitched.

He'd never stepped into the role of father, not wanting to step on J.P.'s toes. But he was a good man, and Mama was happy with him. He let her do all the talking and run the church, preferring to be the quiet one in the corner who set up chairs or broke down tables, whatever was required.

"I'll look forward to hearing more about you, Vander," Mama said, finally breaking their staring match.

"I'm going to show Vander the garden," Shelby called out. "We'll be right in."

Her mama cast one narrowed look over her shoulder before increasing her speed to the house.

"Ready to run yet, honey?" she asked Vander.

"That wasn't bad," he responded.

"I'm not sure she's done with you yet."

Bless the man. All he did was shrug and give her a crooked smile.

CHAPTER 26

VANDER WAS AT EASE IN GROUPS. ALWAYS HAD BEEN. After his dad had been murdered, he'd felt more comfortable talking to adults than kids his own age. What normal child knew what it was like to experience that kind of tragedy? But most adults had lost someone, whether or not it was from violence. They were willing to listen to him when his mother posted her No Talking sign up on her heart.

Catching up with Rye and Clayton was fun, and it felt good to shoot the shit with J.P. and Jake. They were all the kind of men he gravitated toward: strong and comfortable in their own skin. Vander dealt with enough assholes in his profession. He didn't put up with them in his personal life.

Rory and Annabelle were entertaining. Only a girl with a delightful sense of humor could name her dog Barbie.

Then there was Shelby. She was never too far away from him. He sensed she felt protective of him here among her family, and for a man who never felt the need to be protected, it gave him a warm feeling. He couldn't wait to get her home.

Louisa watched him all through a dinner fit for any five-star restaurant in Nashville. He was stuffed by the time he pushed back from the table with the rest of the family.

"Vander?" Louisa called. "I'd like to walk you down to the

river."

Shelby put her hand on him, going on full alert. He leaned in and kissed her cheek.

"It will be fine," he whispered in her ear. "Save a piece of pie for me."

She nodded, and he set off to join her mother. They walked out back and headed through the gardens until they reached an open field, which led to Dare River. She kept quiet, walking with her hands folded behind her back. Vander kept his own counsel, knowing she would speak as soon as she was ready.

When they reached the river's edge, she gestured to the bench situated there, one that held a magnificent view. Water rushed over moss-covered rocks as dragonflies raced across the surface. A trio of turtles sunned themselves on an exposed log under a blue sky filled with puffy clouds resembling cotton balls.

He sat down, and she sat beside him, pushing her gray hair behind her ear. Shelby had her hair, the kind that curled of its own volition. Louisa's was shorter though, barely cresting past her jawline.

"Out of all my daughters, Shelby has always been in the greatest hurry," Louisa began.

Vander smiled, and their eyes met for a moment. He realized hers were green.

"Perhaps it's a mother's intuition, but she seems to be in a hurry with you," Louisa said. "It's got me worrying some."

Vander studied the river and took a moment before replying. "We've both been surprised by the pace of our relationship, but we also know our own minds. If you're wanting to know if this is normal for me, I can assure you it isn't. Your daughter is one of the most amazing women I've ever met, and it's because she's so amazing that I want to spend every moment with her. Usually all I want to do is work. I love what I do, and it requires a lot of social time with clients and the community. Shelby makes me forget about all that in a good way."

She nodded, folding her hands prayer style in her lap. "That eases my mind some."

"Good," Vander said, deciding to be plainspoken too. "What else will?"

Her chest rose, and he could tell she was having trouble getting a breath. "I don't know what she's told you about her daddy, but your profession is giving me some discomfort. Not that it's not an honorable one. That's not what I'm suggesting."

He could see the writing on the wall and braced himself for what was to come. "Go on."

"Shelby has never known anyone with the skills to find a person," Louisa said. "Until now."

"I'm listening," he said.

"I don't want you to encourage her to find her daddy," Louisa said, giving him a sudden case of heartburn. "Even if she asks you straight out, which I fear she will."

"Why are you afraid she'll ask?" Vander asked, meeting her gaze. "Moreover, why are you afraid to have her find him if it's what she wants?"

She flinched. "My reasons are my own—as I've always told the children when they ask me about him. Shelby is the most inquisitive of my bunch, although Sadie has asked questions too. I don't want them to get hurt. Some things are best left in the past. I've learned that the hard way."

"Louisa, I love your daughter," Vander said. "That means I support her. I can't promise you not to support her if she asks me to."

She narrowed her eyes at him. "If you 'help' her in this matter, it could tear apart this family. That is *not* all right by me, and I'm the mama."

A mama with claws, it was clear. "Forgive me, Louisa, but as a man who lost his father at a young age, I can tell you that sometimes the past doesn't stay there. In a few weeks, it's the twenty-fifth anniversary of my father's unsolved murder. There isn't a day that goes by that I don't think about him and wonder why it happened."

"I read that about you online," Louisa said, giving a deep sigh.

A few articles had been written about him opening up shop in Nashville, serving the same community his father had. He didn't express any concern, which made her frown darken.

"I looked you up," she said, continuing. "I'm sorry for your loss. Truly. I can't begin to understand what it must have been like for you, but there'll be no true peace in your life until you let the past go."

Vander stood, his shadow covering her. Anger unfurled inside him, some of it not from her. His mother had said the same things to him.

"From my perspective, Louisa, you don't seem to have let the past go. Not if you're asking promises of me that could undermine your daughter's wishes, notwithstanding her happiness."

"Excuse me?"

"I love Shelby, and she loves me. Yes, we've moved fast, but as my best friend recently pointed out, I usually make my mind up about things straight away. Shelby and I are good together, and I want us to keep being good together. That means I support her and her needs—not yours. I hope you can understand that."

She stood as well, coming only to the center of his chest. "I do understand that, and I respect it. I just don't like it."

He had to give her points for honesty.

She rubbed her forehead like she had a headache coming on. "I want to like you, Vander. You seem like a good man, and from everything I've read about you, you've done an incredible job becoming who you are. I also see the way you treat my daughter, the way you look at her—and how she's been guarding you from me. She's given her whole heart to you."

Somehow hearing Louisa tell him how much Shelby had fallen for him cinched everything between them in a whole new way. They didn't need to rush into marriage, but he could feel it there, waiting on the horizon. For a man who hadn't thought of growing old, let alone getting married, it was quite a realization.

"I'm glad you see that," he responded, coming back to the moment. "Given that, how could you expect me to say anything different?"

She raised a brow. "If you said anything different, you wouldn't be the man for her."

"So this was a test."

"Perhaps," she said, starting to walk back. "You're right about Shelby always knowing her own mind. It's how I raised my children."

"You just don't like it when their opinions conflict with yours," he said, falling in step with her.

She stopped and turned to face him. "If and when you ever become a parent, you'll find yourself struggling with the same thing. I try and be a good person every day. Live a good life. Treat people as I want to be treated. Just like the Good Book says. Vander, I can promise you I would never wish for my children to learn anything more about their daddy and why he left. If I could, I would erase it from my own mind. I hope you'll remember that."

When she took off again, he didn't follow her immediately, sensing she needed time to compose herself before rejoining the others.

He turned around and looked back at the river, soaking in the perfect diorama of the natural order. The water knew which direction to take. The dragonflies knew how to take flight. Soon the turtles would breathe underwater when they took a swim off the log.

Vander didn't believe things happened for a reason. He believed it was his job as an investigator to figure out why something had interrupted the natural order. A father who wanted to raise his son wasn't supposed to be taken away from him.

Louisa was wrong.

Sometimes peace only came from finding out what had happened to make life deviate from the path it should have taken.

As he walked back to the house, he was filled with questions about what had broken the McGuiness home and why a woman as forthright as Louisa didn't want anyone to find out.

CHAPTER 27

THE MINUTE SHELBY AND VANDER CLOSED THE CAR doors, she pounced on him.

"All right, what did Mama say to you? She was pale as a church mouse when she came back from your walk. It took everything in me not to march across the room and ask her."

Part of the reason she hadn't was fear. She wasn't sure she *wanted* to know what Mama had said.

"So it's okay to ask me?" he asked, driving them to the main highway.

She worried her lip. "Vander, let's be real. Of course I'm going to ask you. I'm upset."

"I know you are," he said, "and I'm sorry for it. Heck, poor Sadie looked like she was... What do you call it? Fixing to come undone when I came inside too. And Susannah..."

"Everyone was on pins and needles while you were gone," Shelby said, digging her fingernails into her palms. "We don't like lying to Mama or causing strife."

"Well, your Mama is equally concerned," Vander said, putting his hand on her knee. "Shelby, she's worried you're going to ask me to look into your daddy's whereabouts. She asked me not to."

"She did not!" Shelby said, shocked Mama would interfere like that. "My goodness, that's a horrible thing to do to you."

"And to you," he added, caressing her knee. "But she means well. Whatever she's trying to keep a lid on, she's gripping it with all her might."

"You didn't promise her, did you?" she asked.

"Of course not. I told her I loved you and that meant supporting you. I also said it wasn't good of her to ask that of me, especially since she admitted to knowing how much you love me too."

Her heart welled, hearing him talk like that. She wanted to take her seatbelt off and snuggle up against his side.

"She also thinks we're moving too fast," he said, patting her knee again. "I told her we'd talked about that, but we both know our minds pretty well."

"What else?"

"That's about it," he said with a shrug. "She said she wanted to like me, that she even respected me. But I worried her. You did too. She said you've always been inquisitive."

True that, she thought. "So Mama didn't seem to know we've already looked?"

"No," he told her, removing his hand from her knee to take a sharp turn. "I suppose that's the silver lining in all this. But she thinks you're going to want to. She's a little behind the curve, but she's got your number, all right."

"Lovely!" Shelby said, falling back against her seat. "Oh, this just makes me all the more curious. By all that's holy, *why* won't she tell us her side of things? Dammit, now that Daddy turned coward for the second time and up and ran, Mama is the only one who knows anything." When Vander didn't respond, she turned her head. "I wish..."

She trailed off, feeling the deep sadness she'd been fighting so hard descend upon her. Suddenly she felt exhausted and weepy—and cold.

"Can you turn down the air conditioner, please?" she asked, looking out the window.

"Sure," he said, putting his hand back on her knee and stroking it. "Shelby, I'm sorry."

"I am too," she said, turning sideways in the seat and bringing her legs up as far underneath her as possible.

When they reached her home, Vander came around and opened her door. He helped her out and pulled her against him. She let him hold her until better sense prevailed.

"We shouldn't be making a spectacle by the street," she said, untangling herself and walking to the door, which she then opened with her key.

He closed the door behind her, and she rubbed the back of her neck. Hours ago, she'd told him she wanted to make love with him. Right now, that was the furthest thing from her mind.

"If you'll give me a little time, I promise to rally," she said, putting her purse on the table in the entryway.

He turned her and raised her face to his by tipping her jaw up. "Shelby, when we make love for the first time, we should both be thinking of nothing else. You had a tough day. There's nothing you need to rally for."

She wanted to give in to a good cry right then and there.

He reached up and caressed her cheek. "But I'd like to hold you if that's okay. Maybe stay a while. You don't need to be alone. Earlier when I was upset, talking about my dad, you supported me. I want to do that for you."

Leaning her head against his chest, she wrapped her arms around him. "Don't misunderstand what I'm saying, but having you hold me... Right now, it would be better than making love."

"I know," he said, and she could hear the smile in his voice. "But that will be good too."

She already knew that.

CHAPTER 28

SADIE STARTED MONDAY BREATHING EASIER. SHE'D GOTTEN through another Sunday family dinner with Mama and held it together.

Then her phone rang, and she felt her lungs shrivel up in her chest. Mama! She thought about letting it go to voicemail, but this couldn't continue. She didn't want it to, and Mama wouldn't allow it.

"Hi, Mama," she answered brightly, clutching her coffee mug.

"Hi, honey," Mama said. "I thought I'd see what you were up to. I didn't get to talk to you much yesterday, what with all the excitement about Shelby's new beau."

Sadie's hand jerked at the mention of Vander, and coffee sloshed over the rim of her mug, spilling onto the counter. "Oh, shoot! Wait a sec, Mama. I just spilled something."

Hold it together, girl. She mopped the mess up, wishing she hadn't taken the call. Clearly she wasn't in her right mind.

"Okay, I'm back," Sadie said, deciding the best tack was to get Mama talking. "How's your day going?"

Monday was usually a lighter day for Mama after all the Sunday services. She was fond of calling it cleanup day.

"Have you started next Sunday's sermon yet?" she asked.

"Yes," Mama responded. "It's going to be about letting go

of the past and living in the present."

Sadie gulped. "That sounds lovely." *Get off the phone, get off the phone.*

"Honey, I'm worried Vander's profession as a private investigator will give Shelby ideas about looking for your daddy. She hasn't mentioned anything about that to you, has she?"

Oh, dear sweet baby Jesus. "Mama, why aren't you asking Shelby about this?" she feinted, her heart pounding in her chest.

"I don't think she'll be honest with me."

"Mama, Vander doesn't strike me as the kind of man to put ideas in anyone's head. He's not a manipulator."

"So you like him?" Mama asked.

She cleared her throat. "Yes. He seems like a straightforward kind of person. Shelby talks highly of him." A flash of inspiration struck. "So do Rye and Clayton, and that's saying a lot."

"Your brother said the same thing when I asked his opinion of the man last night."

Uh-oh. Mama was making the rounds. "See. You've always say J.P. is a great judge of character."

"Indeed he is," Mama said. "I just can't ignore this feeling I have. Sadie, I've been praying nonstop since I heard about this man. I fear..."

She didn't want to ask. She really didn't. "What, Mama?"

"I don't want Vander's own tragedy with his daddy to influence him to...well...offer to help Shelby look for your daddy."

Now Sadie understood where Mama was going with this. "Mama, I don't think you need to worry."

"I hope you're right," Mama said, sighing heavily. "Dale tells me I'm worrying over nothing, but I just can't help it. I've told all of you children how important it is to not look back. The past can only hurt you."

Sadie could feel herself growing hot, almost like she

was standing in the center of the road under the sun, the asphalt burning her feet. "Mama, you don't always say that. Sometimes you say you have to face the past in order to heal from it. Look at what you did with Jake. He had to face what happened to his best friend in Iraq before he could let it go."

"That's simplifying things, Sadie," Mama said crisply. "It was the chains of the past and wishing things were different that kept Jake so upset. He couldn't make peace with it or forgive God or himself for what had happened. As I told Jake, the details don't matter. It's putting all that pain and guilt aside with grace that helps people move forward."

Sadie had to bite her lip. Suddenly all she wanted to do was argue with Mama and say something like *How can we let go of the past if we don't know why Daddy left us and why he ran again when we tried to find him?* "Mama, I need to go."

"Oh," she said, and Sadie could hear the shock in her voice. She'd never cut Mama off before. She knew everyone in her family saw her as the soft one, the biddable one. "All right, honey. But you'll tell me if I have anything to worry about, won't you? I'm just trying to do what's best here. As your Mama."

She could feel hot sweat break out across her skin, and for a moment, it was shocking to realize she wanted to throw her phone across the room and watch it break apart into little pieces—just like she was feeling inside.

"Mama, I won't meddle in Shelby and Vander's relationship," she said definitively, no sweetness in her tone. "They're happy and in love, and this puts a dark cloud over things."

"Sadie!"

"Mama, I'm sorry, but this time you're wrong. Goodbye."

She hung up the phone and burst into tears. Her phone rang again, but she didn't answer it this time. The pressure was too much. She dragged herself over to the couch, pulled one of her quilts over her, and bawled her eyes out.

Her head hurt, and her nose was stuffy when she finally

quieted. She blew her nose as loudly as a goose squawking and didn't even care how unladylike it sounded.

She sat in the quiet, her heart hurting, and prayed for guidance. The peace she normally felt while talking to God didn't come. She prayed harder, but soon she was thinking, not praying, and she was all tied up in knots again.

Crossing to pick up her phone, she called J.P. He answered immediately.

"Hey," she said, sniffling. "I didn't know who else to call."

"What's wrong?" he asked, an edge in his voice.

"Mama called me to ask if Shelby had mentioned having Vander look into the past. J.P., I told Mama I wouldn't inform on Shelby and pretty much hung up on her."

"Oh, Sadie," he said. "Mama is worried, is all."

"I know, and I'm trying to understand." She fell silent. "J.P., I'm suddenly so mad. I had a vision of throwing my phone across the room. Why won't Mama talk about it? I've done lost my patience with her."

"It's okay to be mad, Sadie," he said. "When Daddy left us, I threw a ball against the side of the house for hours every day after school. Mama never stopped me, but she never came out to talk to me either. I used to be mad about that."

"I didn't know," she said, her heart hurting for him. "I wish I hadn't been a baby. I would have talked to you."

"Aren't you the sweetest?" her brother said. "When Daddy ran this time, I found myself getting mad all over again. I was short-tempered with the dogs this weekend, and that's not like me. We're all stirred up. How could we not be?"

"Should we just tell Mama now and get it over with? I was praying before I called you—not well, mind—and it occurred to me that maybe we should just hold onto our backsides and jump."

"Let me call Shelby and Susannah and see if they can pop over for lunch," he said. "You don't have to go in to the craft store until this afternoon, right? Since you have your quilting circle tonight."

"Right."

"Susannah hasn't called me yet," her brother continued, "but I expect Mama called her too."

Yeah, that was likely. "I don't like this, J.P."

"Me either," he said, "but we'll weather it okay because we love each other. I'll text you right back about lunch."

Sure enough, he texted her back fifteen minutes later. He'd arranged for lunch to be at one o'clock at Shelby's house, the earliest their middle sister could get away. Sadie offered to cook something, but J.P. said he'd pick up salad and sandwiches. He gave her some more encouraging words, which soothed her heart some.

Sadie arrived at Shelby's five minutes early, only to discover she was the last to arrive.

"Hey," Shelby said simply when she opened the door and hugged her.

Sadie held her tight. Her sister had been radio silent the night before—something that was becoming her new normal now that she and Vander spent so much time together. Since Shelby had been tied to her phone more than any of their siblings, that alone spoke volumes. Sadie was happy for her sister, but she missed her too—they'd always been almost as close as twins.

"Come on," Shelby said. "Come on. Let's get you inside."

Susannah was pouring sweet tea while J.P. unpacked sandwiches from brown paper bags and put them on plates.

"Hi, Sadie," Susannah said, crossing to hug her. "I had to sneak away from my decorating job to be here, so I can't stay long."

Her sister's body was rigid with tension, and there was an edge to her voice.

"Did Mama call you?" she asked when they separated.

"Yes," Susannah responded, crossing her arms. "I don't like this. Not one bit."

"No one does, Susannah," J.P. said, arranging the plates around the kitchen table. "Come sit down, y'all. We'll talk this through."

When they all sat down, Sadie couldn't help but notice the hard set of Shelby's jaw and the rigid line of Susannah's shoulders. "I cried when I got off the phone with Mama," she admitted.

"Are you saying that to make me feel guilty?" Shelby asked. "Are you thinking it would be easier if I wasn't seeing Vander at all? Then Mama wouldn't be so riled up."

The force of her anger and hurt washed over Sadie, and she could feel her chest fill up again with unshed tears. "Of course not, Shelby. I'm happy for you. I told Mama that I wouldn't meddle. I practically hung up on her!"

"Well, good!" Shelby said, her eyes firing. "She's completely out of line."

"I told you looking for Daddy was only going to hurt us," Susannah shot back. "In the end, we didn't find out anything useful except that he's still a coward and a horrible person."

"That's not true!" Sadie said, jumping into the fray. "We met Me-Mother and Shelby met Vander, and as I was praying this morning, those were the only two things I could think of to be grateful for in all this. Except that I was brave enough to do it in the first place."

"It wasn't brave," Susannah said, ripping the white paper off her sandwich. "It was foolish. Look at all the hurt this is causing us. I've cried too, Sadie."

That shut her up.

"We've all cried," J.P. said softly, making everyone turn and look at him.

From his expression, Sadie could tell he meant it, and she extended her hand to him. He fitted his fingers around hers.

"Seems I wasn't so at peace with the past, after all," J.P. said. "God knows, my heart has been heavy. In my prayers, I've asked to be grateful that all these unhealed feelings are rising to the surface so they can be washed away."

Sadie felt tears burn her eyes. "Mama still doesn't want to talk about it. She told me as much again this morning. Part of me wants to shake her."

"Me too," Shelby said, rubbing her nose like she was fighting off a good cry. "And that breaks my heart. Vander and I both said 'I love you' for the first time yesterday, and instead of being joyous, I cried in his arms."

Susannah looked down, visibly softening. "I'm sorry. I know what it's like to fall in love and have a dark cloud over things. I wouldn't wish that for you, Shelby."

They reached their hands out to one another and fisted them together tight. Sadie was glad to be linked with them. She hated when her siblings fought.

"Honestly, I don't know what to do about Mama," J.P. said, pushing his sandwich away. "I've prayed on it and prayed on it, but I haven't found an answer."

"Maybe you should talk to her," Susannah said to Shelby. "She's talked to Vander and all of us about you, but she hasn't talked *to* you."

"I thought of that," Shelby answered, rubbing her nose again, "but she wants me to assure her I won't ask Vander to look for Daddy, and I can't lie about that."

"We're already lying about not knowing Vander," Susannah said. "Even Jake said it doesn't sit well with him. And some of the extended family doesn't know what's going on. I don't like that none either."

"If we'd found Daddy, it would be different," Sadie said. "But I keep reminding myself I'm grateful for Me-Mother and Vander." They hadn't had the full discussion of how to handle Me-Mother's situation yet, but more than one of them had done research into various possibilities.

"It *was* good to meet Me-Mother, and I'm more committed than ever to helping her," Susannah said, touching her arm. "I'm also glad we got to hear a little more about Daddy. And you're right, Sadie, we're blessed God brought Vander and Shelby together this way. I am happy for you, honey. For both of you."

"We all are," J.P. said. "Vander is a good man, and he's

more than welcome in this family."

From J.P., that meant a lot. Heck, he was pretty much giving Shelby his blessing.

Shelby seemed to know it because she got up from the table and hugged him right where he was sitting. He patted her back, and when she let him go, she brushed away tears as she headed back to her chair. Susannah took hold of her hand again as soon as she sat.

Everyone fell silent.

"If you want me to assure Mama I will never look for Daddy, I will," Shelby finally said, breaking the lull. "I can stretch the truth and tell her I won't look for Daddy in the future because it's true. That's in the past."

"It still doesn't address all this hurt coming up," J.P. said, giving her a pointed look.

Sadie took a breath and said, "Mama doesn't want to get over the hurt, J.P., or she would bring everything into the light. I hate to say this, but she's not walking the walk right now."

"Now, wait just a moment," J.P. said, holding up his hands. "We all know Mama's heart. If she doesn't want us to know why Daddy left, she has her reasons."

"Besides, he already showed us the kind of man he is by running away from us a second time," Susannah said. "I say he's not worth our tears."

Sadie mostly agreed, so she nodded.

"Whether or not he's worth it doesn't much matter," J.P. said. "We all feel what we feel, and right now, we all feel pretty awful."

"Yes, we do," Shelby said. "And so does Vander. I want you to know that."

They all nodded at their sister, and Sadie reached for her hand.

"Are we all agreed?" Shelby said with a huge exhale of breath. "I'll tell Mama I'm not looking for Daddy and be done with it? I don't see another way around this."

Sadie thought about it, feeling like she was sitting in the middle of a see-saw being propelled by two different forces—the desire for a resolution and the wish to forget and move on.

"I agree," Susannah said. "Thank you for being willing to talk to Mama, Shelby."

Her sister's mouth twisted, and Sadie knew how much she was looking forward to that exchange. Who could blame her?

"I agree for the moment," J.P. said, "but if this doesn't work, then we revisit it."

"I just want this over with," Shelby said. "Sadie, what do you say?"

J.P. gazed at her steadily, and she closed her eyes to listen to her heart. "All right, I agree. It's not like Daddy's going to up and appear or anything. We looked. He ran. It's done."

"Then it's settled," J.P. said, reaching for his sweet tea. "We should try and choke down a bite. Y'all need to get back to work, and I need to get on back to the house for a call later."

Sadie was going to quilt her heart out when she wasn't at work. "I'm glad we met today. I didn't...think I could handle getting through the day after talking with Mama."

Shelby bit her lip. "I'll go see her after work. Then we'll put all of this behind us."

Sadie sure hoped so, but part of her worried Mama wasn't going to let it go.

CHAPTER 29

SHELBY DECIDED TO CATCH MAMA AT THE CHURCH. THAT way, Mama wouldn't feel obligated to invite her to stay for dinner. Besides, after the day she'd had, all she wanted to do was crawl into Vander's lap and get some of that TLC he was so good at delivering.

Of course, Shelby's plan hinged on getting to the church before Mama left for home, which was beginning to seem unlikely. She was at Gail's house for a meeting, and her boss was chatting idly as if they had all day. While she normally enjoyed Gail's stories, Shelby found herself chomping at the bit.

"What's the matter with you, girl?" Gail finally asked, picking up the opera glasses she'd bought on a recent antique hunt and holding them quizzically to her nose. "You've been acting like you're going to jump out of your skin for at least thirty minutes, and all my dithering isn't doing a thing to distract you."

Gail was trying to distract her? That explained her colorful monologue on her butler's refusal to load the cannonball and add the gunpowder she'd managed to locate, something Shelby had interrupted only to remind Gail again she couldn't do it. "I need to go to a meeting."

While Shelby had told Gail about her daddy running away

again, she hadn't shared anything about the problem with her mama. Her boss' reaction had been dramatic enough to the news about Daddy—she'd even offered to lend Shelby her dueling pistols if they ever found the blaggard. After that, Shelby had thought it prudent to let sleeping dogs lie. She still hadn't told Gail about Vander, mostly because she was worried about how the woman would react. She was already in an emotional pressure cooker with Mama, and if her relationship with Gail suffered, she wasn't sure she could take it.

"This meeting has you stewing," Gail said, setting the glittering opera glasses on her desk. "Want to talk about it?"

Shelby shook her head. "It will be fine. Gail, I really must run. Can we pick things up tomorrow?"

"Of course," Gail said, rising when Shelby did. "You used to confide in me."

"It's...a family matter," she said, grabbing her purse. "Nothing to bother you about."

"And yet, you're terribly upset," Gail said. "Is there any news about your daddy?"

"No," she replied, taking a few more steps to the door.

"Then..." The woman gestured dramatically.

Shelby ground her teeth. When Gail got determined, there was no stopping her. Usually Shelby admired that, but right now, it annoyed the hell out of her. "I suppose you should know Vander and I are dating," she decided to confess instead. "I hope that doesn't bother you."

"Bother me?" Gail eased into the chair Shelby had vacated in front of her desk. "I'm happy for y'all. You're a good match. Like I thought you might be. But you can tell Vander that I would have had copious amounts of wild sex with him if I'd thought for a minute he was interested. Don't want his manhood hurt none."

Shelby was sure her mouth opened like a trap door. Copious amounts of wild sex? Good gracious, Mother Mary.

"I knew he *wasn't* interested," Gail continued with a pout, "but I'm too vain not to tease a man for not wanting me.

Vander isn't the type to be run off by a little teasing."

No, he wasn't the kind of man anyone could run off, including Mama. Shelby thanked God for that.

"But I'll stop teasing him about it when we meet, seeing as how you two are dating," Gail said.

Shelby nodded. "It's happened pretty fast, but..."

"He's a keeper," Gail said. "Strong, handsome, and sure of himself, but he also has a good heart. Perfect for you, really. As someone with two unfortunate ex-husbands, I can promise you he's prime beef."

"I'll be sure to tell him that," Shelby said, fighting a smile.

The woman stood, fingering the eight strands of turquoise beads wrapped around her neck. "At least one of us is having wild sex with him." Shelby barely had time to feel her cheeks heat before Gail narrowed her eyes. "You haven't gotten there yet. I can tell by the blush heating your face. Shelby McGuiness, what in the world are you waiting for? You love the man, don't you?"

"Gail!" They were not having this conversation.

"Don't *Gail* me!" She flounced over and put her hands on Shelby's shoulders. "I can have a suite at one of Nashville's finest hotels ready for you in an hour. Oh, this is your upbringing, isn't it? Shelby, there's being smart about sex, and then there's being wise about sex. What you feel for Vander fits into the latter category. Don't make the mistake of confusing the two like I have. Now, get going and get busy," she said, giving her a little shove toward the door. "I expect details!"

That stopped Shelby in her tracks. "You won't be getting them, Gail. I work for you, for heaven's sake!"

The woman cackled, throwing her head back. "I was just teasing you. Goodness gracious, Shelby, you're easier than Vander. Hah. In some ways. Good night, honey. Say hey to Vander for me."

Oh, good Lord. Shelby was blushing three shades of scarlet by the time she let herself out of the house. If Jeffries noticed, he had the courtesy not to comment on it. Simply closed the door behind her after a brief bow.

When Shelby reached the fountain, she drew out her wallet and opened her coin purse. Right now, it seemed like she was overflowing with wishes: ones that involved every member of her family, herself, and Vander. Well, it wasn't like God couldn't handle them all. In fact, Shelby knew she could pretty much give Him an infinite list.

She picked out a quarter and approached the edge of the fountain. The cherubs looked like they were smiling at her through the gurgling water. "This coin represents all my wishes and them being answered in due course."

She threw in the coin, enjoyed hearing the splash, and watched as it sank through the water to the bottom. Filled with more peace than she'd felt in days, she headed to her Mama's church.

Mama was still seated at her desk when Shelby walked into her office.

Shelby had always loved it in here, from the sunny yellow walls to the inspirational sayings scattered around the room. Today, she didn't feel the usual welcome.

"Hi, honey," her mama said, rising quickly, her hands fisted together in front of her. "Something wrong? I didn't know you were coming."

Shelby closed the door. "Mama, I know what you said to Vander yesterday, and that you talked to the others about it too. I'm here to tell you not to worry. I won't ask Vander to look for Daddy in the future."

There. She'd said it.

Her mama swallowed thickly. "Shelby, I'm glad to hear you say that. You have to believe me when I say it's for the best."

"You always say so, Mama," Shelby said, feeling a hot spurt of anger rise up. "Next time, come talk to me. I happen to love Vander, and I want him to feel welcome in our family. You're undermining that, and frankly that hurts me. I hoped you would be happy for me."

There were tears in Mama's eyes as she approached her. "Shelby, I am. I'm just... I'm glad you came and talked to me. Let's put this behind us. I promise to make Vander feel more welcome the next time I see him, and I'll apologize for putting him in a difficult position. Actually, I admire the way he handled it. He's a strong man with a moral compass, and he respects you. That much was evident."

Mama put a hand on her arm, and Shelby could feel her rocking in place, fighting the urge to wrap her up and hold her like she'd normally do. Shelby moved in first.

"All right, Mama," she said, her voice sounding as tired as she felt. "Let's move on. We have so much to celebrate in our family. We should focus on that."

"Yes, we should," Mama agreed, hugging her tight. "Thank you for coming, honey. You've lifted a powerful weight from my mind."

"You're welcome, Mama," she said. When she eased back, she saw tears falling from Mama's eyes, a rare sight. "I love you."

"I love you too, sugar," she said, framing her face. "I'm just trying to protect y'all. I hope you can understand that."

She nodded, but darn it all if she wasn't tired of wondering what Mama was protecting them from. Determined to put it behind her, she texted Vander once she got back out to her car.

Can you come over in an hour? I'll make dinner.

Then she decided to go a step further because Gail was right. What was she waiting for? She wasn't going to let family drama get in the way of her relationship with Vander.

Plan to stay over.

His reply was immediate.

I'll be there in thirty. Don't think I can wait an hour after that message.

Shelby shivered in the car and headed home with the first smile of the day on her face.

CHAPTER 30

VANDER BROKE ALL THE SPEED LIMITS HEADING TO Shelby's house. She was just pulling up when he arrived.

"Hey!" he said, slamming his car door shut. "I almost beat you."

She looked so beautiful, striding over to him in a violet dress suit accented with a delicate strand of pearls and silver beads around her neck. "It's good to see you, Vander."

It was clear she'd had a day. "Come here."

"Let's go inside," she said, her smile a little tired but still lovely. "You have a propensity to make a spectacle on the street."

He took her hand and brought it to his mouth to kiss it. "Technically, we're on your front lawn."

"Details," she shot back, but her rapport didn't have its normal sauce.

When they entered her house, he took her purse and set it down in its normal place. He liked that he was getting to know her normal places.

"Come on, let's get you a drink, and you can tell me about your day."

"I need to start dinner," she said, stepping away, forcing him to pull her toward him.

"Already taken care of," he said. "I called Jared's, and

they're delivering in about forty-five minutes."

Her shoulders sunk under his hands. "Good. Thank you. I could have made something."

"You've had a tough few days," he said, massaging her rigid muscles. "Do you want some wine?"

"I have some white in the fridge," she said, trying to pull away again.

"Wait, Shelby," he said softly. "Just wait."

He leaned in and kissed her softly on the lips. She wasn't completely with him yet, still wrapped up in whatever was burdening her, so he kept on kissing her gently until he felt the shift in her. Her arms banded around him, her lips softened and moved with his. Then he heard her sigh as she relaxed against his body.

"That's better," he said, finally edging back. "I missed you today."

She put her head on his chest. "And I you. So much. Sometimes, it scares me how much I love you already. How much I'd do to support you."

He tipped her head up, not liking that last piece. "What happened?"

"Best get it out of the way so we can focus on happier things—like us being together." She took a deep breath and then let it out shakily. "Mama was so worried about us searching for Daddy, she called all my siblings. Sadie, Susannah, J.P., and I had a lunch meeting and agreed I would promise her not to ask you to look for Daddy in the future. Technically, it's true."

But she'd also seen it as lying. No wonder she looked so down in the mouth.

"I told Mama that right before I came home. She's promised to apologize to you and give you a better welcome next time you come 'round. Not that I blame you if you want to pass on Sunday dinner for a while. I kind of do right now. Oh, and I told Gail about us."

"You really *have* had a day," he said, massaging her neck,

making her close her eyes. "Maybe we should drink something stronger than wine."

"Tequila is the devil," she murmured, tilting her neck to give him better access. "It gives me a headache. And I don't know if it makes my clothes fall off like in that country song."

"I'll tuck away those important pieces of information," he said, trying not to laugh, loving the feel of her thick hair in his fingers as he massaged her scalp. "How did Gail take the news?"

"She beamed. Thinks we're well matched."

He was in Gail's debt. Maybe he should send a bottle of bourbon over as a thank you.

"She also said she would have been interested in having… what did she call it? 'Copious wild sex with you.' Good heavens, she made me blush. But she's glad we'll be having it instead. She took me to task for being a little slow off the mark."

He fought a smile. Leave it to Gail to intuit that. Nothing got past her. "Shelby, none of that matters to me. We'll make love when the time is right."

"Today, I decided the time was right," she said, opening her eyes and gazing at him. "Truthfully, I'd decided yesterday was right, but we got sidetracked. I won't let us get sidetracked anymore."

"I love a woman who knows her own mind. Makes her own decisions." He kissed her neck. "But you've had a tough day. There's no need to rush."

She twined her hands around his neck. "I want to be with you, Vander. I'm tired of letting other people prick a pin in my happiness. You have to *want* to be happy sometimes. Even in the midst of challenges. I'm hoping and praying and wishing this will all be behind us after today. Vander, I know you don't believe in wishes, but I threw a quarter into Gail's fountain today to honor all of mine. Dammit, I want everything! I'm not settling for less."

Her brown eyes were filled with a captivating light, and he wanted nothing more than to give all her wishes to her on a silver platter. "You're going to have everything," he said, his voice husky. "Starting tonight."

He felt her heart begin to race against his chest, and he ran his hand down her back and cupped her hips, bringing her closer to him. "We both will." Then he fitted his mouth over hers again.

Their kisses were lush and wet and wild, and he could feel her flirting with the edges of her own passion.

"Don't hold back," he whispered against her lips, squeezing her gently at the waist.

"But dinner?" she asked.

"I told them to leave it on the porch if no one answered the door," he whispered right back.

"Oh, you devil, you," she purred.

"Make love with me, Shelby," he urged, kissing her neck. "Unless you want to have wine first."

She angled back and gave him a look that told him clear as could be that he was the stupidest man alive. He gave her a hard kiss in response. Tugging at the buttons of her jacket, he opened it and slid his hands inside, delighted she hadn't worn a cami under it. He liked to think she'd planned that too. She was warm to the touch, soft as corn silk, and straining for more. He ran his fingers over her hot pink bra and traced the lacy edges until she pushed back.

"We have too many clothes on," she drawled, shrugging out of her jacket.

He hadn't expected her to get impatient, but he was learning Shelby was always in a hurry. About everything, it seemed.

She threw her jacket over her shoulder, looking like a siren in her sexy bra and skirt and heels. Heading to the stairs off the entry, she turned and gave him another look. "Coming, honey?"

Oh, she was going to have him on his knees before they were done. He marched toward her and picked her up in his arms, knowing she'd like a manly display like that. She squealed, piercing his ears, and then relaxed against his chest as he took the steps two at a time.

"I flat out adore your exuberance," she said, stroking his jaw, making him wish he'd shaved for her.

"You're about to see how exuberant I can be," he said in a deep voice. "First bedroom?"

"No, down the hall," she said, her finger moving on to the stubble on his neck, driving him wild.

He turned into a room painted a light green she'd probably call green fig or something else deliciously feminine. Billowy white curtains framed the large windows. Her bed was one of those mahogany Southern four-poster types, and the posts were hung with transparent fabric reminiscent of mosquito netting. A mound of white pillows in more shapes and sizes than should be legal covered a lavender comforter. Vander balanced her against his body as he swept all the pillows off the bed.

When he met her eyes, she raised a brow.

"Exuberance," he said with a decided shake of his head, laying her down.

When he moved to cover her, she put her hand on his chest, exerting a gentle pressure. "Hold tight." She slid off the bed and walked to the door on the opposite side of the large room, what he imagined was a bathroom. When she returned, she was blushing. There were five condom boxes in her hands.

He tried not to laugh. "You weren't joking about buying all kinds."

"Exuberance," she joked, but he knew she was wildly uncomfortable.

Choosing the box of extra-thins, he dug out a trio of them and threw them on the bed. He set the other boxes on the floor and kicked them under the bed.

Her brown eyes were wide, and her face was flushed, but she hopped back on the bed and took a deep breath. He sat on the edge, shrugging out of his jacket and unbuttoning his shirt. She watched his every movement, her gaze flicking up to meet his every once in a while, but she didn't help him. He didn't know her well enough yet in this space to decipher if she needed some encouragement or if she simply liked watching. But he planned to find out.

When he was bare-chested, he laid on his side and opened his arms. She came to him in a fluid move, her eyes never leaving his face.

"I love you, Shelby," he said as he tucked her hair behind her ear.

"And I love you," she said, placing her hand on his heart.

Since this was new for both of them, and she was willing but still a little skittish, he leaned in and kissed her slowly and deeply for a long time. Her fingers slid into his hair, and soon she was pressing closer to his body. He was rock hard and impatient, but determined to take this slowly. He wanted their first time to be memorable. He wanted her to feel cherished.

His fingers traced the delicate lines of her collarbone, the warm rise of her breasts. His mouth followed suit, kissing his way down her neck to the soft flesh he'd been fantasizing about since he'd first seen her. He slid his hands under her back and undid her bra, removing it from her arms and throwing it over his shoulder.

"You're so beautiful," he whispered, testing the weight of her breasts, savoring their softness.

Then he tugged on her nipple with his lips, brushing it lightly with his teeth, and she gave a soft moan. He circled it with his tongue until she arched her back, and when she uttered a more urgent sound, he fitted his mouth to her breast, giving it his full and complete attention. From her moans and the straining of her body, he knew she was enjoying it. Soon, he switched to her other breast and gave it the same attention.

When he lifted his head to look into her eyes, she gave him a shy smile. "I rather like that." He'd touched her before, but never this intimately.

Her hesitation to voice her desire moved something inside

him. "Good, because I do too, and I plan to do a heck of a lot more of it."

She raised a hand and stroked the muscles of his arm. "What do *you* like?" she asked.

His whole body clenched, and he broke out into a sweat. "Put your hands on me and find out."

Bless her, she did just that, intent on her purpose but still a little shy in her mission. He ran his hand down her bottom when she put her mouth to his chest, giving him soft kisses. As she moved down to his stomach, those warm, open-mouthed kisses threatened to destroy him. Sweet Christ.

"Let's get the rest of your clothes off," he said, sliding down and starting with her heels.

They were silver and three-inches, if he were to guess, with a double strap that wrapped around her ankle. He expected they were supposed to accent the silver beads in her pearl necklace, which he planned to leave on for the moment.

"These are sexy," he said, slowly unwrapping her ankle.

"Why do you think I kept them on?" she asked, a twinkle in her eye.

He tossed the first heel off and fitted her foot in his hands, caressing the bones there. She gave a throaty purr.

"Oh, I like that too," she said. "I'm hoping I like everything."

He remembered what she'd said about her ex—how he'd never made much of an effort to please her—and felt all the more determined to give her pleasure.

"Always tell me how you feel, and I'll do the same," he said, sliding his hand up her calf and caressing the back of her knee. "All I ask is you remember you're with me and keep an open mind."

She raised up on an elbow. "You're not into kinky stuff, are you?"

Her serious tone had him biting his tongue to keep from laughing. "Like what?"

"Like whips and chains and paddling," she said, blushing again. "I don't think I'd like that. I mean, in some countries, that's what they do to prisoners. I can't imagine it feeling good."

His shoulders started to shake. "You have nothing to worry about. If I need to get out any aggression, I'll go to the firing range. I don't do that in bed."

"Whew! That's a relief."

This time he couldn't help but chuckle. "I wouldn't pass up playing with a few feathers or silk scarves, but I'm pretty much a skin-on-skin kind of guy. Your softness is all the texture I need."

"Oh. My. Goodness." Her drawl was more pronounced as he tugged her other heel off.

"Best lie back now," he encouraged, sliding both hands up the backs of her legs. "I've got plans for you."

"Plans?" she asked, her head popping up again to look at him. "Why does that sound so exciting?"

"Because you're a woman who likes certainty," he said, kissing the tops of her thighs, sliding her skirt up inch by inch until it rested right above the top of her panties. "Even though you're curious too. It's a wonderful combination."

"I like that," she responded, wiggling a bit.

He slid his hands under her bottom, and she jerked in his arms. "It's all right, Shelby. You can trust me."

"I know," she said, releasing a harsh breath. "You just hit a spot I'm...not used to anyone touching."

He made himself focus. His body was urging him to rush, but he wasn't going to take its cues. Kissing her belly, he bypassed the rucked-up skirt and put his mouth on the pink lace covering her. She jolted under him.

"You might need to kiss me again," she admitted softly. "I'm thinking too much."

Yeah, she wasn't used to being touched. He levered up and caressed her cheek. "I'm glad you told me."

"You're not..."

"What?" he asked.

"Upset at me?" she asked, a frown marring her face.

"Not a bit," he said. "We're just getting started, and I'm good at adjusting my plans."

He kissed her again and didn't let up until she grabbed his waist, tugging him closer. She pushed him back, and to his delight, she was breathing as hard as he was. Rolling onto her side, she undid the skirt's zipper and wiggled out of it and her panties at the same time. She was blushing as she threw them on the floor. When she turned back onto her side, she was everything good and sexy and beautiful in the world.

"Better take yours off too," she said, clearing her throat discreetly. "I won't stand for being the only one who's naked."

His lips were twitching as he undid his belt and pants and slid everything down his legs, including his briefs. She bit her lip, her gaze fastened on his dick.

"You're..."

"What?"

"Big," she said, beet red again. "But you have a gorgeous body."

This time he couldn't help his smile. He slid next to her, fitting them together, and ran his hand down her back. "We're going to do just fine," he said, kissing her shoulder. "Better than fine. Let me show you, love."

She leaned her head against his chest and softened into him as he caressed her body. His hands slid down her bottom and the backs of her legs. His mouth tugged on her breasts again until she moaned and arched into him. But it was only when he felt the sheen of sweat break out across her skin that he laid his mouth on her core and made her come.

She moaned and shifted under him as he took her higher, using his mouth and fingers in tandem.

"Oh, God," she called out, her hands digging into his arms as he slid over her body. "Oh, my sweet God."

Music to his ears. He reached for a condom, fitted one over himself, and then entered her gently. She was still hot and wet, but it was a tight fit, and she made an urgent sound as he inched deeper inside her, her face a delightful flush.

"Relax," he urged, fighting for control as all that wet heat enveloped him.

"I'm trying," she shot back, her passion-glazed eyes narrowing.

He leaned forward and took her mouth in a mind-drugging kiss, forcing himself to be completely still inside her so she could adjust to his size. She pushed at him, and he edged back. Her eyes were like starlight and her face was flushed. In that moment, she was the most beautiful woman he'd ever seen.

"Vander!" she said, her voice impatient.

"What?" he growled, surprised at the edge in it.

"Move!" she ordered, wiggling under him.

"I didn't think you were ready," he ground out, thrusting shallowly into her.

She clenched her eyes shut. "I'm not, but I need you to... do *something*. I feel like I'm fixing to come undone here."

He would have laughed if he hadn't been out of his mind with desire for her. Instead, he thrust again, going deeper. She gave a throaty moan and grabbed his hips.

"Yes. That."

He took her cue and increased his pace, setting a delicious rhythm designed to drive them both wild. Soon she was lifting to meet him for every stroke.

"Oh, God, Vander," she panted out, her hands gripping his hips.

Their eyes met, and he could feel it, the rise of pleasure intensifying inside her. He rose up on his knees, thrusting wildly, and she cried out, coming in a rush. He felt his own pleasure gather at his spine, and then it exploded through his system. He was heaving and groaning as he came, and he felt her hands caressing his back as it went on and on.

When he lowered his head to her chest, he had to use the last of his strength not to crush her. She was as sweaty as he was, and smelled sexier than any expensive perfume.

Even though he was exhausted, he raised his head, needing to see her face. She was gazing at him with so much love his chest filled up with more warmth than he'd ever experienced before for another person.

Then she smiled and said his name, "Vander," and he knew he'd never be the same.

CHAPTER 31

SHELBY'S MIND WAS RARELY QUIET. WHEN SHE WAS IN bed, her head usually filled with thoughts ranging from the numbers on a spreadsheet to the list of groceries she needed to buy at the market.

Vander had wiped *all* thought from her mind. Her body hadn't stopped pulsing with pleasure for what felt like the last hour, and it felt downright delicious. After making love, all they had done was suck in deep breaths until their hearts calmed and then caress each other, not needing to say a word. Her heart was so full, she thought she was going to burst. She freaking loved this man.

"You were right," she finally said softly, tracing his sweaty hair with her fingers. What did a woman say to a man after something so cataclysmic? None of her beloved Southern colloquialisms seemed adequate. "We did pretty well."

He raised his head to look at her and gave her the most charming smile ever. "We did more than well. I can barely raise myself up right now, least of all remember my name."

"It's Vander Montgomery," she told him, tracing his arm. "Just ask me if you forget again." She planned to make it happen.

His chuckle warmed her heart. She turned on her side to look at him. *Mercy me, he has a beautiful body.* And it was all hers. She wanted to give a sinister laugh, but thought better of it.

"You know," she said, running her hand over his muscular shoulder. "I've always hated being sweaty. Certainly, I couldn't stand anyone touching me if they were icky. That seems to have changed with you."

His dark chuckle made her toes curl. "Good, because we're going to get good and sweaty pretty often from now on."

She wanted to clap with joy. He edged off her, and she realized he had to attend to...well, the after-business of things. She made a face at the sheets and then did some tidying up as well. When he pulled her back to his chest, she laid her head there and sighed, deciding it the best pillow on the market.

"You all right?" he asked, stroking her hair.

She leaned up and looked him in the eye. "If you're asking if I'm sore, the answer is yes." Her pout was for punctuation. "I *said* you were big."

"You'll grow to like it," he said, practically preening like a lion. "You don't strike me as the kind of woman who likes it small."

She punched him in the arm and settled back down on his chest, hearing his chuckles reverberate in her ear. Goodness, he was heading to hysterical. "You're so bad."

"You bet I am," he responded. "And you need to trust me a little more. I didn't steer you wrong this first time, did I?"

So he was looking to have his ego stroked a little. She could do that. "No, you didn't."

"Be honest, Shelby," he said, toying with her spine. "You shouted my name."

"You're a scoundrel to point that out," she said in a huff, but secretly she loved that they were bantering in bed. It was one of her favorite things about being with him. "But I'm still not doing any prisoner break scenarios with whips and chains for you."

More laughter, all from his rock-hard belly. "Scoundrel, huh? I'll have to figure out a way to live up to that without the whips and chains. I can make you shout my name every time. Just you wait and see."

Had he shouted her name? She honestly couldn't remember. "Two can play that game," she said easily, only to realize she'd have to follow through.

Was she ready to take him to the brink of desire all by herself? When she rose up to look at his smirking face, she didn't have to gather her courage. She *wanted* to make him shout her name.

"Oh, you are so going to get it now," she told him, making him laugh even harder.

He shouted her name the first *and* the second time that night.

CHAPTER 32

VANDER DIDN'T BELIEVE IN WALKING AROUND ON A cloud—it was too dangerously close to a belief in wishes—but his feet didn't feel quite as grounded over the next couple of weeks. He and Shelby were scorching up the sheets at both their places and laughing up a storm.

Whenever a shadow crossed her face, he knew she was thinking about her family. He'd either kiss her softly until it cleared or ask her about it—whatever she needed. As the anniversary of his father's murder approached, a shadow crossed over him periodically as well, but she was as intuitive about his pain as he was about hers. Somehow it was easier when they did it together, and Vander came to appreciate they were more than lovers.

They were partners.

The best combination imaginable.

Shelby challenged him in the best way possible, brainstorming about his cases with him when he hit a wall, something he'd never done with anyone outside his firm. Sure, they bantered about everything from the best way to load the dishwasher to the safest way to make love in her shower after she refused to let him install bars—but he ate up every minute of it.

Charlie couldn't keep the knowing smile off her face

when she caught him whistling as he went through case files or completed paperwork. He found he didn't care. He was happy, and it was new and weird and wonderful.

At first he'd feared all this love stuff would make him soft, but he felt like more of a man than ever. Shelby shouting his name two to three times a day made him want to beat his chest like Tarzan. Then an undercover subject pulled a knife on him, and he disarmed the man as quickly as he'd ever done. This love stuff hadn't made him lose his edge at all—if anything it had given him more of a reason to be strong.

And he wasn't dreading August 30th quite like he usually did every year, and that rocked him to the core.

Shelby's siblings had made an extra effort to welcome him anew. Susannah had invited everyone over for a BBQ—minus the old people, she'd joked. He'd understood: everyone was giving Louisa some time to settle down.

They'd feasted on ribs and grilled corn and polished off chocolate chip pie and homemade vanilla ice cream. Rory and Annabelle had even colored him pictures to take home. The girl had drawn a big yellow daisy with a smiley face while Rory's masterpiece was of his dog playing with a bone. He'd put them on his refrigerator since that's where kid pictures were supposed to go. Shelby had kissed him senseless, and they'd taken each other on his granite countertops as a celebration.

He might not be fully integrated into the entire McGuiness clan, but they were making great strides. Everyone seemed to breathe a lot easier as time passed.

It was a rainy Saturday when his phone sounded, the ring tone signaling a forwarded call from his burner phone. He was reading the paper with Shelby tucked against his side. She was watching some chick flick.

"Did you change your ring tone?" she asked, sitting up.

"It's my undercover line," he said, moving off the couch and picking it up. He noted the Memphis number as he answered. "Hello."

"Toby, is that you?" a familiar voice asked. "Honey, it's Lenore. I need to speak with you about my boy. Between us, you hear?"

"Yes, hello there," he said in his undercover accent. "Give me a second to get somewhere I can talk." He felt a flash of indecision when he met Shelby's curious eyes, but until he knew why Lenore was calling, he needed to honor her wishes. Placing his hand over the receiver, he whispered, "It's a case. I need to take this outside."

She nodded. "Take it in my office. It's hot out."

He closed the door moments later, feeling guilty.

"All right, I'm back," he said to Lenore. "I needed to find somewhere private. I'm with Shelby."

"How is my granddaughter?" Lenore asked.

"Good," he responded simply. "What can I do for you, Lenore? Must be important since you don't have a phone."

"I'm using my boy's new phone," she told him. "He dumped the old one after you called."

His whole body tensed. "Preston's with you?"

"Yes," she drawled. "He was mighty put out I'd told you where to find him. Read me the riot act, and I read it right back to him. He's being an ass. I told him he has wonderful children looking for him and that he was a fool to have run away again. He told me to mind my own business. Said I had no idea what was going on. We went nine rounds, but he finally agreed to tell both of us whatever secret he's been nursing. At the same time. He said you could decide whether or not to tell Shelby and the other children once you hear it."

A sense of foreboding rose up in Vander. His gut had told him all along that there was a dark story behind Preston's abandonment of his family. The weight of learning the truth settled over him.

Shelby wasn't a client anymore. She was his love. His ethics tugged at him.

"You're sure he won't tell Shelby or the rest of them? I don't like this none."

"I'm sure, honey. I done cursed a blue streak. He won't budge."

Damn. "Are you at your house?" he asked.

"Yes," Lenore said. "I know it's a drive."

"That doesn't bother me," he said, "but I'm a little concerned Preston might take off again."

Lenore laughed. "I made him promise me that he won't, but just to be certain, I've set my dog at his feet. That mutt won't let him get away. Trust me."

He looked at his watch. "I can be there around three."

"I'm glad you can come," Lenore said. "It will be nice to have a friendly face around when he finally says his piece."

Worry laced her voice, and he couldn't blame her. "I'll be there as soon as I can. I have to tell you I'm torn about going there alone, Lenore."

"I hear ya, boy," the woman said, "but Pres is mule-headed."

"All right," Vander said, "I'll see you soon. Call me if anything changes."

"I'll sit on him if I have to," Lenore said. "We both know he won't get far if that happens."

She hung up, and he set his phone on Shelby's desk, thinking things through. He didn't like doing it this way, but if Preston refused to tell anyone other than him, he didn't see as he had a choice.

He called Charlie to confirm his thinking.

"I thought you weren't working today," she said when she answered.

"Preston has reemerged," he told her. "He's with Lenore and has agreed to tell us what happened, but no one else. He said it's for me to decide whether to tell the others."

She was silent, and he let her ruminate. "Sticky situation, being as how you're with Shelby. I don't envy you this one, Vander."

"I have to go, don't I?" he asked. "I have to find out what happened."

"It concerns me Preston is letting you decide what to do with the information. Both of us have guessed it's bad, but this makes me think it's real bad. Definitely not a regular dad-walks-out-the-door-on-the-family story."

"I hate not telling Shelby."

"She initiated the search," Charlie told him. "She'd want you to go, I think. She trusts your judgment."

He thought so too. "I don't want to lie to her about why I'm leaving today."

"Her father isn't giving you a choice," Charlie said. "You could tell her against his wishes, but she might insist on going. If she did that, we both know he'll clam up and then run again."

She was right. Shelby wouldn't want to be left behind. "Okay, thanks for talking it through. I'm going to head out."

"Call if you need me," she said, "and call when you have the information. I'm as eager as you are to learn what he's running from."

"Talk to you."

He clicked off and pocketed his phone. Running his hands through his hair, he took a moment to compose himself. When he found Shelby, she looked up immediately. She'd been waiting, he could tell, worrying.

"Everything okay?" she asked, her face tense.

"I had a break in a case," he told her, feeling like shit. "I'm sorry, but I need to go. I'm...not sure when I'll be back. Tomorrow for sure."

She rose and wrapped her arms around him. "It's not dangerous, is it?"

"No," he assured her, stroking her back. "But it can't wait. I really wish they hadn't called on our day off."

"It's okay," she told him, edging back and tracing his jaw. "Your job isn't the nine-to-five kind."

He kissed her sweetly on the lips and then cupped her face in his palms. "You know how much I love you, right? How much you've changed things for me?"

She smiled. "I know. You've done the same for me."

THE FOUNTAIN OF INFINITE WISHES   273

Struggling with himself, he gave her cheek one last caress and took her hand. They walked together to the entryway. He picked up his keys and wallet resting beside her purse.

Kissing her again, he said, "I'll call you when I can."

With another smile, she reached for her purse and took out her own keys. He watched with a mingled sense of wonder and guilt as she drew a brass one off the chain.

"Come whenever," she said, fitting it into his palm. "You're always welcome here. Day or night."

He felt the significance of the action and wanted to meet it with a gesture of his own. Taking off his own house key, he gave it to her.

"I want you to feel the same way," he said, watching as her eyes darkened with emotion. He'd had an extra one made a couple of days ago and had been waiting for the perfect moment. It didn't get more perfect than this. "Can you remember my alarm code?"

Her smile was radiant. "I have a head for numbers."

He told it to her. "And my password is justice."

"Of course it is," she said. "You'd better get going before I make you late. When I see you next though...be prepared to be loved within an inch of your life."

"I can't wait," he said and made himself open the door and walk out.

Four hours later, he arrived in the trailer park after taking the time to change clothes and switch cars. He couldn't very well show up in his Ferrari and his street clothes. Lenore met him at the door with No-no by her side, barking up a storm.

"Hush it," she told the dog, grabbing his collar. "Good to see you, Toby. Thank you for coming on such short notice."

"It's all right," he said. A few feet behind her, he could see a lanky gray-haired man he recognized from two very different photos. "It's good to see you too, Lenore. And Mr. McGuiness, it's a pleasure to finally meet you."

The man had on a denim shirt worn thin at the elbows and a loose pair of jeans without a belt. "Can't say as I feel the same. You've caused me a lot of trouble, showing up like you did. Making me leave my girl. You have no idea what you've stirred up, boy."

Vander fucking hated it when another man called him *boy*. "I'd appreciate you not calling me that, Mr. McGuiness."

"I'll call you—"

"Pres, this is my house, and you'd better treat Toby with respect. Come on in, honey, and give me a kiss. I thought we could talk in the back like we did when you were here last. I can keep No-no inside so we won't be distracted."

"Sweet tea in the same place?" he asked, bussing her cheek with his lips, aware that Preston was stewing beside him. "I'll pour us some while you put No-no in the back."

"Sounds good," Lenore said. "Pres, you go on and sit outside."

"Finally going to let me out of your sight, Mama?" he asked with an edge in his voice.

"Now that Toby is here, he can run you down if you take off again," Lenore said. "Lord knows, I'm not doing much running these days."

The man frowned and headed to the back while Lenore ambled down the hallway with the dog. Inside the kitchen, Vander poured the sweet tea, keeping an eye on Preston through the window. Seeing him in the flesh, there was no mistaking how much J.P. favored him, save for all the wear of hard living. And he saw plenty of Shelby too, which made him feel all the guiltier.

Once they were all settled outside with their sweet tea, Lenore said, "All right, Pres. This man came a long way to hear a story I've been waiting for you to tell me for nigh on thirty years. Get to it."

His mouth tensed, and he leaned forward with his elbows on his knees. "I wish Shelby and the rest of them had never bothered to look for me. I'm no good for the kids. That's why I had to leave. Please, Mama. It's best for everyone to let sleeping dogs lie."

"No, Pres," Lenore said in a hard tone. "You promised you'd tell us, and tell us you will."

The man sighed long and deep. "It's not a pretty story, and I never wanted my kids to hear it. Neither did Louisa. She's going to be as angry as a hornet if she ever learns I broke our agreement."

Vander's curiosity was piqued. "You tell it to me straight. I'll decide whether anyone hears it."

"Fine," Preston said, gripping his knees. "I lost my job in the last year I was with Louisa and the kids. At first I couldn't tell her. I was too ashamed. I had words with my boss, and he drew a hard line. Every time I turned around, the kids needed another book for school or a pair of shoes...and then Sadie was born. I felt the weight of the world on my shoulders."

Unemployment was hard anytime, but Vander had seen lengthy stints of it break families apart. He shared a look with Lenore, and she patted Preston's knee to encourage him to continue.

"I...couldn't find a job," he said, not meeting their eyes. "I did some odd jobs here and there, but it wasn't enough. Louisa was pregnant with Sadie, and she got more and more frustrated with me as her due date came closer. We weren't doing well. Were late on bills. She said I wasn't helping enough with the kids or doing my part to provide for them. And then we stopped...you know. She said it was the baby and all, but I knew different. She didn't want me anymore, and I..."

"She wasn't right to treat you like that, Pres," Lenore said. "A woman should support her husband. I never liked her. Not from day one. This cinches it."

"Mama, please don't interrupt me," Preston said, rocking in his chair now. "I've kept this to myself for a long, long time, and it's hard to tell."

Lenore only response was to purse her lips.

"I got some odd jobs around the church during the week—sweeping floors, cleaning things up." He put his fist to his mouth. "There was a girl who helped out with the kids on Wednesday nights during services. She was...one of those older-looking girls, if you know what I mean."

Vander's heart started to thud in his chest.

"I didn't know she was fifteen," Preston said, staring off in the distance. "She was always nice to me, and she was real pretty. It's no excuse, but she made me feel like I wasn't a failure. She...told me she liked older men, and I..."

"Oh, sweet Jesus," Lenore whispered, putting her hand over her mouth.

"We...had sex," Preston said, clearing his throat with three hard coughs. "I knew it was wrong. I felt guilty as hell afterward. But she pursued me, and I gave in again. After that, I knew it had to stop. She was still in high school, and none of my reasons held up in the light of day."

Vander kept his face neutral, but inside he was seething. He'd heard both men and women justify having sex with a minor—anything from them looking and acting older to them wanting it. Whatever the reason, it was unequivocally wrong. He did the math. Preston would have been twenty-nine. Old enough to know better, especially with four small kids at home.

"I stopped working at the church," Preston continued. "I couldn't tell Louisa why, which only made her madder. Sadie wasn't sleeping much and all she did was cry. I hated being home, even though the older kids never complained, especially John Parker. He was so easygoing. Susannah was the quiet one, and Shelby...well, she was always on the move. I never could keep up with her. I tried to be a good father to them, but...nothing seemed to be going right."

Vander was trying to reconcile this man's story with the family he knew. All of the McGuinesses were happy, well-adjusted people, but obviously this had been a dark time. He was glad Shelby didn't remember much of it.

"The girl..." He coughed in loud bursts again. "Her name was Skylar. She...ah...oh, God forgive me. She got pregnant."

Vander felt the shock jolt his system. *Oh, fuck. Not this.*

Lenore gave an anguished sound. "No, Preston. No!"

The older man pinched the bridge of his nose. "She tried to hide it, but her parents found out. Skylar told them it was mine, and they...they...told Louisa. You can't imagine how she reacted."

Vander had been a P.I. for long enough to see betrayal in all its forms. He'd seen destroyed marriages, husbands and wives decimated by a spouse's infidelity. But he couldn't begin to imagine what a spiritual woman like Louisa must have gone through after learning her husband had slept with a fifteen-year-old girl at church and gotten her pregnant. Everything was starting to make sense to him.

Lenore was crying softly now, and Vander reached for her hand. She gripped it hard while Preston stared at the ground.

"The family..." Preston shook his head and wiped his nose. "They didn't want their daughter disgraced by calling in the law on me. I was lucky that way, and I know it."

Vander had never been a parent, but he knew intuitively he'd want justice. He'd want to make sure the man never did something like that again. He hoped to hell Preston McGuiness had learned this part of his lesson.

"They were going to send Skylar to her grandparents in Texas, but they were adamant that I had to leave town. Her daddy...he said he'd kill me if he had to look at me at church."

That was more like it.

"I asked Louisa to come with me," Preston said, rocking nervously in his chair. "I told her we could make a new life somewhere with the kids and start over. I promised I'd never cheat on her again. She wouldn't hear of it."

Vander's admiration for the woman increased. He had a hard time when women stayed with men who'd treated them like shit.

"I can't see as how I blame her," Preston continued, digging his fingers into his knees. "She told me she and the kids would be better off without me. All she wanted was for me to leave and never come back because she couldn't bear to tell our kids what I'd done. I was so ashamed. I'd done wrong by everyone around me, and I didn't want the kids to know the truth. I told Louisa I'd go and never contact them again. She asked me to promise, and I did. God forgive me, I'm breaking it now."

Oh, Shelby, how am I supposed to tell you this? Tell any of you this? He thought of Sadie and how she cried at the drop of a hat. This would decimate her. It would hurt all of them.

"Oh, Pres," Lenore said, her mascara streaking down her face. "How could you? I raised you better than this!"

"I'm sorry, Mama," Preston said, raising bloodshot-red eyes to look at her. "What I did was unforgivable. Can't you see why I left Haines? Mister, you're trying to open a box filled with hurt. I've already done wrong by my kids once, but if they find out about this... And Louisa will never forgive me—assuming she's tried."

Vander worried his lip when Preston hung his head. Lenore had her hand on her heart and was continuing to cry softly.

"I have another grandchild," the woman whispered. "Preston, did you never try to find out what happened to your own flesh and blood?"

The man shook his head in defeat. "No, Mama. Never. I've never tried to find out anything about my other kids. Why would I look for that poor child I made in a dark moment with Skylar? Besides, her family wouldn't want that."

"But it's your child!" Lenore said. "They're all your children. How could you—"

"Mama, you don't understand how it was!" Preston said, shooting out of his chair. "Marley Watkins didn't want me anywhere near Skylar, and he was right. Louisa was right too. I...Mister, I'm *begging* you to carry this story to your grave. Don't tell Shelby or the rest of my kids."

Vander's shoulders felt like they'd turned to stone, the weight on them was so heavy.

"Maybe Preston is right," Lenore said, squeezing his hand. "I wish...I wish I didn't know. I...I need to go inside for a spell."

She released her grip on him and stood awkwardly, facing her son. Her lips trembled as she walked to the back door, leaving Vander alone with Shelby's father.

"You must hate me," Preston said in a hard tone. "Well, it's no worse than I deserve. I've never had a moment's peace since I left my family, and however much I run, I can't escape it."

Normally Vander wouldn't have asked why someone had kept running in a case like this—it didn't change the facts—but he had to know for Shelby and her siblings. "So all this time, you've been moving from one town to the next...for what?"

The man's eyes blazed. "You can sit in judgment all you like, Mister, but you don't have a fucking clue what it means to be so ashamed of yourself and what you've done that you can't stop trying to run from it. Forget it ever happened. I leave a town almost every year like clockwork as a way of making sure I never get too close to anyone again. That way I can't hurt nobody."

The force of Preston's reply slammed into his chest.

"That changed some with Pauline," the man continued, "but it doesn't matter now. I'm no good—to anyone. Including my kids. I don't plan on ever reaching out to them. They're better off without me. If you have any love for my daughter and the rest of them, you won't tell them what happened."

Suddenly it cut Vander to the quick to see the resemblance this man had to the woman he loved while he repudiated all connection to her except for the genes they shared. He rose slowly out of the chair and stared at Preston. "You said your piece. The rest is up to me to decide."

He left the man standing all alone.

CHAPTER 33

SHELBY AWOKE FROM A DEAD SLEEP WHEN A WARM BODY slid in beside her.

"It's me," he whispered, running a hand down her back. "Go back to sleep."

Her body was lethargic, and she didn't want to open her eyes. "What time is it?"

"Late," he said, pulling her to his side. "I didn't want to be without you tonight. Hope that's okay."

She managed to put her arm around his waist. "I love hearing that. How was work?"

His chest lifted as he heaved a deep sigh. "Tough, but I got through it. Shelby, I love you."

There was something in his voice... She struggled more fully awake. "Can you talk about it?"

"Not now," he said, smoothing her hair. "Maybe not ever. Some things I can't talk about."

"It's okay," she said, kissing the warm skin of his neck, wanting to assure him. "I understand, but I'm here for you when you need me."

His arms tightened around her. "Promise?"

That made her lever up on her elbow. The room was too dark for her to see his face, but she could sense the invisible weight he was carrying. "I love you. Of course, I promise."

Goodness, he must have had a horrible day. "Let's see if I can reassure you."

She trailed her fingertips up his chest to his mouth, letting herself be guided by touch. When she leaned over to kiss him, he rolled her over until she was resting on his chest. He'd been right about how luscious simple skin-to-skin contact was. She reveled in the heat and hardness of his body under hers.

In that practical way of hers, she'd started keeping condoms under her pillow for moments like this. She located one and managed to fit one over him, feeling an urgent need.

He gave a dark groan when she straddled his waist and took him inside her body. His hands gripped her waist as she started to move, and when they shifted to her breasts, she was the one who cried out. He tugged and pulled at her nipples until she was increasing her pace, her desire for him driving her wild.

His fingers found the place where they were joined and caressed her there. She cried out and clenched around him as she came. When he followed her seconds later, she sank on top of him, flushed and sweaty and so filled with love for him—just the way she liked it.

She never wanted to be without Vander or this feeling they had between them.

He tucked her close and whispered, "I love you," and she fell to sleep listening to his heart.

When she came awake, the shower was running. Light was peeking around the edges of the curtains. She grabbed her phone and made a sound. *Seven o'clock? On a Sunday?* She thought about joining him, but good Lord, she hated being up this early unless she had to be.

The shower shut off, and she closed her eyes again. When the bathroom door opened, she turned on her side, shocked to see he was dressed.

"Where are you going?" she asked.

He started. "Sorry. I didn't mean to wake you. I was going to leave you a note."

She frowned. "It's Sunday. Come here."

"I have some work I need to do," he said, approaching the bed. "It can't wait."

"But it's Sunday! I thought we'd spend today together since you had to work yesterday."

He looked down at the floor, and Shelby felt a moment of unease. Usually they were so in sync. He would say something like, "How do you wake up looking so beautiful and sexy?" and then he'd ruin it by adding, "Thank God you have morning breath like the rest of us mere mortals." Something was wrong.

"You have church and family stuff today," he said. "I thought you'd be caught up."

He was always looking at her when they were together, like he didn't want to look anywhere else, but now he was avoiding her gaze. Something was *really* wrong.

Sitting up, she tucked the sheet under her armpits. "Sure, I have church this morning, but I can miss Sunday dinner." She still hadn't decided to attend.

"Two weeks in a row? That's not the Shelby I know. You love seeing your family."

Normally she did. "I wanted things to settle down a little more. So you'd feel more comfortable coming."

He crossed to the bed, leaned down, and kissed her on the cheek, not giving her a chance to pull him onto it with her. Then walked to the door.

"Don't wait for me. Go be with them. I'll call you later."

He was really leaving? "Vander, what's wrong? Because this...something doesn't feel right."

Was it her imagination, or did he sigh at the doorway? Fear washed over her like cold rain.

"It's this case," he said, clearing his throat. "Sometimes they bother me. There's nothing wrong between us, Shelby. Would I have used the key you gave me when I got back in the middle of the night after a horrible day if that weren't true?"

Logically, she agreed. But something was off. She could feel it.

"Promise me you'll come over tonight," she said, clutching the sheet.

"I will if I can," he told her and blew her a kiss before disappearing in the hallway.

She went to church with a heavy heart and hugged Mama extra hard when the woman squeezed her with all her strength. She went to family dinner and chatted up a storm with everyone, but her attention was split thinking about Vander. People asked after his whereabouts, and Shelby told them he was working. It was nice to have everyone send him their regards, including her pale-faced mama.

When she got home, he called, but their talk was brief. He didn't say anything about his day, other than to say he couldn't talk about it.

After she hung up the phone, she wondered what had gone wrong between them so fast.

CHAPTER 34

VANDER FELT LIKE HE WAS WALKING A TIGHTROPE between the duty he felt toward his clients and his impulse to protect Shelby and her family from the truth about their father.

He'd ached the whole way back to Nashville, but the impulse to go to her had been irrepressible. Making love to her had grounded him again, reminded him of who they were becoming. After she'd fallen asleep, he'd lain awake listening to her soft breathing, tortured by the decision he had to make.

When he could take it no longer, he'd showered early to head out before she awoke. Normally, she was a heavy sleeper, and it had cracked part of his heart to leave her, especially since he knew he'd put that hurt look on her face.

He told himself it was best to limit their time together until he'd decided what to do. After he left Shelby's, he called Charlie and told her everything. Rather than give him a flip answer, she told him she needed to think on it. Despite the voice inside him that urged him to *hurry, hurry, hurry*, he respected her for taking it seriously.

She breezed into his office early Monday morning and planted her hands on his desk. "I thought about it all day yesterday. I tried to put myself in their place. Vander, I'm not sure I'd want to know the truth."

Pushing back in his chair, he crossed his arms. "Why not?"

"I was thinking about my family, and I hate thinking about them," she said with a drawn-out sigh. "What if my father had other children, ones he'd never had a relationship with, would I want them to know what he did to me? I know the kind of hurt it caused me. I...sometimes it's not better to know you're related to someone who's done something terrible. It's not like anyone is at risk here."

He'd thought about the situation from a million different angles. Ultimately, he'd be breaking a whole host of agreements other people had made decades ago—not to mention causing plenty of pain to Shelby and her siblings, who'd already been hurt so much.

Plus, if he told them, Louisa might never forgive him. How was he supposed to show up at family occasions knowing she blamed him for sharing the ugly details surrounding the demise of her marriage?

But how could he keep such a big secret from the woman he loved, especially after he'd spoken to her about the importance of honesty?

"Thank you for sharing your opinion," he told Charlie, reaching for his cup of coffee.

"You haven't decided yet," she said, frowning.

"No," he replied, reaching for his phone when it beeped, signaling a text. Shelby.

Hey, gorgeous. I missed you last night. How about I come over early with my new key and make you dinner?

He stared at the display and turned the phone over. Great. Now he was avoiding her. This couldn't continue. She'd get hurt and mad. Rightfully so. He didn't want to treat her badly when she'd done nothing but love him.

He didn't want to lose her.

"All right, leave me be," Vander said to Charlie, looking up at the ceiling. "I need to think."

"Holler if you want to throw darts," she said. "You could crack like a stone you're so tense."

When she left, he dug out a legal pad and wrote down the pros and cons of the problem, like he would do to work out a case. That didn't help. Charlie's take had been enlightening. It shook him that his friend, who had always believed in people facing harsh truths, wouldn't want to know if she were in Shelby's place. Still, he felt the need for more advice.

He settled into his morning, meeting with clients and working the leads on his current cases. But nothing could completely distract him from his problem. He thought about talking to Gail about the situation since she knew Shelby, but the woman was too unpredictable. She might up and tell Shelby herself.

Who could he trust? Rye came to mind, but he dismissed the idea as quickly as it came. Rye could be about as unpredictable as Gail in his own way. Plus he had a baby coming any day.

But Clayton... Rye trusted his secrets with his manager, and Vander knew him to be a man of honor. Desperate to talk it out with someone, he picked up the phone and called him.

"Vander!" Clayton said. "We missed you yesterday at family dinner. Not that I don't understand your absence. Hopefully, Louisa will calm down some. Amelia Ann filled me in on the whole situation. Hope you know I wouldn't say anything."

That made everything easier.

"Of course," he immediately responded. "That's why I'm calling, actually. I need some advice. There's been a break in the case. You need to know up front that it's pretty awful stuff, and I don't want you to tell Amelia Ann if we decide to keep this between us. I don't want to put you in a bad situation, but...I don't know what to do here. You know the family better than I do."

"I'm glad you felt you could trust me," Clayton said, concern lacing his voice. "You have my word it'll stay between us. Amelia Ann sometimes can't tell me things about her work at the legal clinic. It won't hurt us any."

Vander felt relief at that. He didn't want to cause strain in anyone else's relationship. "Let me lay it out for you."

When he finished, Clayton was silent for some time. Then he said, "It's worse than I expected. I mean...Jesus. A minor? And she had a baby? That means they have a half sister or brother out there."

"I know." Vander had thought about the girl and the child too. He'd wondered if he should try and find out what happened after Skylar Watkins went to Texas, but without anyone's permission, that seemed like overstepping.

"I can see your dilemma. You're pretty much fucked all ways, aren't you? Pardon my French."

"No pardon needed," Vander said. "When I'm not sick to my stomach, I want to curse a blue streak. I don't want this to hurt Shelby or any of them, but—"

"You tell J.P.," Clayton interrupted. "He's been the head of that family since their daddy left, and the women all respect him. He's also capable of keeping a secret if needed. I'd talk to him if I were in your place."

Vander had wondered about talking to J.P., but it had a lot of cons. "Shelby would get mighty upset if she finds out I talked to J.P. before her."

"In this situation, I don't see a way around it," Clayton said. "Especially since Louisa has always been so dead set against the truth coming out. Now it all makes sense. That poor woman. I've known her a long time. This would have destroyed another woman, but she... Well, she's one tough cookie."

He concurred. "All right, I'll talk to J.P. Thanks, Clayton."

"You're welcome," the man said. "I think I'll say a prayer for everybody, and trust me when I tell you how rare that is."

"I know what you mean," Vander said. "Thanks again, Clayton."

He hung up and stared at his phone for a solid minute before pulling up J.P.'s contact information and calling him.

"Hey, it's Vander," he said when the other man picked up.

"Hope you don't mind me calling."

"Not at all," J.P. said. "I was sorry you didn't join Shelby yesterday. All of us want you to feel welcomed. Mama will come around, I promise. She's a good woman and always tries to do what's right."

Vander had new insight on that. "Clayton told me I could talk to you about something. How does your day look?"

There was an audible pause. "I can make time. I'm writing a song today, so I'm pretty flexible."

"Could you meet me..." And a public place just wouldn't do it, given the subject matter, especially since he couldn't risk running into Shelby. Charlie would let him use her place. "I'll text you the address. How about in an hour?" It was heading on about noon now.

"Sure thing," J.P. replied. "See you soon."

Vander picked up a pen and rolled it over his fingers. "You didn't even ask me what it was about."

"I figure you'll tell me soon enough," the man responded. "See you in a bit."

That answer cemented it. J.P. was the right person for him to talk to. Thank God, he'd called Clayton. After a quick chat with Charlie, Vander drove to her apartment, equipped with her key and alarm code. Like him, she didn't want the maintenance of a home or yard. She'd warned him everything was mostly clean, but that he'd have to pick up a little.

When he got back to the office, he was going to tease her about throwing her dirty laundry around the house. She was so clean in her work space. It rather surprised him to see the disarray, but honestly, he was happy for the distraction while he waited.

J.P. arrived soon after he finished tidying up, and it took the other man all of two seconds to ask, "This isn't your place, is it?"

Vander shook his head. "What gave it away?"

"The purse over the chair. It's not Shelby's style."

Looking over, he caught the plain black bag J.P. was

referring to. "No, it's not. This is Charlie's place. I'm sorry about the caution. It was…necessary."

J.P. put his hands on his hips, his eyes narrowing. "That doesn't sound good. What's going on?"

Vander's chest constricted as he thought about what he needed to say. "Do you want anything to drink?"

"No, let's just get to it. I'm trying not to be worried here. Is it Shelby?"

Again, Vander shook his head. "No, it's about your father. There was a break in the case…and now I know why he left. It's…" God, how could he describe it? "I understand why your mother didn't want you to know. In fact, that's why I'm not sure I should disregard her wishes. Your dad left it up to me to decide. But all of you wanted to know the truth, and I don't like keeping anything from Shelby."

J.P. looked down like he was studying the floor. "That bad, huh? I feared it had to be for Mama to be so tight-lipped. You don't know her well yet, and she certainly hasn't shown you her best side, but she's always saying you can't heal what you won't talk about. And Mama believes in healing. It's what she does as a preacher."

"I realize that," Vander said. "I didn't quite know what to do. I called Clayton for advice, and he said you were the best person to talk to about it. That you'd know the best course for the family. I didn't feel I did, or that I even had the right to make that decision."

The man blew out a long breath. "We'd best sit down."

They sat at Charlie's glass dining room table, and Vander waited for J.P. to compose himself.

"I don't know that I want to hear it," J.P. said, patting the glass like he was nervous. "But I suppose you'd better."

Vander had told people plenty of horrible things since he'd become a private investigator. One client's spouse had stolen from her checking account when she wasn't looking, and another client had hired him to find his kidnapped daughter, only for Vander to have to report she was dead. Then there was the husband who had hired him to find out why his wife had left him, which had ended with the twist that his business partner had killed her and buried her in his backyard because she'd threatened to tell her spouse about the affair. But telling J.P. what he'd learned was somehow the hardest.

He felt helpless as the man's mouth bunched with emotion during the telling. Not once did J.P. interrupt him. He listened straight through Vander's recitation, only once looking away when Vander told him about the girl becoming pregnant. At that moment, Vander could see the gleam of tears in his eyes, and he felt his own gut burn with empathy.

When he finally finished he said, "I'm so sorry. I don't know what else to say."

"How could you?" J.P. asked, blinking rapidly to clear the tears in his eyes. "I listened to you talking, and it was like listening to a story about someone else's daddy. Part of me kept thinking, *my daddy wouldn't have done that.* But it was the truth straight from his own mouth. My God! When I think about Mama and what she must have gone through... I didn't have a clue. Part of me wonders how I didn't know things were so bad."

"Parents often shield their children from the worst parts of a marriage," Vander said. "Your mother did a stellar job of it."

"I can't even begin to think of the pain this caused her. Or the shame. And that girl, Skylar. My God, we have a half sister or brother somewhere, and we didn't even know it. What must his or her life have been like?" Tears rolled down his face, and he swiped at them. "I'm sorry."

Vander had seen grown men reduced to tears before. He'd also been there himself. "You don't need to apologize. I can't imagine the hurt you're feeling."

J.P. swiped at a few more. "In my mind, I always thought Daddy left because he was too immature to raise a family and be a husband, but to learn this? I don't think disappointment is a strong enough word for how I feel—even if he is sorry."

Preston McGuiness was sorry, and he certainly hadn't led an easy life. But that was no excuse for what he'd done. Vander wondered what the man would do now. Would he continue to move around from town to town like a nomad wrapped up in sins like he'd indicated was his lot in life? Since the man obviously didn't want to see his children, Vander supposed it didn't matter.

"This will kill the girls," J.P. said in a hoarse voice. "And having Mama know we finally know the truth... God help us all."

"Do you want a bourbon?" Vander asked, knowing Charlie would have some around.

"A stiff drink or two might be just the thing," J.P. said.

Vander located Charlie's bourbon and decided to buy her a better selection as a thank you for letting him use her place. He poured two glasses, and when he placed J.P.'s drink in front of him, the man took a long, slow sip.

"I've always told myself I'm not the kind of man to get drunk to numb out bad news," J.P. said, as if noticing his scrutiny. "Rye was the king of that. But now I can see the appeal. I'm still not going to do it, though."

"I wouldn't judge you," Vander said, meeting his eyes as he sat down across from him.

"No, you wouldn't," J.P. said after a time, setting the glass aside. "This must have weighed heavy on you, being with Shelby."

He didn't want to make this about him, but he couldn't deny he was connected. "That's putting it mildly. I love her, and being honest with the person you love is sacrosanct as far as I'm concerned. This doesn't sit well at all."

J.P. nodded and pushed his glass further from him, closer to Vander's, which he hadn't touched.

"Do you know what you want to do?" Vander asked.

Shaking his head, J.P. said, "This whole thing is a mess of tangles, isn't it? If you pull one string, it only gets more knotted up. Christ, give me strength." J.P. stood. "I'll need to sit with this. Pray about it. Hard. But I won't take long to decide. I know this isn't the kind of news you can let linger."

While Vander wasn't sure how he was supposed to see Shelby before he had an answer, he didn't want J.P. to feel rushed. He got to his feet and said, "Time doesn't factor into decisions like this. When you're sure, let me know. I'll be here. Whatever you decide."

The man nodded and walked to the door, letting himself out.

Vander sat back down at Charlie's table, and even though he wasn't the kind of man to drink over bad news either, he downed his bourbon.

CHAPTER 35

SHELBY STARED OFF INTO SPACE AS SHE STIRRED THE BATTER for the Mississippi Mud Cake she'd decided to make for Vander. He'd given her his key and told her she was welcome anytime. Of course, he hadn't responded to her text, but she reasoned he was in back-to-back meetings and hadn't had time.

Being at his house had calmed some of the anxiety that had welled up inside her since his abrupt departure on Sunday morning. His things were where they normally were, and somehow that order was its own assurance. She'd left the office early to shop for their meal and decided to bake the cake at his house. What man didn't like coming back from work to a home filled with the scent of a baked cake? Perhaps it would help Vander relax about whatever case had him all riled up.

Every time her mind told her the problem was her—that he'd grown tired of her like Nick had—she banged the wooden spoon against the side of the bowl. She banged it quite a lot, actually. She said a little prayer that it wouldn't make the cake flat as she put it in the oven.

She returned to the spreadsheets on her laptop and tried to find some peace in all her formulas and numbers adding up like they should.

When there was a loud knocking on the door, Shelby

jumped in her chair. She glanced in the direction of the sound, but stayed where she was. Even though she had a key to Vander's home, she didn't feel right about answering his door.

But the knocking wouldn't let up. In fact, it sounded quite frantic.

She walked slowly to the door, trying to keep her footsteps quiet, so she could peek through the peephole. Could it be one of Vander's clients? She couldn't imagine he'd give out his personal address. When she saw who was knocking, she gasped.

Mama!

She jumped again when another barrage of knocks shook the door. What was her mama doing here? Shelby opened the door to find out.

Mama's whole face seemed to crumple. "Oh, no! I'm too late. Oh, Shelby! I'm so sorry."

Her mama put her arms around her and started to sob. Fear lanced through Shelby's heart. She'd *never* seen her mama like this. She was crying so hard, mascara was streaking down her face.

"Mama! What is it? What's wrong?"

Mama pushed her back, hard enough to make her gasp. "He had no right to tell you. No right!"

She was hysterical. Shelby's stomach gripped. "Mama! What are you talking about?"

"Your daddy called and told me that his awful mama forced him to tell her and Vander why he left."

Pain slammed through Shelby, and she almost doubled over. Everything was falling into place now. Lenore must have called him, and he'd taken off to meet them. It made sense, but her heart couldn't take it. *Vander kept that from me? How could he?*

Mama pulled at her hair, scaring Shelby. "Have you told the other kids? Please, Shelby, *please*. Tell me you and Vander haven't told the rest of my babies. I can't bear it!"

Shelby was shaking all over, and she caught a worried look from one of Vander's neighbors as he walked quickly past the open door. She couldn't bring herself to care. Vander knew the truth about why her daddy had left, and so did her mama. Shelby wanted to know. She deserved to know.

"Tell them what, Mama?" she asked in a hard tone. If Vander didn't plan on revealing what he'd discovered, she was going to hear it from the horse's mouth.

"You know what I'm talking about!" Her mama's voice was high-pitched and pleading. "Oh, the hurt. The shame. I've tried to protect y'all from it. Please, Shelby. Promise me that you won't tell the others."

Her mama gripped her arms hard enough to leave a mark, and Shelby fought the urge to fling them off her. Rage as hot and scalding as boiling water was coursing through her system.

"I want to hear your side of it!" she said, nearly shouting. "I want to hear why you've kept this from us for most of our lives."

"You know why!" Mama shouted back. "Your daddy did the most unspeakable, horrible thing ever—and then he wanted me to leave town with him and pretend it had never happened. He wasn't the man I thought I'd married. I couldn't do that. I *wouldn't* do that! I deserved a better husband, and y'all certainly deserved a better daddy. Even if that meant you never had a daddy growing up, and we were as poor as church mice."

Lead settled into Shelby's bones, and a feeling of strong foreboding prickled her skin. "You tell me what he did, Mama. You say it to my face! I'm old enough to hear it."

Her mama's green eyes locked on hers, and her lip started to tremble. "Your daddy had sex with a fifteen-year-old girl at church and got her pregnant. Is that what you wanted to hear? Is that what you *think* you're old enough to hear?"

Shelby fell back a few steps and hit the edge of a side table. Pain flashed through her ankle, and she cried out. *"No! He* wouldn't do that. *Not that.*"

She realized she was crying, and Mama was crying too. She fell to the floor, every naïve dream she'd had of her daddy exploding like glass shards around her, slicing open her skin and cutting down to her soul.

"Oh, Shelby," her mama said, wrapping her arms around her. "I'm so sorry, baby. I never wanted you to know. Never!"

They both cried and cried and cried until Shelby couldn't breathe and had to blow her nose. Seeing no tissues close by, she went into the hall bathroom and yanked off some toilet paper. She blew her nose loudly and washed her shaking hands.

Mama was standing in the hallway, her whole face a mix of mascara streaks and splotches. "Can I have some too?"

Shelby felt tears burn her eyes again as she looked at her, this woman she'd loved and idolized all her life. Oh, how their mother had suffered for them. Turning sideways, she grabbed a handful of toilet paper and handed it to her.

"Mama," she said as the woman blew her nose. "I never imagined this."

"This is why I've never told you," Mama said in an anguished voice. "I *never* wanted any of you kids to feel the hurt of it. How was I supposed to tell you that your daddy did something like that? We were lucky her family didn't press charges, or he would have gone to jail for sure."

Shelby jolted at the thought. Jail. Yes, he could have been sent there. My God.

"I used to lay in bed at night, sick at the thought of you kids having a daddy who was in prison for statutory rape. You'll never know how relieved I was when that family left town for good a few years later. Seeing them every Sunday at church was pure torture, Shelby, let me tell you. Thank God they sent their girl away."

Shelby felt cold all over as she realized that girl had had a baby—a baby who was their kin.

"I don't think I could have stood the sight of her," Mama

continued in a harsh tone, tears streaking down her face. "It makes me feel so much shame to say that. I try and be a good Christian woman, but even after all these years, I haven't completely forgiven him or made peace with what he did."

Shelby understood. She hated him with all her might. "Mama! What about the baby?"

She shook her head, biting her lip. "I never wanted to know, Shelby. I'm...sorry."

Her head was hurting from all the stress and the crying. "Mama, we need to tell the others," she finally said.

"No! Your daddy was wrong to give in to Lenore. He was sure as hell wrong to tell Vander. Dammit, Shelby, you told me he wasn't looking into this."

She felt another slice of pain. Vander had come back from Me-Mother's and slipped into bed with her without saying a word about it. "I...I lied to put you at ease. We all agreed not to tell you we'd tried to find Daddy. Mama, that's how I met Vander."

Her mama put her hand to her mouth. "You lied about all of that to me? Oh, Shelby."

"You wouldn't tell us anything about Daddy, Mama!" She realized she was raising her voice again and went over to shut the front door finally. "We wanted to know. We *needed* to know."

"All of you? Even John Parker?"

"All of us went to meet Me-Mother, Mama," she said. Then added, "Lenore."

Her mama's eyes fired. "You met that awful woman? Shelby, she's one of the meanest women I've ever known. If you could have heard what she said to me at our wedding or when your daddy left..."

"Maybe she's changed, Mama. At first she seemed cold, but she was kind to us later on. We...liked her. We've talked about helping her out."

Her mama hung her head. "I've prayed and prayed to ask God to protect you, but hearing what you did... I'm afraid I've already lost you."

Shelby wrapped her arms around her. "No, Mama. You haven't, and you won't. But we...we just wanted to know what happened, and you would never talk about Daddy."

"I hope now you realize why," she whispered. "Oh, Shelby, please forgive me. I love you so much. All of you kids."

Tears poured down her face as she stroked her mama's hair. "Mama, there's nothing to forgive. We love you. It's going to be all right."

She sniffed. "When I think about what your daddy did, part of me can't help but wonder what my part in it was. I thought he was such a good man, but what man with an ounce of decency would get intimate with a child? That's something I could never, ever understand!"

Shelby couldn't either, and the mere thought of it made her ill. "I don't understand it either, and it certainly doesn't make me feel good knowing it. But Mama, I'm glad I finally know why Daddy left us. It means I can let go of all the stories I made up about it." And she could curse her father's soul and feel grateful he hadn't been in their lives, even though she knew it was awful of her. But he'd done something unforgiveable, and she just couldn't be a good Christian right now. Maybe not ever.

Her mama wiped her running nose. "Then I guess there's a blessing in all this. I feared there wouldn't be."

"Mama, we need to tell the others," she said. "You can't keep carrying this secret, trying to protect us all. We're old enough to know the truth, and you need to let us carry the weight with you. Maybe if we carry it together, it won't feel so heavy."

Her mama cradled her face. "God blessed me so much when he gave me you. How wise you are."

Shelby felt tears streak down her face anew. "You taught me, Mama."

Mama wiped her tears away, something she hadn't done since Shelby was a child. When they embraced again, they were both calmer. Shelby didn't know about Mama, but her heart wasn't hurting as much.

An alarm pierced the silence, and they both jumped a foot. *Fire. Please proceed to the exits.* The automated voice had Shelby running to the kitchen. Black smoke was pouring out of the oven.

"Oh, dammit, I forgot to set the timer," she said, shoving potholders onto her hands and opening the oven door.

A phone immediately started ringing, but Shelby focused on taking the cake out as she coughed and blinked back tears. The cake was charred and black and smoking up a storm.

"Go answer the phone," Mama said. "It's the alarm company. I'll deal with this."

She raced in the direction of the ringing, wanting to put her hands over her ears as the smoke alarm continued to peal. "We're okay," she answered. "Sorry! I burned a cake."

"Are you sure you don't want us to send a fire truck?" the alarm company representative asked.

"No," Shelby immediately responded. "There's no fire. Just a burnt cake."

"All right. We'll just need your password."

She blanked for a moment and then said, "Justice," which Vander had told her after he'd given her his key.

"Thank you," the man on the line said. "I'm turning it off now. Please call back if you need anything else, Mrs. Montgomery."

Shelby started at that, and pure elation shot through her—quick and brilliant as a shooting star—as she hung up the phone. Mrs. Montgomery. Then she fell back to earth. Not in a million years. How was she supposed to trust Vander after he kept something this important from her?

Her mama came out of the kitchen. "I put the cake in the sink and turned the faucet on. It stopped the smoking."

"Good." She supposed that was good. But as she walked back into the kitchen and eyed the groceries she'd set on the counter, she thought about all the worry Vander had put her through—how she'd taken the evening off work to make him a meal—and a hot rage blossomed inside her.

Her cell phone started to ring, and she knew who it was. If Vander's alarm company was anything like hers, they'd contacted him both at home and on his cell. Well, there was no way she was talking to him right now.

"Mama, let's go," she said, walking over and grabbing her purse.

"But Shelby, we need to clean up this mess," her mama said.

"Mama, I don't think either one of us wants to talk to Vander just now."

Shelby wasn't sure she ever wanted to talk to him again. How dare he lie to her like that! How dare he let himself into her apartment and then her bed without giving her the information he knew she'd waited years to learn? He was always talking about honesty and his integrity. He was a hypocrite.

Her mama nodded. "I see your point."

They walked out together.

CHAPTER 36

VANDER ARRIVED HOME TO THE SMELL OF CHARRED cake in the air and an unholy mess in the kitchen. The alarm company had notified him of the fire alarm going off, but they'd also said the person who'd answered his phone had known the password. Shelby, it seemed, had indeed gone over to his house to cook them dinner.

The burnt cake wasn't the only mess. Vander had been on his way home from a meeting with a long-time client in Dare River when Charlie had called to say Louisa McGuiness urgently wanted to meet with him. According to her, the woman had sounded frantic on the phone. After texting J.P. to make sure the man hadn't spoken with his mama—he hadn't—he'd told Charlie to give the woman his home address so they could speak in private. Of course, he'd gotten delayed in rush hour traffic—and then come home to this.

Vander wondered what in the hell had happened. Shelby must have been here when her mama arrived, and the burnt cake wasn't a good sign. Neither was the fact that Shelby wasn't picking up her phone.

Conjecture wasn't going to get him anywhere, so he detoured to Shelby's house.

She wasn't home.

He dialed J.P. again. "Hey," he said when the man picked

up. "Sorry to bother you, but have you heard from your mother or Shelby?"

"Yes," J.P. said, his voice tired. "Mama asked all of us kids to come over tonight. She said it was important, but didn't give specifics. Did you speak to her yet?"

"No, we missed each other," Vander said. "Whatever your mother wanted to speak with me about, it can't be good."

"I guess I'll find out at eight," J.P. said. "Mama asked spouses not to attend."

That was interesting. "No word from Shelby? She's not answering my calls." He quickly told J.P. about the burnt cake and dinner fixings on the kitchen counter.

"That doesn't sound like Shelby," J.P. said. "I'll tell her you were looking for her when I see her tonight."

Vander feared the worst. If Louisa had been frantic, surely she knew some, or all, of what her children had been looking into behind her back. If she'd somehow found out about his talk with Lenore and Preston...

"It's not like her to ignore my calls."

"I'll talk to her, Vander," J.P. said. "I need to go. Tammy thought we should have a special meal as a family after I told her what you told me today."

"You're lucky to have her support," Vander said, wondering how she'd taken the news.

"Indeed I am," he said. "I'll talk to you later once I know something. Hold tight. This is tough on everyone."

"I'll be thinking about you and your family tonight," Vander said. In fact, he wouldn't be able to think about anything else.

"Thanks."

After the man hung up, Vander took out his key and let himself inside Shelby's house. She might be ignoring him, but she hadn't asked for her key back yet.

Two could play this game.

CHAPTER 37

WHEN MAMA TEXTED SADIE TO REPORT THERE WAS A family meeting tonight, she was working on Shelby's abacus quilt. Surprise and foreboding made her prick her finger. She immediately called Shelby, but her middle sister didn't answer. Susannah didn't know what it was about, and J.P. only said it was best not to speculate when she hounded him, so Sadie pretty much rocked herself and paced until the agreed-upon hour arrived.

Mama looked about as worn out as Sadie had ever seen her when she opened the door. Her heart started to pound in her ears when she saw the fatigue in Mama's bloodshot, puffy green eyes.

"What happened?" she asked, clutching her arms. "Is it Dale?"

Mama shook her head. "No, honey. Come inside. I only have the strength to tell y'all once."

Shelby emerged quietly from behind Mama, and Sadie locked gazes with her. *This has to be about Daddy.* Shelby's face held the same pallid color and strain as Mama's. So, her sister already knew.

Mama hugged her tightly and then Sadie walked over to Shelby and embraced her with all her might. "It's about Daddy, isn't it?" she whispered.

Shelby nodded and burrowed her head in Sadie's neck.

Her sister was hurting, and so was Mama. *God give me the strength to comfort them, and please comfort me for what's ahead.*

J.P. was already seated on the couch, holding Susannah's hand. Her sister was biting her lip, her strain evident. Sadie grabbed her brother's hand when he held it out to her, and she and Shelby squeezed in on the end of the couch, staying close to each other.

"Thank you for coming," Mama said, clenching her hands together in front of her, standing before them. "What I'm about to tell y'all is one of the hardest things I've ever had to say."

Sadie held her breath, her chest tightening so much it hurt.

"I know y'all have wanted to know about why your daddy left us for a long time." Mama sucked in some air and put her hand over her mouth for a moment before rubbing her neck. "I had my reasons for not sharing the details. I hope once y'all hear the truth, you'll understand I was only trying to protect you. I also pray to God y'all can forgive me for any pain my silence caused."

Oh, Mama. Sadie wanted to jump off the couch and wrap her arms around this wonderful woman she loved so much.

"It seems God had a plan for the truth to come to light, and I've been an impediment to that." She looked down and paused for a moment. "But that ends now. I learned today your daddy told his mama, Lenore, and Vander the truth on Saturday."

Sadie gasped and turned to Shelby. "Vander told you, and you didn't—"

"Vander didn't tell Shelby," Mama interrupted. "Your daddy called to tell me he'd broken his word to me and to say he was sorry. Hearing his voice after all these years...and learning he'd gone and told something we'd agreed long ago to take to our graves... Well, it was another betrayal in a long line of them. I didn't want you to know the kind of man he was, but it seems as though the time has come for me to share the truth. As Shelby told me earlier, y'all are adults now. Plus, you had hired Vander to find out what happened to your daddy."

"You told her?" Sadie asked Shelby, who nodded quietly. It was as if her boisterous sister had gone mute.

"Mama, I'm sorry!" Susannah said, her voice breaking. "I didn't go along with it at first, and in the end, I knew it was wrong of us to look."

Sadie gave her eldest sister a sharp look, hot rage pouring through her again, a kind she'd never experienced before. Susannah *would* try and soften her involvement so Mama wouldn't be upset at her. "We did what we thought was best at the time, Susannah. You went to Me-Mother's too!"

"Please don't argue," Mama said, holding out her hands. "This is hard enough. We all have strong feelings, and they're only going to get stronger once you hear what I have to say."

"Vander told me everything earlier today," J.P. said, causing everyone to turn their heads and stare at him.

"He told you, and not me?" Shelby asked, her voice cracking.

"You should know he was mighty upset about things," J.P. said. "In his defense, he didn't know which way to turn. Mama, he understands why you kept the truth from us for so long. He didn't want to hurt you or any of us—or his potential place in this family with Shelby. Especially with you, Mama. But he also felt we had a right to know the truth since we'd hired him originally for just that."

Yeah, if Mama had been difficult with him before, how sour would her attitude have turned if Vander had told them whatever ugly truth she'd hidden for decades? Sadie didn't envy the man none.

J.P. leaned forward to look at their sister. "Shelby, honey, Vander loves you. So much. He called Clayton for advice, and Clayton told him to talk to me since I was someone y'all looked up to."

"You really know *everything?*" Mama asked, tears streaking down her face.

"Yes, Mama," J.P. said, standing up and taking her small shoulders in his hands. "I'm so sorry. There aren't words enough to say how much."

She put her arms around him and started to cry, and Sadie was itching to shout, *Hey, what about me? I don't know the truth.* But Mama never cried like this—and so she waited while her sister shook from head to toe next to her. Shelby must be hurt and mad as all get out. Well, so was she.

"All right," Mama said, untangling from J.P. "I need to tell y'all in my own words from start to finish. If you can hold off until I finish...it'd be easier on me."

And so Mama began, beginning with Daddy's unemployment and the stress it had put on both them and their marriage. When Mama choked out the details regarding Daddy's affair with the fifteen-year-old girl at church, Sadie sat back against the couch as the pain and shock crashed through her. *How could he do that? How could anyone do something so vile? And with a girl? At church!*

Sadie heard Susannah make a strangled sound when Mama told them the girl had gotten pregnant. Something funny happened to Sadie then—she felt like she was floating, and while she could hear Mama's voice, it suddenly sounded like she was talking underwater. The pain wasn't crushing Sadie anymore. In fact, she couldn't feel her body.

Mama was crying and suddenly put her hands to her face. Still, Sadie floated in her reverie, jarred only slightly when J.P. and Shelby dropped her hands and stood up, making the couch move. She tried to turn her head, but it moved so slowly, almost like the air had grown thick with humidity. But that was strange. They were inside the house.

Susannah was crying by herself, her arms wrapped around her sides. Then Mama was sitting beside her eldest sister and enfolding her against her chest, rocking her and stroking her hair.

Someone jostled her shoulder, and she turned her head to see J.P. kneeling before her.

"Say-dee," he seemed to drawl.

Shelby sat down next to her on the couch and put a hand on her knee. At first she looked at her sister's hand but couldn't feel it, then she suddenly felt the touch. Shelby's hand was hot. And then she everything inside her was hot too.

"Sadie!" J.P. called out and snapped his finger in front of her face.

Pain shot through her system as though a switch had been turned on. And then she felt it...the hot, clawing hand twisting her insides. She bent over at the waist, cradling her stomach. "*Oh, God.*"

J.P. stroked her back while she cried as spasm after spasm roiled through her gut.

"Shh..." he kept repeating over and over again.

"Oh, honey," Shelby said, resting her cheek on Sadie's shoulder. "I know it hurts."

"It hurts so much," she whispered as the sharp pains continued. "How could he do something like that?"

"I don't know, honey," J.P. said softly. "I just don't know."

The razor blades cut through her as she let go of every dream she'd ever had of the daddy she'd never known. "I hate him! I hate *him!*"

"That's okay, Sadie," J.P. said, keeping up the comforting sweeps of his hand on her back. "You feel what you feel."

The heat rose within her until she felt like she was standing in a forest fire. She pushed off the couch. "I can't take this! I want to hit him." Mama looked over at her sharply. "I want to know *why!*"

"Oh, baby," Mama said, rising and wrapping her arms around Sadie. "I know you want to know. I wish could tell you."

Her chest thickened until she could hardly breathe, and a rush of pain rose in her chest. She cried out again, and this time tears erupted—hot, painful, drenching tears—the kind that made her fear she would drown in them.

She pressed her face into Mama's shoulder as the world narrowed to nothing but her pain and the unstoppable release of it. Her head filled up. Her nose ran. She coughed and cried and then coughed some more. The happy dream of her daddy walking her down the aisle turned into the tawdry scene of him banging a fifteen-year-old girl at their old church.

From time to time, someone would press a tissue in her hand, and she would blow her nose and throw the tissue on the floor because she didn't care. She didn't care about anything.

The flood transformed into a river and then narrowed to a stream, and then she was nestled against her mama's chest. Mama was humming in her ear, and somehow hearing that sound, one she remembered from childhood, soothed her some. Her daddy might be the worst kind of deadbeat asshole—good heavens, she didn't use that word lightly—but her mama was the best. And so were her siblings. She was so lucky. She tried to latch on to that.

"I'm so glad you didn't go with Daddy," she whispered in her mama's ear.

Mama edged back and soothed away her tears. "Oh, my sweet girl, I'm so sorry for this."

She shook her head and looked over her shoulder when she felt a hand touch her lower back. It was J.P., whose dark eyes were wet with tears like the rest of them.

"I'm so glad you were the man of the house," she told her brother.

His mouth turned up, and he caressed her cheek. "We're blessed we have one another."

Mama gestured to Susannah and Shelby, who were hugging each other beside them. "Come here, y'all."

They wrapped their arms around one another, making a circle, offering and receiving comfort. Sadie was sure there would be many more discussions about the events Mama shared with them tonight, but for the moment, no words were necessary.

Sadie didn't know how long they stayed that way, but the pain lapping at her heart was now surrounded by love...and that was bigger than all the pain in the world.

"We're going to be okay somehow," Mama said, sniffing.

"We're more than okay, Mama," J.P. said in his deep, reassuring voice.

And Sadie knew he was right like usual.

CHAPTER 38

WHEN SHELBY FINALLY CRAWLED OUT OF PEARL AFTER midnight in her driveway, her body felt like she'd gone nine rounds in the boxing ring of life. Her emotions were all over the place, and she'd already decided to call in sick tomorrow and wallow just for the hell of it.

Mama had invited all of them to spend the night, but Sadie was the only one who'd taken her up on the offer. Shelby had wanted to be around her own things. And if she had trouble sleeping—which she expected she would—at least she could wander the halls or make tea without disturbing anyone.

When she opened her front door, she dropped her purse on the floor, not having enough energy to set it on the table. Too much effort. She dragged herself up the stairs and stripped off her clothes on the way to the shower. She made the water hot, and when she got under the spray, she let it wash over her.

The pain seemed to rise up all over again. God, when was it ever going to stop? It was bad enough to learn about Daddy's horrible sins, but to hear that Vander had spoken to Clayton and her brother rather than her... The heart that had been filled with love and sparkles for him was now filled with anguish and gravel.

Shelby sank to the floor of the shower and gave in to her emotions all over again as the questions swirled in her head. *How could her daddy have done that? That?*

She cried until the water turned cold, and since she was starting to shiver, she pulled herself up and shut the shower off. Crying like this made her feel weak and pathetic, but even J.P. had cried, so perhaps there was no shame in it. He'd always been the rock, their stronghold, but this had hurt him as much as the rest of them. Perhaps more so because he remembered Daddy the best, being the oldest and all.

After drying off, she decided she was too tired to brush her hair out or put on moisturizer. Wrapping a towel around her, she left the bathroom and jumped when she saw Vander sitting quietly on the edge of her bed.

"I would have held you while you cried, but you were naked, and I wasn't sure how you'd feel about that right now."

Her bones were aching, and her heart swelled with renewed hurt. "How could you have talked to Clayton and J.P. and not me?"

He took her robe from the bed and stood. "You're shivering. Put this on, and I can tell you why. I made you tea."

She pushed the robe away and looked at him. His face was grave, but his blue eyes were steady on her face.

"I don't want your help," she said, her voice pitched to hurt. "In fact, right now, I don't even want to look at you. I thought you loved me. You talk about how important honesty is in a relationship, then you do this. How can I trust you again?"

"I know you're tired," he said, moving toward her slowly, like she was an animal that might shy away. He slipped the robe around her shoulders before she could flinch from him. "And cold. God knows how much you're hurting. It killed me to hear you cry like that and stay out here. Shelby, I do love you, but this was complicated. Surely you can see that."

J.P. had tried to talk to her before she'd left, saying Vander had been between a rock and a hard place, urging her to listen to what he had to say. She'd given him a pat response.

Now, she said, "You men! I hate it when you treat us

women like we're too soft or dumb to handle tough news."

Vander's eyes fired. "This wasn't about gender. I didn't want to break your mama's silence after I found out why she'd kept quiet, but I also didn't want to keep the truth from you when you were so desperate for it. Shelby, there were more people involved than just you. If it had only been you, I would have told you in a second."

She studied him, her eyes burning from fatigue. "Would you have? I'm not sure I believe that. You were trying to protect me—just like Mama was. I don't want or need protecting. Not from you. And not from any other man. You destroyed my trust in you."

"*I'm sorry*," he said, his mouth twisting. "I know I hurt you. I usually have a clear vision of what to do about things, but this time I didn't because it involved you. Shelby, I love you and want you in my life for a long time. I don't see that changing. Ever. Do you know what that means?"

She felt tears streak down her cheek. He was going to allude to marriage at a time like this?

"It means I didn't want your mama to hate my guts for telling you a family secret she'd kept her whole life. It means I didn't want there to be friction between you and your family. Shelby, you love them, and my involvement with you complicated matters. I'm sorry I didn't speak with you, but I just...didn't know the best way. I thought J.P. might. I hated putting that decision on him, but it felt like he was the best person to entrust it to."

Other times, she might have agreed with him. But not now. "And what if J.P. had decided it was best to keep quiet about it? Would you really have kept something that important from me for years?" The thought sickened her. "For our whole lives?"

"I want to say no, but honestly, I don't know, dammit! Shelby, please...I'm trying to be honest here."

A harsh laugh escaped. "Honest?"

He pinched the bridge of his nose. "I'm asking you to

forgive me and move forward. The truth is out now. And you know I love you. Everything I've said, I've meant."

Her chest radiated pain. "It's not enough. How can I trust you not to go around my back if you think it's 'best' for me?"

His hands cupped her shoulders, and he bent over slightly to make them eye level. "Let's make a new agreement. I swear I will never keep anything from you ever again. From this day forward."

The words echoed the vows she'd heard at weddings, and it broke the remaining pieces of her heart. "I thought we'd already promised each other that."

He closed his eyes for a moment and sighed deeply. His hands fell from her shoulders. "Get some rest. You're exhausted. We'll talk again."

His kiss landed on her cheek, and she fought the urge to hug him to her, to make everything better through touch. But that wasn't the way.

"If you want, I'll stay with you," he said, keeping his cheek inches from her own. "We've comforted each other before. You don't have to forgive me to take human kindness from me."

But she did, and she made herself step back. "I think you should go."

He ran his hand through his hair. "All right, but when you're thinking about all this, just remember one thing. I love you, and I've haven't said that to anyone since my dad died."

Her lip quivered, but she made herself remain silent. His admission didn't change what he'd done, even though her heart broke for him.

"You damn well know how long that's been, Shelby. Think about that."

With one last scorching look, he walked out.

CHAPTER 39

VANDER WASN'T A MAN WHO SEETHED, BUT HE'D DONE nothing but. Shelby refused to see his side of things and believe he'd done everything out of love. In the office the next morning, Charlie brought him a dozen pointy darts with a knowing look.

He'd texted her an update after speaking to Shelby the night before, and Charlie had called him even though it had been late to offer the Charlie Comfort Package he'd come to rely on in tough cases. That package included her cracking obscene jokes about elephants and their trunks and brainstorming what Caribbean island he could run off to for some time away. She was a good friend and had promised to beat the pants off him at darts.

And so they kicked off their day by taking turns throwing darts at the felt board in their private work space off the conference room. He shed his jacket and rolled up his sleeves, but the pressure in his chest didn't abate any.

When Charlie called it quits for a client meeting, she gave him a long look and said, "As a strong and sometimes bull-headed woman, I can tell you not to give up on Shelby. Figure something out."

He glared at her. "I'm trying, dammit."

"*Try harder*," she said, leaving the darts with him.

After a few more drills to the bulls-eye, he composed himself and headed back toward his office, only to discover Louisa McGuiness in their waiting area. He stopped short. Their eyes met. Her face was pale. Wrinkles he hadn't remembered seeing cut strong grooves in her face. Over the pounding of his heart, he made himself walk forward.

"Louisa," he said, hoping his face was devoid all expression. "I didn't know you were here."

"I told your assistant not to bother you until you finished conferring with your colleague," she said, clenching her hands.

He noted the gesture. "Why don't we talk in my office? Can I get you something to drink?"

"No, thank you," she said politely, so he showed her to his office.

He told himself to keep his cool. After closing the door, he extended his hand to the more informal meeting table to the right of his desk. She sat in the chair as if expecting it to be rigged with dynamite.

"What can I do for you?" he asked.

She put her hand to her heart, her eyes filling with tears. "I owe you an apology. I've been nothing short of horrible to you, and I wouldn't blame you if you thought I was a horrible person."

He shook his head. "Louisa, you're not a horrible person. In fact, you have my admiration. I see a lot of people experience betrayal, and not all of them turn their lives or the lives of their children into something worth writing home about. You managed all of that, and from where I'm sitting, it's pretty incredible."

She took a moment to compose herself. "You have no idea how much those words mean to me—especially this morning." Her mouth lifted with a half smile, and then she reached for his hand. "You're a kind man to say that, Vander. I can see why Shelby fell in love with you, and why the rest of my children hold you in such esteem. I was a fool to treat you like I did, and I hope you can forgive me and put it behind us, so I can show you how happy I am to have you be with Shelby and come around our family."

He didn't know that he'd be coming around anymore after last night, but that didn't change what she was saying. "You were protecting your family. There's nothing to forgive, but I appreciate you saying that nonetheless."

"Shelby must be pretty angry with you," Louisa said, shaking her head. "I'm afraid that's my fault. You were put in a terrible situation. If I can do anything to help…"

The last thing he wanted was more back-channel conversations. He'd had his fill of them. "Shelby will decide what Shelby will decide. I only hope she'll remember how much I love her and realize that this situation…will never happen again."

Louisa barked out a laugh and brushed at tears in her eyes. "Good heavens, I hope so. I feel black and blue this morning, but more at peace than I have since their daddy left. I thanked God for that this morning, and I thanked Him for your role in bringing it about."

Other people had told Vander such things, and they always made him uncomfortable. Coming from her, he wanted to squirm. "I was just doing my job, Louisa."

"I see it differently, Vander," she said, finally releasing his hand. "I'm sorry about the burned cake we left for you."

He'd thought it a fitting metaphor for where his relationship with Shelby stood right now. "It's why I love her. She doesn't mince words."

"Not often, no," Louisa said. "Please come to dinner on Sunday. I'd invite you to church, but Shelby tells me you don't attend—which doesn't bother me in the least, I want you to know."

He studied her. "I believe you mean that last part."

She nodded. "I do. Well, I should let you get on with your day. Vander, I…thank you again for not holding a grudge against me and for trying to do right by Shelby and my family."

The pressure in his chest seemed to increase the longer

her green eyes rested on him. He didn't know if he'd ever see this woman again. That would be up to Shelby. He hoped he would, though. "Thank you for coming, Louisa. Most people wouldn't have thought to, especially after the day you had yesterday."

"God doesn't want us to let our bad behavior stretch out," Louisa said as they walked to the door. "Mine had already lasted way too long. Have a good day, Vander. Don't give up on my daughter."

"I don't plan to," he told her.

"Good," Louisa said. "What's your favorite meal, by the way?"

He thought about it for a moment, knowing why she was asking. "Fried chicken, corn, and mashed potatoes and gravy. Nothing better than that, if you ask me."

"We'll have that this Sunday," Louisa said. "I'll expect to see you there."

There she went again. *"Louisa."*

Her smile was the first easy one he'd seen. "I have faith in you two. Plus, I'm doing a lot of praying, and my prayers are usually answered."

"When aren't they?" he quipped, opening the door.

"When love isn't at the root of the matter," she said, making his hand fall to his side. "That's not the case with you and Shelby. Goodbye, Vander."

"Goodbye, Louisa," he said, and then jumped an inch when she leaned up and kissed him on the cheek.

"Don't worry," she said, smiling wider now. "You'll get used to it. Rye, Clayton, and Jake have, and they're all as tough as you are."

She walked off before he could compose a reply. Charlie popped her head out of her office.

"You okay?" she asked, looking in the direction of Louisa as she headed down the hall for her meeting.

He shrugged. "I have no idea. Go back to work."

His current case files didn't distract him. All he could

think about was Shelby, and what he could do to make her see reason. She was stubborn, but under that, she was hurt. He needed to make her believe in him again. In them.

Light flickered on the ceiling, reflecting something from outside. It seemed to dance across the room like liquid gold. Suddenly it hit him.

He knew how to win Shelby back.

CHAPTER 40

SHELBY'S INTENT TO WALLOW THE DAY AWAY PROVED futile. J.P. called her to share his *perspective* on what Vander had done. That's what her brother had the audacity to call it. She'd cut him off and told him she needed to make up her own mind.

Not too long afterward, her mama had called as well to tell her she'd swung by Vander's office—holy heavens alive—and ask for his forgiveness regarding her actions, which he'd given without hesitation. While she was reeling from that information, her mama had informed her she was making Vander's favorite meal—fried chicken and all the fixings—this coming Sunday, and Shelby had better make sure he was present to enjoy it.

When her mama had finally let her get off the phone, Shelby was fit to be tied. How dare her family interfere like that and tell her what to do! Had they all learned nothing?

Being with Vander was her decision, not theirs. For once, they needed to butt the hell out.

Then Gail called, and Shelby was certain Vander had enlisted her help somehow. Yet her boss was all business—she had insisted she needed to see Shelby ASAP to go through the profit and loss balance statements for all her businesses since she'd had a brainstorm the night before about opening up a new business—a juice bar on the Vanderbilt University campus. Gail thought it would require little overhead and sell like gangbusters with the more affluent, health-conscious crowd. Shelby agreed to swing by after lunch, not seeing another choice.

When she arrived at Gail's, the security gate seemed to take forever to open, and she realized she was feeling surly. Her boss didn't know why she was in a bad mood, and she didn't need to lead with it. If Gail sensed something was up, she'd pounce on her like a mad terrier until she spilled her problems, and Shelby wasn't ready for Gail's kind of leopard-print couch therapy. The woman would probably swing her white feather boa around as Shelby talked about her daddy.

She parked her car in the circular driveway. After grabbing her purse and valise, she made sure not to slam the door. The fountain was gurgling, and Shelby turned her head to look at it. The cherubs seemed to be frolicking in the spray like usual, and suddenly the magic and playfulness of it made Shelby grind her teeth.

She really *should* throw a coin in the fountain. Heavens knew, she had plenty of wishes to request right now, but the last thing she wanted to do was throw a coin in that fountain today.

When she thought about all her dreams—the ones she'd had about finding her daddy and being with Vander—they seemed so foolish now.

Vander was right. It was stupid to wish for anything. It was even stupider to throw coins into a fountain. What a waste of good money.

Shelby turned around and started up the brick path, struggling to ignore the pain in her heart.

"Aren't you going to throw a coin into the fountain today?" she heard a familiar voice ask.

Turning her head in the direction of the sound, she watched Vander materialize from behind one of Gail's white Plantation columns and head down the steps. He held two white cloth bags in his hands, and for the life of her, she had no idea what was in them.

Not that she cared.

She told herself not to care he was here either—or that there was a look of intense longing in his beautiful eyes. It was best to take a step back and shut this down right now.

"I was just thinking you were right," she told him. "I was stupid to think it worked."

Her heart broke saying it, but in truth, her heart was breaking all over again just from seeing him.

"I'm sad to hear you say that," he said, reaching her. "I was just thinking how right *you* were. In fact, I have some catching up to do. Would you help me?"

"With what?" She glared at him. "I'm not going to change my mind." But she was softening, dammit, hearing him talk like that, seeing him look at her like he always did.

"Your prerogative," Vander said, thrusting out a bag, which jingled suspiciously, and fitting it in her hand. "But I would like your help."

When she took the bag out of reflex mostly, her shoulder wrenched, and she realized what was inside. "You brought a *bag* of coins?"

He started walking to the fountain's edge. "No, I brought two. Come along. I need to get started, or I'll be here all day." Dropping the bag, he opened it and drew out a handful of coins. There were quarters and dimes and nickels and pennies inside. Hundreds of them from what she could see.

"You've plumb lost your mind," she said, her aloof waning.

"Don't the poets say love makes us all a little crazy?" he quipped, his mouth tipping up. "Now, for my first wish. Please don't critique me. It's my first time, and I'm nervous enough as it is. This is a big moment for me."

There was no playfulness in his voice now, and she watched as he selected a quarter in his right hand.

"I'm starting with this coin since it's the biggest I have."

Their eyes met, and she couldn't look away.

"My first wish is to watch the woman I love grow old and to have her smile at me until her teeth fall out," he said, tilting his head to the side as if gauging her reaction.

"Do I know her?" she made herself ask, and even to her ears, she sounded like a bitch.

His face fell, but he threw the coin in. Then he selected another. A dime this time. "My second wish is for her to forgive me when I ask and to never hold a grudge, knowing I love her and would never hurt her intentionally."

Pain radiated in her bones. "That's a low blow."

His chest lifted like he was struggling to breathe as much as she was. "Doesn't make it less true." He threw the coin in. "Maybe this isn't the right approach."

Lifting the bag of coins he'd set on the ground, he approached her and extended his hand. She stared at him, trying to decide if she should give it to him. If she did, it would mean she'd forgiven him like he'd asked.

"The coins, please?"

She shook herself. He hadn't wanted to hold her hand. When she thrust out the bag, the coins jingled again. He grabbed it and took off for the fountain, both bags making a pleasant music as the money danced inside them. At the edge, he undid the top of the other bag and then hefted them up into his arms again. He leaned forward, and suddenly she understood what he was going to do.

"Stop! You can't throw in all those coins. You'll clog up the fountain."

He turned back and looked at her. "So what?"

"Don't you understand? Jeffries will kill you, and God knows what Gail will do to you. That fountain cost over a hundred thousand dollars. It's Italian!"

"But these are all the wishes I have for us," he said, dumping the first bag into the fountain without a qualm. "And Gail thinks what I'm doing is the most romantic thing she's ever heard."

Her heart rapped against her chest, and she felt tears burn

her eyes. "Damn you."

His mouth twisted, and she knew he was fighting emotion too. "Don't say that. Shelby, I love you." He waited a beat and swallowed thickly. "Seems I need more wishes. Good thing I brought more coins."

Hefting up the other bag, he dumped in all the coins, shaking the bag for good measure to dislodge the last few.

"These wishes are for our life and our happiness," he said, sitting on the edge of the water.

The afternoon sun caught the aqua in his eyes as he gazed intently at her. Her heart was taking flight, the heavy weight of pain being transformed by the love he was offering her.

"Shelby, I have so many wishes for us. You've made me believe in them again. You make me believe every wish I have can come true."

Suddenly she couldn't see through the tears in her eyes, and she couldn't choke out a reasonable reply. She dropped her valise and dug into her purse for her wallet. She marched over to the fountain and opened her coin purse. She shook all the coins she had into the fountain. When there were none left, she wiped her tears and looked at him.

"I don't have as many coins as you do, but the ones I just threw in there represent all the wishes I have for us too. Dammit, I love you!"

He pulled her to him, and she went into his arms so hard and fast they toppled into the fountain.

"Hey!" she cried out, feeling the water soak her suit all the way up to hip level.

"Sorry about that," he murmured, kissing her cheek. "I think I took the worst of it, what with you being on my lap and all."

She flicked water at him. "You're an idiot," she said and took his face in her hands. "But I love you. Even when you piss me off."

He touched her cheek, his eyes serious. "But do you

forgive me?"

She gave her best pout. "So long as you promise to never, *ever* keep anything from me again."

He wiggled in the water like he was trying to get more comfortable. "Sorry. There's a pile of coins under my ass. Yes, Shelby, I promise to never, ever, *ever* keep anything from you ever again. Is that enough 'evers' for you?"

"Yes," she said, fitting herself on his lap better, trying to maintain some sense of decency even though she was sitting in Gail's fountain like it was an everyday thing. "You'd be wise to expect that I'll come up with a punishment you won't be able to endure if you do it again."

"I couldn't endure losing you," Vander said, tracing her cheek with a wet fingertip. "That's the worst punishment you could ever dish out."

"I guess that's not happening now since I have such a forgiving nature," she said, linking her hands around his neck. "You're an idiot, but a romantic one, it seems. I can't believe you dumped two whole bags into this fountain—and then somehow managed to dump us in with them. You usually have such good balance."

He looked away, biting his lip. Off in the distance, she heard Gail's unmistakable cackle.

"You did this on purpose, didn't you?"

He shrugged. "I figured you wouldn't run off and ruin your leather seats if I got you wet. I had more things I wanted to say to you, and sometimes you...well...blow hot and cold."

Maybe later she'd give him a hard time about his allusion to her changeability—but only because she loved to banter with him. He saw her as she was and loved her, and it didn't get much better than that.

"So it was a strategy. You're devious," she purred. She knew how his mind worked too.

"And you like it," he said, leaning his head down until his mouth was inches away.

She pressed her lips to his, completing the journey.

They kissed in the fountain, their wishes for each other all around them.

Epilogue

THE DOWNTOWN ALLEY WHERE VANDER'S DADDY HAD been murdered made the hairs on the back of Sadie's neck stand on end. The brick walls were cracked from floor to ceiling, and two overflowing dumpsters were wafting a horrible stench.

She reached for Mama's hand and felt a reassuring squeeze.

"What are y'all doing here?" Shelby asked in a shocked voice.

Her sister was standing beside Vander, who seemed to be curled into himself somehow, not standing as straight as normal. In his hands was a silver flask with the initials JM on it. He looked over at them.

"We thought you might like some more support today," Sadie said, glad the idea had come to her in prayer time. Thankfully, everyone else had agreed to attend. "To honor Vander's daddy. Being that it's the twenty-fifth anniversary and all."

J.P. put his arm around Tammy and nodded to Vander. Jake did the same, his hand to Susannah's back. Dale delivered a heartfelt smile from his position beside Mama. Clayton gave him a chin nod, and Amelia Ann made an attempt at a smile.

"Family supports each other," Mama said, and that had Shelby wiping away tears.

Mama truly meant it, and Sadie felt tears well in her eyes too. When she and her siblings had told Mama they'd decided to move Me-Mother into an assisted living facility, she'd told them she was proud of them. She might not be on speaking terms with Lenore, but she'd assured all of them she was okay with them having a relationship with their grandmother. The relief they'd felt was tremendous.

"Thank you for saying that, Louisa," Vander said in a hoarse voice. "This...it's always a difficult day, but somehow being here with Shelby...and now all of you...it isn't so hard."

"I'm here too," Charlie said, putting her hand on her hip as she came forward. "Hopefully you won't fire me. Sadie assured me of my job security."

"But I didn't say that..." Sadie said before she saw the woman's smile.

Vander rolled his eyes. "I think you're safe, Charlie."

When Charlie had told her Vander had never let her come to the alley with him on the anniversary, Sadie had almost changed her mind. But she'd pressed on, knowing it was the right thing to do. He'd been there for them during the worst of times. They could do the same for him. He was Shelby's man now and that meant he was family.

The smell of garbage touched Sadie's nose, and she put her hand under it, hoping to offset it a bit.

"I usually..." Vander coughed to clear his throat. "I say a few words and then take a drink of my dad's favorite bourbon. His grandfather gave him this flask when he graduated from the police academy."

"Go on," Shelby encouraged. "Just say whatever you would normally say if we weren't here."

He barked out a painful laugh. "In the early years, that might have shocked the ladies present."

Another tortured sigh filled the silent alley as Vander gathered himself.

"This is...a little weird for me," Vander said. "I'm not used to having people here. Charlie knows why I come here. My mom would never understand. In fact, she would think I was crazy if she knew. Some of you might think it's a little crazy too, and that's okay."

"Don't apologize," Jake said. "You honor those you've lost in the way you need to."

Vander nodded in his direction. "Thank you. I've come here every year since my freshman year at Vanderbilt because I wanted to remember who my dad was and what had happened to him. This alley..." He coughed again. "This stinking alley... My dad didn't deserve to be murdered here in cold blood. He didn't deserve to have his killer escape justice. I...I've been trying to help the people of Nashville like my dad did. It's why I became a private investigator."

Shelby wrapped her arm around him when he paused and hung his head.

"I've been trying to make peace with what happened to my dad, to make peace with how he was taken from me when I was just a kid."

Sadie felt tears roll down her eyes, and she noted she wasn't the only one crying.

"It wasn't fair," Vander continued. "And it wasn't right. There was no justice in it. But I can help people make things right. I can help people find justice."

Sadie saw Clayton glance at Amelia Ann. Her honorary sister was obsessed with helping people find justice too.

"You helped us make things right," Shelby said, laying her head against his arm. "You helped us find out the truth about our daddy, and it healed our family."

Sadie thought the healing had started, but she wasn't sure it was done yet. She still wondered how Daddy was bearing the knowledge his secret was out. Sure, he didn't know Mama had ended up telling them, or that Vander had told J.P.

From Sadie's perspective, how could Daddy *not* want to know what had happened? The suspense would have killed her.

"I do my part for the people in this city," Vander continued.

"Like my dad did. And I do it knowing I could end up here."

"Don't say that," Shelby said urgently, turning him toward her. "Don't you ever say that!"

He traced her cheek with the hand not holding the flask. "I used to be okay with that. I thought I wouldn't mind if I ended up the same way. But after meeting you, I don't feel that way anymore. Shelby, I told you my first wish was to grow old with you, and I mean that."

She laid her head on his chest. "You're fixing to make me come undone."

"We can't have that, can we?" He smoothed her hair and took a moment. "Dad, I don't know if you can hear me, but...I have a good business and good people I work with. And I've found a woman I love more than anything in life. She's made me wish for things I'd stopped wishing for a long time ago. Love and family and a sense of belonging. Dad...I know what I'm going to do with the rest of my life now."

Sadie felt more tears stream down her face.

"Dad, I have a great life now. I'm happy. I hope you like hearing that...if you can hear me."

"He can hear you, Vander," Mama said softly, giving Sadie chill bumps. "And he's proud of the man you've become. How could he not be?"

Vander swiped at his nose as Shelby brushed tears off her cheeks.

"Thank you for saying that, Louisa." He lifted his flask. "Here's to you, Dad. For being so big in my memory and for continuing to inspire me today. I...miss you. And I love you."

Sadie couldn't dash at her tears fast enough as Vander took a sip from the flask and then handed it to Shelby. Her sister drank deeply and coughed before handing it to J.P.

"You don't have to drink unless you want to," Vander told the group.

"I'd be honored to," Tammy said, giving him a watery smile.

She took a quick sip and handed it to Jake, who continued

to pass it along—even Mama took a drink—until it ended with Sadie. There wasn't much left, and she made sure to barely touch her lips to the flask, not liking the taste of bourbon one bit. The fire burned her mouth.

"Vander, if it's okay," Mama said beside her, "I'd like to invite everyone to observe a moment of silence for your daddy and you and his family."

He nodded, and they all bowed their heads. Sadie knew Mama normally would have prayed out loud, but she was honoring Vander, who wasn't a church-going man.

Sadie gave Shelby a smile when their eyes met. Her sister was especially teary, and Sadie couldn't blame her. Usually she and Vander were teasing each other. Today, in this awful place, they looked like they had the kind of love the wedding vows talked about, the "in good times and in bad" type.

It was the sort of love Sadie knew lasted forever. She prayed to God every night for the right man to love her like that. Maybe she needed to go over to Gail's fountain like Shelby and Vander had and throw in a coin or two. It kinda sucked to be the only one of her siblings who had yet to meet the love of her life.

Suddenly someone's phone beeped.

"Oh! I'm so sorry!" Tammy dug her phone out of her purse. "I told Daddy and Mama to only text me if someone happened with Rory and Annabelle."

"Too bad Rye and Tory couldn't make it, what with her feeling so poorly." Mama said. "I can't believe her doctor is letting her go more than a week late. Must be one of those new natural kinds of medical folk."

Sadie knew everything was fine from what Tory had said. "Mama, her doctor says most first babies are late and doesn't believe in intervening unless necessary."

Even if it was driving Rye crazy. Sadie had never seen him so strung out.

"She's in labor!" Tammy cried out. "Tory's in labor."

"She is?" Amelia Ann asked. "Oh, wonderful! I'm going to

have another niece or nephew."

"Well, my goodness," Mama said. "What a blessing. And on such an important day."

Vander gave a half-smile. "Before Shelby, I didn't believe it when people talked about synchronicities like that. I do now. I like the idea of a new baby coming into the family on the day of my dad's death."

Shelby rubbed his arm. "Might be nice to have some joy on this day after all of the hurt."

He put his hand over her arm. "It might indeed."

Sadie thought about the new baby and all of the people waiting so eagerly for it to arrive. But then her mind gave her the image of another baby, one she wasn't sure had ever been wanted. Her half-sister. She couldn't stop thinking about her. Knowing Skylar Watkins' name had made it easy to conduct a Facebook search—one she hadn't told anyone about yet. She was still praying on it.

"Please go on, everybody," Vander said, draining the flask. "I appreciate you coming. Shelby, you should go too. I can meet you later."

Everyone started to leave the alley, but Sadie held back, waiting for her sister.

"I'm staying with you if you want to take a little more time here," Shelby said quietly.

Vander heaved in a huge breath, like it was torn from inside the deepest part of himself. "No, we'll all go. I'm finished here."

He looked around the alley slowly, and Sadie wondered what he was seeing. Did he see the crumbling brick or the overflowing dumpsters like she did? Or did he see his daddy lying on the ground in his own blood?

"Actually I think it's *finally* finished," Vander said, and he bent over and laid the flask down gently on the ground. "Goodbye, Dad. See you on the other side—if there is one."

He took Shelby's hand, and together they walked out of the alley, only stopping to take Sadie along with them.

Dear Reader,

I hope you loved the newest Dare River installment as much as I did. The McGuiness family continues to expand my heart with their love and closeness for each other.

If you enjoyed this book, I would love for you to post a review since it helps more readers want to pick up this story and enjoy it themselves. When you post one, kindly let me know at ava@avamiles.com so I can personally thank you. Thank you for spreading the word!

Are you wondering about Sadie's story? I can't wait to explore the next part of this series in THE PATCHWORK QUILT OF HAPPINESS.

If you love Dare River, you might check out my Dare Valley and Once Upon a Dare series, both connected to our Dare universe. Thanks again for being part of the family.

Lots of light and blessing,

Ava

PS: To learn more about Sadie and Adam's story called THE PATCHWORK QUILT OF HAPPINESS, sign up for my newsletter on www.avamiles.com.

Also, watch for the next Dare Valley story, HOME SWEET LOVE (Moira & Chase).

And check out the next installment of the Once Upon a Dare series, FINDING FAITH (Faith & Sam).

ABOUT THE AUTHOR

International Bestselling Author Ava Miles joined the ranks of beloved storytellers after receiving Nora Roberts' blessing for her use of Ms. Roberts' name in her debut novel, the #1 National Bestseller NORA ROBERTS LAND. So far, millions of readers have discovered Ava's fiction and nonfiction novels. She's hit the bestseller lists and reached the #1 spot at Barnes & Noble and ranked in Amazon and iBooks' top charts. Women's World Magazine has selected a few of her novels for their book club while Southwest Airlines featured NORA ROBERTS LAND in its in-flight entertainment. Ava's books have been chosen as Best Books of the Year and Top Editor's Picks and are being translated in to multiple languages.

Made in United States
North Haven, CT
19 July 2022

21559584R00200